# ABOUT THE AUTHOR

JP lives in Western Sydney with his wife and daughter; one dog with back issues, another with anxiety issues and another who is an escape artist, attempting to flee from their constant love, affection and security.

Before inking stories, JP focused on writing songs for the melancholy masses and in complete contrast, also developed vibrant and catchy children's songs.

He has worked in education, human resources, business development and communications, but is often dreaming of otherworldly adventures and experiences.

You can find him trying to emulate chefs on the food channel, planting native bush foods in his backyard and chasing the sun through rivers and national park trails.

Website: www.jpmcdonald.com.au
Instagram @jpmcdonaldwrites
Tiktok @jpmcdonaldwrites
Facebook @jpmcdonaldwrites

# THE INVISIBLE TETHER

JP McDonald

Cover Art by Les @Germancreative
Edited by Samantha @ Miss Eloquent Edits
Design and Layout by Daiana
Title designs by Harryarts / Freepik

# CONTENT WARNING

This story contains content that might be troubling to some readers, including but not limited to, depictions of and references to death, suicide, self-harm, depression, anxiety, substance abuse, childhood trauma, child abuse, plane crashes, drowning.

Please proceed with caution if some of those subjects might be triggering for you.

# Dedication

*For Amelie,*
*My love for you transcends words.*
*Chase your dreams and together we will make them a reality.*

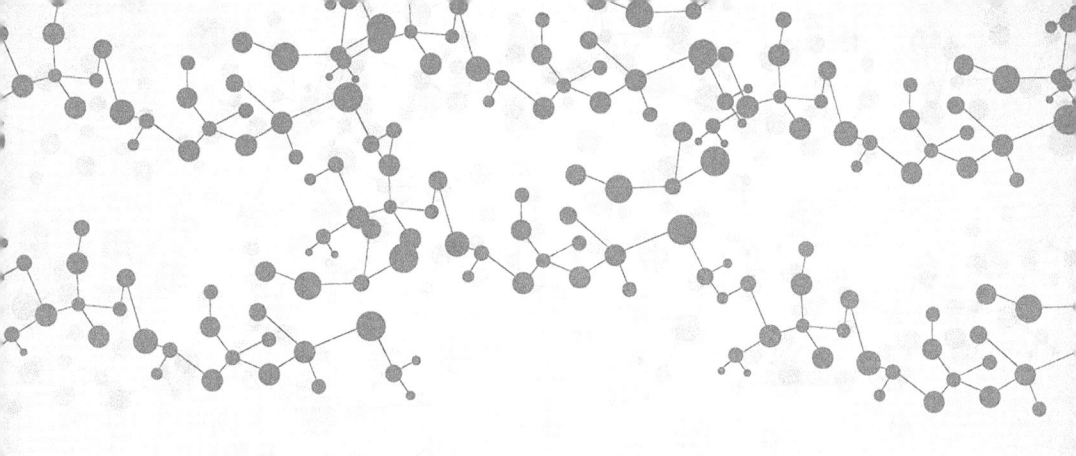

# CHAPTER 1

A muffled crack pierced the soundscape: a sudden accent in the monotonous droning symphony of the engine. My headphones were melting ice as they slipped through my fingers to the carpeted floor.

Stifled screams came from behind the veiled cockpit's door, the sacred space tainted by unhinged aggression. The taste of pine and ammonia thick in the air, sweat beading on the back of my neck. A primal screech of its wounded prey followed two prominent bellows from the throat of a gun.

The plane erupted in a haunting chorus of gasps, faces white as old, discarded bones, the air dense with dread, infesting the plane like a virus. Our hearts bound together in fear, a unified, adrenalised reaction: an invisible tether.

Waking from a deep sleep with a sudden jolt, my eyes adjusted to a flickering television screen. A remote dangled, flaccid, in my right hand.

The news team sifted through the day's important headlines. A deep, troubled voice mentioned mysterious murders, a new reason to suggest shark-culling as a young surfer lay bound to a hospital bed, a David and Goliath sporting tale between the two local football teams.

My weary eyes blinked several times, adjusting to the harsh light that filled the lounge room. The sleeping bag I used solely for naps on the tired, navy-blue couch spilled over my torso, leaving my legs exposed and gnawed upon by the ravenous spring chill. Sitting up, I twisted my neck to the side, loosening tension that had become a persistent ache in an otherwise healthy body. Turning to my right, I accidentally knocked one of the dusty metal photo frames to the worn, beige carpet. Picking it up swiftly, it lingered in my hands and my mind. The dust on the glass was a fog cast across a glacier-fed lake. Such beauty in the image before me, sliced through layers of feelings and reminders that endured still. It was a lovely family portrait—before the family had shattered like the glass, which encased the portrait.

*Holographic frames don't crack! It would be a shame to stick with a tired, old frame.* I recalled the catchy advertisement in about every programming break. Damn those advertisers and their catchphrases. Mum resisted the frame upgrades; she couldn't abandon the aesthetic of an overcrowded glass coffee table, like the one beside me. I guess I inherited that from her, not buying into the hype of new products, regarding the past as an appreciation of what was. In a world where we constantly wanted trivial things, I was happy with my upcycled, recycled—or *treecycled* mentality.

The familiar musical composition of Mum clanging her pots and pans in the kitchen triggered a speedy transition from depressing daydreams to stark reality. My stomach moaned in desperate resentment as the dominant smells of garlic, sweet paprika and tomato reached my nostrils. I shuffled over to catch a glimpse of her in preparation mode. The gleaming pearl kitchen bench held captive a rustic wooden chopping board. A knife lay panting on its side after a chopping marathon. Hexagonal white tiles on the splashback caught the small flecks of pale red rue after launching themselves like kamikaze pilots out of the boiling pot and onto a cooler surface. Mum's blonde hair bobbed up and down as she shuffled from the stovetop to the pantry, adding in pinches of salt while humming *It Will Be Alright* by Jimmy Barnes from the good ol' days. My lips curved upwards, and the swollen dam of my cheeks broke, revealing an involuntary smile that felt real. Watching her cook was like watching an artist bare their soul on a page. Her canvas was the food, and we tasted her culture's rich tapestry and love with every meal.

I heard her call out, "Cooper, are you awake? I need your help setting the table."

My response was not forthcoming. The dinner table could wait. Pretending I was still asleep seemed like a safe and relaxing option. The news then returned from a brief commercial break.

"World-renowned scientist Gordon Grey has successfully cloned the chimpanzee," said a blonde, generic-looking newsreader.

I stared in astonishment. He did what? My finger found the volume button. *Tap, tap, tap.* The TV screen showed images of a man in a white lab coat, grey hair parted on the left, intriguing and affable brown eyes sunken into the wisdom of his face. He spoke cautiously behind a barrage of microphones.

"We have made a significant breakthrough for the good of humanity." He paused, allowing the cameras to capture the moment for social media.

"The steps that we have taken in cloning the closest human relative will ultimately lead to replicating the true human form. This will propel us forward into the future and will abolish the threat of human disease, rendering human suffering obsolete. We will live in a world that is clean, effective and peaceful."

Gordon Grey vanished from the screen, replaced by two chimps in opposing cages. A booming voice accompanied these images, prompting you to ask yourself, *Is anything noticeably different?*

Truth be told, there was not. As I sat there, eyes glued to the screen, I shifted uncomfortably, feeling a chill spread throughout my body.

Was this what they called intuition? A part of me had never given these futuristic, science fiction-type of ideas the time of day. But in 2025, what others deemed futuristic had become, well, *present*-istic.

In 2018, China was the first to clone macaques, but chimpanzees were close to ninety-nine per cent of our DNA structure. So, were humans next? Would they clone humans?

My slim-fitting grey shirt felt tighter all of a sudden. I changed the channel before my pulse quickened. No need to draw imaginative conclusions into what it might do for the future. *Breathe in deeply and work on what your therapist has told you. Savour the moment; be present.*

A fair-skinned female news reporter with a seductive twinkle in her eyes stood in front of Sydney Airport. She introduced the "new and exciting" appearance of the latest P-134 jet. What a coincidence. I would be boarding that very plane tomorrow, flying to North Queensland for the annual University Games.

People touted the University Games as a week full of competitive sporting tournaments; however, it often turned into a week of extreme partying and drinking. The severity of alcohol consumption at this event wouldn't provide a showcase of skill or sportsmanship. Instead, it would highlight which university teams had the best tolerance for competing with hangovers.

Aside from the news on the recently developed aircraft scanning the airspace, the TV couldn't hold my attention; reality shows littered every other channel.

My sister had come in to help set the table, so until mum had finished cooking, the best option was to go to the only place on our property that captivated me for lengthy periods of time: the place I called "Serenity."

# CHAPTER 2

The family property was nestled in a semi-rural area, an hour west of the Sydney City Centre. Large basalt rock formations encased the untamed bush, trailing down towards horses who gleefully traversed the greener pastures. Copper-brown dirt mounds converged upon a simple motorbike track linking the open spaces to the worn paths, shadowed by proud eucalyptus trees. The lack of development around us meant that the air was pure, and it tasted sweet, with lingering hints of lemon myrtle and red boronia.

My mother had always appreciated open spaces and had convinced my father that living so far from the city would "enrich the children's lives."

On a Saturday morning, she would say, "C'mon, kids! It's time to enjoy a conversation with nature!" The sullen whispers of leaves in brash billows. The calls of a kookaburra encouraging laughter and mischief. The cicadas signifying the arrival of the summer.

"The true essence of life is in these simple conversations, kids," she would say, as we ran down towards the dam, rolling our eyes and giggling at the subtle life lessons.

Aided by the noise of dinner preparation, I managed to slip out of the house without Mum hearing me. It felt like an age since we were kids, yet we still rolled our eyes whenever Mum would say something embarrassing.

The motorbike shed loomed before me, and as I started upon the charcoal gravel path, it brought other memories of when my father was alive. He had enjoyed riding motorbikes, and as a result, encouraged me to do the same with him when I was younger. He frequented gala races, even when he was a teenager, and as parents often do, he attempted to push his dreams onto his son. Even though I enjoyed riding with him and was more than competent in several manoeuvres, I had always kept my distance from its competitive nature. The father-son connection was all I saw. I look back fondly on the days we enjoyed together; however, all unique relationships must end. This one, in particular, was an abrupt one, resulting in an emotional whiplash I would suffer several years into the future.

On an unusually foggy morning in late spring, my father, Christopher John Belrose, went to the Blue Mountains on a motorbike trip with his mates. A sharp corner emerged on the relatively moderate track, and he tried to correct his mistake, but the brakes locked, and the cliff face was unforgiving. The shadowy abyss beckoned him to his death and those same shadows sought me out and encased my heart in sorrow. Each time it beat, vibrancy faded, and the shadow grew. The once beautiful family portrait had shattered. I struggled through the funeral process: the burden of a eulogy, the realisation that I'd lost my best friend, the lowering of his coffin into a meaningless hole in the ground.

It took a while to adjust without having a father figure in my life; in fact, now that I reflect, it is something you never get over. I had searched for meaning while trying to find myself along the way, shared a room with my good friend, loneliness, fumbled through a twisted path wrought with depression and navigated those nagging suicidal thoughts. There was always a certain boundary I couldn't cross, and I guess it was the world needing something more from me.

Luckily, for my sister and I, Mum was a strong woman. Without her, we never would have survived. But I suppose that is how relationships within a family work; when things fall apart, you become the fence post, the hammer, the nail: different things at different times.

The motorbike shed vanished behind me as the sunlight beamed onto my face through the treetops. It warmed my heart, and it hauled a smile from the depths of a waterlogged soul onto a weathered face. I trudged down the path towards Serenity, abolishing thoughts of longing for a father. I was twenty and old enough to start my own family, if I so desired, which I certainly did not feel inclined to right then.

My boots devoured the gravel, chewing and crunching on the insipid pebbles, trudging past soggy clothes dangling on the line. I stole a glance to the left, where my music practice room was. It was detached from the house in an old, converted shipping container, built to withstand loud noises from within. It housed thousands of dollars' worth of equipment, including basic recording modules, complete with a range of instruments.

As I continued down the familiar dirt path, my two horses, Dexter and Faruke, galloped playfully around the paddock. To the left of them, the resident family of ducks willingly broke the surface of the dam to dive down and search for food. I approached the mouth of the motorbike track, which over the years, had become a breeding ground for assorted weeds and young grass roots to sprout into existence. From here, it never took long to stumble into Serenity. In fact, the first time I embarked on that journey, I did just that.

I quite stupidly accepted some playful competition with my father while circling the track one morning. I was about twelve, attempting to outdo the deceptively agile 'old' man.

Who knew that failing would open my eyes to Serenity?

We had engaged in a precious battle, zipping in and around trees and pursuing shortcuts, holding the lead for mere seconds at a time. My father's dusty red motorbike was up ahead, just about to round a corner on the inside. I attempted a move that would see me drift along the outside, overtaking him once the path straightened out once more. Opening the throttle, I accelerated too hard. Before I could comprehend my error in judgement, I was sliding across broken twigs, leaves, and shrubbery, rolling end-over-end towards stoic tree trunks and a potential array of my own shattered bones.

I landed hard, perilously shaken upon my back, staring at a vivid blue sky, impeded by several branches. My breath was a raging stream as it approached the crest of a waterfall, but it reminded me that I was very much alive. Dad's engine roared triumphantly and tantalisingly in the distance. I rose cautiously from the earth, ensuring my bones were all intact, and I glanced around. My bike lay crumpled, forlorn against a tree about five metres from where I lay. I had slid several metres myself, perforating a group of weary but sturdy shrubs that had created an impressive enclosure around the area I had mistakenly entered.

The briny smell of lichen lingered from within earth's womb; sharp fissures and granite fists adorned its entry. Wind swirled inside, like a breathy melody from the flute of a faun who had whimsy in his heart. I had stumbled into the mouth of a cave.

Hidden away for years behind the seemingly impenetrable fortress of the shrubs, this was part of the wild, untamed bush territory on the property. My wits had returned from the little motorbike accident, so I rose to my feet, eager to explore what lay within the cave. It was imperative to be cautious and careful when searching the property's newer areas. Ironic, I know, seeing as though I'd nearly injured myself on a track I knew so well. However, my cautiousness withered, and feline curiosity overwhelmed me. *What was the euphoria that I felt when I peered in and around the cave?*

With tingling sensations and goose bumps, I inched forward. A covering of pennywort crept toward the deep shadow covering the cave, while a clump of withered dandelions sighed at the absence of light. The eerie tunnel of darkness invited me in. Slowly, the shadows dissolved with each small step I took. Sharp echoes bounced off the slick walls as the warmth dissipated and the air thinned, taking in a damp, mouldy scent. The faintest light twinkled ahead, like Saturn on a clear night. Continuing carefully, determined to see where the light was coming from, I felt truly immersed by a sense of harmony with nature, almost forgetting that my bloodied and bruised body had wandered into the comforting unknown.

The path curled around, and I followed the light, a beacon in the otherwise disorientating darkness. Stones shuffled underfoot, the cold washing over my bare skin, goosebumps; apprehension brail. The single ray of sunshine beamed through a tiny crevice at the top of the cave into a small pool of water. Moss and algae were two best friends, dangling their feet into the shimmering darkness of the pool.

If a divine hand was actually real and able to yield instruments to craft a perfect space, this was it. The feeling that surged through me was peace, Serenity found.

The light inside was dim, but it illuminated everything inside: the naturally smooth walls, splintered with wrinkles of character, the complimentary space surrounded the shimmering water feature, the delicate and wondrous glow from the sun's projection as it bounced off the water and onto the walls.

A change flowed within me, and as I found my way out of the cave to the finishing line where my father waited to brag about his victory, I lay claim to a different prize that day, and it suited me just fine. It was a new hideaway on my property that I would call "Serenity."

Serenity's generous, undeniable beauty has not grown old over the years. The sun's reflection still dances in dainty revolutions, the warm water trickles and swishes throughout all seasons and the cool, humble air provides comfort and insulation from the severe summer heat. The scent of mould still lingered, but my mum's homemade candles of sweet jasmine and lavender fought with valour for the top spot.

Shaking off the memory of Serenity's discovery, I reached the once impenetrable fortress of shrubs, pulling back the weaker branches to pass through unscathed. I listened intently to nature's foreign language: the coarse whispers of the wind in the trees, the water in the dam lapping towards the bank, the birds serenading one another with a gentle song. It was the most peaceful place I knew. Turning away from the world's beauty bathed in sunlight, I focused on the beauty that divinity kept in darkness. Step-by-step, I made my way into my second home.

I had recently converted this ideal place of peace into something that resembled a compact 'room,' placing a mattress in the corner for the nights I had slept there, an acoustic guitar and a small cupboard with food and notebooks inside.

That night, when I left the TV programmes behind, I stayed in Serenity for a couple of hours attempting to relax. Certain moments in life materialise, where you often need to just lie down and read a book, gather your thoughts and recharge your batteries. *Me time* had exceeded the duration in which my own stomach would allow, grumbling in disgust at my defiant desertion. As I walked back towards my house, the smell of garlic and cooked tomato's wafted through the cool night air.

After a lukewarm dinner, I talked briefly with my sister, Brooke. I stayed in her room chatting about my trip, what lovely lady I had my eye on and what clothes I should bring. My phone buzzed inside of my pocket, interrupting our talk. Excusing myself, I wrestled with the inside of my pants until the phone popped out.

*Nikki calling.*

*This is odd*, I thought.

I picked up the phone. "Cooooooops!" she whined hysterically.

I rolled my eyes.

Nikki was a lot of work. She had a sense for over dramatising situations, and I didn't always react well to such bursts of attention-seeking behaviour. I needed to be delicate with her, though, as having her wrath turned on me was not worth the trouble. She applied a certain knowledge and ability while studying a complex computing and software engineering course at university but was one of those people who would be considered book smart but not street smart.

Histrionic disorder aside, she remained a loyal and understanding friend usually, so in this case, I casually replied, "Hey, Nikki, what's up?"

Then came the dreaded sobbing.

I spent the next twenty minutes consoling her, as she explained how her mother didn't allow her to attend our trip, due to "family reasons." I knew that was code for "being angry at Nikki's relationship with Matt." Nikki, a daughter of proud Aboriginal parents, was dating someone unattached to their culture. To make matters worse, her parents were leaders in the community, so the relationship was a great source of tension in their household.

Dani, her best friend, fiercely protested Nikki's family's decision, and of course, chose to stay home with Nikki as a result. I failed to understand the logic behind Dani's decision. Nevertheless, I attempted to downplay the week ahead, all the while itching for the chance to hang out and wreak havoc with my uni buddies.

I hung up the phone to her sniffled goodbyes and reluctantly promised her that we would meet up when I returned. By the time the phone conversation had ended, I was, once again, on my mattress in Serenity. I gathered my things to pack in my backpack; it was bedtime.

Luckily, I left Serenity that night in a clean enough state, because the next time I was there, I had several companions with me, one huge problem and no way of knowing what to do next.

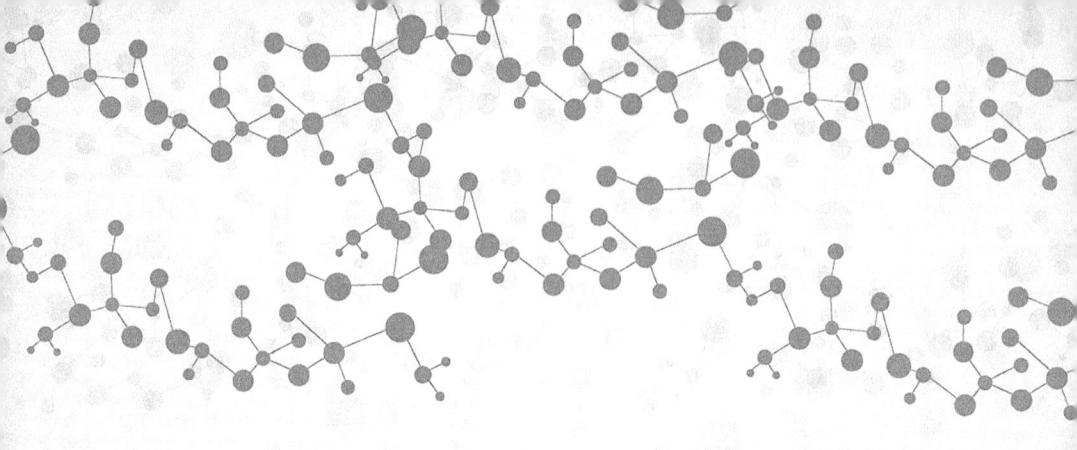

# CHAPTER 3

The door creaked as Mum rushed in.

"Cooper, it's time to get out of bed; your uni games trip is today!"

I rolled over onto my other side. Of course, I knew it was uni games. What else had I been looking forward to for the last few weeks? Still, I decided it wasn't important enough to warrant waking up that early.

No more than five minutes had passed before I heard the familiar chorus of the door opening and Mum yelling once more. The concept of a 'good morning' has never lost its irony. I didn't delay the inevitable any longer, though, throwing the covers off in an exaggerated huff, accompanied by an eye roll that no one else could appreciate. Standing at the foot of the rustic queen-sized bed, I rubbed my eyes and allowed their focus to initiate functionality. I stretched my arms above my head; multiple cracks from my spine ticked like a clock inside the room. Dragging my feet, I headed towards the shower to revitalise my senses. I floated past Mum, who was still yelling something incomprehensible.

The water droplets lashed my exposed skin, doing their best to awaken all senses. The aroma of the coconut and jojoba body wash swirled around me like a jellyfish in the open ocean. It reminded me of where I wanted to be: a white sand beach, cocktail in hand, snorkel goggles resting on top of my head and salt encrusted on the outer edge of my lips. I rushed to finish after that, intent on getting to the airport. My wardrobe beckoned me, and I answered the call. The burgundy of the slim-fit T-shirt resembled that of a fine wine, pitted against grey scale rose tattoos that trailed down my arms. *Will Zoey notice that I'd been taking more trips to the gym?* I wondered. Wincing in discomfort because I didn't skip leg day, I chose the black organic cotton jersey shorts for comfort, not aesthetics. Even though the famous six-pack eluded me, I'd been working on feeling fit and somewhat toned. After throwing a grey hoodie on, I jogged to the bathroom and surveyed my own reflection in the mirror. I strategically tousled my dark brown hair with some sort of hair product that my sister owned. This kind of hair product appealed to me; I didn't have to know its name, only that it worked because my sister used it.

A modest, untidy clump of hair fell across the top of my forehead, covering persistent blemishes that hadn't vacated for the month. The sides of my hair were cropped short in a low fade, but the dishevelled chic ran rampant across my face with three-day-old stubble.

Mum interrupted my thoughts with her familiar yelling, discernible only as some foreign language. I finished washing my face and leapt out of the bathroom. I ran to grab the suitcase from my room, hauled it uncomfortably through the hallway and opened the door.

A startling, bitter breeze hit me first. As I peered through the catacomb-like treetops, the sun appeared like a gold coin glinting in a pellucid pool of water. Raising faux tortoiseshell sunglasses to my face to hide the russet brown in my eyes, I silently praised nature for another radiant morning.

"Stop dawdling and get in the car, Cooper." Mum snapped, frazzled, as she unlocked the car's doors and ran to the driver's side.

*This will be a fun ride,* I thought. Flopping onto the passenger's seat and resting my head against the window. Off to the airport, we go.

Mum dropped me off at the terminal gates, tears welling in her dark brown eyes as she embraced me one last time.

"It's basically a week, Mum. Relax." My soothing sentiments tinged with an irksome tone.

"Cooper, don't tease me. You know that you and your sister are all I have left."

*Why do you have to bring that up now?* I thought.

"I'll send you a text when I land and maybe a photo of us all hungover on the beach or something?" The lighthearted quip was enough to subdue her sadness.

"Oh, goodness; don't get me started on alcohol consumption. You all indulge a little too much for my liking, I think . . ."

I pressed my forefinger to her mouth. "Now is not the time for this conversation." I hugged her tight for the last time and hopped out the door.

"Bye, Mum, enjoy a bit of 'you' time!" And with that, I slammed the door.

Turning around, bag in tow, I caught her smiling and waving wildly. Laughing, I haphazardly gave her the spirit finger wave and entered the airport without another glance behind me.

Once inside the terminal, I hung my sunglasses on the curved neckline of my shirt, searching for directions to the gate. I passed by all necessary security points unscathed but couldn't locate anyone from my team around. It was when I ventured over to the airport food court that I spotted most of my tutor group, the team and coaches standing close together.

Gus Gauci's thick Maltese eyebrows shadowed his darting eyes, recounting a story full of embellishments to Zack Johnson. Zack's curly black hair bobbled as he shook his head vigorously in disbelief. His beady brown eyes narrowed at Gus' bulky frame, who had fought his point to the very end.

Lost in my observations, I felt a faint tap on my shoulder. Turning around, I caught a glimpse of her voluminous blonde hair and gentle brown eyes. It was Kasey Bean. She kissed me on the cheek and squeaked.

"Cooper, this is going to be so much fun!"

She pulled away, a provocative smirk decorating her face. Makeup accentuated her features perfectly: lacquered lips framed by the sparkling rosè in her cheeks. She bounced on the spot, eager for my reply. Smiling back at her, I muttered warily, "Yeah, it'll be okay." I shrugged, my excitement buried in layers of apathy.

"Oh, c'mon, you sad sack; it's gonna be heaps of fun, spending this much time with everyone . . . especially me!" she squealed.

Before I could answer, she had spotted Zoey Chan over my shoulder, screaming and shuffling towards her in high heels, extending slender arms into the air as if she were basking in the radiance of the rising sun. Kasey's bright red dress clung desperately to her body, making it difficult for her to run freely.

Zoey's hair was a rich hot chocolate, spilling below her shoulders, splattering concentric curls across the neckline of her plain black singlet. Her long eyelashes carried the hint of sin towards the deep autumn of her eyes. Kasey's embrace appeared to send a gentle shock through her as she stumbled back to steady herself. The sound of laughter comforted them.

In contrast to Kasey, Zoey had a natural allure that seemed so effortless. With a genetic combination spanning just about every continent, she didn't need to over indulge with products or embellishments. She smiled at me over Kasey's shoulder, and I waved with an arm that was a little too straight. *Why did being attracted to someone bring out the loser in all of us?* My eyes darted nervously from left to right, as I squeezed a stupid thin smile out of my face. I pulled out my phone and pretended to check my social media accounts to look 'cool' again.

Zoey and I had been getting closer of late: messaging most nights, calls every now and then, one-on-one discussions when out on the town. I felt like there was something there, but at that point, it was unspoken. A sultry stare, a subtle touch, a stolen conversation, a lingering thought.

A peaceful voice that floated like a morning fog materialised over the loudspeaker.

"Flight 404 to Cairns – boarding now."

Everyone rose simultaneously. As I directed my attention towards my other friends, Zack and Gus rushed over to greet me with a handshake. I stole several sneaky glances in Zoey's direction on my way to the boarding gates, conscious not to wave like an idiot again. She threw her head back, laughing with the rest of her friends. *Maybe I should stop staring at her and do the same*, I thought.

Me, Zack and Gus walked towards the gate to present our tickets, all the while catching up about the recent days' trivial social media exchanges. Our coach pulled Pj aside for a stern word. He was caught throwing lollies at grounded passengers sleeping on the airport's floor. Classic Pj.

He bared his teeth in an impudent smile as a scowling Coach Hart returned to reprimand him. Shrugging his shoulders, he swept his shaggy brown hair away from the mischief clouding his eyes, clearly ignoring what Coach Hart had to say.

As I sat down in my designated seat, Pj pushed through the lineup of patient passengers, his robust figure creating ripples of fury in his wake. His unbuttoned red and white baseball shirt flailed with his swift movements, his eyes lost to the extent of his wide, childish grin. Ruffling my hair to greet me and knocking Zack on the back of the head, he crashed down into our row's aisle seat.

"Can you not do that?" Zack seethed through gritted teeth.

"Oh, lighten up, buttercup," Pj teased, squeezing Zack's cheeks as Zack swatted him away almost instantly.

"C'mon, you two, don't make me turn this plane around," I joked

"I just want to chill out, and this guy comes in like a goddamn cyclone." Zack's frustration was clear.

But Pj was already trying to annoy the person sitting in the seat in front of him, yanking the hat off his head and throwing it across the plane to Gus.

"At least he has found another target – that isn't you."

"He is bloody relentless." Zack shook his head.

The captain's friendly voice came through the speaker overhead, making sure we knew the flight details and weather reports before taking off. Zack turned to me.

"Did you speak with Zoey this morning?"

The awkward wave hung proudly in the art gallery of my memory.

"No, I sort of waved hello, but that was it."

"Have you got a game plan for you and her this week or what?"

I narrowed my eyes. "I don't know in what world you think that love is a sport – enough to plan for anyways."

"Well, so many girls and guys play it like a game. I think you're the one in the wrong world, brother."

"I suppose I have heard; there is a so called art to 'courting a fair maiden.'"

Zack laughed, "She is anything but a fair maiden. Some of the disagreements I have had with her, I can't even get a single word in."

"She definitely takes no prisoners. But that's part of her charm."

"Good luck with that." His laugh was colourful and true.

"Anyway, I'm just hoping that things progress naturally. There is definitely a spark there – it's just . . . I hope it burns bright rather than fizzes away."

"I know you well, buddy, and if there is a spark there, then you'll somehow spill a bottle of water over it and put it out before anything else comes of it." Zack teased.

I shoved his bulky frame with a smile in my eyes, "Like you can talk. You're drowning yourself in a lake of your own lonely tears."

The plane had reached the beginning of the runway, and the pilots had engaged in the final few checks before takeoff.

Pj's attention was back on us, joking with Zack about trying to 'pick up' the flight attendant as she began the safety procedure. I was hardly in a mood to participate in their ridiculous behaviour; maybe I was a bit of an old soul. I turned to my phone, eager to find a playlist that would help me relax.

Taking off was usually the part that evoked the most anxiety. However, for us, the problems began about an hour into the flight.

# CHAPTER 4

The majority of our group sat near the front of the fuselage. Coach Hart, with his spiky grey hair and a whistle resting against his chest like a medal he won in his hay day, reclined in the first row with our assistant coach, Heather Mildred. She swept wispy blonde hair behind her ear as she smiled, with a careless joy that only came from wanderlust fulfilled. The plane was at around half capacity, with a couple of different university teams possibly opting for a later flight.

The aroma of a warm breakfast wafted through the plane: scrambled eggs, mushrooms, bacon, hash browns. The healthy options: a small cup of orange juice and a less-than-crisp pink lady apple came as an afterthought on the side. Normally, we would consider it a decent breakfast, but about five to ten minutes after consuming the food, my stomach groaned like a time-worn boat struggling to navigate the restless ocean. It didn't affect me enough to want to go to the bathroom; instead, I resumed the paused playlist, shrugging off the nausea.

Before I closed my eyes to sleep, I tried to locate all my teammates. Mia sat next to Gil, her shoulder-length cherry-coloured hair undulating graciously as she shuffled her tarot cards. Her mahogany eyes twinkled like a fresh coat of varnish, and a broad smile, baring teeth and gums alike, materialised as she painstakingly attempted to explain their meaning to a dumbfounded Gil.

A generous auburn fringe fell over the top of his wrinkled brow, digesting Mia's dark arts. He scratched the right side of his head, cut shorter to create a lopsided effect, and ultimately, threw his hands up, insinuating he didn't understand the tarot cards and perhaps didn't want to. The cross on his gold chain bearing down onto his chest, a not-so-gentle warning to stay off a blasphemous path. He, instead, moved to tracing his finger across the flight path on the back of the chair in front of him, mapping out where we were and where we needed to go.

Zoey placed a Band-Aid to cover a cut on her leg next to Kasey, who was applying makeup to her face for about the seventh time within the hour. Gus sat just behind them – next to Desh, my final good friend on the team.

Desh's enigmatic eyes focused on a first-person shooter game on his tablet. He was not normally one for frivolous games, but I assumed his cousins in India had convinced him to play against them as a way to stay connected across the globe. He tapped the back of the gaming device and complained to Gus. "Isn't this new plane meant to have state of the art Wi-Fi connections? This is lagging like crazy."

"How old are you again?" Gus mocked.

Hands that could tame the earth ran through the sharp slithers of his short black hair, stopping at the base of his neck, with long, rigid fingers circling in a massaging motion.

"You have a point." His thin lips curled into a smirk and grew with Gus' laughter.

I smiled and directed my attention back to the phone, though the two clowns beside me, who poked and prodded one another, interrupted my attempt to forget my stomach issues and relax. I ignored them so that I could unwind before we were happily causing havoc in Queensland.

It was just a couple more hours until we all landed at our holiday destination, liberated from the pressures of normal life.. . .

A muffled crack pierced the soundscape: a sudden accent in the monotonous droning symphony of the engine. My headphones were melting ice as they slipped through my fingers to the carpeted floor.

Stifled screams came from behind the veiled cockpit's door, the sacred space tainted by unhinged aggression. The taste of pine and ammonia thick in the air, sweat beading on the back of my neck. A primal screech of its wounded prey followed two prominent bellows from the throat of a gun.

The plane erupted in a haunting chorus of gasps, faces white as old, discarded bones, the air dense with dread, infesting the plane like a virus. Our hearts bound together in fear, a unified, adrenalised reaction: an invisible tether.. . .

Coach Hart rose from his seat, hesitating at first with a bent back and a furrowed brow. He moved forward with careful steps until he reached the cockpit door. With tentative rasps, he sought answers.

"Is everything okay in there?" he inquired.

A glaze seemed to cover his flustered face.

I held my breath. What was he thinking? There was no doubt in my mind: we heard gunshots.

The lock on the door clicked, and once more, everyone on the plane watched and waited. Denial, our truest friend, gave us comfort in the wake of crippling fear. The door swung back, revealing a flight attendant: silky brown hair matted and wet, black mascara trailing down her face as if she had been standing in the rain.

"Everything is most definitely okay. Can I be of any assistance to you, sir?" she managed to ask.

As I watched the flight attendant and Coach Hart speak, a dip of the plane and a jolting movement caused patrons to slide from side to side and even fall into the aisle, appearing to be unconscious.

*What was going on here?* As the butterflies in my stomach returned, flapping chaotically, tremors took over the plane. My heart hammered in my chest, my shirt damp and constricted against my skin. This was not normal.

Coach Hart raised his voice.

"What happened in there? It sounded awfully like two gunshots."

The flight attendant's phlegmatic eyes twitched and burnt with red smouldering flames. The plane had ceased its timid dissention, now lurching violently in midair. Screams erupted from the passengers as they cowered beneath their seats; some lay motionless on the floor, others stood tall, attempting to view the scene near the cockpit door.

Jasmine, who was sitting in the row behind me, cried out desperately.

"Wake up, Kate! Wake up!"

Kate, a member of a rival team, was limp and unconscious, blood trailing from her nostrils and her mouth. *What was happening?*

Coach Hart then caught my attention, motioning to the passengers to keep calm.

"Don't panic. I'm trying to figure this out," he bellowed.

The flight attendant came forward, taking centre stage for her closing monologue.

"There is no need—you will all soon be dead," she declared.

Another wave of nausea nearly paralysed me. I could taste fear. It was bitter. Like raw cacao powder without the sweetener—like corked merlot, stagnant, foul. It was hard to swallow.

The flight attendant gestured to us all as we gazed at her, worry obfuscating our otherwise usual, benevolent stares.

"You will never have the chance to see what great will come of this new world."

With that remark, she revealed a pistol, concealed behind her and thrust it in between Coach Hart's eyes. He didn't even have time to react. She immediately sent a bullet right through him. The back of his head exploded, a prominent exhibition of blood to a dissonant soundtrack of exasperated panic. The thick red substance spewed forth like lava, coagulated and intense, bursting out from the back of his head.

My soul recoiled and shrunk behind a heart made to withstand this type of emotional ambush. But my heart faltered. It dove into the ocean of my pride, swallowed by the deep blue.

Steven Hart's legs became flaccid as he made his lingering descent towards the floor of the plane. Blood decorated his face in large droplets and flowed from the back of his head, immediately soaking into the carpeted floor.

Steven Hart: my first dead body.

My death virginity, taken on a plane. Something I had never expected. Zack buried his fingers into my thigh, but I hardly even felt it. What I witnessed numbed my senses. Panic rose and burnt within my chest like a furnace. The nausea was worse now, but my body stood firm when my heart did not. It held together while the situation threatened to tear me apart. The flight attendants' voices rose above all the crying, the screams and calls for mercy. She spoke with such force, transcending the wave frequencies of chaos and fear. The plane howled, warning dozing and unsuspecting prey. "We are the New Breed, and elimination will be your only future!" screamed the flight attendant.

No one knew what she meant; no one cared about what anyone was saying at the time. My own thoughts were too scattered to comprehend.

One thought zoomed past another. *Will I die here? Is there a future for me? What the fuck just happened? Why did a flight attendant kill my coach? Can someone land the plane? Why is . . .*

Gus vacated his seat, interrupting that final insignificant thought. My focus turned to him. The sturdy, young man had reached the aisle, standing with his arms away from his sides, his blind determination ratified by clenched fists and a clear, focused stare.

He braced himself with a steady and deliberate breath inwards and eagerly shot off towards the flight attendant. His shiny, shaved head bounced with each stride, bringing him closer to impact with the maniacal flight attendant.

Her gaze fell upon Gus as he approached her. As she raised her gun at him, he corrected the distance with longer strides and leapt towards her. She didn't get to fire a shot, as his solid frame crashed into her rigid body.

I held my breath as she crumpled beneath him. Gus' impact knocked the gun from her grasp. He rose majestically off her broken body, and with dominating prowess and strength, proceeded to plough his fists into her bewildered face.

A shocking scene unfolded before me, as the remnants of her head hit the floor with a moist thud. Gus forced himself up with the ferocious fists that had obliterated the face of a woman, grabbed the gun off the floor, and with one swift movement, released the bullet into her heart.

Brilliant red sparks sprayed onto Gus' face, his eyes wide with indignation and conviction. *Had I just witnessed this?* Gus had just killed someone. Clearly, my adrenal gland was not working, I froze with shock. As I juggled my thoughts, Gus snapped out of his trance. He turned to us all, the regular passengers crying, screaming or attempting to pray, and Gus yelled in a booming voice, "I need someone to help me land this plane, it's going down!"

Could I move?

My fingers twitched in response to the question.

The evidence was there.

It didn't look like anyone else was going to, as I searched the rest of the plane. Maybe I did have an adrenal gland after all. I had to repress the fear. I had to ignore the feeling that someone else would save us. It was time to do something other than stare starry eyed, shocked and scattered.

I bid farewell to a pale-faced Zack, who was slumped in his chair beneath the cover of his tattooed arms. Running down the aisle to meet Gus, we stood for a second and surveyed the bodies of Coach Hart and the flight attendant.

"What did you do man? You just killed someone." I stammered.

"I did what I had to do; she was crazy." He grabbed my shoulders. "This is not a time to debate what just happened. We need to move, we need to act."

Desh arrived from the row behind me, and we locked eyes, nodding at each other in silent appreciation. I steadied myself to open the cockpit's door.

A spiteful splatter of death ruined the cockpit's metallic grey sheen. I swallowed hard, determined to keep my pride and my breakfast.

Slumped at the controls were two bodies. I ran towards them.

One pilot: hole through the right eye, splintered skull on display, chunks of brain exposed, blood trickling onto the epaulettes and stripes on his shoulder.

The second pilot: keeled over, holding his stomach, shot but still alive.

"Holy shit, are you . . . are you okay?" I said, panting and desperate.

He coughed, breathing ragged and strained. "Kid, just listen to me. She fucking blew the radio and damaged the autopilot. We're somehow going to have to land this plane."

"What do you want me to do?" I screamed.

Gus pushed me out of the way and turned to the dying pilot. "Tell me what to do; I'll get this done."

"Take the controls on the left-hand side and look at that altitude metre right there." He spluttered and coughed as he extended his right hand towards a small globe not far from the centre.

The floor shook with startling severity, violently throwing Desh and I into smears of blood on the back wall. I reeled away in horror. The plane bellowed, willing itself to withstand the laws of gravity.

"Pull up on the yolk – ah, the controls," the pilot strained to say.

Gus heaved on the control, pulling upwards, his muscles bulging until his skin was stretched and taut. His teeth locked together, the creases on his forehead defined as he gave the very essence of himself to the task.

Desh and I regained our balance, and we flanked the pilot, waiting for a chance to contribute anything helpful at all. The buttons on the panels flashed, alarmingly. Vivid colours fused together and hurried passed us; there was no identifiable structure as I squinted out of the window around Gus, who had worked on levelling the plane out according to the altitude metre.

"Can you see any clearing up ahead, kid?" the pilot groaned at me.

Desh and I searched out of the window.

"There – up ahead to the left; it's as close to a clearing as I can see," Desh yelled, his voice tinged with the spawn of hope.

"Aim for that. It's your . . . best chance to . . . survive," said the pilot.

"Now, pull that throttle down . . . and the . . . landing gear will be released."

I obeyed orders, and the plane responded with a low groan of its own.

Gus turned towards Desh and I, the uncertified co-pilots.

"Get out of the cockpit now. I'll do the rest!" he screamed.

Desh and I stood firm.

The second warning from Gus came as a plea, not an order.

"Get out of here, guys. I'm serious. GO NOW!"

I refused to move. I knew I was closer to the door, but I didn't want to leave him. Thankfully, Desh made that decision for me. He grabbed my shirt and pulled me out of the cockpit.

Sprawled on the floor, we lay next to the bodies of Coach Hart and the flight attendant. I shuddered, rising to follow Desh down the aisle. He pointed in the direction of my seat. "You better get ready for impact!"

Stumbling into my chair, I stole a despairing glance at the cockpit door.

Pj held his head in his hands, looking at the floor, breathing rapidly.

I shook him out of submission and yelled, "Brace yourself!"

Pj tried to say something, but his voice trailed off as my own mind encouraged a barrage of thoughts.

I never wanted to face death, to know the light of day would never shine again. I never wanted to let the feeling of air circulating my lungs abandon me, or know that I would never feel love flood my heart like a monsoon rain.

I stole a glance to my right. Zack was not sitting in his seat. As I searched for a curly black head of hair, I rested my darting eyes upon Zoey instead.

A comatose state had overcome her and she stared with a blank expression at the ceiling; tears were footsteps treading cautiously the steep decline of her magenta cheeks.

Rising to my feet, I launched myself in her direction. All the while, the plane strained to level itself out. The engines roared in pain and frustration, crunching together violently as the yolk control shook in a final effort to achieve stability.

Coming down hard upon Zoey, we crashed to the floor in the small space between the seats on the plane. With my last movement, I covered her with my body to ensure she was protected from harm.

A flash of blinding light.

Deafening silence.

The end had arrived.

# CHAPTER 5

Violent spasms rocked the plane in every direction; glass shattered above my head, and like a cloud from hell, it rained upon me. A huge power surge shot through the plane, splitting each and every structural substance into hundreds of pieces. The metal plates screamed as they tore from the roof and the floor. Luggage and bags came crashing down, some landing on my back and shoulders with a force that took my breath.

Time had become a construct, my thoughts unregistered through a black sea of nightmares. I tightened my grip around Zoey, her nails digging into my back.

The noises were deafening, and they continued for what felt like hours or seconds – I just couldn't tell. The screaming originated from the engine; nothing audible resembled human life. The plane still seemed to glide across the earth, with the bumping, crashing and tearing of the structure. Burning rubber and smoke offended my nostrils.

My body, wedged between both seats, kept Zoey and I safe from being thrown across the entire plane. I kept my eyes closed, as if that would protect me, but soon enough, the plane came to an unexpected halt.

The horrific noises, stained with the fear of death, ceased. Poised on the ground minutes after, I listened intently to the tired creaks of the plane, the ticks and tocks, the clattering metal falling from the roof.

Pins and needles enshrouded my body, indicating my nerves still worked. I knew I was alive – *I think, therefore I am.* The ordeal appeared to be over.

Lifting my head, my eyes were level with the obliterated window, pale green leaves wedged into the cracked glass, still damp from the kiss of the morning dew. Loose clothing clung to my bruised and weary back, so I shook them off as I craned my upper body higher. A sob leaked from underneath me. I eased my arm up and lifted myself off Zoey. Her amber eyes were glowing bulbs, illuminating the shock and fear that spilled from her every pore. Although her tears had long since departed the realm of her face, she held her hands out to me, needing to feel warmth surrounded by a cold situation.

Relief raced through me; I had successfully protected her. As her warm body ignited my own, I scanned what was left of the plane's interior. The entire back section of the plane was gone, replaced by the bitter green of a forest. Clothes, bags, glass, tree branches, bodies, metal and seats lay piled on top of one another, creating an obscure sculpture of disarray and destruction. Our seats were intact; propelling metal sheets or discs had sliced the others in half. My eyes recognised chaos; I was well-acquainted. Bodies lay contorted, fused together with objects that didn't require a beating heart.

My eyes became a sponge, absorbing and adjusting to a strange, new world. Although my head pounded, I could make out the devastating scene. I fought the sudden, penetrating urge to look away. There was nowhere to hide. Although I wanted the innocence in me to return, triumphant and wielding a sword, vanquishing the disquiet just like they were menial foes, I knew as I inhaled the smoke of the burning bodies, that it would scorch who I had been, and the misty exhale were parts of me that I'd never know again, floating into the ether.

I turned my attention back to Zoey, lifting her up gently, careful not to cause more injuries to her. As I rose to my feet, I lost all balance. I steadied myself on a ravaged chair, regaining some traction to carry Zoey towards the plane's exit. I didn't know who or what I was treading on; there was no clear aisle anymore. I didn't want to look for a path between broken bodies and blood, I just needed to get the hell out of there and find the quickest route possible.

As I came to the main exit door in the middle of the plane, I followed the instructions on the side of the door, heaving it open. Luckily, I was fortunate enough to find that the emergency exit ramps were in working order.

"Go and rest near that tree over there," I told Zoey. "I'm going back to look for some more people."

She was shaky and nervous venturing into the bush alone, and I cursed myself for being so callous, assisting her as we shuffled over to a towering blue gum to rest.

"Wait here. I'll be back soon." I spoke gently, squeezing her hand with sincerity.

She didn't say anything but threw her head back against the tree, pale-faced and breathing heavily. Far beyond anything, I wanted to stay with her and heal together, but I sensed my friends from inside the plane, silently pleading with me to find them. I turned without another glance behind me, mustering all the strength I could. As I walked back towards the plane, the engine still roared, but it seemed timid; perhaps it was dying.

From the outside, the fuselage looked relatively intact, apart from the missing tail, of course, but internally, the scene was a complete catastrophe. If a car crash was meant to ravage the body, well, I had reached the penultimate level with what I had just experienced. As the plane went down, I was a satin sheet caught in a hurricane, and in the aftermath, my poor muscles throbbed with every step I took.

And I thought the after effects of leg day were bad.

The sharp ache in my head distorted my vision, swirls of smoke and dust made it difficult for me to breathe. As I rubbed my eyes, I caught a glimpse of my hand. Red scarlet smeared across my skin from a wound on my forehead. It trickled over my right eye, carving a path onto my soiled face, its warmth burning me as if it were the sun's rays reaching out to engulf the earth.

As I found myself back in what appeared to be an aisle, only the cold embrace of horror rushed through me – of total, crushing disbelief. For a moment, I wondered, *How did I get here?* It took me a minute to register it, but it just didn't seem real. It couldn't happen to me – to us.

The only thing that released me from my trance was Desh's voice. He stood tall and proud among the chaos that surrounded him, holding Mia in his arms as he advanced towards me. She was unconscious, but as they came closer, she was still breathing.

He gave me a stern order. "Cooper, just find as many people as you can and send them out the hatch."

The task of finding survivors overshadowed my relief to find him alive. I hated this reality. I hated that some of my friends were dead. But I had yet to find out who.

"Desh, are you okay?" My voice was sandpaper on untreated pine.

Blood trailed down the hickory hues of his cheek like viscid tears fused in time. "I'm barely holding it together." He struggled with Mia's weight on his shoulders.

This wasn't the time for heart-to-hearts. Our ventricles could sit across from the other when time would allow. "Set her down next to Zoey, and I'll try and find the others."

This was a heartbreaking journey, one that spanned a short distance, but lingered long in the memory. I walked down the aisle, covered in debris, searching for any sign of life. The ache in my head impaired my vision, just as much as the sight of my university mates' lifeless bodies sprawled on the floor like old, discarded toys.

I reeled back in horror. Jasmine Mazio sat upright in her seat in peace. The strands of red rust in her hair revelled in the light of the sun. A large chunk of metal sparkled maliciously, embedded in her throat. Rich blood flickered and spat out in intervals, like a broken tap spilling onto her lap. A weak sound escaped me, like the whimper of an orphaned cub. I had to repress the shock and sadness and continue on to search for survivors. Would finding someone alive take away the hurt of seeing Jasmine?

I had to stop letting this get to me. I had to find the strength inside myself to move forward and repress the grief straining at the surface. Strength was the hardest thing to find that day.

Walking down the aisle, I called out in wispy breaths, searching for people through eyes filled with bitter tears. The stench of rust overpowered my senses, but it wasn't the torn metal inside the plane; it was the blood on the floor, on the walls, everywhere around me. I fought nausea, bile rising, burning my throat.

I caught a glimpse of movement to my right. Underneath piles of twisted copper, I spotted Gil. In his arms lay Craig. In that moment, I admired the love Gil had for his friends as I helped them up. To my dismay, Gil was the only one to rise to his feet. Craig fell back to the ground again, limp, dead. A long metal bracket that had broken off from the plane had driven heedlessly into his chest. His eyes were still open, staring out the window, admiring a world that had little admiration for his previous existence. Gil grabbed onto my back, but death devoured my strength; death that penetrated each glimmer of hope. Craig was so damn innocent, and now – gone. He saw risk as a foe, so he never did anything remotely reckless, yet here he was, dead before me.

I cried, but I didn't care, and with tears staining my face, I turned away from Craig to help Gil. There was nothing more to do but focus on the living. After helping him to the door, he strained to smile and squeezed my arm. "I can manage from here. Thank you Cooper." He met the ground gingerly and shuffled off to join Zoey, Mia and Desh against the tree.

I turned back. Movement in the aisle caught my attention. It was Hayden. We played poker and roulette together at the casino, on the odd occasion. He lay under a pile of metal and broken glass; his hand was the only visible body part amongst the debris. I could only tell it was him by the sound of his voice. He called over and over, "Help!"

I ran to Hayden and grabbed his hand, pulling him out as far as I could. Strands of flesh from a severed stomach sought its counterpart, like roots exposed above the earth reaching desperately for the nourishment of soil. He looked at me; his eyes screamed for answers that I did not have.

He opened his mouth to say something, but all that came out was blood. It flowed out of his mouth and onto his clothes, already stained with the putrid substance. I was too traumatised to say anything; there was absolutely nothing I could do for Hayden. His eyes bore deep into me, asking the same question: *WHY?*

Shaking off the shock, I held his hand and started to speak.

"Hayden, you're okay, buddy. Just take in deep breaths with me." I inhaled through my nose and exhaled out of my mouth.

He tried to do the same, but he lurched forward, throwing his arms over me, gasping for air.

"I've got you, buddy." I pushed through clenched teeth.

Hayden's eyes bulged, and he begged me to help, but the volume of blood he vomited across my shoulders couldn't possibly sustain life. I held him tighter as he shook, singing the chorus of a song about the sun, in hope that it would paint his last moments in brighter colours. I would never know if it eased his pain. Like the draining of water from a warm bath, blood gurgled inside his throat, and he exhaled for the last time.

Tears welled up in my eyes, and this time, they flowed stronger than before. I collapsed in the aisle, atop the torn sheets of metal and cried as if the dam of my emotions had broken beyond repair. I allowed myself to let everything go as Hayden's body fell from my arms.

Desh's hand touched my trembling shoulder.

"Man, we couldn't do anything more," he said. "This is breaking me, Cooper, but I can't find anyone else."

His eyes twitched with the suppression of grief. He brought me to my feet and placed his arm around me. As we turned our backs upon the scene where our lives changed forever, we threatened to walk away.

An angelic voice in severe distress called my name, begging us not to leave. I whipped around, wiping the tears from my eyes, allowing my enervated body to follow her voice. She was underneath several seats and metallic shards. After helping her out of the rubble, I hugged her tight. She was unresponsive to my touch, riddled in disbelief, not knowing what to do.

"C'mon, Kasey," I whispered. "You're okay now."

Her mouth quivered, and she fought against coming undone, but her legs gave way. I found enough strength to catch her and pull her close to me as she sobbed. Even though Kasey's tears seeped into my torn shirt, I felt a sudden jolt of joy because we had found someone else alive. Desh and I helped her out of the plane. "Cooper, go down there to look after everyone while I try to find some more survivors. I just need to believe there might be somebody else," Desh remarked with severe composure.

At that moment I dared to dream, *what about Gus?*

Desh reached out to catch Kasey as I ran for the cockpit door. Heaving it open, I called his name.

There was absolutely nothing left of the front window. Clumps of leaves and thin broken branches were snagged on the tiny shards of glass that remained. The control board looked like a giant had reached in and tore it out. Wires, bulbs and buttons were criss-crossed and cracked, a colourful palette of useless objects now, once important enough to transport lives from one country to another.

Then I saw him. Sprawled next to the open door, his mouth agape and eyes wide. I almost smiled and told him to get up, but he was impaled on a tree branch; the flexing arm of a tree, who gave the world so much life had in this case, taken one. It had smashed through the window and into his chest, severing him in half. His internal organs were strewn across the floor like vines of poison oak infesting an elegant garden. My shoes were submerged in his blood. Not only anger welled up inside me, but the horrifying scene haunted me. The heat of chilli tickled my throat, the sour taste of malt vinegar rose, burning acid towards the roof of my mouth. I rushed out of there and vomited profusely. Tears were now a permanent fixture on my pale face.

Gus had done something wonderful for all of the survivors and I. He saved several people, while sacrificing his own. Gus was a true friend and a hero.

I climbed down to the bottom once more to find Zoey, Kasey and Gil sitting in a staggered formation, looking dumbfounded, shocked, horrified and broken. Mia lay across the earth, unconscious but breathing.

I walked straight over to Zoey, who had her hands folded across her stomach and a blank look upon her face. I put my arm around her a moment after I sat down. There was nothing I could say, no words that could provide comfort to the situation. She didn't say anything, either; she just turned her face into my chest and made it her home.

Noises came from inside the plane. Desh and Pj stood at the hatch door, carrying Zack in their arms. I was so relieved when I saw Pj and Zack, though it all escaped me when I realised how much of a bad condition Zack was in.

Although Pj looked fine, he was limping significantly due to a large laceration on the back of his calf. I let go of Zoey, easing her away from my chest so that I could help Pj walk. Desh lay Zack on the grass next to Zoey, who placed her hands upon his shoulder. His body willed itself onwards, but a gentle hiss and the low groan of wheezing breaths had us deeply concerned.

Desh shifted his eyes at me and bent his head towards the plane. As he walked, I imagined that he wanted me to follow.

Desh spoke. "There are no more survivors. No one else is alive; this is it." He sighed. "You and I can go back in to collect whatever supplies we can find."

His voice was a plain white painting hung in a cavernous hall.

I nodded as we made our way onto the plane again.

The search was brief, as the plane's engine exhibited signs of life once more. I almost didn't notice it sputtering because of the growing familiarity of the constant drone. The first warning sign was a slight surge of electricity that rocked the plane.

I snapped a decisive look at Desh, and his eyes were wide.

"We need to go!" I yelled.

Everything we had gathered was in three large backpacks, so we grabbed them and bolted. We didn't even bother climbing down the ramp; we jumped off the plane, hell bent on getting out of it. As we hit the ground, the engine became a savage lion defending its territory. The propellers found a rhythm, dragging us in.

The others were already off and running further into the bush. Mia and Zack were being dragged along the ground to safety. The propellers gathered speed and severity as we stumbled past the tree where we had all been sitting. It was only a matter of time before our legs would collapse, and the propellers would drag us into their welcoming blades, serving us up as bush sushi.

The plane exploded, and I turned around on instinct. An orange ball of destruction lit up before my glassy eyes. Fiery remnants of the plane danced in the sky like shooting stars, cascading towards the earth all around us. We continued to surge ahead, but I fixed my eyes on the beautiful chaos behind us; autumn in its palette and in its intention to end our life cycle. A spiralling tool of death, fixed an eye upon me. Desh tugged me down to the dirt just in time to see it slam into the tree ahead of us. Before I had a chance to thank Desh, thank God, thank whoever, the tree starting to tip over above us. This time, I yanked Desh to the left. As the hulking trunk slammed into the ground beside us, it released an exhausted breath, anointing us with a light sprinkling of soil. We lay there, the sounds of the explosion dying in our ears, our hearts hammering inside our sweaty bodies, on my back, in the bush, next to a fallen tree looking towards the heavens.

The sky was a grey collage of elusion and destruction.

'Fuck you!' I screamed. Even now I don't know who I was screaming at. Maybe it was God. Maybe I was just angry at life itself? Life, who knocked upon my door, trying to sell me the dream. Life, who I would normally invite inside. We would share a cup of tea and a delicious fruit flan, of course. But right then, I would have placed a welcome mat for death. I would have beckoned death to burn me in that scalding cup of tea, rather than share putrid, fraudulent moments with a traitorous life.

When I think of all the people I've lost, death would've been easier. But the easy road is seldom the most forgiving, for challenges heed a certain elixir for the afflictions that asphyxiate us.

When I realised that no one was going to answer my screams, I flipped onto my stomach and looked upon Desh, whose sombre and exhausted face stared up at the torn sky. "Let's get out of here," I managed to say, balancing on my elbows.

He turned to me but didn't say a word. I gave him my hand, and we both used each other to rise up from the beaten earth, groaning in a baritone harmony.

I barely registered the shapes of the others in the distance, only the select few who were lumbering back to check that we were okay. With each forced step, my sight shimmered and waned. In a delusional state, I imagined that I would soon wake up to the sounds of my Mum begging me to get ready. When faced with duress, humans turn to denial. I had blindfolded myself with my own fear. It was all too much to handle.

Zoey and Pj came back to see if we were okay. They didn't fuss about it; they grabbed hold of the backpacks and shepherded us about a hundred metres further to where the rest of the group sat. Each of them stared at Desh and I, abolishing courteousness, eyes glazed, parched mouths, resembling the living dead. I sat down next to Gil, who was staring into the distance.

We were all silent. That spoke volumes.

Mia's shallow breaths drifted towards my ears as she lay peacefully on her back, eyes closed in a world where we could not visit her. The forest scent combined the awakening zest of eucalyptus and the grit of rotting wood, ravaged by moss.

Inside of our hearts, and in the finest layers of our skin, we were an absolute mess. Relief might have kissed us upon our soiled foreheads; disbelief may have run its spindly fingers through our matted hair. But the shock of it all ran deeper, and the silence proved that survival was not about moving one foot in front of the other, it was about giving our hearts a reason to pump; giving our frightened souls a reason to return.

The silence would linger no longer, as my husky voice emerged from the forest floor.

"Desh and I grabbed some water and a medical kit. They're in the packs over there. We should all use what we can to patch ourselves up."

At the mention of water, their heads turned towards me like a group of sullen meerkats scanning the earth for signs of life. I smiled inside because it was too much effort to form an actual smile. Ambling over to one of the bags, I uncovered the bottled spring water, brought to us courtesy of the airline. Handing out bottles to everyone, I conjured up the, don't-disappoint-Dad routine.

"Be smart about this. We don't have much of anything, so just take a couple of sips at a time."

"Where's the goddamn alcohol?" Zoey complained. "I need a drink of some real shit."

I ignored her.

After everyone had their fair share of water, I opened the medical kit in an attempt to play doctor rather than Dad, surveying the countless wounds. After I applied some disinfectant to Kasey's arms and legs, she went around to the others and helped me. *Bless her sweet soul,* I thought.

We inspected that laceration on Pj's right calf. It looked terrible. When I asked him what had happened, he shrugged it off and said he woke up on the floor with a cut on his leg. I gave Pj the bottle of disinfectant and a pain killer.

"It's important you keep an eye on the wound to minimise infection," I warned.

"Cooper, last time I checked, you were studying communications, buddy, not medicine," he sneered.

Kasey interjected, "Last time I checked, rude assholes didn't get any help from people who were doing a nice thing."

Normally, I didn't need others to fight my battles for me, but in this case, the battle for my life had taken all of my energy.

I put my hand on Kasey's knee and breathed in deep.

"Yeah, okay, that was poor of me," admitted Pj. "Sorry." And he trudged off, shoulders slumped and eyes affixed to the earth.

The rest of the patients weren't too bad considering; Mia was still unconscious, so Kasey dampened her forehead with a wet cloth, and Zack only had a broken arm, luckily. We made him a splint and told him it would have to do. It was amazing that he only suffered a broken arm because, when we first saw him, it was as though he was moments from death.

"Let me be the first to break the dumbfounded pleasantries and ask: what the fuck just happened?" Pj's chagrin didn't last long, as he trumpeted into the calm bush setting.

I stared at each face gathered in the group. The adrenaline that pumped throughout my body had subsided, but the severity of our situation was ever present. I was emotionally exhausted, and I wasn't sure of what to say.

Thankfully, Zoey spoke up.

"Well, our plane crashed; we survived. Many others died. Now, we're in the bush with no clue where we are," she said.

"Does anyone have a phone we could use for GPS or at least to call someone?" Gil asked politely.

Several hands shot towards their various pockets.

"No signal here," wallowed Zack.

The exact same response followed from the rest of the group.

"Well, what do we do now, then?" Gil searched us all.

Feeling useless, I chose silence instead of offering up anything constructive.

"Let's look at this logically. Our plane has crashed, so, chances are, people will look for survivors within the hour at least. If we don't see any sign of a rescue in that hour, we will set up some tents to get some sleep for the night and work out another plan in the morning," Zoey suggested, reasoning with us.

Her thoughts seemed to be firing at a quicker rate than the rest of us.

"Yes, our plane crashed, but we can't forget that our coach was murdered, and a flight attendant caused our plane to go down," said Desh.

"That flight attendant – did she not say something about a New Breed? What was that about?" asked Pj.

"Did anyone hear her properly?" Gil inquired.

"I did," I said hesitantly. My mind was still scrambled, so I wasn't sure if I had heard correctly. It seemed like it didn't make sense.

"It was about a New Breed, yes, but a New Breed of what – I'm not sure." I managed.

"This is so fucked," spat Zack, running a clawed hand through his matted black hair.

He was right. The situation was as Zack so eloquently put it, but despite everything else, hadn't we just survived a plane crash?

Weren't we the handful of survivors while others perished?

"It's not all fucked, Zack," I croaked.

"We're alive, and that's more than anyone else on that plane can say –"

My raspy voice trailed off as I fought the onset of tears.

The explosion's smoky haze had settled around us now, tainting the pure, wild air of the bush. The granular texture of charcoal settled on my tongue, and it was the acrid taste of death that crawled down the back of my throat.

Everyone bowed their heads and abandoned voices, perhaps in search of an inner reflection or an intrinsic exploration of grief. Silence came once more to embrace us as we sat together in a circle. Sometimes words filled the air like the skyscrapers littering an urban wasteland. In this case, I wanted to demolish what impeded my panoramic view.

# CHAPTER 6

We waited for an hour, but nothing happened. It was as if the rescue crews thought that we were beyond saving.

*How did we even know that the flight was registered? The flight attendant could have erased our flight data from all systems.*

Spending a night in the deserted bushland after such a horrific ordeal left us terrified and anxious, but it seemed as though we had no choice. The sleeping equipment we had salvaged from the plane made an appearance in the middle of our circle. There were four tents, five sleeping bags and some extra clothes and jumpers we could use as blankets.

We set up the tents as best as we could. I was absolutely useless at putting them together. Instead of enraging myself with countless failed attempts, I gave the job to Kasey, who somehow knew what she was doing.

"I was a girl scout for like, all of primary school," she bragged.

*Not your run of the mill beauty queen*, I thought. We chose our camping area several metres into the bush, where the trees provided constant shade and shelter. When we had finished setting up our tents, we sat upon a large log positioned at the core of our camping ground. While we waited for something to happen, Kasey took control. To my surprise, she organised our sleeping arrangements.

"Let's look at this realistically: we have more people here than sleeping bags. So, some of us have to share. First, we have to see, like, who is comfortable sleeping in the same sleeping bag?"

Zoey raised her hand.

"I'll go with Cooper tonight."

I looked at her from the corner of my eye, but she didn't take notice of me.

Kasey watched me sternly, as if to say, "Are you okay with that?"

"Ah, yeah, sounds fine to me."

A decent attempt at nonchalance, if I did say so myself.

"Okay, well, I guess I'll bunk with Gil, if you – like, don't mind," said Kasey, flickering blue ocean eyes that could drown a skilled sailor.

"No issues with me," he muttered, unfazed, drawing shapes in the dirt with a stick.

Desh cut in.

"I'll sleep without a sleeping bag tonight. I'll grab the jumpers and whatever else there is and then the next couple of nights we'll all alternate?"

"Okay, we'll see how that goes tonight, but in the meantime, you and Mia will share a tent so you can watch over her. Pj, you can be with Zack."

I admired Kasey for her resilience. I hadn't seen this side of her before, and it was a surprise to see that she could prevail under pressure.

"Well, I guess we will see each other in the morning, then." She let out a small sigh.

Zack croaked, "Oh, man, what a day." He squeezed the bridge of his nose and rubbed his red eyes. Kasey floated to his side and put an arm around him. It prompted the rest of us to seek a warm embrace, to share a pained smile, to give something positive to one another. It helped instil strength in us before we separated for the evening.

Zoey and I climbed into our tent and wasted no time laying out the sleeping bag on the ground.

"Hey, so, listen. If you're not comfortable, we don't have to - " Zoey interrupted my spluttering.

"Coops, everything that happened today was just crazy. We don't have to complicate anything. It's just science; keeping close will keep us warm."

"Oh, okay, well, don't be afraid to kick me out."

I finished, nervous and embarrassed.

Zoey smiled confidently.

"I won't."

I nodded in appreciation.

"I need to go out for a cigarette; this whole situation is doing my head in, but I'll be back, okay?"

Zoey rose gracefully, and I bowed my head, acknowledging her departure. I was a bit dejected, knowing that the whole reason she wanted to share a sleeping bag with me was for science. It wasn't romantic at all. But then, a microsecond after, I stopped myself. Here I was, pining after a love-fuelled experience after suffering through the worst day of my life. As I recalled the day's events, my pulse accelerated; my breath gathered intensity. I ran out of the tent as fast as I could, cradling a Ventolin puffer like a childhood teddy bear.

I leant, wide-eyed against a sturdy boulder, but I was shaking. One minute, I was daydreaming about love, the next: a nightmare of death brought cruel whispers of anxiety. It was difficult to swim through the night then, difficult to breathe under the waves as they came down upon me, unrelenting and forceful.

When I closed my eyes, death was there, smiling. Hayden, Craig, Jasmine and Gus, all calling out to me for help. Memories and imagination fused and fought for the right to my reality. Tears fell as loneliness clung to me in a desperate embrace. *Would I ever be the same?*

*Would I ever get back to who I was before? How can you possibly forget friends and move on? Why did I have to live without them?*

All these questions I'd asked myself before. But was it easier now that I'd already experienced the loss of my father? No. The answers abandoned me then, so why would it be any different now?

I think that this is what humans do: push the problems into the dark corners of their heart, allowing denial to bathe them, clothe them, repair them, until the dark corners are no more, but the room of the heart itself becomes encased in shadow. I didn't want my heart to live in a shadow world. I wanted it to nurture bursts of colourful embers, hues that burnt brighter with age and truth. *Don't let this ruin you*, I thought.

Zoey hovered passed me as I trembled against the boulder. I cupped my hands to my upper arms, rubbing up and down, implying that it was the unforgiving night air that brought the shakes.

"Hey, you, sorry about that; addictions are a bitch. I only have two left, anyway. So, I guess I'll be giving up shortly. I just wanted to check – are you alright?"

*Zoey was here. I could take my mind off things now, couldn't I?*

I snapped back into feigning everything was okay.

"Yeah, yeah, everything is good. Just thought I'd catch a bit of the night air, but it's colder than I expected. Let's finish the tent stuff, why don't we?"

A crooked smile spread across her face, awash in the moon's gentle light. "Okay, c'mon, then."

She knew I was broken; she definitely knew. She was too smart to be fooled.

Long after we had settled in for the night, human screams and whimpers competed with the insect acapella and the squeals and rustling of the flora. My friends and I were obviously finding it hard to get through the first night, after experiencing so much devastation earlier in the day. I slept about two hours that night. The last remnants of my sanity threatened to slip away from me, but focusing on the present was a tactic I needed to try. I found peace in Zoey's warmth against my skin, her heart beating so close to mine. The smell of floral perfume faint on the back of her neck wafted towards me, and the moment beckoned for just one kiss. But I knew that with the events of the day such a kiss would come for the wrong reasons. I kept close to her all night, thinking of yesterday, when I was at home dreaming of sleeping next to her like this, in a totally different situation.. . .

Dawn was fast approaching, and I hadn't found enough peace of mind to fall asleep. I tossed. I turned. I repeated those actions, but I still couldn't find rejuvenation. In utter frustration, I heaved the sleeping bag off my body, exiting the tent with boiling blood. Several clouds loomed above our campsite, threatening a downpour. The wind did not whisper it howled. The taste of burning rubber and smoke, still alive on my tongue. Nothing was as beautiful as it had been the previous morning. I surveyed the campsite before choosing a relatively smooth log to sit on. After finding a long stick, I drew circles in the dirt, attempting to synthesise the information gathering in my head. All night, I clung to the thought of death. The topic was getting stale. I needed to hand-pick something that warranted productive thinking time. Remembering the plane taking off yesterday – was there anything there? *No.* Coach Hart dying in the middle of our flight. *There may be something there perhaps?* I probed around until I found a memory that deserved greater reflection: *What had the flight attendant said before she turned into a homicidal maniac?*

"We are the New Breed, and elimination will be your only future." *New breed.* These were words that I could only assume made reference to some sort of animal, but in context, seemed highly unlikely. She didn't look like an animal. She never once got down on all fours and pounced around the plane. She looked and acted very much like . . . one of us.

Too many questions brewed inside my head, with no answers in sight. The constant back and forth grew tiresome. I craved to know what everything meant. Most of all, I was anxious about what the near future held for me and my friends. I looked towards the sky. I was not alone anymore. The sun had opened its eyes, peering cautiously over the land, illuminating the crash site further in the distance. *Bad memories.*

I heard someone struggling with their tent zipper behind me. I didn't care to turn around. My current mood did not lend itself to small talk and social pleasantries. I, however, favoured the idea of continuing my newfound friendship with the dirt, drawing a catalogue of obscure shapes and patterns. I have realised that, when complications arise in my life, I will either lash out in anger or crawl inside of myself. It wasn't something that made me particularly proud.

Was it the caustic relationships of my youth that have broken me down? Maybe it was growing up without a father figure to guide me through the emotionally constricting times? Look at me, psychoanalysing myself. What positive could I have gained from that?

This complication, however, was one I had never experienced before: a plane crash, several friends dying at the same time, stranded in the bush somewhere between Sydney and Cairns. As you could imagine, my feelings were tainted, and my heartstrings were taut. So, I just shut myself down and let the absence of thoughts and feelings comfort me.

A firm grip on my shoulder caused me to look upwards at Desh's solemn stare.

"Morning," I muttered grumpily.

He sat down beside me. "No sign of rescue yet, which is quite a surprise to me. How are you holding up anyway?" I didn't take my eyes off the stick drawing circles in the dirt. "Not the best, mate. How about you?"

"Well, to tell you the truth, if I think about it too much, I honestly find it difficult to comprehend."

I nodded.

"Yep, I hear you. That is why I'm trying not to think too much."

My thoughts were now dormant at the bottom of my head, twitching and itching to be heard. But I didn't need them, nor did I want them at the time. The 'New Breed' could wait. My feelings could wait.

Then, Desh opened up a whole new can of worms I hadn't even considered.

"Do you think our families are okay?"

I stopped drawing circles.

"Why would they be in danger?"

"It was just the way the flight attendant was talking. It was as if she had been following a grand plan, something that would affect more than a plane with a couple of uni students."

My mind hadn't taken me to the same destination as Desh's. He was traversing mountains and cliff-jumping, while I sat by the pool, reading an intriguing novella. Worlds apart! Regardless, I needed to repress those types of thoughts and feelings down inside again.

"I hadn't thought of it yet, to be honest," I said, hoping they were all safe.

After minutes of silent reflection, another wounded soul wandered out to join us. Gil exited his tent, looking tired and weary. He suggested to Desh and I that we explore the area around us. It was an idle, practical thought from a university student who perhaps watched too many movies about being stranded in the bush, a practical thought that would take my mind off other pressing matters, I suppose. We only took a couple of minutes to gather our packs, setting off east of our camp and completing a full circle. We did our best not to disturb those who were lucky enough to sleep in. Some would say that the whole time we walked around, sweating in the sun, was a waste of time, losing precious energy and precious fluids. But I took comfort in my interaction with the earth: the rhythm of my footsteps as we passed gumtree after gumtree, broken stick after broken stick, jagged rocks and dead leaves, the odd Cyathea fern rising from the undergrowth like a proud warrior. Sure, I exhibited my customary clumsiness, tripping and falling over every tiny bump. But all in all, I was at peace, hearing nothing but the music of nature, undisturbed by cars or people in suits: the way it was always meant to be.

The piece of music came to an abrupt end when we had come full circle back to the camp.

When we returned, we uncovered a hovering cloud of sadness, sprinkling droplets of rain upon the heads of our friends. It didn't get any better. We gathered in a circle, going back and forth about the plane crash, the flight attendant, death upon death. I didn't want to talk about the same thing over and over. Sitting in my tent alone was appealing. Staring at the green nylon walls was appealing. Anything but dealing was appealing. And I was good at pretending. For a minute or two, I rescued a princess from the clutches of a mutated man; I surveyed an ancient land and became their noble king. I was a leopard scaling plains in Africa. No doors were locked for me. However, the more I pretended, the more that voice inside pleaded with me to deal with what was going on.

When I relented and welcomed that voice into my head, I couldn't help but cry yet again. I slept as the tears buried themselves into the cemetery of my face.

When I opened my eyes, the murmurs of conversation arose outside of my tent. I could have gotten up and out of bed, but I had no energy. I didn't want to see anyone. It felt like I was lying on my back for days, staring at the pointed ceiling of the tent before Zoey ambled in.

"Are you awake, Coops?" she whispered

"Yeh, I'm here," I mumbled, not taking my eyes off the ceiling.

"I brought something small for you to have a nibble on."

I still didn't bother to look at her. "I'm not that hungry."

"Just sit up, please, Coops. You need to eat something," she said with a hint of forcefulness in her voice, assertive but not quite rude.

I tentatively obliged.

As I stole a glance at Zoey's hands, two small bread rolls and a fruit cup that she had salvaged from the plane supplies were thrust towards me. Her eyes were amber crystals dancing as one underneath a sultry sky, set ablaze with determination and strength. Black hair was pulled back in a braid, tossed over her right shoulder, and she caressed the back of her neck with a timid forefinger while I ate. Her lips pursed, and she sighed with exhaustion. The weight around her seemed just as heavy, but resilience made it appear like a feather.

I graciously accepted the food from Zoey, nodding at her in appreciation. I was not all that hungry, but my mood would surely increase with food inside of my stomach. Silence fell across the tent as I tried to ingest the stale bread. Staring at my feet, my arms, anything but those endearing eyes. At last, I finished and offered my thanks once more.

"No problem," she muttered, comforting me. I hadn't quite seen this compassionate side of her before. Her unique party personality always drew me in, but here she was, letting the masquerade slide off her face. I liked what I saw even more. Zoey's pale red lips parted in a smile, which exposed the slightest echo of the mischievous girl I knew.

"You know that it is hard for us all, Coops, but you aren't helping yourself by shutting out the world."

Yeah, she had a point. But my feelings – I needed to protect them.

"At least we have food and don't have to gnaw on dead bodies, like a kind of tangy charcoal chicken," she joked, wearing a goofy, open-mouthed smile.

Narrowing my eyes at her, I shook my head from side to side.

"That is so wrong!" I exclaimed.

A twisted smile graced Zoey's face. "Too soon, right?"

Her dark sense of humour served her well during a difficult time.

She placed her warm hand on mine, and it sent an alert, trailing along capillaries into the centre of my heart. The laughter had subsided, and all that remained was a pitiful smile. My heart braced itself for impact. Just as I was about to squeeze Zoey's hand or brush a stray hair away from her cheek, she turned away and released her grip. Our moment was lost. As she exited the tent, she called back, "You look exhausted, Cooper. Try to get some rest, and I'll be back shortly."

I slammed my head down on some rolled up jumpers that served as a pillow and rubbed my temples. *Just when I think a moment of splendour is upon us, she goes and says something like that?* It's as if she's saying, "Hey, champ, you look like shit. Catch you on the flip side," ruffling my hair and punching my arm like a big sister would. At least it distracted me from the darkness.

I woke the next morning, more positive than the previous night. Zoey had her arm draped across my chest, and although it felt so good, I suspected that she had moved that way while she was sleeping and didn't even realise. I left the comfort and security of the tent, interested to see what the new day would hurl at us. Understanding that I needed energy to get through the day, I ate my favourite: stale rolls for breakfast. Luckily, I did because Gil thought it would be a good idea for us all to do some more exercise. This time, to search for a possible water source nearby, concerned that the plastic bottles would soon run out. The only people who didn't participate were Zack and Mia. Mia still hadn't awoken from her deep slumber, rendering her incapable of participating in exercise. We each worked in shifts to check on her. When it came to my turn, I sat with her for an hour. Not much happened: slight mumbling, tossing and turning – nothing to write home about. The only thing we could do was wait and have faith that time would bring her back around to us again.

Zack was a different story altogether. His arm seemed to be better. And by better – I mean, it was not broken, quite contrary to what we expected a couple of days before. It appeared as though Zack was a hypochondriac. He milked the pain in his arm to get out of the small duties we had assigned to him. A large gum tree shaded him as he reclined against its sturdy trunk, catching a glimpse of the group members who brought back water bottles from the newfound spring. After carrying my fair share of bottles, I meandered over to where he sat.

The envy was clear in my narrowed stare, but I could at least focus my energy on something positive while he lived in the cage of his mind. I had never understood the mental power of the gym or exercise before. I did it to stay healthy and to look relatively decent. It was a perfect distraction first and foremost, but it also encouraged endorphins to swim around your body, delivering parcels of positivity throughout. I playfully kicked at a bruise on Zack's leg to wake him up. He just screwed up his face like he'd sucked on a ripe lemon and exclaimed, "Ow, dude! That hurt!"

I chortled, sitting down next to him, as he puffed out his developing chest and squared his shoulders.

"How are you feeling, man?"

"Well, not too great now that you kicked me," he replied bitterly.

"Oh, c'mon. I merely tapped you." My condescending tone most likely hurt more than the kick.

"Yeah, but a bruise means it's still not sweet."

"Yeah, yeah. Anyway, speaking of bruises and bones that aren't broken, how are you going, little injured bird?"

He spat out laughter. "Look, I don't get it either. I come out of the plane, my arm clearly broken, feeling that pain all through my whole body like I'm going to black out. I'm lying down under the tree with Zoey and whoever else, and then I don't know. I just started to get better." Zack took off his hat and ran his hands through his hair in frustration. "I can't explain it," he said.

"Honestly, I don't know if you're full of shit or if now, all of a sudden, you can heal yourself."

"I'm unbreakable it seems," he bellowed, scaring off a curious skink.

"Well, if you're so unbreakable, get up and help us carry some of the water back to camp," I spat, with equals parts of humour and frustration, yanking him to his feet with an open palm.

"How's the nightlife in tent city, anyway?"

52

My forehead creased, not understanding. "C'mon, Cooper, with you and Zoey sharing a goddamn sleeping bag at night. If there were any sparks flying, surely that tent would light the fuck up."

"Yeah, sure. Two nights in the bush after the worst day of our lives, and we're totally bonking already."

He laughed, flicking a wrist at me. "I don't necessarily just mean those sparks, although I'm sure that would be great for you."

I recalled the night before: exhaling against Zoey's earlobe, her body shifting against me, a moan so soft, like a hint of wind before a chaotic storm. I held her in a tight embrace, and she fell deep into me, as if into a black hole of primal desire. But we were half-asleep or seeking warmth. Who knew? It was most definitely warm. In fact, I'd go further to say it was getting heated.

"There are cuddles, and it feels a bit more than just sharing body warmth. At least I think so," I added in haste.

Zack's thin lips spread across his face in a teasing grin.

I spotted the two girls talking to each other underneath the tallest gum tree near our campsite. It was time to get away from Zack and leave his creepy little grin behind me.

"Keep walking and get more water for us, you little shit. If you don't come back with at least three litres, I'll break your arm myself, Mr Unbreakable," I warned playfully.

"Sure, sure, buddy. Give it your best shot," he shot back.

The attempt at being social after my self-imposed isolation now moved into phase two. Kasey and Zoey were talking about the crash, exchanging theories as to what may have happened. Zoey seemed frustrated by Kasey's lack of evidence for her theories. Zoey's sarcasm said it all. "Yes, so aliens came *all* the way from Roswell and took over the aircraft."

"Wasn't it Bosewell?" Kasey asked with sincerity.

Zoey's eyes widened, and she craned her neck towards me slowly, like an owl scanning the canopy. Her jaw dropped as she turned her hands over, as if asking me why.

I smirked, then shrugged and kept on moving past the sounds of Zoey berating Kasey about her lack of knowledge.

No sign of rescue showed itself, and we had accepted that we would have to find our own way out of the bush sooner or later. Positioning myself between nothingness and the conversation, half-listening and half-staring into vacant space, I reflected on how time had passed us by so damn fast; it was as though time was our greatest adversary. The coming of a mortal enemy could always be heard. But time had no footsteps. It didn't leave imprints in saturated sand. However, it could creep up on you without warning, stealing your youth, your hope, your dreams. It didn't allow you to live without taking something. Maybe I was paranoia's latest victim, but I felt a looming shadow follow me wherever I went. Was it time itself reaching out to me, waiting for a chance to reveal my final moment? But if time was my enemy, wouldn't life be my enemy, too? Because, without time, there is no life, and without life, there is no time. Maybe death was the only salvation from my everlasting enemy?

As we gathered old logs and dead branches to light a fire, time scrutinised our actions. Luckily, we weren't restricted to primitive methods of lighting fires, such as creating friction between two sticks. Zoey was an occasional smoker and kept a lighter in her pocket. Burning eucalyptus replaced the timid stench of death from the plane. The fire cackled a hideous laugh into the evening, bustling with insects and critters coming out to play. We drank a toast to our friends and all the other people who had perished in the plane crash, whispering words into the night as a gift to their sleeping souls.

I know that, I, for one, liked to imagine that they all reclined on twinkling golden thrones, allowing fresh grapes to dance into the pits of their stomachs. But it was my imagination that provided a delicate banner of hope to be cast across my doubtful perception. I was one of many who struggled with the idea that there could be a heaven. Unfortunately, I lacked the faith that provided a cloud-like cushion from grief and unique, trepidatious circumstances such as ours. In hard and desperate times, it is always good to believe in something, as to receive comfort and peace from a reputable source. My faith was an unwelcoming desert, unyielding and unrelenting in its quest to desiccate the luscious earth. Gil believed in God and was passionate about Him. As for my other friends, they never brought it up.

As the flame flicked her luscious eyelashes in sparse flirtations, we each shared stories of the great times we had at school and university over the past couple of years. Reliving those humorous moments was a positive experience. It was an experience that gave us the materials to build a path in front of us, to walk away from the crash site and push on into the ferocious, unsuspecting future. Flames turned into embers, fighting death, occasionally blinking with heavy eyelids, so the group dissected and retreated to the loving arms of slumber. Kasey, Pj and I stayed up talking quietly about how the plane crash had shifted what we thought was important in our lives. It was interesting how one significant incident could change plans beyond reproach. After an hour, Kasey left Pj and me by ourselves. Unexpectedly, Pj opened up to me.

"Do you think we're gonna die, man?" he asked, his eyes sweltering with concealed anguish.

"I don't know," I remarked, wondering how odd it was to have Pj staring into my eyes with such purpose. "I guess all we can do is fight to continue living."

"What if the fight is gone?" he said. "Weren't people meant to rescue us? Why can't someone fight to make sure we are safe?"

I hadn't seen this side of him before, and it spooked me.

"You may think the fight is gone, but I tell you: one thing to fight for is *us*. Simple as that, man. It isn't just you anymore; it's all of us, together."

He shifted on the log, indicating his emotional restlessness, though I continued.

"I know how you're feeling, buddy. You won't meet another person who is more afraid of death than I am, but at the end of the day, if this hasn't taught you to just live as hard as you can, then I don't know, mate. Besides, if someone doesn't come for us, then we can work out an exit strategy when our supplies are nearly gone."

I was absolutely terrified of dying. But we had survived . . . so far.

We were eight out of a decent number of people on that plane who survived. Maybe Gil had spoken to God and given him a couple of extra lambs or whatever currency heaven deals, giving us a free pass.

Pj sighed and tossed his head to where the stars burnt in the expansive sky. I could make out faint droplets of tears forming in his eyes. Pj had always appeared so impenetrable, a primitive male archetype. So, when this frailty within him surfaced, weakness washed over me. It's strange how people around you often make you who you are. From Pj, my strengths emerged. I was sure he never quite understood what his friendship and his charisma instigated within me. I thought about what qualities I helped uncover in people. Were there any? As I sat there with Pj, unable to move, I acknowledged our extremities and our crippling weakness – the person you think you need actually needs you more. I squeezed his shoulder to transfer the strength that he had given me back to him. I didn't know how else to react. It was Pj. He never needed any kind of comfort before, so, as awkward as I was, my simple gesture let him know he would never be alone. I remained beside him until the ghost of sleep threatened to haunt our eyes. I climbed into the sleeping bag with Zoey; she had already fallen asleep. Again, warmth spread through me as I put my arm around her body. Feeling brave, I pulled her close to me and closed my eyes. She expelled a sleepy groan but allowed herself to be held. I thought of how photographs always stood the test of time and how I needed a camera for moments like these. *Were photographs the only way to conquer time?* They captured a moment and stopped its progression. It was a small victory admittedly, for we couldn't physically return, but we could allow those photographs to prompt memories. Photographs and memories: the conquerors of time perhaps?

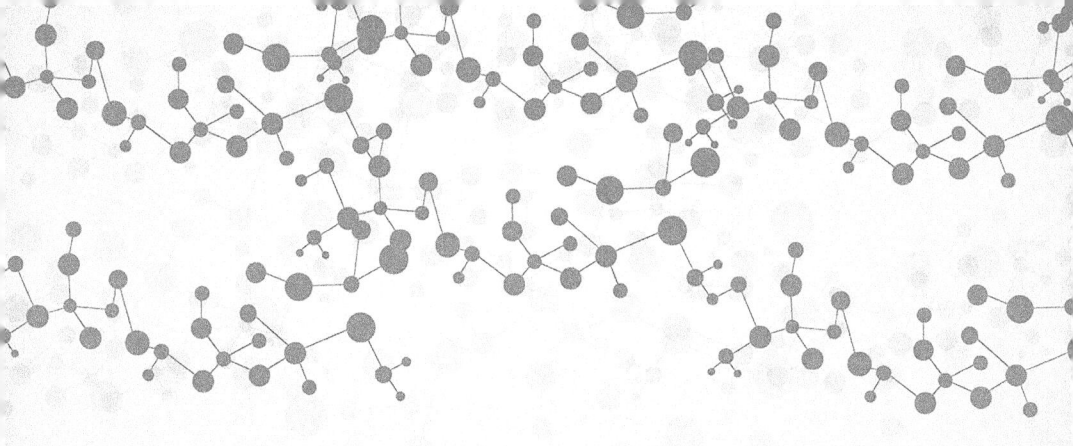

# CHAPTER 7

I woke in the morning on day four, with Zoey still in my arms. Her body pressed against my own betrayed the strong will of my hormones. My eyes scanned the curves of her body, the gentle thrum of a pulse visible on her neck as my shallow breath marked the spot I wanted to taste. Lust snaked its way into my thoughts, and I couldn't trust myself. I shifted over onto the other side of the tent, breathing in and out to quell the heat that pulsed within me, dressing myself awkwardly before exiting.

Stumbling into the campsite, a photographic moment presented itself. My friends were smiling in a circle around fire-blackened logs. The sound of timid laughter spread across the bush amphitheatre.

I tiptoed over to Gil.

"Hey, mate, why didn't you wake us for a bit of exercise?"

"I figured you needed the rest," he replied, gesturing to the log. "You were up late last night."

I nodded.

"You can make up for it," Gil said as he rose unexpectedly, "by coming with me to have a look around the plane."

I looked at him, taken aback.

"Ah, it kind of blew up, didn't it? There won't be all that much left."

He brushed my scepticism aside.

"I still want to have a look at the wreck to see what turns up, salvage anything and everything we can."

"You think this bush retreat is going to last a long time, then?" I asked, undertones of worry colouring my croaky morning voice.

He just smiled at me with an air of pity, placed a hand on my shoulder, squeezed and walked past me.

"Um, I guess that's a yes, then?"

I called after him as he gave me a thumbs up without even turning back around.

Zack stopped me as I headed towards my tent to put on my shoes.

"Keep warm last night, buddy?"

He prodded my chest with a rigid finger.

I had kept my lustful interactions with Zoey at bay for several nights. But it was clearly getting harder. No pun intended.

"Mate, are you going to ask me for updates every morning? If so, get ready for a whole lot of nothing."

"Well, what do you expect? The most excitement I've seen since the crash has been watching that lizard get on top of that other one," he said, pointing to a pale olive and brown lizard scurrying off into the undergrowth.

"Let me tell you: even if something goes down, you will not be 'seeing' anything, you creep."

His laugh was a warm camomile tea on an autumn morning.

"I'm just saying it would be kind of cool, though, if you two could, you know, get together at least after all this shit went down."

I stopped him even before the 'shit' had settled in the air.

"Oh, look. Clearly, my whole body is pushing me forward, but it's something my mind might not be able to handle right now."

"You've felt strongly about her for a while; it's not like it's just come out of the blue."

"Yeah, but I can't really gauge if she is interested or not. Besides, it kind of doesn't feel like the right time. I see Zoey as more than just a lust-fuelled roll around in a tent."

"Alright, alright, man. Be chill." He put his hands up.

Gil came into view, sneakers tied tight and backpack on. "Oh, there you are, Cooper."

Looking him up and down, I asked, "Are we leaving now?"

"Yeh, mate," he snapped. "Let's go quickly and quietly so we don't get everyone jumping on board."

"Wait," I said as I grabbed hold of his shirt. He galloped past me.

"What exactly are we looking for?"

He turned back to face me.

"Any remaining supplies – you know, just . . . some bags or anything, really."

"Alright, so we are pretty much taking whatever we can get our hands on?"

"That's it, buddy. C'mon let's go," he replied energetically.

I shrugged my shoulders at Zack, and he waved by wiggling his fingers. "Have fun," he mouthed as I followed Gil.

I didn't like the idea of going back to the plane, but I guess someone had to do it, as signs of rescue still hadn't surfaced.

As we were nearly out of sight, Kasey spotted us and raced over.

Between breaths, she inquired.

"Where are you two going?"

"Just for a walk, Kase," answered Gil, avoiding her eyes.

"I just *have* to come! I feel as though I'm getting, like, fatter everyday sitting on these stupid logs."

Her enticing bottom lip slid upwards in a seductive frown. With an exaggerated roll of the eyes, Gil agreed for her to come on one condition.

"We leave right now, and you ask *NO* questions!"

"Of course, of course," she answered, her perfect white teeth gleaming in the morning sun.

With that, we headed into the bush, back to the very place of our rebirth, from the ashes of those who weren't so lucky. We were only about thirty metres away from the plane wreckage when the stench of fuel and burnt flesh twirled like a ballerina of the underworld. Kasey slowed as we approached the plane wreckage and started to nibble at her manicured nails, usually polished with a vibrant pink, now chipped and faded. The look in her eyes indicated that she didn't want to be there. I took her hand as the apprehension in her blue eyes shimmered like a lake moved by a steady breeze.

The smile I gave to her represented a steely resolve, an indication that it unified us. Oxygen returned to her deflated lungs; rose quartz decorated her cheeks once more. It appeared as though the fear within her was whisked away by the gentle touch of a friend. We walked hand in hand until the ravaged shell of the fuselage grew in stature, greeting us with the blackened stain of a smirk. No windows remained intact, the plane's compartments scattered throughout the surrounding bush. Gil led us towards the remnants of the main section. Kasey strangled my hand tighter than ever.

We passed an exhibition of charred bodies distributed throughout the chaotic crash site: unidentifiable remains, severed limbs, broken or askew, torsos seared and bloodied, picked at by various critters. Upon the earth, they remained rotting, waiting for the angel of death to impound them inside Eden's sanctuary.

Kasey kept her eyes fixed on her bright red sneakers. Not because they were interesting at all, but because it appeared as though she would break, as her bottom lip quivered through a clenched jaw. Feeble tears crept down her cheeks, so I held her hand tighter to show her I knew exactly how she felt.

With aching hearts, we sifted through the wreckage to uncover scarce food, bottled drinks – some of them alcoholic – matches, lighters, a flare gun and more than a few bags. We sorted the most important items into our own packs, making a silent promise that we would return later to claim the rest of what we needed. As I zipped up the last item into my pack, the three of us huddled together, taking in the desolation one more time.

Gil turned first, sweeping the fringe from across his eyes and tucking it behind his ear. He bid farewell to the scene of our turmoil, flipping the hood of his jacket on top of his head before moving back to camp. Kasey followed, her white crop top sullen with flecks of mud and dirt as she stopped to crane her head at a termite mound, probably wondering what architect of nature commissioned such a project.

I came up behind her, the palm of my hand meeting the crease of her back, coaxing her forward. We held hands once more. The touch of someone close, often gives you strength to persevere through harrowing times. Kasey and I had found meaning in a symbiotic relationship.

Moving away from the crash, I breathed a sigh of relief. But was it relief? Relieved that I could now leave it behind me and never look back?

Even if I wanted to protect myself from the pain of loss, I should at least remember the good times, right?

The occasional wave of grief threatened to immerse my heart, sinking towards the depths of a liquid graveyard. Not only did an overwhelming sadness encompass me, but anger and a deep-seated darkness scratched at the surface. It took the last bit of strength left within me to repress it further down into the confines of my shell, where it could never see the light of day. I grew tense and rigid. Thoughts turned to vengeance and the desire to find answers.

"Coops . . . " Kasey whispered close to my ear.

"Would you, ah, please stop squeezing so hard please?"

I looked down and realised that I was no longer just holding her hand; I was strangling it.

Releasing my stronghold, I drew my hand away.

"I'm sorry, Kasey . . . I'm just a little angry and I . . . didn't . . . realise . . ."

Kasey's eyes narrowed; a concerned stare transformed her face.

"It's okay. We'll get through this together. Just concentrate on getting back in one piece. I've seen you lose your temper on the sporting field, so I know what it can be like for you. Just try to breathe deeply." She accepted my hand once more, and I breathed in deep, filling my lungs with clean air.

Kasey constantly surprised me. Her care and compassion – unreservedly – took my heart and gave it a bed to rest, with satin sheets and feathered pillows. With her inner beauty revealed, I realised that truth and vulnerability accentuated her features, more than make up ever could. Her true beauty was so evidently on the inside.

We returned to the campsite bearing gifts. The others didn't ask us about our journey; they, however, praised us for acquiring all the lost treasures for them. The urge to laugh bubbled and oozed within me, disturbing the surface of my face. We had a small win but a win all the same. As I walked over to where Desh handed out the supplies; things were starting to feel normal again.

Did I say *normal?* How absurd. Sitting in the bush, emotionally and physically bruised, was not normal for us. We hadn't even uncovered the truth about anything yet. But I soon realised that this was as normal as we were going to get for a long time.

I climbed in next to Zoey when it was time to farewell another day in the bush. Placing my arm underneath the sleeping bag, I was careful not to linger anywhere inappropriate, but acutely aware that my heart thumped into her shoulder blades. It was like the more I thought about not wanting to make a move, the more my heart said, "To hell with the mind. I'm going to make something happen."

Zoey then shifted, turning to face me, her stale breath tickling my nose. My heart was quiet all of a sudden.

"Cooper, I'm pretty sure we're on our own here," she whispered, the insects outside playing the evening encore of their greatest hits.

"What do you mean? I'd say the rest of the group were starting to work well as a little team," I said defiant, realising, that maybe I had misunderstood her.

"No, I mean no one is coming for us, Cooper. Ever. We're going to have to think of a way to get ourselves out of here." Zoey frowned, annoyed at me.

Her legs shifted and moved, entwining with mine, like the beginning of a tapestry. Our ankles acquainted themselves as skin met skin. Heat rose from the base of my toes, like a pressurised geyser.

"I'm no survivalist, Zoey, so what exactly do you suggest?" I inquired, my heart hammering in my chest.

"Well, I've watched my fair share of survival documentaries, and I'm thinking that, so far, we've done okay! We've had access to food, water and shelter."

The strength of her voice diminished.

"But that is going to run out soon. Desh and I have already contemplated traps for catching wild animals when resources look thinner, but that is a whole new ball game. We just have to do more," she reasoned.

"Like, set up smoke signals and things that people will see?" I answered, confidence blossoming. I'd watched my fair share of documentaries, too.

"Yes, but just do something . . . anything to plan our way out of here."

We had been face-to-face now for what felt like ages. The amber in her eyes danced as the moonlight crept in through the small tent window. The weaving of our tapestry: complete as both of our legs were tangled together. I forgot to reply; her stare held my attention.

"Any ideas, or do I take your silence for apathy?" Her lips curled into a smirk.

My frazzled mind went with, "Just a long day. My brainstorm sessions are best with breakfast."

"In that case, see you at the breakfast table, then." Zoey spun back around in one swift motion, grabbing my arm and pulling it across her.

"Goodnight, Cooper," she whispered.

I didn't know which emotion to validate as I struggled to sleep: guilt, lust, love, fatigue. They all tussled for primary position. Why bother trying to pinpoint one particular reason for wide eyes and a restless heart? I sighed, letting everything in. Maybe feeling overwhelmed would put me to sleep?

A scream in the distance startled us.

Shooting up from the dusty earth, Zack and I raced towards the tent. The sun sat high in the sky; it was around midday, and Zoey was on Mia watch. After fumbling and fussing with the zipper, I pulled down to open the tent flaps. Zoey was sitting next to Mia, rubbing her back. Nobody was screaming anymore, but as I searched Mia's flustered face, I knew that something was wrong. When her eyes settled on me; I was a stranger. I didn't see an adorable smile on her ample, rosy cheeks. I, too, saw a stranger, sitting wide-eyed and afraid.

"Mia, are you okay?" I spoke softly. "Can you hear me?"

At the sound of my voice, she twitched, springing to life.

"Who are you people, what do you want from me?" she cried.

Her breath was dense and disjointed, her eyes flashing like headlights on a congested highway. The words she spoke lingered in the stale air within the tent; no one wanted to answer her.

Mia raised her voice, "I'm warning you – whoever you are, don't follow me. I need to find out where I am."

She rose from the ground, knocking Zoey onto her side, staggering out of the tent into the unforgiving bush. I didn't heed her warning; I followed closely at her heels. Browns, greens and blues flew past us both as we delved deeper into the great unknown. Mia only stopped as a result of her leg muscles failing her: seizing up from lack of movement over several days. She dragged herself underneath a giant gum tree as I slackened my pace, panting hard and approaching her from a safe distance. She shivered, small beads of sweat creating a shimmering necklace around her chest. Her eyes were wide with paralysing fear. I inched closer to her, as composed as I could appear.

"Mia, it's me – Cooper. I'm in your mixed netball team at university."

Before I could say more, she interrupted me.

"You're lying. I don't know you. I told you not to follow me; just leave me alone!" she yelled without taking a breath.

I turned to observe the small crowd of my friends who had gathered around us both. Mia nervously shuffled her feet and continued muttering to herself, tears pouring down her face.

"I don't know where I am." she said louder, with feeble inflections.

As I inched closer, I held my hands upwards, showing my harmless intent, though she stiffened and backed up against the tree. Out of the corner of my eye, Kasey appeared, while behind her, my friends gazed intently.

I soothed my voice. "Mia, you're okay; you are safe with us. Even though you may not remember us right now, I can promise you we will not hurt you."

She stared at all of us, afraid and unsure. I was convinced she had no clue who we were, or who *she* was, for that matter. I extended an open palm towards her.

"Come here. I'll get you some water and something to eat."

Disquiet capitulated in Mia's eyes, covering her pupils like an eclipse. But she took my hand, and I clasped it firmly to let her know that I could be trusted. We all walked with her back to the campsite, where I gave her a cool drink of water and a blanket to keep her warm. Kasey had her arm around Mia the whole time. Zoey seemed distant, almost as if she were afraid of something. I should have known then that you don't just wake up from a comatose state and be as lucid as Mia was. But Zoey would only realise her true involvement later.

Those days were a mess. We had all made our assumptions about Mia, but we had agreed on just one. We estimated that her temporary unconsciousness had created some issues with her short-term memory. When she saw her own reflection, it was as though she appeared frightened of what she saw, almost like she hadn't expected to look the way she did. Mia knew her name because she responded to it each time we called her, but she couldn't recall any of her post high school years, which meant that her memories of us were non-existent. It upset us all, but we kept at it.

The second day after she awoke, she knew our names; the day after, she smiled. In my selfish haste, though, I wanted the old Mia back. So many of our friends were now lost to us, and I truly hoped that she would find herself again.

Kasey and Zoey stayed with Mia for long periods of time – day and night. Though our very own sleeping beauty awoke, I still had a lot of trouble making it through the day. Depression and grief lingered while trying to shake these feelings, deciphering the 'New Breed' remained high on the daily to-do list.

During the day, I wore my masquerade of happiness. It meant fewer questions; it meant raising the spirits of others. But the mask eroded at the glimpse of the moon. I took short walks to process my thoughts and allow the internal pain to flow out of my eyes and down my cheeks.

Were the tears actually releasing the pain or were they exorcising the innocent Cooper, the young Cooper, who had never known sadness and anger like this before? I actually felt as though I was really losing something within me, a childhood innocence that I've held onto for years.

It was time to let it go and build over the fragility with something stronger. I needed to find strength through this adversity. When I came back from one of my short walks on the eleventh day, it was roughly about one in the morning. As I crawled into my tent and settled in next to beautiful Zoey, her dark brown hair splayed across our pillow of dirty jumpers, that familiar scream echoed throughout the silent, sleeping bush.

# CHAPTER 8

I ran as fast as my exhausted legs would allow. I arrived at her tent before anyone else did. Mia was a rigid pole, erect and unmoving. Her skin was a perfect pallid picture of terror as tears leapt from the branches of her eyes. I bent down, slotting into a space next to her and placed my hand against her back.

"Honey, what's wrong?"

"They are dead, Cooper; they killed them all."

Her voice shook like a delicate shrub in a storm.

"Mia, who is dead?" I asked, perplexed.

She repeated that same phrase once more, eyes fixed upon a greater horizon until she left the disturbing trance behind her.

"The bad people . . . they killed my family . . . they are dead."

She sobbed.

"They were eating dinner, and the door just collapsed inwards. They stormed in with guns, and they shot them all!"

Mia was inconsolable.

"How do you know this was real?" I tried my best to stifle my scepticism.

"It happened, Cooper. I felt their pain." She stopped talking, but her eyes pled with me to believe her.

*She felt their pain? What was going on here?* She can't possibly feel people from miles away.

"Mia, who killed them?" I inquired.

"Uniformed men and women with guns and familiar faces . . . They all had the same face."

That was all that we could pry from her. Kasey, Zoey and Desh stayed by Mia's side while the rest of us returned to our tents to recharge. Sleep was difficult. In my tent, I attempted to decipher the thoughts, the feelings, words and pictures that waltzed in perfect circles, entwining and colliding like a cryptic fog leeching across my mind's eye. I closed my eyes. Mia's admissions took the form of imagined images: uniforms, death, blood, guns and familiar faces. Nothing made sense. As sleep covered my eyes like a blindfold, I succumbed to an enlightening dream. My cynicism about Mia's visions floated into the clouds once my dream took shape.

I was in the university common room speaking to Jasmine and Mia. *Was this a memory, or was it just my imagination?* I couldn't tell. I loaded a fresh ream of paper into the photocopier, wet black ink mixed with the smell of cumin and rice filled the air, a microwave the culprit in the corner. As I scanned the room, several people that had died on the plane smiled, laughed and chatted to one another. It wasn't long before I was lulled by a false sense of normality, my smile reflecting the ease of university life. Silence descended upon the common room with an effective awe; friends turned sour, threatening me. My smile faded.

Why was I the target here? Their scars were bridges of pain connecting the avenues of broken dreams to their untimely death. Their scars were transcribed reminders that life, in actuality, is more brutal, more unpleasant than deepest fears realised. Their hollow eyes spoke the sorrowful sonnet of a visionary denied a future. I searched their faces for a trace of friendliness, for compassion, but it was as though they cursed my existence for remaining scarless and breathing. It was no longer euphoric at all. From across the lengthy common room, a profound and resonant voice spoke to me. As my dead friends encircled me, Gus appeared as an angel of reason, an essence of shimmering gold encasing him as he hovered towards me.

"You have been asking yourself about the New Breed, have you not?"

I recalled that I must have fallen asleep, and this was a dream. Gus provided me with a startling realisation that it could be nothing other than that.

I didn't even have to answer his question, for he already knew my thoughts

"Intervention is a requisite in moments such as these. Moments that threaten to disturb the security of humankind. So, I am here, establishing that you are threatened, and you must know of your enemy in order to tread the path to conquer them."

I kept my eyes focused on his face: an angelic face painted in wisps of shimmering silver.

"The day has come where humankind will face their greatest challenge: the uprising of the clone . . . or the New Breed – if you will," Gus continued.

"Dressed in uniform, they appear just like you do. This is why you must act with diligence, becoming relentless in your pursuit to claim what is rightfully yours. If you wish to live a normal life once more, you have to eliminate the replicas made from your own flesh. You will find the necessary tools buried within yourselves to aid you on this crusade.

Do not falter; you must heed this warning and make haste. They must be stopped."

A shadowy figure approached Gus; the figure held what appeared to be a gun. I opened my mouth, threatening to scream, shaking, pointing at it. Gus did not adjust in time before the figure fired a single shot, the bullet bursting out of his left eye socket in an explosion of blood. Standing proudly above his body was not just a shadowy figure. He resembled Gus in every way. He then looked into my eyes and fired his gun.

My eyes opened with a jolt. I was breathing hard, trying to comprehend what I had just seen and heard. *Could it all be true?* Unnatural noises that didn't belong in dense bushland disturbed my thoughts. I reacted to what I thought to be an ominous situation, slipping on a black jumper and making my way outside the tent, vigilant. Creeping towards the noise, I was trying to understand that the New Breed meant clones. Yep. Okay, got it.

*What the actual fuck? How could this be reality?*

Then I remembered Gordon Grey, the man who had recently cloned the human's closest relative. I thought back to the day not that long ago, where I had watched him on the news, his silver hair shining as the press captured his momentary notoriety. The speech he delivered echoed some bullshit about saving humanity and abolishing disease, did it not? Wow. This was happening, wasn't it?

It started with us: little ol' Cooper and his friends from Western Sydney. Had there been any other cases? I had not heard of anything, but how could I really know? Surely, there would be some sort of government cover-up if there had been. My precious thoughts were connecting smoothly, but I had to sever them.

I stared from afar at the plane wreck in dismay. Beams of light spilled out into the shadowed night, like an enervated eye searching for a place to rest. The perilous, pulsing light illuminated several discarded contents in and around the bush's perimeter.

*So, where was this source coming from?*

I narrowed my eyes so that I could decipher the figures I was observing: ant-like humans dressed in dark khaki uniforms held sturdy torches, pulling apart significant bits and pieces of the plane. Was it the army coming to rescue us? One thing that Mia had seen in her dream tiptoed into my head.

"Uniformed men and women with guns and familiar faces . . ."

At that moment, it all dawned on me: these uniformed, army-looking types were not people at all; they were the clones that Gus had spoken of. If this was the case, they were not here to help us. They were only here to clean up their mess and possibly 'clean' us up!

I forced myself to believe everything Gus had said to me in my dream, considering I was staring at 'uniformed men and women.' But the more I thought about it, the more ridiculous it seemed. Even as I stared at them, I felt like a crazy person, believing something so far-fetched. I thought that, often, seeing was believing, but it was like a part of me still wanted to defy what my pupils had processed. I asked myself, *Should I take this as a sign of some sort – that somehow I needed to take action?*

But what could I do? Gus had spoken about 'tools inside of us.' What the hell did that mean? Understanding what he had meant eluded me; it wasn't as if I could just ask him about it. He was dead, after all. But it was very clear to me that we had to work out what was going on. No one else was going to save us; we would have to save ourselves.

Turning away from the plane wreck, surging with unexpected life, I walked briskly back to the camp to warn the others that our situation had changed. Mia's tent was first on my list.

When I arrived, I found Mia, Desh, Kasey and Zoey sleeping, huddled together. I lowered my hand to wake Mia, hovering inches above her shoulder. Her eyes burst open, which startled me and threw me off balance. Mia turned over, raising her body up and out of the sleeping bag. Her movement woke the others as they rubbed their eyes to face the situation. As they were coming to terms with the unnatural humming noise in the distance, Mia grabbed my hand.

"Cooper, I think I remember some things . . . but it's in a weird order," she whispered with a quickening tempo.

Although we needed to discuss pressing issues, I let her explain herself as Desh's face contorted, trying to smooth out his confusion over the noise.

"Okay, Mia, what do you remember?" I asked, impatience burning my tone.

"I remember you all now. I know who I am, and I remember when we were standing in the terminal, but that's all."

"Okay, so you don't remember being on that plane, correct?"

"No, I don't remember that part, but it's not important now. You should tell them, Cooper."

I narrowed my eyes and turned my head to one side. It was odd that she knew I needed to tell them something. Maybe she could tell by the urgency of my tone and by the look on my sweating, concerned face that something wasn't right. I turned away from her and spoke to the huddled group, who awaited and expected terrible news.

"Someone is here for us."

Frivolous smiles graced their pitiable, unsuspecting faces. What I was about to say would crush the little bundle of hope they held so dear to their aching hearts.

"But they are not here to save us."

I paused, witnessing those smiles fall hard upon the barren earth of their expectations.

"These guys are . . ." I searched for the right words, "something like an enemy. Don't ask me how I know – I just . . . know. So," I sighed, "we are going to have to learn what their weakness is by observing them. This is why I'm going to take a longer look at what is going on."

"How could you possibly know anything about an enemy?" Zoey objected, her craving for logic getting the better of her once more.

"Please, don't argue. I just need to find out what is going on. I can explain everything later," I sighed.

"Is it me, or does this saga remind you of some sort of *Men in Black* bullshit?" Zoey complained.

"I knew we should have left here a week ago. They say, 'stay close to the crash site,' but my instinct told me to move further away!" she complained.

Mia turned to Zoey and Kasey, bringing them in close to divert the conversation.

I ignored Zoey as Desh stood up. "Let's go, my friend." He placed a hand on my shoulder and whisking me away before the girls could ask any more questions.

Before he left, he whispered into the tent, "Stay here and alert the other guys and whatever you do, just remain here until we come back."

We arrived at the place where I had first observed the clones only several minutes before. Inconspicuous, Desh and I stood behind thick shrubbery, gaining understanding of the system that the clones employed while keeping well concealed. And if I had doubted that they were enemy material before – well, I was sure they were after watching them.

Groups of four would carry the evidence and dump them into different trucks. Truck number one and two contained the dead bodies and body parts while the remaining trucks stored all evidence of the wreckage. Luckily, Desh had borrowed Gil's bird-watching binoculars to enhance the view. Their grim faces appeared as the fickle moon, glowing in a dark blue, midnight sky. The clones could shoulder a substantial load alone, and they communicated to one another with precise hand signals and direct commands.

Their blasé tossing of body after body into the back of truck number one triggered me to tell Desh about my dream. I needed another opinion, another point of view, as I had connected reality to a dream. The resolve in his eyes was evident as he nodded, listening intently.

"Look, if this is all true – which, to be honest, seems highly likely –" he said, pointing at the clones, "then we have got a hell of a fight on our hands, haven't we?"

I nodded, thankful he didn't size me up for a straitjacket.

After observing this for several minutes, we headed back towards the campsite to figure out our next move. As I inched closer and closer to the campsite, the despondent darkness of the night cast its shadow over my uneasy footsteps. I was afraid of how often shadows spawned from branches, large rocks and seemingly insignificant bushes. They followed my movements, providing an ominous warning of what was to come. The campsite had a significant gathering of all occupants, appearing similar in several qualities: wide-eyed, anxious and exhausted. Members of the group rose to their feet as we made our way towards them, asking questions like: What did you see? Is someone here to kill us? Are you sure that if someone is here, that it's not a rescue team? What do they look like?

Desh and I attempted to settle them down, asking for their cooperation by sitting on the log in the middle of our campsite. We addressed them as a group, answering those questions and several more.

The first and most important fact we had communicated to them was that we needed to pack up the campsite and move further into the bush as to avoid potential trouble. We dispersed into our respective tents and packed the essentials. I watched Zoey as I placed my diary in the backpack. Her eyes told me a lot of what she was feeling. It was amazing how much you could uncover just by looking into someone's eyes. I had never noticed it before the plane crash, though.

Zoey stuffed clothes into her pack with a scowl, ripe with disdain, clearly annoyed about our complacency. Time sorted through our final moments, displaying them at the buffet table of life, forcing us to make a choice. I chose to have a future.

When we exited the tent, with our bags packed, I summoned the courage to take her hand. My gesture to Kasey earlier this week was to provide comfort; taking Zoey's hand, however, meant something more. Within me, weakness and strength dissolved into one another, like sugar swimming through filtered water. It was pleasant because it was new, a desire fulfilled. Her eyes told me she felt it, too, with an unexplained flicker of happiness flashing through her determined stare.

She turned to her left, looking deeper into the bush where our 'family' had assembled. Her smile faded like a timid ripple in a placid lake, and a stern expression replaced it. Zoey intended to make it out of here alive, leaving no one behind. As we walked into the bush, following the same path that Gil and I had taken a week before, we did our best to cover our tracks and dispel any evidence of survivors.

"No offence, Cooper, but I'm finding it hard to believe all this," Zoey said. "You know that I need some hard evidence to believe claims like these."

I loosened my grip on her hand, feeling vulnerable as she paused, searching the crevices of her mind for something comforting.

"But I'll ride this wave with you and stick up for you. I know you're not the type of person to lie to us all."

Tightening my grip on Zoey's hand once more, I followed the footprints of our friends. We chose a place to lay our heads under the cover of trees, shrubbery and dense rocks, which provided near perfect concealment. As we erected tents, we each appointed two people to walk back to our previous campsite to keep an eye on the clones.

Pj and I volunteered to take the first shift. As we set off, we spoke quietly about my dream and how it possessed an inextricable connection to what Mia had said in her tent. In Pj's eyes, there was no denying it, we had to assume that the "people" were, in fact, clones, and they were obviously on a mission to find us. After that, who knows what they would do? It had become more apparent as the hours wore on that this was going to turn into a fight for our lives. Pj was helpful – uncustomary to say the least – and assumed the role of a devoted soldier to the cause. He never once berated me or questioned the validity of my assumptions. I loved him for that.

As we skulked behind the cover of ferns and overgrown weeds, the severity of the situation was on full display. The clones had an array of menacing guns. Unfortunately, I hadn't encountered guns many times in my life – only a handful of times, when Dad would cull the rabbits in spring so that I could not always define and identify them. But the word 'gun' itself evoked a crippling fear within me. A gun was always the catalyst for death in action and adventure movies. I think that, deep down, there was a feeling that this situation was movie-like. As soon as I had exorcised my fear of guns and their catastrophic potential, Pj reached inside his backpack and pulled out two handguns. I searched his face in disbelief.

"Man, where the hell did you get these from?"

"Oh, um . . . one of them was the flight attendant's, and the other one was lying next to a body at the back of the plane," Pj replied, shrugging his shoulders, unperturbed.

I couldn't believe he had salvaged two actual guns!

"Well, what do you expect us to do with these?"

His composed nature and maturity spilled into the air in thick gusts of wind.

"Cooper, they are only for protection. I'm not intent on going in all guns blazing, but I am intent on defending us if anything happens."

"Alright, alright . . . well, how many rounds do we have, then?"

Pj smiled. "Only one if we're lucky . . . between us."

I sighed, realising that I didn't know how to use a handgun. Prior to this, I'd only worked with rifles.

"Um, do you even know how to use these, man?" I inquired, dangling the metallic instrument of death between my forefinger and thumb.

He smiled that all-knowing smile of his and placed a hand on my shoulder.

"Remember the time me, Zack and Gus went to that wedding up in Hamilton Island?"

I recalled their drunken pictures posted on social networking sites.

"Well, we spent a couple of hours at a gun range. Quite good practice, wouldn't you say?"

He responded condescendingly.

That must have been how Gus had known what to do with the flight attendant on the plane. I acknowledged him by asking for a demonstration on how to cock the weapon. Once he taught me all the necessary ins and outs of loading a gun and preparing it for combat, I smiled and turned to face the plane, ignoring his smug satisfaction. The gun weighed heavily on my mind and my right pocket. The clones tore the plane apart, numerous cutting tools sending mesmerising gold sparks into the otherwise dull bushland. They summoned five monstrous trucks to dispose of all the particles and pieces speckled throughout the area.

After about an hour of constant observation, my eyelids succumbed to the temptation to sleep. Unfortunately, Pj took the early mark before I could and left me fighting the urge to lay down and snuggle with an ant or two. As he bid me farewell, he signalled that he would send someone else over. My head lulled onto my chest in a lethargic nod of appreciation. I squinted to the left of me over the canopy as the sun began its reign over the land to signify the new day. The clones, it seemed, did not notice the sun's natural splendour. They continued on like dutiful soldier ants, packing bodies and plane parts into the trucks. Heavy footsteps thumped behind me. I turned and strained to see who it was: Mia's earthy linen pants billowed around her ankles, exposing her worn brown sandals. She had one of her customary vegan leather headbands fastened like a halo atop her head, keeping her hair, touched with the colour of freshly cut plums, manageable. Scanning the area for a comfortable seat on a rough patch of grass beside my pack, she greeted me with a swift and sweet smile.

"How are you holding up?" I whispered. We still hadn't found a moment to talk about her memory retention.

"I just don't know, Coops. My mind is like a scrambled egg. One minute, I don't know who you are – the next, I can tell you your favourite colour and even your middle name."

I nodded, about to respond, but she continued, "It's David, by the way."

I covered my mouth to mute my laugh.

"Well, at least you remember a lot more now . . . just take that as a positive."

Mia stared into the unforgiving distance, populated by hard working clones. She sighed.

"Cooper . . ." she hesitated, "I think I can sometimes see what is going to happen. I know this sounds silly, but . . . I get these dreams that are so real, and I just know that it's not just a dream; it's like I'm being warned of something."

My first glance into her eyes was that of disbelief. Then I remembered my dream, and the pieces connected. Each different dream led to the truth about our perceived reality. I could not fault her integrity, nor condemn her honest and embarrassing admission. To be fair, it was incredulous – ridiculous even – that people such as Mia or I possessed a knack for predicting events in the future. As I reflected upon this uncanny ability, I remembered Mia's dream about her family before I cast that thought aside.

"You do believe me, don't you?" Her voice quivered like a flame atop a candle, fighting a cold, conquering breeze.

"Of course I believe you Mia because, to be truthful, I am in much the same situation, I guess."

I explained my dream to her. From where we sat, next to one another, as moths to an invisible flame, Mia searched the plane wreck for confirmation that the uniforms were the same that she had seen in her dream. With a resigning bow of her head, she verified my concerns: the uniforms were, in fact, present within her dreams. In turn, it proved her family's death and confirmed that she might actually be able to see into the future.

Her weakness, her grief, came to the surface and collided with a brooding fear of an enemy that was less than three hundred metres from us. The burden of the plane crash, the death of her family, the absence of a home and normality, finally gave her pause to cry. Tears of resentment and festering horror gave life to dry, cracked leaves dying of malnourishment strewn upon the earth. It seemed apparent to me that, for all these reasons, Mia's crippling affliction rooted itself into the crevices of her bruised and beating heart. As I searched her glistening eyes, I wondered whether that would be enough to erase her compassion and selflessness for just a single moment, a moment where she had to choose to end the life of an enemy. Would her purity and innocence penetrate any reason, any cause for vengeance? Mia was always harder to read than most, so I was clueless. Even as I mused over Mia's ability to kill or be killed, I thought about myself.

I had never killed a person before. *Could I distinguish the difference between a clone and a real person?* I guess, at the time, there was no simple answer. I needed to succumb to the moment and allow it to decide my fate.

As I stared at the enemies that plagued my mind, the remains of the plane lay in pieces, glinting in the morning sunlight. It brought back memories of the calamitous event that had taken good people and severely scarred the survivors.

I had completed my fair share of grieving each and every day for all of the friends that I would never be able to see again. Their proposed future eradicated in a single moment. Usually, that is all it takes to change everything. Mia and I stared at the trucks until our vision distorted. As the monotony enveloped me, my mind ticked into overdrive, threading ideas through the interstices of an attentive brain. It was then that I formulated a plan to leave the bush, to head back to our hometown to find out what was going on.

Mia and I walked with a spring in our step back to the others to run the plan by them, careful to cover our tracks. As we approached our campsite, Mia stopped in her tracks, slapping an open palm onto my mouth, covering it like a paramedic sealing a body bag.

An infectious melody tainted the tranquillity of the bush, filled with warning shouts and pleads of mercy. My stomach rapidly fell to a flat floor, sending segments of life sliding like synchronised ice skaters across the smooth, icy surface. A metallic taste crept onto my tongue and towards the back of my throat; a banquet of anxiety fit for a restless king. Mia and I crouched low and shuffled behind bushes close enough to see what was going on. All our friends were there, held captive like a litter of stray cats at the pound, standing and shaking in a line with their backs facing us. Behind them stood two clones dressed in that familiar uniform. Piercing blue eyes sparkled with the caress of the sun's golden hand, their stares fierce with a clenched jaw and furrowed brows. Hair cropped short, so it was hard to tell what colour it was, but dark features were prominent upon both faces. Faces that were exactly the same. The formation in which my friends stood reminded me of the way Nazi soldiers lined up unsuspecting victims in order to carry out executions by firing squads. They cradled machine guns in their arms, like a cherished extension of their own bodies.

These particular clones bellowed into wireless communication devices.

"I repeat: we have discovered escapees. Can we receive confirmation to terminate them?"

The moment had come, where actions overruled the internal debate. The actions were physical. When adrenalin calls upon rash decisions, it is usually your physicality and lack of thinking that saves you. What saved me was my ability to embrace the moment, to discard the implications.

Gripping the gun that lay in the right pocket of my jeans, I liberated it from a cast iron hand of amity. I recalled the moments before, when Pj had tutored me, following the same procedure. I had only a millisecond to take my aim, so I prayed that a misdirected bullet wouldn't find one of my friends. I exhaled a disjointed breath and welcomed the absence of thought, empathy and future ramifications, squeezing the trigger to send the train of death from a dormant station to collect its first passenger for the day. The kick of the gun was sharp and unexpected, wrenching my shoulder from its socket, sending a shockwave through the bones that held me.

The second wrinkle in a collection of three on his forehead was a perfect point to aim for, though, with a dash of serendipity, the bullet pierced his upper torso. As he fell to the ground, the other clone swung around almost as fast as the bullet had exited my gun. I dove to my left, cowering beneath a lump of granite, hearing and feeling numerous bullets flying over my head. Hapless arms covered my head as torn and shredded leaves drifted in tiny pieces to rest upon my recoiling body. *The train of death awaited my arrival*

A second or two of metallic clicks resounded from his direction, signifying the need to reload. This was my opportunity to gain an advantage, but just as I was about to poke my head out from the granite protection, a deafening sound of bullets shattered the quiet once more. I assumed that this was the end, shrinking behind a large rock like a poor, pathetic puppy dog. This was not the day that death would hold me tight, pulling my head into his chest, silencing my sorrowful sobs with gradual suffocation.

A heavy thud came my friends' direction. Ashamed, I had forgotten their predicament once the bullets had threatened my existence. As I inched my head upwards, slow enough to rival a snail bounding across the road to freedom, divine voices called our names in shaking, nervous squeaks. Their divinity and the premise of their livelihood instilled energy within me to rise from the foetal position. They were all there! At least, I thought so, making sure to double check that no one was missing.

They stood in a broken semi-circle, towering above two static clone bodies rooted to the unforgiving ground. Pj and Desh were panting, guns muted by the completion of the task. Mia lay on the ground, sprawled out, gauche, attempting to shield herself from the rain of bullets that had ripped apart the bush. I crawled over to where she lay to help her stand. She wore a ghostly mask as I linked arms with her, stumbling over each other to complete our circle of friends. We embraced, fusing our souls together, connecting our fear and temporary relief in a unified bond.

Although relieved, we were in grave danger, which latched itself onto our current situation. The clones must have heard the bullets, and without a doubt, would send reinforcements to make sure the termination was successful. The only solace we found was in the way the clones undertook the attempted executions of my friends and I: the bullets they had wasted were somewhat accounted for. All the while, it left us with a small head start. We would save our stories for later and pack up our stuff for the last time. I broke the silence into several jagged pieces as we dismantled tents and strapped packs to our backs.

"I came up with a plan to get out of here."

They all looked at me with hope in their eyes.

"That's right." I said with a wry smile.

"We're getting out of here today, and this is how…"

# CHAPTER 9

Who would have thought firecrackers could save our lives? I certainly did not. Firecrackers were known to create problems around congested suburbs with delinquent teenagers. Low-level explosives with a short fuse: what a fun time! The fourth song on my playlist, *The Heart Is a Muscle* by Gang of Youths, came on as we boarded the plane. At this stage, the clone flight attendant was at least half an hour away from changing our lives forever.

Pj squeezed my arm. One of my headphones popped out of my ear.

"What's going on, man?"

A wicked grin scarred his face.

My heart sank beneath waves of anxiety. *What was he up to?*

"Check this," he whispered.

My heavy gaze fell onto the palm of his hand, open beneath the arm of the chair. In it were four medium-sized firecrackers. I darted my gaze back at him, now rigid in my seat.

"What were you thinking? How the hell did you get them past security?" I whispered through gritted teeth.

"Just underwear, bro." Pj giggled like a delinquent child. "It was so worth it!"

I shook my head at him, pursing my lips in dissention.

The sounds of his chuckles died as I placed one headphone back in my left ear, trying to forget what I had just seen.

With the knowledge that Pj was, in fact, attempting to nurture his delinquency and inner demon child at University Games, my plan took shape. I would create a diversion using the firecrackers that Pj had smuggled onto the flight, aided by a flare gun that we had recovered from the plane. This diversion would send the majority of the clones into chaos, charging into the vast, savage terrain of the bushland while we would climb into one of the trucks, transporting our sorry souls to a location far from the danger zone. As proud as I was about taking the initiative to get us closer to home, the plan relied on fortuity and pure hope.

When I had explained the finer details of the plan, we summoned our combined character strength and prepared for the great escape. Our first task was to tidy the turbulent mess that had enveloped our campsite. The dead bodies of the clones, bloodied and crumpled upon the barren earth, already tantalising the salacious soil with their suppressed nutrients. We moved to conceal the bodies with anything we could find. It provided a brief camouflage that we suspected would last long enough to make our escape. We could do almost nothing about the shredded leaves and broken branches but we raced around, collecting empty shells and rejected bullets that were strewn across the campsite.

As I placed the last of the bullet fragments into my pockets, a crackling sound split the air: a two-way radio. The muffled sound, buried beneath the various natural decorations cast upon a fresh corpse, but as it lay tethered to the dead, the radio exploded with life.

The grip on my shoes failed me as adrenalised astonishment assisted my motionless legs to become celestial, tensile wings that enabled me to soar through the air. I did not become a graceful angel of God, stumbling with each step I took on moist leaves, on deceitful dirt, searching for that tiny black monster growling and hissing at us.

As I pulled back the iron bars and released it from its enclosure, the message pulsed – as clear as a two-way radio would allow.

"Is everything under control? We heard wild gunfire, over," said an unknown voice.

I stared at the radio, bewildered, scanning my mind for an answer.

The voice repeated these words a second time, this time, urgent and with conviction.

"Is everything under control? We heard wild gunfire. Please respond. Over."

From deep within, I conjured up an academy award-winning performance, presenting a deep, confident voice to imitate the clone on the other side of the radio.

"We executed four of the five escapees; however, the remaining target has retreated west of the bush. It is imperative that we send as many squad members as we can towards that section. Over."

I turned my hands upwards in the direction of my friends, speckled in different corners of the campsite, like chess pieces on the anarchical board of life. If I believed that the crossing of fingers would delicately sprinkle beads of luck upon me, then I would have broken them just to keep them there.

We waited, breath scarce for an answer.

"Affirmative. Squad members have been deployed, General. Over."

Oh, man. The dead clone was a general!

This was bad . . . or was it good? I then took advantage of the situation.

"Send the trucks away in fifteen minutes from now, as they're nearly full. After that, have the squad members return here when they drop the contents off at the base. Over."

Almost instantly they responded. "Yes, sir. Over."

There was no time to do a victory dance to celebrate my efficient thinking. We still had to plant the firecrackers and create a fuse. Setting off with our equipment in tow, we gathered a mass of dead leaves and grass to assemble them in an enormous pile, rivalling the heights of a mid-sized gum tree. Time constraints limited how significant the pile could have been, but when we had accumulated the required amount of vegetation for the plan, we positioned the firecrackers.

They were evenly speckled throughout the dead leaves and branches; larger ones close to the edges, while the smaller ones were deep inside. Pj had shown me at least five medium-sized firecrackers on the plane but he had smuggled a further five larger ones in his shoes.

We just had to hope that it was enough to get us by.

As we dispersed to various parts of the surrounding area, most of the group headed straight towards the vantage point. Pj and I stayed behind to await visual confirmation of our arranged target.

We decided that everyone except Zack would remain at the vantage point so that he would return to us to confirm the positioning and probability of completing our task.

Our plan was to alarm the clones of a precarious situation instigated by the firecrackers. Once we succeeded with our surprise tactic, the goal was to lead the clones into the unknown bush to capture the fabricated menace. But no one would be there.

We would, instead, be on the road to freedom, safe inside one of the trucks.

We anticipated the actions the clones would take, but we didn't have any other choice. It was either try this or fight a hopeless battle with guns and an affable resolve that would – let's face it – end in death.

My hands shook as nerves took hold of my breath and body. Tasting the acidic burn of reflux at the back of my throat, I turned to Pj, impending doom accentuated the wrinkles on my forehead.

"Pj, quick! Let's do it! Set it off now!"

Pj knelt down next to the congestion of natural tinder: dry leaves, dead grass and pine resin.

He held the lighter in front of his face.

An open flame quivered, suspended in the midst of the moment, bracing itself to rage, to expand, to destroy and to give new life.

The flame transferred its energy from the lighter to the fuse, and we became scarce, creeping low to the ground through shade and shadows. The rest of the group was at the vantage point, waiting rather impatiently for Pj and I to join them. We didn't even exchange pleasantries before Gil turned. The group followed our fearless shepherd, guiding us towards distant paddocks full of lush, greener grass.

The final piece of the puzzle was a failsafe. If, by chance, the fire could not burn for long enough to cause the explosions, I had to make sure the firecrackers ignited. Desh and I remained the only ones left behind to administer the failsafe. The task was one of extreme difficulty. If the original fire did not ignite quick enough, I had to shoot a flare at the pile of vegetation to create the explosions, imitating the sound of gunshots fired by a solitary terrorist. This would, in turn, lure the clones to the wrong side of the bush, leaving an open path to a departing, deserted truck.

I nestled my feet into the damp earth and extended my arm, closing one eye in an attempt to assess the angles and directions of the shot.

It was almost forty to fifty metres to the target. I had to make a conscious effort to ignore the pessimistic side of my mind that told me, *Hey kid, you'll never make it.*

You have to believe in your ability in those situations – one hundred per cent, or, I find, there is no use even trying.

After minor adjustments and locating my comfort levels, I inspected the flares path. It wasn't as much of a clearing as I had anticipated; several tree branches obstructed my view. I waited and waited until Desh's whisper brushed the outside of my right ear.

"Dude, the fire isn't catching; you have to do it now."

He was right.

The fire had diminished, and was losing its strength. It was never going to ignite the firecrackers.

I took a deep breath in and exhaled slower than usual.

My heart was a startled bird, beating wings into the metal bars of my aching chest. I raised the gun and abandoned all thoughts and processes, pressing my finger down hard upon the trigger.

The flare whistled through the air like a flock of birds painting the horizon with synchronised movements. A large tree branch became an obstacle, occluding the peripheral glare into a parallel world, as the flare rocketed straight into its villainous embrace.

Severed into two separate pieces, the branch sent sparks flying like the night sky on a perfect New Year's Eve, then it ricocheted and veered off into nothingness.

As the noise of the flare shook the silent serenity of the bush, I cursed under my breath.

I couldn't believe I had missed the shot.

I couldn't believe I'd wasted another moment.

I couldn't believe we hadn't been caught.

With disbelief clouding my mind, I loaded another flare into the cartridge as sweat tumbled off my forehead.

I raised the gun once more; however, I didn't even have the chance to press the trigger. Desh extended his arm past my ear and snatched the gun from me like an arrogant thief in a crowded market at dawn.

I looked up in bewilderment.

"What the fuck, Desh?"

He didn't notice me as I narrowed my eyes into a puzzled, hateful stare. A trance of some kind took hold, as he raised the gun to face our target, steady and determined. Without aiming and testing the wind speed or direction, he squeezed the trigger.

The flare whistled a lingering melody of liberty once again, this time plunging straight into the centre of the pile of dead vegetation. We stared at the target for a second as it absorbed the flare into its skin. An apprehensive flame poked its head into the air, peering with disdain at overhanging leaves and tree branches.

That visual confirmation was all we required to move ourselves onto the next part of the plan, but as the flames grew in confidence, several fireballs painted the bush with orange tears and golden eyes. Awe encapsulated us as our own eyes became mirrors, reflecting the fiery splendour and transferring the refracted image into the core within ourselves.

We couldn't waste any more time, though; Desh and I had to move.

I pulled our sharpshooter by the shoulder, jolting him out of his trance, and we sped through the bush, ensuring to conceal ourselves as best as we could. After several seconds of running blind, we found the rest of the group.

Their bulging, anxious eyes were stationary insects decorating the still morning with minimal designs and colours. Those eyes were the only beacon I could see in the shadowed bush, as it prepared for the sun to rise.

From our position, the chaos unfolded, like a precious love letter scribed with a passionate hand. The clones had seen the flares whistle across the bush, witnessing a raging fire. They were no fools. Although confused, they sent most of their squadron to where Desh had fired the flares. It was only when the firecrackers expelled their sweet song into the air that the clones abandoned their regimented reason in search for a gun-toting maniac.

As the apparent gunshots rang out into the bush, several other clones charged towards the flame, yelling for others to follow. One clone turned to those guarding the trucks and ordered, "Wait another five minutes then drive off."

*Was this our chance?*

The trucks were metallic soldiers standing between our death and our safe return home, a menacing demeanour present at this close range. Each truck had been grouped together further away from the constant gnawing activity of the plane crash. The clones assigned two guards to the stationary trucks, sending the majority of the troops into the bush to find the source of commotion, which gave us the slight advantage of avoiding capture.

There was no time to waste, as the last of the firecrackers exploded in the distance. To the huddled group, exhaling feeble wisps of air in nervous anticipation, I whispered, "Let's go."

I nodded at Pj first.

He took the first step onto the battlefield, creeping towards the first clone like a lioness hunting for her pride.

Desh "covered" Pj with one of the machine guns that we had salvaged from clones we had killed. I had the handgun with three bullets that remained cocked, shaking in my hands.

Pj approached the right side of the truck, when, out of a cloud of smoke and dust, a clone materialised.

He moved at an unnerving speed towards Pj, crouching beneath one of the larger wheels, waiting for a perfect time to open the back of the truck. Before the clone knew what was in process, Desh released a bullet into the back of the clone's head, sending him into the fiery depths of hell.

Desh's aim was perfect today!

As the clone fell onto his face, Pj spun around. His eyes darted from the clone to us. Then, with a gigantic grin, he signalled a thumbs up. Above all the noise and chaos of the firecrackers, the shot became part of the background noise. As Pj lowered his thumbs, he gestured for us to walk to the truck, which was now secured and safe.

In groups of two, we withdrew from the cover of the faithful bushes and crept towards the truck. By the time we all reached Pj, everything was going well. I suppose that, for a brief moment, I believed that we wouldn't run into any trouble.

Gil and Pj led the group, clutching guns tight against their chests, threatening to vanquish the life of any clone that dared to cross our path.

Gil's devotion to Christianity and his gun created a juxtaposition that, less than two weeks ago, seemed entirely preposterous. In that fate-filled moment, I had never pictured any of my friends the way that I was observing them: faces frozen in determination and dread, hands trembling under the weight of guns, eyes fixed upon shedding the blood of a living organism – a living organism that was not human. Maybe the non-human element made it okay? Didn't it?

Maybe that was why Gil was content holding a gun, holding an organism's potential death in his bony arms.

I moved my eyes to Desh. That familiar glazed look had drifted across his face. It was a trance again, a trance that centralised brutality, a trance that illuminated the enemy and the enemy alone.

He gripped the gun and muscles pulsed across his forearm. I abandoned trance-mode Desh and stole a glance at Zoey. She appeared calm and aware. Then again, she was always good at repressing her true emotional state.

Shaking my head, I focused on what we needed to do. The handgun became an extension of my arm defending my friends and I against the clones. Lacking professionalism in the gun-toting department, I followed Pj and Desh as they led the group.

Zack and Mia dragged the clone's lifeless body towards the truck. Kasey wouldn't touch the bloodied mess; her face twisted in disgust as she whispered, "Ewww" and "Oh, my god" in randomised spurts.

We reached the back of the truck and helped pry the door open. By this stage, the firecrackers had ceased their familiar racket throughout the bush, encouraging us to move swiftly.

Zack and Mia dumped the clone's body into the truck and climbed in. Each one of us searched for danger, with jagged movements and shifting eyes, as silence had befallen the area.

I was the last one to step inside the truck, breathing a premature sigh of relief as I climbed onto the hard metal surface. My second foot had just touched down, thoughts fixed upon our next move.

Then, I felt the impact.

I didn't have time to react before I found myself sprawled on the ground next to an infuriated clone. The fear in my stomach wrapped up my existence with a bow and ribbon, presenting it to the clone as a gift for his perfect timing.

I didn't bother to scream as the clone straddled me, constricting my chest. In this moment of disbelief, I didn't have enough time to raise my hands to protect my face, so he threw his clenched fist into my unprotected cheekbone.

As each impact thwarted my ability to remain calm, I became fixed to the ground, blindsided by the crippling shock of the situation. When his bulging fists continued to pound my face without respite, enough was enough.

What was I doing, allowing myself to get pounded to a pulp?

I allowed rage and adrenaline to pulsate, replacing the shock to my body. As he drew back his fist to punch me a fourth time, I clenched my own and thrust it hard into his face underneath the left eye.

It seemed to startle him but didn't contain his vigour.

Although I was no longer a slave to the pain, I could feel that my sight had grown hazy, like a green mist had swallowed the morning sun.

I must have waited too long between punches because before I knew what was happening, he reached for his gun. He struck me once above the right eye, and at that moment, I felt truly defeated. It tasted as though I'd swallowed several gold coins as the blood filled my mouth. Paralysation encompassed me, not only from the impact itself but also by a wrenching trepidation, the moment where the only thing left to do is pucker up and kiss the earth goodbye. The barrel of the gun pressed into forehead, its cold steel nestled against my thick, sweating skin, morbidly soothing me.

The crack of the gun rang in my ears for the next several hours.

I saw darkness. Unfocused shapes twisted and distorted under a pool of profuse liquid.

Blood poured with enthusiasm, covering the surface of my face, eyes burning with the acidity of an unwelcomed substance. I didn't know whose blood it was, I could not even comprehend the idea that death had spared me.

Was it the bullet that had transformed my life into a silent film: distorted, muffled and without vibrancy?

Or was it the fact that the clone had knocked the wits out of me?

A heavy mass obstructed my breathing. Even through blurred vision, I could see that this was the clone's body and its mutilated head. Someone I didn't recognise pushed the body off me and hurled me into the back of the truck. I landed in an awkward position, however, the numbness in my body kept me satiated for the majority of the ride.

I heard the truck door close almost silently, ticking as the metal rails stroked one another, bringing darkness to us all. My hearing was already so terribly muffled that I could only just make out faint voices and footsteps outside the truck. Blood and tears trickled down the side of my face, and I knew that my eyes couldn't tolerate being awake any longer. Darkness then devoured me and sent me into the perilous warp of unconsciousness.

# CHAPTER 10

Consciousness prevailed.

The humming of an engine filled my ears, the taste of blood filled my mouth and a hand rested on my forehead. It was difficult to find the strength to say anything. Hisses and mumbles disguised whatever I had tried to say.

The person above me responded quickly to my sudden conscious outburst, whispering in my ear.

"We're in the back of the truck, so just lay there until we tell you and try not to make a sound, okay?"

Accepting the advice, I lay back. The potholes in the road jolting me with the occasional right and left turns, shifting my body across the floor of the truck.

A figure in the darkness waved their hands about and whispered to everyone. "All of you guys, come over to me."

I didn't bother moving. Protecting myself from pain was more important than understanding our next move. After they finished, the person returned to my side, and in the pale light, I saw that it was Zoey.

She knelt down next to me, and this time, put her hand in mine.

It felt like a warm stream of water gushed through the tunnels within me, filling me with strength. Her touch – and even her presence – made me feel better.

"We are going to have to start moving now," Zoey whispered in my ear. "Gil thinks he knows where to go somehow."

I squeezed her hand to acknowledge that I understood.

"We have decided to smash the glass, kill the driver and take control of the wheel."

I jerked my head towards her, my disbelieving look lost in the darkness. *Was everyone crazy, or was I the only person that thought killing another clone here was a huge risk?*

I shook my head at her, thinking, *No way! You have to be kidding!*

She shrugged her shoulders.

"What other choice do we have, Cooper?"

My plan of escape may have brought us closer to death, as opposed to the other way around. I hadn't considered what to do once the truck had taken us away, conceiving plans in a terribly half-assed way.

My silhouetted friends peered out of small perforations in the truck, gauging where we were. My eyes had become accustomed to the light or lack thereof. The stench, however, hit me then, just as hard as one of the clone's fists did when I first stumbled onto the truck.

I also became conscious of the truck we had opted to board.

You know the one?

The one stuffed with all those dead bodies!

Yes, that one! The smell of death was rancid, bitter and sharp, causing the bile in my stomach to rise. I shuddered to think of who or what I lay on. Before I had a chance to survey the truck in detail, Desh called to everyone in a whisper.

"This is it; we are going to have to move now!"

Letting go of Zoey's hand, I struggled to my knees first. Taking a laboured breath, I pushed with shaking hands and groaned all the way until I stood on both feet.

It was easier than I had imagined, though. No muscle fragments tore off the bone, my face no longer felt as though it was beaten with steel road; I was revitalised and rejuvenated somehow.

The truck jerked to the left. With a small screech of pain from the tires, the vehicle hurled us to the opposite side, cascading with a heavy thud into the solid metal sheet. I couldn't cry out in pain because the fear gripped me with such force that I felt numb.

The engine's hum faded away, and the truck ceased its movement, coming to a distinct halt.

*Why had the driver stopped?*

A faint whisper startled me.

"The drivers have all stopped to refuel; this is our chance."

I rose from my self-imposed grave and whispered in a perturbed tone, "The other clones will hear the gunshots, and then, we will be in serious shit."

"Tell me what other choice we have?" whispered the voice, angrily.

"Okay . . . fine," I snapped, embarrassed.

"Who will kill them with me?" The voice belonged to Desh. A long silence followed until Zoey said, "I'll do it."

Why had I not volunteered for such an enjoyable activity? My exhaustion was quite the palatable excuse.

I pulled myself up off the truck's floor and groped around for my gun. The fatigue, doubt and fear had all surfaced, but I was only passing on my gun to the girl next to me, cloaked in the darkness of her own resolve.

Zoey would have to kill in cold blood, and I wasn't sure if I was nervous for her or if I was curious as to whether she could go through with it. I couldn't paint her as a satisfied sadist.

The taste and smell of death inside the truck was replaced by the ferocious bite of fear as we all exhaled nervous, stale breaths.

The clones yelled out to one another as the petrol flowed into the truck. Brutal spite raged in our eyes as we carefully watched him opening the driver's door and sidle inside.

His radio boomed with life.

"They seem to have evaded our capture."

Zoey and Desh kept silent, attempting to focus the rest of their energy on shedding the cold blood of the clone all over the interior of the truck. The clone turned the key in the ignition, and the engine coughed and spluttered, signifying the moment to kill. Desh and Zoey pressed their guns to the glass and fired.

The gun's kickback threw Zoey into the rear of the truck. Glass shattered and danced around us. In the pale light, it glistened like water at Bondi Beach on a balmy, summer evening under the gaze of the moon.

Chunks of glass remained, standing pompously among the weaker of its kind. Desh cleared them out with the handgun to join the rest of their shattered family.

The remnants of the clone's head were displayed all over the windscreen. Solid chunks of flesh and bone mixed with chestnut-brown blood splatter.

Zoey groaned from the back of the truck.

"Is anyone going to drive us out of here?" I cried out in a hoarse whisper.

"Go on, then, Cooper. Hurry up," Zack snapped from behind me somewhere.

I glared at him for a split second then focused my energy on the clone's headless body. As his body quivered still, blood sprayed onto my face as I climbed through the shattered window.

Heaving the rest of the clone's body into the back with my friends, I ripped a sleeve off my shirt to wipe the cracked windscreen clean of all the internal organs and blood. The engine was still running, and although the windscreen was blurry, I put my foot down on the accelerator, desperate to get closer to home.

The radio murmured once more. "Check your vehicles for the escapees, it is confirmed that they set up a diversion and may have boarded one of the trucks."

I smiled at the radio, several other trucks responding with confirmations that their truck was clear.

I followed them by adding the same response.

Driving away from the refuelling station, I had to fight back the tears as they pushed against my insides, craving liberation. Sure, we had satisfied our anger, sadism and revenge, but I still felt guilty. Taking a life betrayed childhood lessons. You could never give that life back once it was gone.

Even though I never pulled the trigger a moment before, it brought back memories of an hour prior, where I needed to either live with regret or kill someone – or *something* – to save my friends.

I'd killed my very first being. That was quite a big deal for me.

Blood dampened my pants, squelching with the movement of the rickety truck. It was revolting. The stench of week-old soup contaminated the small compartment, and I focused on my breath to ensure I didn't vomit. Never in my nightmares had I felt such a cocktail of negative emotions.

The good thing about nightmares is that, whenever you wake from them, it is always to a comfortable bed and a kind reality.

But my nightmare was my reality in this instance.

For about two hours, I followed the other trucks, driving the main roads until Gil called out from the back, "Cooper, if you follow my voice, I can tell you where to go."

"Oh, really? Have you been here before, mate?" I shouted.

He paused. "Well, not really, but I sort of know where we are. I guess that sounds weird, but just trust me."

I shrugged my shoulders. I didn't know any better, so I placed myself at the mercy of Gil's newfound internal navigation system.

"How long shall I follow these guys, then?"

"I would say another couple of hours or so, then we'll take a different route," he responded.

"Where do you think we ended up crashing, then?"

"It was pretty close to Coffs Harbour. There is a national park called Guy Fawkes National Park, and I think we were in there," he assured me.

Another half-hour on the plane, and we would have crossed over into Queensland. I appreciated this stroke of luck – if that was the proper term.

I longed for my mother, my sister, my Serenity. Heading back home excited me, which was out of character for me. Normality beckoned, which meant happiness and healing were within reach too. It didn't matter that we hadn't had a proper holiday or chance to relax.

When I placed my feet upon the path leading towards my home, the horrible events of the past week would fade, and I could focus on grieving and healing.

At the same time, though, there was still a lot more to do between now and putting my feet up at home. I had to lose the trail of trucks so that I could gain access to a clear run into our suburb. I didn't know what to expect when we arrived, but I repressed all the poignant feelings inside my heart and focused on a small glimmer of hope, salvaged from the storage of my childhood innocence. That diminutive bit of hope led me to believe that my family would still be okay.

But chances were slim. There was no denying that fact.

Two hours later, I turned down Lancastor Street, losing sight of the trucks. As I accelerated, I made the first left with a deafening, inducing a screech from the tires. I kept a frantic pace, turning down many streets that would eventually take me to my humble home.

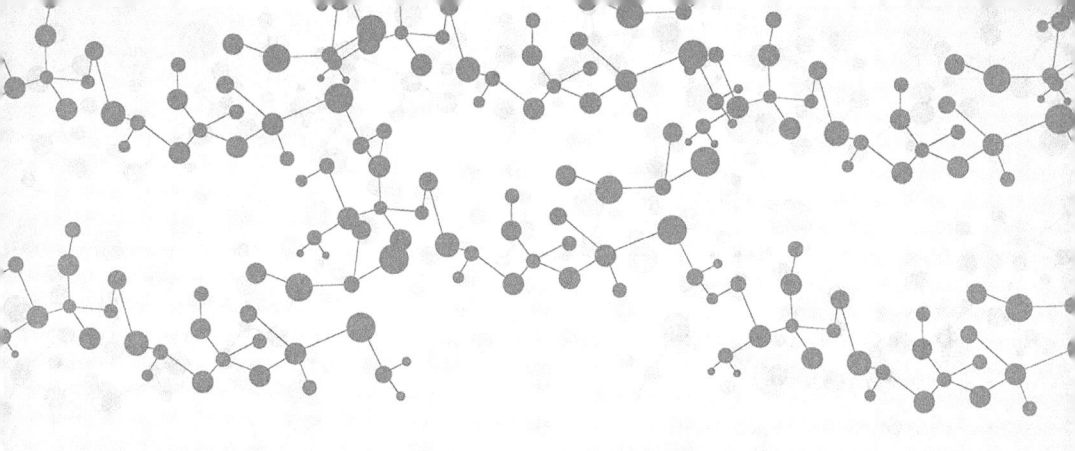

# CHAPTER 11

We drove down Vince Road and approached my house. We'd been in the car for around six hours. The driver side window was down, and the sun flashed a golden smile just for me. I could hear him say, "Cooper, my man, you're nearly there, you've nearly done it."

I winked at him. "Shouldn't have doubted me, Sun. You shouldn't have doubted me."

Everything was going as planned until the radio from the deceased clone transformed into a volcano, erupting with a formidable voice.

"Where are you, 675? Why have you deserted your post?"

The voice faded into wisps of white noise. It appeared as though we had become trapped inside a tunnel, although that tantalising glimmer of light at the end was nowhere in sight.

Suspended in nothingness, we siphoned motivation from the voices of the dead. If only a speck of light would grow and show us the way to peace and safety. Where was the sun now? I thought.

Reality took hold of my shrinking hope and transformed it into a spiritual demon that infiltrated my soul. Fear was that demon: the very quality that could convince someone to abandon all hope and retreat. But I did my best to ignore fear, attempting to shut out everything and maintain my focus. I was driving down a road, a road that could take us to freedom or lead us to the very end.

Before I was able to soothe my fear, something interfered again. Maybe it was Gus, just as it had been before. Maybe God and the angels took notice. All I knew was that my consciousness was slipping away. It was as if I were still experiencing my reality, driving on an open road towards my home, but my spiritual self had abandoned me. It floated into the air, floated onto the car's bonnet, resting on its elbows and twirling its legs in the air.

Taught hands still gripped the wheel, so, at least, my physical self was still intact. Green sparks were laser beams pulsating right in front of my eyes. Overbearing voices, copious and wicked, enveloped the air surrounding me. It was apparent a dream state had begun.

From a diminutive speck on the ground, the green sparks grew. A mountain of evil took form; the green lines silhouetted the figure against the darkness that consumed my mind. A burly man took shape out of the glow, his gaze fierce and unassuming. Flamed hands complemented his muscular arms reaching out in vibrant bursts towards my face.

A fire ignited in the core of the hideous man as he made his way towards me. He was as tall as a skyscraper in the city of the dead. His fiery eyes stared directly into my pupils, cursing my wretched soul with a wicked smirk. Revealing a lengthy, sweltering sword, he swung it at my face, lacerating my cheek underneath the left eye.

Blood gushed from the wound and trickled down my neck, like chlorine water running off a swimmer's back as they exited the pool.

Standing before this monster, this descendant of evil, I cowered into submission. I was an obedient servant, succumbed to its will, for how could a simple man measure itself against such an entity?

It bellowed in a distorted, dissonant voice.

"Fear is your mortal wound, and it bleeds eternally."

At first, the declaration perplexed me. Though, as my furrowed brow resolved its creases, this entity pointed out the perpetual weakness of humanity

Fear gathered and built upon itself in hearts and in minds: ceasing development, quelling imagination, instilling doubt and obliterating hope. It was ironic that this entity had attempted to enlighten my understanding of the human existence while evoking that same weakness within me.

*Maybe it was not a warning at all? Maybe it was infiltrating my mind, evoking fear in my spiritual being in order to defeat me in reality?*

The silhouetted figure wrenched back its arm. Its hand nurtured a raging, smouldering fireball. With malicious disdain, the figure thrust the fiery image of my own death at me.

I attempted to scream, opening my mouth as wide as I could, the rumble inside my throat producing a shrill, piercing scream that would soon taint the silence.

My stomach exploded, the capacity of my lungs expanding, intensifying as a swarm of locusts emerged from within. The locusts rapidly swarmed out of my mouth, each pair of wings rustling and scratching my bleeding gums.

Ravenously, they devoured me from the inside out. The luminosity crept up behind me, and blinding light penetrated my eyes, spreading throughout holes in my body until I burst into millions of pieces.

I slammed on the brakes, sweat sliding from the top of my head to the curve of my jaw. Hands trembled as I gripped the steering wheel. I was back in my physical body.

"Cooper, what the hell are you doing, man!?" Zack yelled from the back.

I ignored him and looked around; subconsciously, I had continued driving while the terrible image ravaged my mind.

A desirable thirst for air emerged within, as I became conscious of my heavy breathing. Slowing it down, I eased the beloved oxygen into my body. How did the dream-like hallucination fit into everything?

The green-glowing man, the burning fire – what did it all mean?

I thought of what kind of fear it evoked in me. I guess it was more of an acknowledgement that fear was the very weakness that burdened each being. As I remained stationary, someone else was breathing heavily. I listened closely.

The breathing was in tandem with my own, struggling to slow, feasting on oxygen as if it were a home cooked meal. An unknown feeling flooded my heart and mind. For some reason, without even looking at who it was, I had a suspicion that it was Mia and that she, too, had seen that green-glowing entity.

All at once, muffled voices erupted from the back of the truck.

I could only make out, "Mia, is everything alright?" and "Oh, Mia looks ill."

I turned to face Mia. She had anticipated my stare. Locking eyes with one another, I became a sponge absorbing her inner emotions, feeling everything she felt, truly understanding her.

As I stared, everything around me fell into a deep shadow. All I could see were Mia's eyes beaming in the darkness. Her eyes were small fireflies in a cave of mystery, alive with fear and diffident wonder.

Before I could grasp what had happened between us, she turned away. When she broke our stare, the light returned, restoring my vision. I blinked and shook my head to gain traction in the physical realm once more. I searched outside my driver's side window to see where we were. The street sign read Frankie Street, adjacent to mine.

I had found something to settle my nerves and quench my fear.

*Okay,* I said to myself, *just breathe; the dream was not real.*

A street separated me from my home. At the thought of normality. My nerves closed their weary eyes; my fear hid beneath a veil of momentary welfare, remaining alert and attentive. My own indestructible logic returned.

I turned to the back of the truck.

"Hey, guys, I reckon you should all get out now and start walking while I park this thing . . . it will be safer that way."

Desh yelled to me from the back of the truck something that sounded like he had agreed.

I could park and conceal the car in that street then walk to the house under the cover of darkness so as not to lure our enemies straight onto my doorstep. I wasn't sure if my house was safe or not.

The back door slid open, and feet shuffled upon the gravel road. In the rear-view mirror, I watched the last couple get out of the truck.

Mia's eyes were the last things I saw, ablaze with dread and concern in a gaze that did not waver. A tanned hand grabbed her shirt and pulled her away, which put an end to our staring contest yet again.

Without sufficient warning, darkness and loneliness engulfed me. Arduous emotions swirled inside, adding weight to an already heavy heart. Emotions were puzzle pieces that connected us to an overall projection of our current selves; a projection that had the ability to alter one's personality, if left to ravage internally. If only someone had found a way to obstruct their imposition, to perhaps impede their penetration of the soul.

But it was and is unfeasible to do so, they have a way of infiltrating each and every situation, each and every circumstance.

Left alone in the truck carrying all those dead bodies, the only thing that I could have done with my emotions was repress them. I prepared to park the truck and make my way back home with the emotions buried deep.

As I accelerated, and the truck bounced onto the asphalt once more, I recalled what I had felt and experienced with Mia: a simple but powerful connection that I longed to know more about. Although this connection interested me, I understood that more pressing matters were at hand.

I shook my head, narrowed my eyes and fixed a determined stare upon the road ahead. The truck leapt into life, a vivacious ghost of hope and authority wistfully gliding across the open road. I was focused on driving, but nowhere near prepared for the peril that lay ahead.

It just goes to show that you should always prepare for the worst. Because I had not expected it, peril found my eyes, missile locked into them and laughed hideously. It was a contemptuous, scornful laugh, shrill and vile like the drivers of the very machine heading towards me.

A hideous green monster galloped forward – only, this time, it wasn't a dream. It was real. I stared at it: hapless prey, cornered by its pursuer, targeted for termination. My mouth dropped wide open; my heart sank into depths of despair. Fear, the collective human weakness, incinerated my last ray of hope.

The headlights flashed on high beam for a split second, warning me to stop, but there was just no way that I could. I knew what kind of "things" were in that truck, and I had a vague idea of what they would do to me if I surrendered.

On that revelation alone, I made my decision. As a slight over exaggeration to reinforce my decision, I slammed my foot on the accelerator. The truck took a second to surge forward, gasping as if I had just woken it from an afternoon nap.

My impulses urged me on, but my conscience was screaming at me: "All you're gonna do is kill yourself!"

*Fuck you!* I screamed at my conscience.

Nothing was going to stop me. I was raging inside. My eyes bulged and my blood boiled. Although I had compromised my safety and well-being, my friends were okay. So, in that regard, those last few seconds brought me peace.

I had to assume the worst. These clones knew we were the escapees who had evaded their capture. It was verified the moment they shot at me. The passenger side clone had her torso exposed out and over the window, holding a loaded rifle in her hands. I cursed under my breath, knowing that I was staring into the barrel of death itself.

Bullets rained onto the windscreen like a villainous hailstorm, vanquishing a radiant summer day. I bent down as low as I could to evade the angel of death from caressing me.

Brooding eyes peered over the shattered windscreen as I inched my head up. Stealing a glance at my hands, tiny bits of glass peppered my skin. Before I could curse once more, I found myself heading straight for letterboxes on the left side of the road. I swung the steering wheel back aimlessly, not before I had knocked at least three over, including one or two unfortunate garden gnomes enjoying the afternoon sun.

The truck veered right and left; and only with my shaking hands was I able to steer it back on course. It was a miracle that I didn't end up smashing into a house or two, as another round of bullets thumped into the seat next to me.

I glanced up, startled at how close the bullets had come to causing a mortal blow. Ignoring the narrow escape, my eyes adjusted to what was in front of me.

The last thing I remembered was how close their truck was. The determined faces of the clones grimaced in anticipation of an impact. My last thought solidified itself to the important parts of my mind as a memory.

*Is that a green glow that I see around them?*

It didn't matter at that moment because the sheer determination of their truck had defeated me, for it served one purpose: impact.

My first impulse was to turn the wheel as hard as I could to avoid the truck. It didn't work.

The clones smashed into my passenger side, forcing the truck to sway at an impossible angle, propelling me in the direction of the earth. Shock spread throughout my whole body. Windows smashed to my left and right; metal roared, chewed me up and spat me out, revolted.

The washing cycle engaged; I spun towards the living room of a house. Pressed against the dashboard and levitating above my seat, my head thumped against the steering wheel, and I blacked out.

The heat of the sun crawled across my skin. I was no longer in the truck.

A warm sensation started at my toes and slowly crept up my tingling legs. Although disorientated, I was able to register small flames cultivating inside of the truck.

A cacophony of ticks, tocks and snaps resounded around me amidst the crackling flames. Forcing my crippled arms to move, I dragged myself across the tiled floor to safety.

*Tiled floor? It couldn't be. Where was I?*

I became a snail, not only because of my pace but because of the thick blood trailing me as I slithered away from the burning wreckage.

With my last effort to stay awake, my heavy eyes wandered to my arms. Pieces of glass were embedded in my skin, like mosaic tiles in a Gaudi piece, glistening with cellular disruption.

Darkness then wrapped its fingers tight around my face. It was there, on the kitchen floor in someone's house, next to the burning wreckage of a truck, where I lost consciousness for the second time that day.

# CHAPTER 12

A bright, bubbly blue sky filled my periphery as I lay on my back. I was almost lulled into a trance by the aesthetic delicacy before me. But the skulking grey mass of smoke tainted the baby blue.

Soon, that wispy plague spread across the whole canvas of the world. The blue was no more.

My chest heaved to an imaginary beat, accompanied by the dissonant melody of flames burning and tyres squeaking.

Since smoke tainted the sky, I turned to survey my surroundings: grey metal, rubber and a photo frame? A part of a letterbox, papers . . . scattered in disarray.

The tranquillity faded as the sensation of pain climbed up and down my arms, like I'd brushed up against a cactus.

I groaned, closing my eyes to shut off the pain.

I couldn't bear to look. The pain still held me tight.

Was it the worst feeling?

It appeared so. Squandered upon the grass, shards of glass embedded in my charcoal arms; multiple lacerations stinging my face. But it wasn't the worst.

Physical pain, in the moment, left us in turmoil; though, in a day or two, the pain quelled into a distant memory. It may leave a scar upon silky skin, but internally, there is no skin to scar; there is no barrier to break through.

Emotional pain was something that could sting you forever. Whether it is the death of a friend, regretting actions in the past, holding onto hatred or feeling as though you had been forsaken. It won't leave a scar, but it will change the course of your life, often unbeknownst to you.

As I lay on the grass, sweating, spluttering, coughing, wincing as the terrible pain held me tight. I knew that I would choose to endure the same thing a thousand times over, just to have the lives of my friends returned.

The more I thought about the people I had lost, the better my recollection of the recent events strengthened. Straining to think of how I had come to that moment, I stared at the plagued sky, with a photo frame beside my arm.

Turning my head to face the right, Zack handed me my answer.

He stared at me, wide-eyed and stunned. His eyes drew me in. Staring into them, what appeared to be a ray of light beamed down, illuminating him from what surrounded us.

All at once, I saw what he was feeling.

Don't ask me how, but I saw it. I knew I was exploring Zack's emotions. It felt very much like the feeling with Mia, not ten minutes prior. I felt his uncertainty, his fear, his worry. But above anything else, I saw a small but significant change in him. As I concentrated to see what it was, he tore his eyes away like a page from our paperback stare.

Once he did this, everything returned to normal.

Zack had looked away to update the group on my condition – I learnt later.

Before I realised Zack was talking to someone else, my friends had gathered around me.

I looked at no one in particular, but Kasey was the one who spoke first.

"Cooper, can you hear me?"

She kept repeating this until I grunted a barely audible "Ehh."

"Do you think you can move at all?" she asked, her voice shaky.

I took a deep breath, my lungs shallow.

"Reee . . . bad . . . eh . . ."

"Normally, we wouldn't rush you, but we need to get out of here."

Her voice cracked, and she was choking back tears.

"O . . . eeee . . . " I wheezed.

Hopefully, they understood this as: Yes. Although you need to assist me.

I closed my eyes and braced myself.

Their hands dug underneath the ground and curled around my body before lifting me. I tried to think of other things, but pain writhed within me.

Pain as they carried me home.

Pain so intense, my breath was scarce. My vision darkened.

Pain.

They carried me all the way around to the back of my property, propping my ruined body up against a tree. The back of my head scraped against the rough bark as I faced them on their haunches, panting.

*Was I that heavy?*

My head was a merry-go-round.

Up and down, round and round, up and down, round and round.

The ride stopped as my head slumped forward, my chin resting on my chest, still heaving, still wheezing, attempting to breathe but failing. Even through my distorted vision, I could admire why my arms were still ablaze with wrenching pain.

Seeing the damage with my own eyes, the pain intensified. It made me remember the times when I was hurt as a child. If I didn't see the damage

I had done, the pain was never as severe. Once, I rode my bike without a helmet. The wheels lost grip over a slippery section, and I was thrown from the bike, smashing my head upon the tired brown earth. I rose from the ground, disguising embarrassment with laughter. Though, when I rubbed my head to soothe the pain, a warm, watery substance leapt from a small gash at the top of my head. Then the tears began to tumble.

This was much the same thing, but instead of tears, a flourish of anger and a desire for vengeance surged. I used my functioning neck muscles to rest my head back against the tree and search the sky.

My watercolour canvas soothed me once more.

By the time I realised where we had gathered, I saw that the ducks were nowhere to be seen.

The dam, usually bustling with life, had been abandoned.

It prompted me to think of the lives of my family, of whether it would be such a good idea to run into the house straight away.

I needed to introduce my friends to Serenity, for it was the safest place to stay. We could explore my house when we were all rested and able.

Summoning their attention, non-existent words fell limp from my mouth. I didn't even realise, though, that they were debating whether to walk up to the house or hide around the property. No one was sure how far any of this madness had spread.

"I . . . know . . . where . . . to . . . go," I mumbled.

I pointed with my newly sculpted arms towards the dense bush where Serenity hid.

Zack understood. He knew there was no better place to hold out for a few days. My friends all offered to help carry me, but I shrugged most of them off. I enlisted the help of Zoey and Gil to aid me, battling through exhaustion and the pain in my arms.

As Zoey and Gil held me, my legs gained strength. Numbness replaced the pain; the tingling started at my toes and crawled towards my thighs. By the time I reached the base of Serenity, my legs were lighter and walking was easier.

The feeling was something I'd felt before only a few hours ago – *in the back of the truck, perhaps?* It was bizarre.

I turned to my friends as I approached the entrance. Their faces, sullen, weary and downcast. Behind them, the sun dipped beneath the hills like a cookie into a glass of milk, sending the moon out to take its place. The chorus of sirens and helicopters filled the soundscape.

Zack volunteered the walk first, becoming a tour guide, as he was one of the people to have gone there with me. As I swayed on the spot, clutching Zoey and Gil, a coughing fit threatened to burst. I covered my mouth as the pain rocketed through my body. I took my hand away and stared down at shimmering, rich red blood, pooled in my palm.

"Ohhhh!" I grimaced.

Something was terribly wrong. The thud of my heart echoed throughout the chambers in my body.

Zoey lifted my shirt and gasped. Her face seldom shielded her emotions.

"Whart's ron?" I strained.

"Coops, lay down, please."

As they lay me down on the ground, the world still spun. The breath within me retreated and shadows sought a permanent residence.

Zoey whispered something to Gil, and he left me there alone with her. Watching him leave, I glimpsed at Desh following Zack into Serenity.

Zoey put her hand in mine.

I closed my eyes.

*Man, she made everything seem so much better,* I thought.

Holding her hand returned my strength.

I lost track of time as I lay upon the ground, the cover of night well and truly upon us.

"Try sitting up," Zoey whispered to me.

I rose stiffly, but surprisingly, I was without pain.

In fact, I felt as though my breath had returned, and my headache had faded.

I took a couple of deep breaths.

"I actually feel . . . better."

Zoey nodded, "I'm glad," pausing as she motioned to the fortress of the shrubs. "Shall we follow the others?"

I stole a glance at Zoey before we pried through the shrubs and trees to get to Serenity. She looked pale and weak, but how was I supposed to aid her? I was a liability myself.

As Zoey and I stood at the entrance to Serenity, I wondered whether all my friends had felt the same tranquillity?

I limped down the path in the direction of the luminous glow ahead, en route to the makeshift room.

The surroundings brought me comfort, and a sense of belonging – something I hadn't felt since the crash.

My friends didn't particularly share the affection and adoration I had for my second home. They were much more interested in finding a place on the mattress and placing their heads in their hands, attempting to unwind after such a tumultuous day.

Zoey was the only one who was not among the bodies that now covered the mattress. She rested her hand upon my shoulder. I turned around and examined her face.

She looked exhausted. Small abrasions covered her once rosy cheeks, creating a swarthy complexion from the dirt; forced brushstrokes painted her smile, attempting to conceal a hidden truth.

When I looked into her eyes, the same feeling hit me – just like it had with Mia and Zack.

Everything around me swirled and twisted into a nebulous glow that enveloped my vision. A solitary, blinding light penetrated the shadows writhing between us and projected her thought process and feelings.

I saw her worry, her heartbreak, her sadness, her guarded secrets.

Unfortunately, for my prying eyes, she took her stare away a second before I could attempt to open the small box of secrets suspended in her gaze. The desertion of her stare was enough to stop whatever feeling had overcome me. However, she turned back to me and said, "Cooper, let me clean your arms. I imagine they are hurting quite a bit."

I looked at her again. This time, I did not attempt to see anything more; however, I knew that she was hiding something. Clearly embarrassed, but I just couldn't understand why.

"I sup . . . pose so," I muttered with a painful grimace.

Zoey smiled and took me by the hand.

The very moment she touched me, a warm sensation spread all over my body again.

Covertly, she took me to the darkest corner of Serenity and sat me down. Taking a bandage out of the first aid kit on the floor beside her, she looked into my eyes. My 'power' kicked into gear. This time, it was precise and penetrating.

I saw her emotions as if they were on display: two solitary pictures hanging at opposite ends of an art gallery. Walking between them, I felt the emotions as if I were Zoey.

The two pictures represented forms of doubt and trust that she was experiencing at that very moment. Somehow, I was there, inside of her stare, inside of her, knowing and feeling them, too.

I had crossed the lines of reticence.

As she continued to wrap the bandage around my arm, I heard her whispers inside my head. They echoed as if they, too, were in that same large gallery.

Four words repeated over and over. "I hope this works, I hope this works . . ."

Zoey sighed and placed her hands on my arms.

Intense pain rocketed through my system again. I closed my eyes and repressed screams that scratched at the surface. Just when I thought I couldn't take it anymore, a palliative, comfortable heatwave spread throughout my entire body.

As I opened my eyes, I couldn't release my stare from Zoey. I was cleansed, as if a river of purity had alleviated my agony.

Zoey still had her eyes closed, lost in a trance of concentration. When her amber eyes flickered, she took her hands off mine, and that diffidence and insecurity returned to her sunken face. I brought my hand to her cheek and swept her sleek hair behind her ear. Bashful, she smiled, and her eyes drifted towards the floor.

As I moved in towards her, floating on a confident cloud of desire and adoration, I caught sight of something shining in the incandescent glow of the moon. I looked down at her hands and realised that she was bleeding. In haste, I clutched her arm to examine a sizeable cut to her wrist, but she jerked her arm away, fumbling at wrapping a bandage over the wound.

Scarlet red blood materialised gradually upon the ivory swathe.

"Zoey, what is happening to you?"

"It's nothing – please, I'm fine. It doesn't even hurt," she muttered, avoiding my eyes.

"But you're bleeding; let me help you."

"Cooper, I'm okay," she insisted. "Just tell me if you are . . . better? Is the pain gone?"

I hesitated, thinking about this for a second.

Holy shit. The pain was no longer.

"Yes, it's all gone," I spluttered in disbelief. "H-h-how . . . did you do it?"

She paused, as if contemplating telling me.

"You're going to think this is silly; even I cannot believe this because, it is, well . . . ludicrous. No evidence as to why it happens . . ." she said before breathing a heavy sigh. "When we were in the crash, I cut my wrist terribly." She gestured to the blood-soaked bandage on her left wrist.

"I woke up in your arms, and I noticed that a small piece of metal was stuck quite deep in my wrist. I was still in shock, so I didn't know what to do. Adrenalin does funny things to your mind. So, I yanked it out, which is, of course, a stupid thing to do."

She paused, recalling the traumatic event.

"So, of course, the blood just kept pouring out. I can remember just feeling like that was it: I was going to die from blood loss. As you carried me off the plane, I felt a hot liquid run through me, with a tinge of pins and needles, I guess. When you put me down, I looked at my wrist and there was only a scar. I guess your touch helped heal me. In turn, I have realised – especially this week – that I can now . . ." Zoey hesitated, as if saying it aloud would make it real, "heal . . . things."

She shifted awkwardly, turning to the opposite side of Serenity.

I inhaled a deep breath, feeling refreshed, almost pleasant . . . truly . . . healed.

Zoey continued. "I'm starting to find out that every time I . . . 'heal' something, my wound opens and bleeds."

"It doesn't hurt; it just bleeds a lot. I first found out when I helped Mia to wake up. I might have also fixed Zack's arm, but I can't be sure."

She stopped and looked at the ground, avoiding eye contact.

It took me a while to absorb everything she had just said.

Zoey suffered a mortal wound, but now, she could heal people?

She was the one who brought Mia back and helped Zack. What a gift this was.

I was still dumbstruck as Zoey's eyes drifted towards mine, extending her hands to grip my face. We could do nothing but embrace the divinity that pulsated through her hands.

Before I could speak, she came so close to me that her warm breath caressed my face. Her finger drew over the fresh cuts on my cheeks with the softness of a feather floating from the wing of a baby bird. Moving slowly, her touch was tantalising, causing ticklish tremors to cascade down one side of my body.

I closed my eyes, but the deprivation of Zoey's vulnerable beauty pained me. But her willingness to heal in such a loving way surprised me, and it made me consider that tenderness might be a prelude to a deeper affection.

When she pulled back, I opened my eyes. I saw a shadow of love, stifled by doubt and apprehension. Zoey's confident facade shattered right before my eyes.

I saw hope in her endearing brown eyes. Something I thought was lost after all that we endured. I salvaged what time we had left in the moment, reaching out and softly touching her chin, arching her head up so she was level with me. We breathed in unison, the air of desire with its intoxicating musk filling us to the brim.

I inched closer and kissed her on the cheek, my lips parted, leaving a damp impression of a long-awaited moment. Zoey's body tensed with anticipation, a sharp inhale stole her composure. I then turned to face her. For precious seconds, we studied the intricate colours of our stare and breathed in scarce succession, as if the air were precious. We thrust forward simultaneously, as if competing in the race of love, sharing the spoils of desire atop the podium.

The kiss was not as I'd imagined. Zoey's lips were dry against mine, and the stubble on my top lip seemed to startle her. After the initial shock of being unusually unkempt, our lips parted, mine caressing hers, sensual and delicate. She collapsed into my arms as our tongues engaged, passionate but sparingly. It was beautiful, careful and colourful.

With all my injuries now a painful memory, Zoey's miraculous healing power swept through me, colliding with the newfound feelings of careless love and affection. The heat, the warmth and the passion scorched my heart.

We could never recreate moments like this with words, with music, or with art. Each of those methods encouraged simple imitations and perceptions of what moments mean to us. I suppose that memories, however feeble, can be our only avenue back to a mark that changed us or a cherished point in time.

When I opened my eyes, colours that I didn't know existed before were splattered upon the walls of the cave, creating a rainbow archway that bound Zoey and me to one another. The colours, unlike memories, would never dull with the curse of time.

Footsteps echoed behind us, and the rainbow disappeared. Arms fell by our sides as Pj and Gil entered our colourful corner of the cave.

Zoey pretended to finish applying the bandages and whispered, "Keep them on so that nothing looks suspicious."

I nodded, indicating that her secret would be safe with me. I would need to investigate my own secret further before I was to discuss it with her, but it would open a door to share some honest conversations and vulnerable truths, a connection that I very much wanted to explore.

"All done." She steadied my arms, turning to Pj and Gil. With a brisk smile in their direction, she walked away.

"Geez, your face looks a lot better than it did before!" remarked Pj.

"It feels better, too," I replied, uneasy. "Zoey has . . . ah . . . significant healing remedies, I suppose."

"Well, it's great to see you alive and well. We all thought the worst when we pulled you out of the car . . . I mean, lucky we got there in time, otherwise –"

"There will be enough time to tell the story tomorrow, Pj. Anyway, we were just checking to see if you were okay," Gil said.

As Gil turned around to leave, Pj made faces behind him.

I smiled. Pj showed that he still didn't believe in taking life too seriously, despite all the recent horror we had experienced. I suppose that the stronger characters show their true strength when faced with adversity. Pj exuded defiance and fortitude.

The Pj that threw eggs at houses and yelled at people on the side of the road was the prankster Pj, who acted far below his age. As a result of this situation, more in him surfaced, a certain growth that indicated manhood was on the horizon, leaving the immature, selfish adolescent behind.

The changed man that Pj appeared to be was a man who had heart-to-heart conversations with people when something was wrong, a man who chose to believe in you when others might not, a man who could still see the light in defiant, bleak circumstances.

As I sat there by myself, in the corner of Serenity, thinking of how Pj had changed, a certain change unveiled itself in all of us, illuminated by Zoey's surprising revelation.

Even I had to admit that I could do something unnatural, inhuman – if you will. I guess that something special had happened to me on that plane; it handed me a gift. The gift was not only the sparing of my life, but a power to see something more in people. As I made a conscious effort to truly embrace it, everything around me threatened to change.

My eyes adjusted to palettes that I could never distinguish before. It wasn't just the influence of Zoey; it was more than that.

The world lit up in its true form. But was beauty a true characteristic of the world as a whole? Perhaps this was a question that could never have a definitive answer.

Beauty encapsulates an essence of the natural: a waterfall at the centre of an ancient rainforest, an autumn sunset kissed by curious clouds, two bonded penguins snuggled amidst a snowstorm.

But this world nurtured humans who would destroy another life with the spray of a bottle, the stamping of a foot, the trigger of a gun – just because they could. Humans destroyed anything if it threatened to disrupt their lives in the most diminutive of ways. So, why did they create a life-form in their image?

Was it to further their existence or provide an opportunity to boast?

But not every human stood atop the castle and threw breadcrumbs to the bottom feeders below.

The best qualities shine brightest surrounded by adversity.

Love, loyalty, devotion, empathy: all were qualities measured by their radiance when darkness called to them loud and proud. Almost always, lights would beam down, colours would caress and the beauty within those qualities would reign supreme.

Humans could find beauty within, if channelled correctly. The world could show us said truth and cleanse us with its natural gifts.

But it always came at a price. To have what is beautiful, we must first endure affliction.

So, as I sat in the corner, recalling the feeling of Zoey's lips upon mine. *Was it my chance to have something beautiful after so much pain?* I wondered.

Something gnawed at me below the surface of reality and shook its head.

*No, Cooper. The pain is far from over.*

I rubbed the cotton bandage tied haphazardly to my wrist, thinking that we would need to bulk buy a box or two to prepare for what was to come.

It was a shame that bandages couldn't cure emotional pain, too.

# CHAPTER 13

I t was Gus who came to me again; so, it had to be a dream.

Smoke billowed around him from a fat cigar wedged between his forefinger and thumb. He sat in an elaborate chair, carved from the finest dark mahogany wood, in the centre of a large room. A charcoal suit adorned his imposing figure; thick, bushy eyebrows snaked across his resolute stare. A single candle in the room burnt as a beacon of hope, reflected off his clean-shaven head.

Smiling with a warmth that he was not known for in life, it brought me a sense of comfort in the presence of a dead man. He beckoned me forward; I obliged but scanned the room in apprehension.

"They will come for you."

He delivered with conviction and gravitas.

"There is no use hiding in your place of peace. They will destroy all the beauty, all the dreams that humans have ever had."

The mere thought of opening my mouth encouraged Gus to raise an open hand into the air, as if commanding me not to speak.

"You must first understand them. Then you must believe that you can stop what has already begun. You have discovered the tools or gifts that were given to you to save your existence. But remember, time is a vast ocean, only willing you to sink to its depths.

"As a reminder, you will soon find a timepiece. Take it and wear it to remember that time is always against you."

He stopped and looked straight into my eyes. I could not see into him. An invisible force stifled my power.

I had so many questions for him, but the words suffocated at the back of my throat.

"Do it for all that has been lost, if you won't do it for yourself."

He turned to his left and blew out the candle.

Pitch black.

I opened my eyes, startled by the dream.

Pitch black.

I twisted, the jagged, uneven surface of the cave digging into my back. A combination of a restless sleep and a warm, sticky night formed beads of sweat on my brow, my grey jacket now moist and clinging to my body.

With a faint sigh, I located the zipper to ease the warmth created by its insulating capabilities.

Gus was right.

Come to think of it, dreamy Gus was always right.

Time was an adversary.

We couldn't control it. No matter how many people thought we could, it was the only worldly power that controlled us.

I must have slept for a while – Lord knows I needed it.

Pushing myself up off the ground, I headed towards the opening of Serenity, searching the heavens, imploring the skies for an answer.

Gazing at the stars presented me with precious moments to think about: Gus and the watch and how I would attempt to discuss it all with Mia. She seemed to be the best person with whom to discuss anything remotely out of the ordinary. Reading the stars quelled the desire to resume sleep, although the thought of Zoey and me in bed together evoked inappropriate images. I shook my head to rid the mind of amorous thoughts to concentrate on the path ahead.

When I approached the cave's mouth, a solemn silhouette shimmered in the surrounding darkness.

"Mia?" I guessed.

She spun around, and her eyes were all I could see. They were ablaze like a bushfire on a scorching summer's day, though shadowed smoke did not waft across her stare.

She may as well have been transparent. I could hear a faint echo of her thoughts as a whisper in my own head. *The North Node is in Scorpio, so I suppose that is why we are seeing our transformations more clearly.* She mused at the sky, unaware of my thought intrusion.

I was surprised at how well I could hear them.

"I'm trying to find some answers," Mia declared, pointing to the stars.

I stood beside her, our shoulders touching. "I can't even begin to understand how you can interpret this stuff."

"It's just like anything really, a bit of practice, and you find your feet." She turned to face me, shrugging her shoulders.

"When we were carrying you here, a rosella flew directly overhead. I interpreted it as an auspice."

"What the hell is that?" My tone was aggressively curious.

Mia laughed. "It's like a good omen. It gave me a bit of hope I guess."

"Hope from a flying bird, I love this. Bring on a flock of seagulls," I joked.

We soon became simple oak tree soldiers, engulfed in the tranquil silence of the forest frontline, forever staring at the horizon, waiting for something to come.

Silence has always fascinated me.

Silence: a perfect duality, significantly empty but complete. We exist, surrounded by everything and nothing; we say no words. No definitive sounds exist, but an entity engulfs and deafens us. There is just something about the way we see things when there is nothing to hear.

In movies, we see silence as awkwardness, but I understand it as an acknowledgement of what isn't there, of what we cannot comprehend. I see it as a calm before the storm, a moment in which reflection can cleanse.

As Mia continued to scan the skies for signs. I remember Gus's warning in the dreams and imagined that timepiece: a green flash scanning its glass face, waiting for me in its hiding place as precious seconds ticked by.

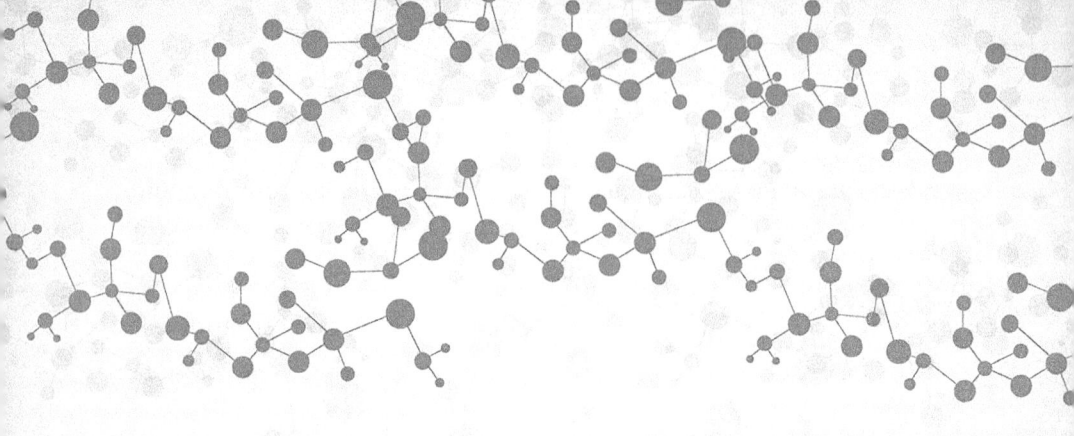

# CHAPTER 14

T he moon skulked behind foetal clouds, succumbing to the clutches of the conquering sun. Bending creaky knees, I folded my legs to sit on the cold rock next to Mia as I soaked up the deafening silence.

"Do you want to discuss anything with me – you know, now that we're here . . . just the two of us?" she inquired.

"What do you mean?" I answered.

"I can just sense that you have something to discuss," she replied.

*What topic should I explore with her?*

Maybe Gus.

No.

That was in my head. I needed to decipher him myself.

Next topic . . .

Zoey and that kiss?

No. Too personal. I wasn't the type to brag.

I had the perfect topic, but I was unsure of how to bring it up.

"Ah, I guess I should tell someone about this." I paused.

"Just don't think I'm weird, but I can kind of see what people are feeling and thinking just by looking into their eyes," I said with the speed of a commentator at the races.

Bowing my head, I took an extreme liking to my feet, not wanting to look her in the eyes.

I expected Mia to shuffle sideways until she fell headfirst into the jagged rocks adorning Serenity.

"Hey, well, I can kind of see the future, but I don't exactly have a choice in what I see," she concluded with a nervous smile.

I chuckled.

"Well, I guess whatever this is, it's too early for us to really control it, right?"

"I suppose it's hard to control something we don't understand." Her worry lines defined.

"Do you think we are ever going to understand why some of us are experiencing these changes?"

"I have thought about this a fair bit. My guess . . ." she paused, as if daring me to produce my own assumptions, "is that something happened during the flight. I'm not sure what yet, but even before we crashed, I felt sick and so did a lot of others around me."

I recalled feeling ill after our meal and trying to distract my mind with music.

"Oh, wow. I didn't even consider anything like that," I admitted.

"Well, either way, we aren't getting an instructional manual detailing what happened and how to deal with the after - effects!" Mia laughed.

"I guess we need to just figure it out ourselves, then."

She shot me a glance, eyebrows bent inwards, thoughtful.

"Okay," Mia quipped, "look into my eyes now and tell me what you see."

As I met her gaze, I didn't expect to feel anything different. My hesitant nature spawned vigorous doubt.

"Mia, the world isn't going to change here."

"Come on," she said forcefully. "Do this properly, Cooper."

I sighed, feigning disinterest. But the water of potential knowledge simmered as the heat increased.

"Okay, well, look at me, then," she said, her patience fleeting.

As I narrowed my eyes, a hazy glow enveloped the room. The familiar feeling surged inside of me, twisting and pushing against my body, which struggled to contain its energy. My breath, stolen from me like a distant memory.

The feeling refocused my vision, and my entire placement within the world reached out from within me, surrounding Mia in an aura embrace. I felt her presence inside of me. A foreign entity amidst what I knew so well. I felt just about everything that she was: her satisfaction, sadness, her sense of foreboding, her . . . jealousy.

As soon as I reached out and touched the pinnacle of her jealousy, I aborted the absorption. The green haze swirled back inside of my body, lungs filling up with air once more. I was myself once again, feeling my own feelings.

Confusion and excitement pulsed within my body. Mia must have sensed that I had found something personal, as she broke her stare to stop my prying eyes from exploring further.

*Too late*, I thought. *Perhaps, I'd already found what you didn't want me to see.*

I needed to say something to break the silence, but no words could stop me from turning over the thoughts in my head.

Luckily, Mia saved me.

"Well, Cooper, I guess it's not just me that has a sort of "power." I'm pretty certain you can also add Zoey to the mix."

I looked at her, unsure of what expression was worthy of the moment. Once again, I had no words.

"I can see things, Cooper – maybe not like you, but I see a little bit of what she does in the future. And – let me tell you – we will need to keep her close because, without her, many of us will not survive."

I contemplated this thought for a moment, relieved that I had something else to think about.

"Okay, I admit I felt something different, something, perhaps, supernatural? I just find it hard to think that Zoey, you and I are the only three that have this . . . new . . . talent thing?" I managed to say.

"I have not yet seen anything to prove or disprove any sort of abilities with the rest of our friends. Maybe it's something they haven't figured out yet. Visions only come to me when I'm not expecting them." Mia protested.

"Are you suggesting that, by telling our mates, they might uncover some sort of ability that had been concealed until now?" I inquired.

"I suppose it couldn't hurt." She shrugged.

"Alright, let's figure out a good time in the next couple of days."

As I said this, I knew it would give me time to figure out how it would go down. Besides, I wasn't in the mood for sharing secrets before the sun had risen higher into the sky.

"Well, I'm heading back to bed for a couple of hours. I'd rather not watch the sun come up this morning," I shared with Mia.

"See you in the 'proper' morning, then." She avoided my eyes.

"Okay. Oh, by the way, shouldn't we run this by Zoey before we tell everyone?"

She turned to me. Only for a second did it flash across her eyes once more, stirring and fizzing away.

"Yeah, I suppose so." Mia shrugged and faced the rising sun.

I nodded my head towards her and turned away, a lopsided smile gracing my face. I had uncovered the source of her jealousy. It was all about Zoey and I. Weren't there more important things to worry about? Our entire world was on the precipice of danger.

But the empathy within me stirred and cried out. *Cooper, don't be a hypocrite. You just kissed a girl. You have had impure thoughts about Zoey this whole time.*

Ouch, empathy. Way to silence me.

It was true, though. I needed to acknowledge that, even though I'd never considered Mia in 'that way', she obviously had been holding onto these feelings for quite some time without being comfortable enough to discuss them with me.

The love lives of a group of friends were often so complicated.

Throw in a plane crash, a newfound enemy, a bunch of dead friends and concern for other family members, and – well, *complicated* doesn't even begin to explain it.

When I opened my eyes, Zoey was already awake.

She smiled at me, her voice raspy and hoarse. "Morning."

Before I could reply, she leant forward and kissed me. It was brief, but it was gentle and loving. As she pulled back, I smiled.

Somewhat surprised, I inquired, "What was that for?"

She shrugged. "Life is too short, wouldn't you agree?"

Did I agree?

If it involved kissing and what else came with that, then, of course, I agreed.

"So, I guess our feelings are out in the open now?"

This was a question I didn't need to ask, for I already saw them in her dark, alluring eyes.

"What do you think?" Zoey asked through a coy smile.

"Well, I'm hoping that whatever we have here doesn't end up as some cute crush thing. 'Cause, the truth is: I like you, and I take it that, with the couple of intimate moments that we have . . . enjoyed together . . . that you're kind of . . . feeling something, too," I explained, mustering as much composure as I could.

"After so many months of flirting and not knowing how to bridge the gap, I'm kind of glad that we can be honest right now," she stated, shoulders relaxed.

"Well, as you alluded to, what is the point of waiting? It's not like time is slowing for us." A dash of pessimism threatened to cripple the moment.

"As long as we can agree that I made the first move," she declared.

"Umm, please. I'd say it was equal!" I exclaimed.

"Ahhh! You wish!" Zoey slapped my upper arm playfully, then nestled her face into my chest. My chin rested against the top of her head, and the warmth of the moment brought a smile that I could not contain.

"Hmmmm. How hungry are you?" I asked.

"Wow, You're thinking of breakfast in bed already?" she joked.

"Yeah, I don't know if I'm that romantic, but if you're happy to eat, I'm happy to make breakfast for you and everyone else."

"That would be nice." She smiled like the sun would have smiled.

I told Zoey to get ready while I got up to prepare breakfast. The sleeping bag exposed the goosebumps upon my flesh. Shuffling towards the cupboard, I searched around for a gourmet breakfast.

A couple of tins of canned spaghetti – not too bad.

Salt and vinegar rice crackers: not breakfast material, but who is being fussy?

Vegemite and crackers looked like a good, wholesome breakfast.

Zoey sauntered in behind me before wrapping her arms around my stomach, her dark hair tied in a plaited braid pulled to one side, exposing her arched neck. Her amber eyes were playful, and her smirk would've tasted of the sweetest toffee.

"How nice would it have been to have breakfast in bed?" she whispered into my neck then paced to the table. Her breath sent shivers through me.

I prepared some extra dishes for the group, who were up and about, their stomachs appealing for fulfilment. Zoey grabbed the last few plates to help me distribute to the remaining family members.

I mouthed at her, "Bed after this – no breakfast?"

She whispered in my ear, "Hmmm. No breakfast, and no bed, unfortunately."

Turning without gauging my reaction, she placed the last plate in front of Mia.

*Cheeky*, I thought. Sitting down on the cave's cool, uneven floor.

"I felt totally powerless," Gil said, bowing his head.

"As that truck came towards you, all we could do was wait and see what you would do."

I didn't even realise he had started to recount yesterday's events for my sake, as I was too caught up in my own thoughts.

"Luckily, you swerved at the last minute. Head-on collisions are never pretty."

Zack chimed in. "But the truck, man. It spun about twice in mid-air and rolled with you ending up smashing through a fucking brick house!"

Gil narrowed his eyes at Zack for swearing at the breakfast 'table.'

"I'm awfully sorry for cutting this interesting conversation short, but I'm thinking that I need to possibly check out the house and see if the shower is working," I interrupted. "I believe this takes the record for the longest time without one. The cold spring water in the bush just didn't soothe the soul."

"Yeah. Well, you are at home now, aren't you? I guess you can do what you want," Kasey spat, apathetic.

"I thought we had agreed to be cautious?" Zack puffed his chest out, ready for a fight.

"Relax, buddy." I put my hand on his shoulder.

"I will be careful," I reassured.

"Save some water for me, then, hun," Kasey sang, changing her tune.

I turned to her, smiling wide and muttered, "Will do." I left the corner of the cave, eating my breakfast on the go.

Zoey caught me just before I reached the mouth of the cave. Thoughts were turning to how sweet she was for wanting to kiss me goodbye when she put her hand on my forearm and locked eyes with mine.

"Just wanted to tell you to be careful. No doubt these clones are looking out for us still, and they know we're in the area. It's not your smartest idea, but have a look around – just don't walk around like you own the joint," she warned, swivelling on her heels without the hint of a forgotten kiss.

*But I did own the joint?*

Frowning, I walked towards the fortress of shrubs. She called something out to me about finishing our talk later on. At that point, I tried focusing on finding a shadowed path towards my house to appease the group and not draw attention to myself.

But it was worth reflecting on whether this was a clever choice: going to the house by myself, risking danger. A weakness of mine was tunnel vision. If I have a desire for something, I must have it right then and there. Even when presented with convincing arguments that suggest my behaviour is risky and ill-conceived, a certain sense of denial always prevails.

In this case, I was basically home.

I wanted a hot shower.

I wanted to add to my diminishing wardrobe.

I wanted to know if my family was okay.

The sun revealed the path back to the house, and for a fraction of a moment, everything felt normal again. It was as though I could hear those pots and pans clanging again, with Brooke in her room panting on the exercise bike.

But reality was cruel. I could not follow the path. Instead, the surrounding bush sheltered me, my new scarred arms, my new two-week-old beard, my tattered clothes. My life would never be the same.

Ever since I had employed my special, little gift, out of all the wreckage and total devastation, we could almost salvage something beautiful again. I didn't know how attractive it would be and what purpose it would serve, but I wasn't just walking towards the cemetery gates; a peaceful meadow loomed over the hill. It was now a question of how I could bypass the army of death that marched in perfect formation towards me.

After spending curious moments crouched behind a veil of plants, watching for any sign at all, I was satisfied that I was the only person in the vicinity of the house. I reached the front door and stared at the battered metal doorknob.

After pushing the door, an icy hand brushed my face as I entered my desecrated house. It smelt of their betrayal. Sharp and pungent aromas of disinfectant clashed with warmth and love. Air particles, once pure and pleasant, now soiled and mutilated. As I brushed aside the visual confirmation that a foreign presence had infected the house, I went to the cupboard to salvage some more canned food.

I passed the photographs hanging perfectly in the hallway evoking memories of happier times. This was my home, a place where I used to feel safe and secure. But I guess it was never a home without Mum or without Brooke. It was an empty shell of brick, wood, metal, concrete mix and mortar. It was hard for me to look at the photographs, unaware of what had happened to them. My thoughts were merely speculative but stained with realism.

Turning away from the faces in the frames, I hastened to the pantry doors. The food comprised tinned spaghetti, corn kernels, soup, asparagus, peaches in syrup – basically anything that had the potential to appeal to the senses while stewing in a can. I gathered up environmental shopping bags to carry the food down to the masses at Serenity then placed them at the backdoor as to not forget them.

Walking towards the bathroom, I passed my bedroom on the way. Clothes, frames, books and consoles littered the floor. I filled up two backpacks worth of clothes to take with me. No doubt my own clothes would serve as the only available fashionable garments in the small popular town of Serenity.

I placed them in the corridor, just outside the bathroom. As I walked into the white-tiled wonderland, I uncovered my own dishevelled reflection in the mirror. My hair was no longer strategically positioned, dark tufts of brown stood on frayed ends, and the sides clumped over the top of my ears like grass creeping over garden borders.

My once manicured stubble had grown into a beard, altering my amicable appearance with smudges of dark swirls like a faulty inkjet.

It had been close to ten days since I had seen my reflection, and truth be told, I was afraid of the eyes that met me in the mirror.

Was it my facial hair that exhibited menace? Or was it my eyes replaying the moment my soul bonded to the dark? I looked away and turned on the shower. Change was all around me – my home, the house, my eyes, my ordinary life and my extraordinary experiences.

It was all new.

New and shiny.

As my clothes became the newest addition of rubbish on my bathroom floor, I let the warm water dance on top of my naked body. The hair on my arms rose, bracing itself for the first contact with water. Droplets fell, disintegrating at first contact with the floor.

I closed my eyes, thinking of how new and shiny didn't bode well for me. I much preferred old and tattered. I liked rag dolls and furless teddy bears, but I lived in a world full of Barbie dolls and Matchbox cars that were never taken out of the box. The driver's seat beckoned someone to manoeuvre tight corners and take the chequered flag, but at the time, no one presented themselves. I kept my eyes closed and let the water support me, soothe my skin, cure my aching muscles and eradicate the grime.

I twisted the knobs to shut off the water.

What a shame. I had enjoyed the feeling. Had anything in that past week felt so good? I couldn't remember. Well, aside from the kiss.

After stepping out of the shower, I gathered fresh clothes to wear and readied myself to get back to Serenity, where the town would sing my praises.

*Would I be elected mayor? Surely*, I thought.

The chugging sound of a truck's engine approached the house from a distance.

I sped through the corridor and the front door, picking up the bags along the way. A new and shiny truck lumbered down my driveway. I crept behind mum's front garden surrounded by bags of food and clothes. I waited patiently for any sign of life.

It was definitely there, walking up the pathway towards my door. I couldn't believe my eyes.

Mum! Brooke!

I was so close to jumping up out of the bushes and shouting several sweet nothings into the air. But a familiar figure behind them stifled my urge to call out.

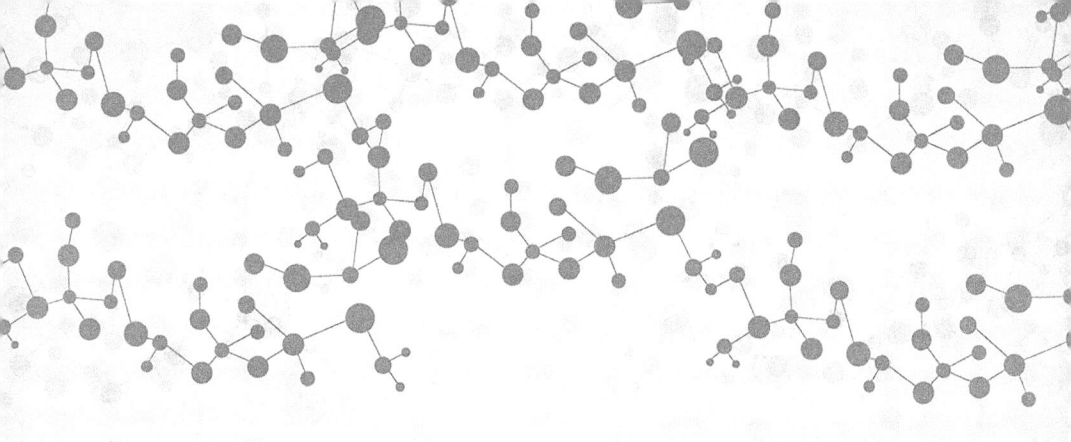

# CHAPTER 15

F amiliar, youthful and determined, yet carefree and resolute. His jawline, prominent and strong on a clean-shaven face, his slick brown hair combed across the top of his head. It was me! But it wasn't *me*.

My mouth hung open as a new and shiny version of myself walked through the door. Unfortunately, the preparation for such a moment does not exist in the handbook of life.

I did not take to the situation as I thought I would. I was numb. I couldn't hear much of what they had said to one another, but the longer I stared, the more it did not matter.

The familiar, ominous feeling bubbled up inside of my stomach: the same feeling that I had with Mia not long before. It spread throughout my blood and my skin, swelling to my sight as a stirring blur, encircling the clones of my family and I. Their surroundings became distorted, defining their physical form.

A green glow emanated from within them, their eyes like fluorescent green laser beams on New Year's Eve, spiralling into the distance.

I could feel them; their cold vice grip strangling my very core. It felt as if something lodged itself into my eye; I had to blink several times. Although it was uncomfortable, it was imperative that I used the moment to come to grips with this gift. Slowing my breath, I opened my eyes once more.

The power worked differently with clones and regular human beings, it seemed. I could hone in on the emotions of humans at a glance but could only identify a clone.

We couldn't take this power for granted. Obviously, it was difficult to tell humans and clones apart. But I could keep us safer by being able to identify who or what to avoid.

The shock wore off, and as each breath filtered through my lungs, my heart and my mind became active. I crouched behind the house, but I needed to leave before jeopardising my position.

Getting back to Serenity to warn everyone of what I had witnessed became my number one directive. I stole another glance just before I left. This time, the sensation wasn't so overwhelming.

The bright green flickered in their eyes.

The bright green marked the enemy.

The bright green would mark them for death.

A wicked smile crept across my face but faded as clone Cooper walked down the corridor towards the bathroom. The steam on the mirror would linger.

I would take the back streets to the deserted town of Serenity. In no time, I was out of first gear, carrying clothes and food for the townsfolk. No election party for Mayor Cooper tonight. My very first crisis meeting would take place.

The dim complexion of Serenity provided enough sight to acknowledge the shadowy figures of my friends.

"Guys, we have a problem . . ."

People have said in varying situations, "When the time is right, you'll know."

The time had arrived to announce our powers to the rest of the group.

It was all or nothing; my admission would test our cohesion as a group. They had gathered around a Monopoly board, and I was about to tarnish the greatest amount of fun they would've had in a significant amount of time.

I usually loved being the centre of attention with the spotlight on me as I sang or played guitar on stage, but this was different. Several eyes fell upon me, asking questions without words, revealing their deepest fears and concerns with just one glance.

The seconds ticked by. One by one, our secrets became common knowledge. Mia took the podium first in a surprising display of courage and spirit. "The fact is, guys, we don't have a lot of time to tell you these things. When we do, some of it is going to be . . . well, a little hard to believe. I'm just saying that it would help if you could support us a bit here," she requested, displaying a customary hint of her timid nature, despite her bravery.

Most of the darkened faces nodded in acceptance.

"Okay, well, here goes."

She exhaled, closing her eyes for a second to steady herself.

"I can see parts of the future." Without pausing or lifting her eyes from the ground, she continued. "I cannot choose what I see; it just comes. All I know is that what I see will happen – if I do nothing to change it – that is. Some things have already come true."

Silence fell upon Serenity.

I spoke next, continuing on from where Mia had left off. "The real reason that we have chosen to speak to you like this is because, as you know, I've just experienced a problem while collecting some food sup –"

"Dude, I'm sorry, but how do you expect us to believe this bullshit?" Zack retorted.

"Zack, shut the fuck up. I want to know what is going on. You can take your bitching and moaning elsewhere," Pj blurted.

I tried to calm the situation.

"Okay, Zack, think what you want; I just need to tell everyone here what's going on, then you can decide what to do with yourself."

I looked away from him and chose the rough walls of the cave instead.

"There are clones in my house as we speak. I saw them with my own eyes."

Gasps and soft murmurs erupted around me, but I tried not to let it perturb me from delivering my all-important revelation.

"I ran away before I could figure out what to do, but I wanted to talk to you all first to get a grip on what we could do . . . together, I guess." I steadied myself.

"As Mia said herself, she has developed a certain extra sense – if you will. It has happened since the crash, and now that she has told you, I think I need to let you know that both Zoey and I can do something . . . new and unexpected as well."

"I can heal people," Zoey blurted out, before I had a chance to reveal anything.

She flushed and looked upon the ground.

I continued what she had begun to say.

"I can read what people are feeling."

Zoey's eyes narrowed, her stare insinuating her dismay that I hadn't informed her.

I looked away from her; bodies shifted uncomfortably.

"I guess we wanted to tell you, hoping that, if any of you feel something . . . different about yourselves, you'd speak up now."

Zack spoke up again.

"I'll tell you how I feel different: I haven't had a fucking shower or seen my family or had decent sleep. All of a sudden, when we are careful, Cooper goes off to have a shower and happens to see some clones. Now, we can't even go into the house. Not to mention this absolute bullshit about being some kind of superhero. Prove it to us, then!"

Gil fired a response at Zack.

"Mate, they aren't circus freaks. If they say they can, then they can . . . We need to dedicate energy towards finding a solution, not fighting with each other."

"I don't give a shit what you think, Gil. I'll walk right outside and kill those fucked up pricks with my bare hands . . . I'll do it now!" Zack shot up from where he was sitting, gesturing towards Serenity's entrance. His fists clenched; a red rash of rage spread across his cheeks.

He was in a state of denial; grief lingering like an unwanted friend. Zack was in pain and needed to take it out on someone.

I took a different approach with him.

Sidling up next to Zoey, I whispered, "Would you be able to heal me now?"

"Um, yes. I guess so. Why?"

I walked straight past Zack towards the cupboard in the corner of Serenity, opening the door to reveal a menacing fifteen-centimetre blade.

Several gasps echoed.

Zack turned towards me and stuck his chest out.

"Is that how you're going to stop me?" he yelled in an ominous tone. Ignoring his question, I responded, "You want proof, right? Then I guess you can stop acting like an asshole."

I placed the knife blade against my skin, pressing it across myself, meticulous, wincing in pain as it paved a path of destruction upon the inside of my arm. Skin parted like a solitary tree under the force of a lightning strike. White flesh peeled, split in two, sending rockets of sharp pain through me. It took several seconds for the blood to arrive at the surface. When it did, it stained my arm in steady bursts.

The knife slipped from my grip, spinning through the air and crashing onto the floor. My hands were shaking as my heart thumped against my chest. Desperate to ignore the searing pain, I closed my eyes, and my breathing slowed. The sound of whispers and shuffling footsteps rose to my ears.

Without the need to open my eyes, I knew Zoey was there. Her presence evoked an extra sense within me. Cool hands met my skin, producing a tingling sensation that reverberated off my internal walls. It cocooned my damaged arm as the feeling intensified, sending its true repairing force inside and out of my body until all traces of the blood and pain were a distant memory.

I opened my eyes to find Zoey clutching at her own wrist but finding only dried blood and another fresh scar upon my arm. I searched her, attempting to show her my appreciation.

A weak smile crawled across her face. I guess she understood.

Turning to the crowd of my friends, I looked directly at Zack, who had shrunk in size and stature.

Holding my arm high above my head for everybody to see, I bellowed, "Is this proof enough for you!?"

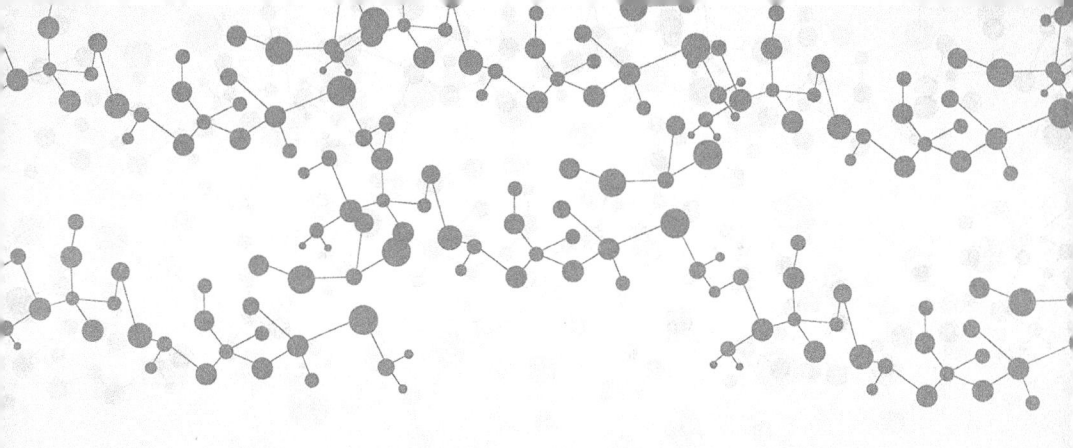

# CHAPTER 16

Zack hung his head in defeat.

Desh sat in silence, far away from my little stunt. He ignored all the antics and remained unfazed when I told them that the clones had come into my house. He didn't sit in disbelief when we spoke about our gifts. He didn't even stop me from making a scene.

He remained seated, calm, composed and poised.

At school and at university, he was always more devoted to study than the rest of us. He would often stay after class to understand significant formulas or equations that required more focused attention.

Desh was in the midst of formulating his own equation, one that would help us find out the true intention of the clone army.

After I bellowed, "Is this proof enough for you?"

Desh's eyes narrowed as he stood, imploring every person in Serenity.

"I know what we have to do in order to figure out what is going on here."

Silence covered the cave like a drawn curtain shielding penetrating sunlight.

I had just performed a nice magic trick for the citizens of Serenity, and here Desh was: taking my spotlight and not providing any applause?

How rude!

I stared at Desh, contemplating what to say next, but he resumed his speech. "I know there are these new revelations – and okay . . . they are quite startling – but this should not be our focus right now. Our focus should be finding out just what these clones – or whatever they are – are attempting to do to us, to our families and even to our world, and I have an idea about what we should do."

Desh was, of course, one hundred per cent right. Regardless of the circumstances, we needed to use our collective energy to shut the clones down, not use it to fight amongst ourselves.

I think he understood everybody feared what could happen. We'd all seen our friends die, so who knew if we could survive anything more than what we already had?

Sometimes being afraid and anxious can manifest into negative and damaging emotions like anger or frustration, which we often direct at others unintentionally. Zack was most likely terrified of the significant changes in his life, just as I had been. The ones we love are the people we take it out on. It doesn't mean we love them any less. It is the complete opposite: the more we love somebody, the greater chance there is of us leaning on them for support, through means that others misconstrue, proving ineffective.

I appreciated Desh for his clear head and focus. While all the rest of us gave in to our aggression and fear, he remained on task to find a plan that could save us all. The air softened as we each realised the error in our ways.

With our undivided attention, Desh could divulge his plan.

The week that ensued shed some light on what we were up against.

# CHAPTER 17

O
ur plan of attack was defensive and simple. But often you will find that true success is achievable with thorough, careful – and most importantly – uncomplicated steps.

Desh's plan became our unified vision, and we worked through mundane tasks to find out what we were up against.

Desh gestured for us to huddle as he informed everyone of their tasks and separate responsibilities.

"Here is what I think we need to do. I know some of us want revenge for what has happened so far." Desh's gaze darted in Zack's direction then slowly moved it towards me.

I smiled, acknowledging his warning.

"But we need to be intelligent about what we can physically do without knowing anything about our enemy. If you research the great wars throughout history, there was never any attack without knowing the opposing forces first. This is much like any competitive sport we play."

He pointed at Kasey.

"When you played netball, did you ever talk about a certain player you needed to mark closer than others?"

She nodded.

"My point exactly. We need to calculate risks before we make a move. Once we know what we are up against, then we'll figure out what comes next. Our lives together are worth more than seeking blind vengeance. I also don't want these things to eradicate humanity, so we will find a way to end them. We just need to plan it."

We looked around at one another. The mood had shifted.

I clarified, "Okay. So, basically, we need to observe first and figure out what to do from there?"

"We'll do it in pairs with shift work if you like and report back every little thing that we learn about them."

"We have access to old school cameras if we need them," I replied. "Obviously batteries or charging may become a problem further down the track."

"Great idea. Okay, well, the cameras will be used for only particular circumstances. Our phones are pretty much useless, as the batteries are dead. So, they're out. Are we all in agreement of what needs to occur? Does anyone want to change anything?"

We separated for the night, all in agreement for the coming days.

*Day One*

Desh's face was not the most enticing of faces to wake up to, but there, he was crouching over me as I cradled Zoey in my arms.

I moaned and rolled over, allowing Zoey to turn onto her side and rub her nose, grunting something indecipherable.

"What is going on Desh?" I croaked, my face buried in the pillow.

"Morning, buddy. We need to get everyone started on observations and briefing."

I turned to look at him through squinted eyes, wondering why he was talking like an army general. His smile was wide and broad.

"Errr, okay, I'll get up. Just get out of my face with that idiotic smile."

"Meet you soon," he chirped as he bounded off to another unsuspecting victim.

When I had summoned enough energy to put my clothes on, I helped drag Zoey outside to meet the others, who had gathered in a circle around the rock pool.

"Morning, all. Just to let you know, I have been up all night figuring out certain schedules and also taking preliminary observations and precautions."

He turned to Mia and Gil, "*And* I had some help from both Mia and Gil, whom I appreciate."

They bowed their heads in respect.

"From what we have gathered so far, the clones have begun to pass themselves off as humans and, basically, go about life in much the same way you or I would. Everyone should use today as an opportunity to try to understand what it is they're doing. The partners will be Zoey and Pj, Kasey and Zack, Gil and Coops, Mia and I. For now, we'll just keep it that way until something changes. Zoey and Pj are up first. Remember, we all need to make sure to stay out of sight; be vigilant and careful. No risks, *especially* today."

He handed them binoculars, a handgun and two cameras, all of which they needed to place in a backpack.

"This is the equipment we have. Please do not waste anything. Those who are not rostered on for observation are eligible for free time. Any questions?"

I think Desh had spoken for long enough, assuming the role once more, of army general taskmaster. Seeing many of my friends make faces at each other during his speech, it came as no surprise that I was not the only one who thought Desh was a little over the top.

We each moved off to our 'designated areas,' Zoey and Pj clearly keen to start a new task, as they star jumped and jogged with a Rocky-esque swagger towards the opening of the cave in jest.

I took Zoey aside and embraced her, squeezing her just enough to give her strength.

"Be careful, please," I whispered into her ear.

"All I'm doing is watching!" She casually let go of me and resumed her brisk walk to Serenity's mouth, ready to face our enemies.

Maybe I was being a little over dramatic, perhaps? Desh's pep talk had me a little more on edge than I needed to be.

Zoey often referred to herself as a chameleon, adapting quite successfully to fit certain situations. Here she was, the first to embark on our initial mission, and she presented herself as calm and collected. Not blending into the walls of the cave but thriving in a new situation without a spot of bother. When would I get to see the real her in every situation? Would that be the defining moment when I'd know that our relationship was real?

Gil and I were meant to be on "free time," however, we watched Zoey and Pj from behind the shrubs at the top of Serenity, flanked by Zack, who had calmed down since his outburst the previous night.

I suppose we were all curious as to what would occur.

It was a bizarre situation, though, as we were watching two people who were essentially watching two or three other people. An inception of observation.

I glanced at Gil's watch; it read 7.36 am. I had a slight feeling that the coming days were going to drag on, and I was not wrong.

*Day Two and Three*

The revelations were sparse on the first day.

In fact, the concept we explored most was tedium. Its presence seeped under our skin. It made us yearn for a midday nap. It made us want to run out to the clones, bounce up and down in front of them, just so something would happen.

Even though we did not take that exact route, we understood that, although tedium infected the majority of the day, there would most likely be a moment that would change everything. A moment that would give us the greater understanding we desired.

Gil and I were quite productive on our shifts. Our notepads were content, displaying our minute-by-minute observations with pride.

We all soon discovered that the clones would act as though they were living a regular human life. My Mother's clone would maintain and look after the property, gardening and even hanging the washing out on the line. We made a note suggesting that the domesticated clones might not pose a threat to us.

While Mother clone looked after the property and the house in the daytime, the clones resembling Brooke and I travelled to university for the day and returned before four in the afternoon. They interacted in similar ways to what we would, but the facade was evident in the sense that they didn't possess the intimacy that a family would, often appearing superficial and forced.

*Day Four*

When the day broke, and the sun did not appear, it was time for us to initiate something. During Desh and Mia's shift, the clouds erupted with tears of longing for the sun. They came down hard upon the clothes on the washing line, swaying with the subtle disturbance.

I spared a thought for our poor friends huddled towards the back of the motorbike shed, crouching in a river of mud. Knee-deep and huddled together, they spotted the dark grey army truck we had all come to know and love – or rather, know and fear, bounding towards the house.

Two clones emerged from the vehicle. It was late afternoon when they arrived, lingering until the moon shone in the blackened sky, as drops of rain caressed the sodden, muddy track.

While Gil and I were forced to double back behind the recording studio in order to conceal our tracks, I turned a thought to the equipment inside and how I missed recording various ideas late in the evening.

A small yet triumphant light bulb flickered within my mind. Maybe I didn't have to suffer the whole time here without recording something!

We waited until midnight when we were positive that the clones were asleep. I brought my keys down from Serenity and entered my recording studio after a long, painful absence.

I had tucked my portable recording unit inside one of the cupboards for quite some time. The advances in recording technology rendered units like this obsolete. Luckily, this brilliant hunk of musical equipment had a built-in microphone for moments that warranted recording conversations, spying on enemies - that sort of thing!

Acquiring this piece of equipment was the easy part of the plan; setting it up, however, involved risking our safety for the first time since observations had commenced. As far as I was concerned, we had already come as far as we could by watching them. We needed to make something happen.

Questions begged for answers.

Why did the important clones attend meetings at the house until early hours of the morning?

Out of all the places in Sydney, why were they meeting at my house?

Before I left to undertake my little mission, I ran the idea by Desh and the rest of the group. They, too, believed that it was time for change.

Pj and Gil were my little helpers – or back up, if you will. Pj bolstered the precious handgun that contained three bullets while Gil and I carried the recording unit towards the house. We crouched beside the back door where I had first seen my cloned family. I finally felt invigorated again. Nervous still, of course, but I was doing something that would help our cause.

The keys jingled as I raised them to the lock at the back door. I inserted the key as delicately as I could, not having the faintest idea about the sound that it would make in the dead of night. Twisting ever so slowly, a thunderous crack of the lock littered the air.

I severed my breath without hesitation. The clones would be aware that we could be somewhere near this place, somewhere within the neighbourhood, right?

Wouldn't they be on high alert? I wasted precious moments just waiting, afraid of being caught. My thoughts turned a blind corner.

*You know what? Fuck it. I'm going in.*

*Pj is behind me with a loaded gun!*

I shoved the door open. To my surprise, it didn't squeak as it swung forward. I reached out, catching the door just before it slammed into the wall on the other side. Pj and Gil hissed a "wait, be careful" at me with exaggerated hand signals, but I had no intention of waiting any longer.

Creeping inside the kitchen, the persistent buzz of the refrigerator filled the soundscape. The trash beckoned for me to open it and peer inside. It was practically empty. I picked up the slimy food scraps, but I was not squeamish. I just wanted to complete the mission.

I dumped the scraps on the floor before turning on and placing the recording unit in the trash. I threw the food scraps back in, atop the recording unit to disguise the bulky metal contraption.

I carefully placed the lid back on the trash can upon hearing a noise in the hallway. I caught my breath and froze. I was a boundless, beautiful deer in headlights.

Gil and Pj were still crouching outside, their mouths forming frantic phrases and gesturing wildly for me to come back to them. I leapt up from my crouching position and sprinted towards them after another creak came from the hallway. As I returned to the path, flustered and out of breath, Gil attempted to close the door, but the hinges relinquished their beautiful silence and exhaled a squeaky breath into the air.

"Fuck." I swore under my breath, yanking the keys out of the door, clicking as it connected with the wooden frame of the house.

The hallway light flicked on, and we were sprung, surely.

"Follow me," I whispered to my stunned friends.

I ran low to the ground, towards the front of the house and dove into the bushes. The collective weight of Pj and Gil crashed on top of me and we waited in an odd clump of bodies, breathless for what could have been half an hour before we dared to move.

Whoever it was that had turned on the light must have been a little paranoid – within reason, I might add – and had just wanted to check the area.

I needed to be sure that we were clear to head back towards Serenity. We couldn't crouch in the bushes until the morning light stumbled upon our backs, exposing us in all our semi-hidden glory.

Creeping out of the bushes again, I was careful not to make a sound. I looked towards the backdoor for a sign of life, but there was none. Whoever it was that had been there before, presumed it to be safe and went back to bed.

Breathing a sigh of relief, I signalled that we needed to get back to the rest of our family, who had awaited our arrival. We didn't speak a word the whole way back to Serenity, too agitated for small talk.

The thought of sleeping next to Zoey calmed me. As a result, I bypassed the millions of questions directed at me, leaving Pj and Gil to entertain the masses.

I took Zoey by the hand and led her to accompany me in the garden of peaceful slumber, where there were no clones, where moments were seldom frantic or heart-wrenching. They were tranquil and easy.

*Day Five*

After earning a day off for my heroic efforts from the night before, agitation got the best of me, urging me to discover anything on my recording device. I had hoped that my great risk had not become a grand failure.

Kasey and Zack rushed into the living area at around ten in the morning. Kasey looked as though she was about to explode.

"News already, Kasey?" I inquired.

"Oh. My. God," she blurted out, elongating each syllable as she spoke.

"Um, one of those trucks, like, just took your clone away."

She bounced up and down, her gaze ping-ponging between Desh and me.

This time, I took her lesson in speaking the English language and accentuated each syllable. "OH KAY, did you perhaps want to elaborate?"

Zoey stirred behind me. The way that Kasey added "like" into most sentences aggravated her.

Kasey sighed and stamped her foot on the floor, sending a reverberating crack around the walls of the cave.

"Um, fine I will." She paused, flicking her tongue and gathering her thoughts.

"Well, about fifteen minutes ago, two clones — one of them was that same man from the other night — came down to get your clone. Your clone seemed all ready to go. Like, dressed in that disgusting green uniform and everything. I made sure to tape it with the video camera, so maybe later, when we have the audio stuff, we could try to match up what was being said."

Desh raised his head from a book he was writing in.

"Okay, thanks heaps, Kasey. Great work," Desh uttered then resumed his important study.

Kasey looked at me, her bright puppy dog eyes glistening with rejection. I shook my head at Desh and gave her a wink and a thumbs up. She smiled with the rays of the sun, shrugging her shoulders in a way that some would call "cute" and departed to her corner of Serenity, leaving Zack trailing behind.

I went back to my sleeping bag to rest a little more, for night would spawn stars that reflected answers guided by my own hand. Maybe a prayer would help us get to know our enemy?

No, I'd leave that to Gil.

Night fell upon us like a sinister cloud, forming the darkness and spreading across our beating hearts. I was nervous and excited about the possibility of discovering more about our enemy. Unfortunately, my job for the night was not to rescue the portable recording unit. My assignment was 'free time'.

I waited for Zack, Desh and Kasey to bring the unit to us. That night, they did not have to enter the house at all; they only had to retrieve it from the bottom of the driveway because of bin collection in the morning.

The three of them returned, eager to share their new discovery. The discarded orange peels and chicken fat pieces had only tainted the shiny exterior of the recording unit.

I ripped the bag open and carefully dusted off the disgusting excrements that the clones had used for garbage. The recording unit was still flashing red, which signified that it was currently recording. The hard drive had not yet reached its capacity: news that warmed my heart.

I smiled and thumped the stop button.

My friends had gathered in a circle around me, wide-eyed and eager to discover something remarkable.

As I plugged the recording unit into Serenity's personal entertainment unit: a standard set of old, USB-powered computer speakers. Breathless, I pushed the rewind button.

The great feature about the recording unit was that we could identify the soundwaves, so I fast-forwarded almost six hours of creaks and footsteps until I reached the first registered sound.

I pressed play and waited. As we listened to water swishing in the sink, familiar voices drifted across the kitchen in my house. It sounded like my mother and me.

"Morning, Cooper One. Are you ready for this morning?"

"Morning, Mother. I believe I am as ready as I can be."

"Did they request that you wear the uniform?"

"Yes, I have to wear the one that Sergeant Tonks One provided me with."

"Okay, I'm fixing you up some breakfast. You should get ready now."

"Sure. Thank you."

The sound of water splashing. The dishes scraping together resumed. Footsteps trailed off down the hallway.

My friends were sitting, open-mouthed. We were actually listening to a real clone conversation. The monotony of their voices surprised me. No warmth snaked through the icy tundra. No passion fuelled excitement. It was as if they conversed because they had to.

The voices became clearer.

"Mother, it looks like they are out in the front now. It is time for me to depart."

"How long did they say you will be required for?"

"We will be back to brief you on stage two developments at 1800 hours tomorrow. There are many options we need to explore to put an end to human lives. The measures we are taking will affect us in the short-term, but we must push forward with the overall plan."

"Understood Cooper One. I will see you at 1800 hours tomorrow night. In the meantime, make sure you fulfil your duties."

"Goodbye."

The door slammed shut. The sound returned to the irregular swishing of the water.

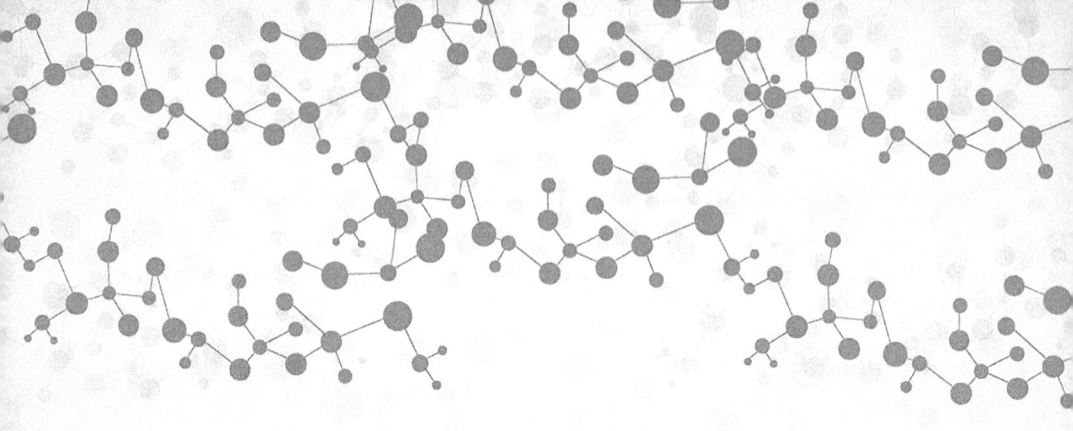

# CHAPTER 18

That one small phrase resounded in my head long after the recording unit had been switched off. Stage two developments. The schedule presented us with a small window of opportunity at 1800 hours that night to find out about them.

This specific revelation had given us great hope that the past five or six days were not wasted on vicarious notions of attack. Soon, we would be equipped with the knowledge to make a significant move against the enemy. We were no longer required to hide in the shadows. If we were craving the blood of the clones, this would be the defining moment where we would flip the switch on our Rambo mode and become instant killing machines. But would it be that easy?

Sure enough, Gil and I were scheduled for observations and roaming duty at 1800 hours. I couldn't grasp the major details of what could occur and what we were required to do. All we knew was that clone Cooper One was returning home, accompanied by an all-important Sergeant Tonks One, who possessed information on recent developments within the clone structures.

All in all, it seemed as though this "mission" of sorts was a big deal within the context of our own plans. Gil and I needed to make sure that preparations were suitable and effective to increase our chances of success. The time on Gil's watch read 4.30pm or 1630 hours, and Zoey was nervously fussing over me at the entry to Serenity. The apprehension crept through the thick air at dusk, visiting each and every nearby group member.

Zoey moved gracefully to whisper in my ear "Be smart; don't do anything I wouldn't do."

Her lips flicked the bottom of my ear; a sharp tingle cascaded down my sides. I responded without words, settling only for winking at her as I turned after Gil, who had already made his way forward.

Gil and I traipsed towards the back of the recording studio in pockets of silence. The thought of what we needed to do wracked my nerves, despite the mask of confidence strung tight around my face. In less than two hours, an important member of the clone army would be several feet away from us. For some reason, we had been thrust into the limelight without any instructions whatsoever.

I guess it was just the same as before, wasn't it?

Sit and watch. Listen and wait.

But it couldn't be the same. It was intensified by the personnel, by the severity of what we were about to uncover.

As darkness crept across the property like a jaguar on the prowl, the truck rolled down the dirt path recklessly, stopping several feet away from the front door of the house. Gil and I exchanged solemn looks of solidarity. I raised the binoculars to my eyes and peered into the truck. What I saw was utterly confusing and surprising.

The man behind the wheel was clone Cooper One. Sitting calmly in the first passenger seat was who appeared to be Sergeant Tonks One, who we all had seen once before at the house. His pale green hat fixed firmly atop his square head. In the three-seated army truck, I was not prepared for the man seated in the furthest passenger seat. His face was familiar to me, and his features encouraged me to remember the day this whole thing began.

*"World-renowned scientist Gordon Grey has successfully cloned the chimpanzee," said a blonde, generic-looking newsreader.*

*I stared in astonishment. He did what? My finger found the volume button. Tap, tap, tap. The TV screen showed images of a man in a white lab coat, grey hair parted on the left, intriguing and affable brown eyes sunken into the wisdom of his face. He spoke cautiously behind a barrage of microphones.*

*"We have made a significant breakthrough for the good of humanity." He paused, allowing the cameras to capture the moment for social media.*

*"The steps that we have taken in cloning the closest human relative will ultimately lead to replicating the true human form. This will propel us forward into the future and will abolish the threat of human disease, rendering human suffering obsolete. We will live in a world that is clean, effective and peaceful."*

Gordon Grey himself sat next to Tonks, holding a folder full of documents. He was pointing to several sheets, attracting Tonks One and Cooper One's attention. I pulled the binoculars away from my eyes in astonishment.

Gil nudged me.

"What's going on man?" he whispered.

I didn't answer.

"Is there a problem?" he pressed again.

My reply was not with words; I passed him the binoculars.

"Darn, I recognise that other one . . . who is he?"

"Gil, that is Gordon Grey, the creator of the chimp clone!"

It dawned on Gil as it had dawned on me, his eyebrows rising higher than a skyscraper in the midst of a dense city block, his breath becoming scarce.

"Oh man," he exhaled, "this is so much heavier right now."

As I watched from afar without the aid of magnified lenses, each clone emerged from the truck, slamming doors then directing their movement towards the house.

Gil turned to me as they knocked upon the front door of the house. "They just left those documents inside the car and didn't lock the doors; we have to go get them!"

"What do you mean?" I hissed.

"I mean, we have to go to the car and take a look."

"Gil, I don't think . . ."

He was off as soon as the front door had closed.

I rolled my eyes in an exaggerated expression that only I was able to appreciate and followed him. He pointed towards the driver's side as he crept through the lingering shadows of the shed and adorning bushes. I figured that was his way of telling me to follow him, so I obliged.

Opening the door with caution, my ears pricked at the sound of the faintest creak in the deathly silent surroundings. Gil opened the passenger door and navigated through the two folders tossed haphazardly upon the dashboard. He passed me the digital camera from within his pocket.

"Here, man. Take videos of these so that they won't know we weren't here. Pretty sure they do this in the movies."

I snatched it out of his hands, fumbled the on button to video mode and pressed record. I scanned the "confidential" folder. I looked up at the front door of the house, my pulse thumping against my neck, scared out of my wits that I could be facing the end of my life in the ensuing minutes.

The first few pages were laden with text, and we didn't have the luxury to sit there and read every word, so we had to skip ahead.

The third page caught our immediate attention.

It was a poster or a press release of sorts, containing the faces of those that had become "an immediate threat to the country and the well-being of regular citizens alike." A group of eleven terrorists dubbed 'The Evil Eleven,' who, if found dead or alive, "would earn a significant reward."

The video camera's recording light flashed red every few seconds as I scanned the familiar faces on the page: my face, Gil's face, Pj's face, Zoey's face.

We were all there.

As the camera panned across the page, it displayed three more faces at the bottom of the poster that were not within our current circle of friends. I knew for a fact that they had not even been on the plane.

Nikki, Dani and Whitey.

Nikki's parents did not permit her to take part in uni games. As a result, Dani had remained at home in protest. Ben "Whitey" White had come down with an illness one week prior, isolating at home due to doctor's orders.

I whispered to Gil, "Dude, look who is on this page."

"I know, I know, this is crazy." Gil replied anxiously. "What do you think it means?"

"I don't know, but you better keep turning pages before anyone realises we're in here."

Gil flipped to the next page. As I scanned each paragraph, slow enough to read text with the camera, a pattern unfolded. The text pages were the details of their plan, and it appeared that some kind of invasion was on the horizon. The fifth page was a map of what had to be their base.

As each page flipped over, I became more and more anxious to get the hell out of the truck and back to Serenity. I peered down at the last page that Gil had revealed and scanned with the camera, when the sound of voices disturbed the pleasant night air. My head jolted upright, eyes staring straight at two green figures marching towards the truck.

"Fuck!"

Gil and I both ducked beneath the wheel and dashboard.

"Holy shit. We're fucking dead men." I panicked.

Reaching into my pocket, I rummaged around, fighting with the cotton to pull out the gun. The cotton pocket won because, before I had a chance to release the steel, several gunshots from the distant bush pierced the air, interrupting the soft murmur of the clone's voices heading towards the truck.

I peered up over the dashboard to steal a glance at what was happening. The backs of the two clones rushed towards the sound: Serenity.

Pulling Gil by the shoulder without restraint, I yelled, "Get out of the car now. Follow me!"

I grabbed the door handle and yanked it open, spilling out into the moonlit driveway. Gil rolled out with his thin, spindly arms at odd angles like a spider tiptoeing the surface of a lake. He swept his fringe behind his ear, freeing the blue in his eyes that shone with the aquamarine of a topaz gemstone. I ran in a cold sweat towards the back of the recording studio, and he followed, diving onto solid ground and out of plain sight. Gil and I lay surrounded by dirt and weeds, panting in fear.

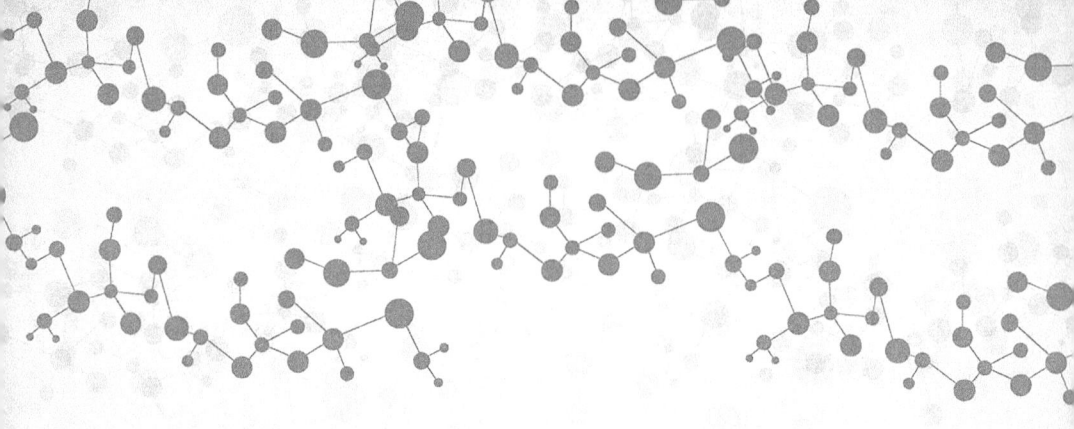

# CHAPTER 19

Gil and I faded into the shadows to make it to Serenity without arousing suspicion. It would only be a matter of time before they would bring in reinforcements and find clues as to where we were.

By then, the light had almost vanished from around the property, which gave us a slight advantage. They searched with torches in the far distance, so we were safe to run to Serenity when the opportunity arose. Our friends were there to greet us, waiting anxiously for our arrival. Steel and iron painted their faces as they became the rigid welcome mat to Serenity.

I glanced at Mia, and she answered my question before the words had left my mouth.

"We let off those shots. Otherwise, well . . . you wouldn't have made it back, Cooper." She breathed.

I nodded. It was handy to have someone in our group who could see the future!

"We each packed as much as we could, so we could start to move out of here. I can't see where we need to go, but hopefully, one of us will know somewhere we can stay for a couple of nights."

She handed me my backpack. "Here you go, now follow us down the . . ."

"Wait, Mia."

Apprehensive, she turned and faced me.

"How many guns do we have left?"

"We have two, Cooper. You know that."

"I had just had a thought."

It was a crazy thought.

"In the motorbike shed, there were two guns: one shotgun and a hunting rifle that Dad used on odd occasions."

Mia turned to face me, lowering her eyebrows.

"Cooper, seriously, you'd be achieving a miracle to get in there, let alone come out alive. Haven't you just literally dodged a bullet or two?"

As I looked out across my property up ahead, several beams of light flickered in the distance, tainting the usual tranquillity it possessed.

I pushed Mia aside.

"No, we need to protect ourselves against other threats. I've seen what they are planning, and you will soon realise we need everything we can to pose some sort of a threat to them."

Wrestling the video camera out of my pocket, I thrust it towards her and arched my eyebrows.

"Take this and keep it safe. If I don't come back, I insist that you find a nice quiet place to read and process all the information."

A heavy sigh escaped her. "We'll meet you behind the dam in ten minutes then, okay?" she conceded.

Turning away from Mia and the others, I yelled, "I will see you there. Oh, and by the way, if I was in danger, you'd see it and you'd save me!"

I didn't get a chance to see her reaction, as I jogged towards the outskirts of the property, sticking to the kind-natured darkness.

As heavy footsteps approached behind me, I whirled around, expecting to see Zoey or Mia doing their best to stop me.

"Kasey, what are you doing here?"

She took hold of my hand without saying a word. I searched her expansive eyes, and the terror materialised like a timid ghost, shimmering then fading away. My vexatious skin had shed, so I sought to provide her with comfort, smiling.

"I'm here because I thought you might need some company. How can you carry two guns by yourself?"

Musing on this thought, I found my voice. "True, but do the others know you are here?"

"Desh insisted it was a good idea. We all know he couldn't come — like, every group needs a leader."

Hmmm how did I miss out on the leader position?

Aside from jealousy raring its head at an inopportune time, I felt a wave of admiration for sweet, simple Kasey who risked her own safety to help me. Or – rather, to help us. This was surely her defining moment.

She didn't have to be as intelligent as Desh or Zoey to make a difference; her heart was good enough. Sometimes that meant more.

We approached the bike shed hand in hand, keeping an eye on the three torches scanning the north side of the property, closing in on the path to Serenity. The old rusty door of the bike shed, speckled with patches of copper, loomed as a portal of hope.

Grief pinched me as I placed the key inside the lock. My mind trailed back to when my father opened the same door on Sunday mornings, rust not as prominent back then, the colour of the door, painted a bold colt blue. Pushing forward, cool air stung my eyes, and the odour of fuel pinched the back of my throat. I felt my father's presence sift through the shed, laying eyes upon his favourite motorbike dormant in the far corner, ripe with dust.

Boots scraped against the cracked concrete as I moved to the motorbike that had waited patiently for my return. I absentmindedly caressed its faded brown leather-bound seat, and it shivered with the touch of a rider's hand; the little amount of petrol left within the tank swished.

Kasey called me over to the other corner, where, behind a fridge filled of old beer, lay two perfect weapons that had the potential to protect us all. Bending down with an exaggerated sigh, I packed the scattered bullet boxes into my bag.

It took me a few attempts to pack everything to the point where the zippers came to meet, like long lost lovers starving for affection. Without taking my eyes off the floor, I held up the gun for Kasey to take.

After several long seconds of waiting for her response, I looked upwards on instinct, sensing something awry. Kasey stared at the door; her mouth had become a broom sweeping the filth from the floor.

I shot up like an eastern brown snake, ready to strike at the face of Cooper One. I didn't have neurotoxins coursing through needle-like fangs, but I had a determination to lay claim to the best Cooper: the Cooper that would remain. He seemed to be unarmed, though if I shot him, the noise would surely lead them all to us, and we might be gunned down before leaving the shed.

*I'm going to run at him,* I thought.

A starting gun cackled hideously in my head, and I sprang out from my platform, dropping the shotgun and relieving my right pocket of a knife as I ran. He, too, reached for the knife concealed at his side.

We came together. His blade penetrated the side of my stomach as I flailed and slashed in circular motions, exposing my body to his cunning manoeuvre.

As the impact knocked us to the ground, he pinned me down, digging his elbow into my throat. He had forgotten about disarming me, focusing on killing me. It was proof that, although clones were strong, it had left them lacking situational intelligence.

Kasey suddenly loomed up behind Cooper One; her claws sharpened by a friend in danger. She slashed out across his eyes in a flurry of desperation, howling like the last semblance of sanity had been strangled by her darkened soul. His dominance over me was broken, thanks to her. His elbow buckled, and he reached towards his eyes to protect himself.

Seizing an opportunity, I raised my right hand and swiped across his neck with a sharpened blade before he could bring his own knife down upon me. His eyes grew wide and his body slackened. Oxygen returned to my lungs as blood poured onto my heaving chest in regimented bursts. He convulsed for the last time, ending his existence face down on top of me.

Adrenalin pumped through my veins as I threw him to one side. I was a magnet, and blood was my metallic bride. She draped herself upon me, consummating a dying love.

My thoughts scattered.

I had been stabbed. My side. Painful. Nauseous.

Kasey sobbed as she helped me to my feet.

My vision was slow and laboured, as the blood crept like a gluttonous lion down the side of my stomach, out of a fresh, gaping wound. I stole a final disgusted glance at Cooper One: a perfect physical reflection of myself, aside from a deep gash that had made a treacherous journey across his throat.

Was this the image of my future death?

It was an image I thought I would never see, an image that I never wanted to imagine. But there I was, looking upon what was essentially my own dead body, face staring upwards as a bow tie of blood protruded from his wounded throat. The knife lay on the ground, glinting passively; his other hand grasped something small and grey.

*What the hell is that?* I thought.

I bent down, wheezing like a deflating balloon. The grey metallic cylinder was a tracking device of some sort. He had pressed a large red button to release a pulsing, delicate bulb, blinking unassumingly.

I mumbled to Kasey in between shallow breaths as I pointed to the device.

"Gotta go now. Just forget the guns."

She ran to my father's bike.

"Shall we use this?" Her beautiful, questionable gaze fell upon me. Blonde hair sprayed wildly across the regal and proud cheekbones that framed her face.

All I could think about was that I needed to find Zoey in the next couple of minutes. Not just because I missed her affection but because she needed to save my life. I attempted to think positively, coercing myself into believing that I would get to her.

Why hadn't she come with me to make sure I was alright?

Did I not mean that much to her?

Why was I thinking that way? Sure, I meant something to her; this was the stupidest thing I could have done.

Did I even let anyone else know I was leaving?

Did she see me?

Probably not.

Deep regret seeped within my current denuded palette.

I mounted the bike with clear difficulty, slipping on hands that wore a warm glove of blood.

Kasey helped steady me, her dainty arms not only bearing the weight of my useless body but willing me forward to keep me alive.

As I stole a glance towards the door, through the hazy windscreen of my eyes that were splattered with morning sleet, faint beams of light trailed towards the motorbike shed. Kasey jumped on the back, and I thrust my foot down to kick-start the motorbike.

The engine coughed and wheezed a mighty breath but trailed off into nothingness. I tried a second time, a vigorous and mighty kick, sweat and blood fusing beneath my torn beige shirt.

This time, the engine roared with life: a mighty king of the jungle. Upon its back, I was restless, knowing that it was time to return to our pride: to safety.

I needed Zoey more than ever, as my eyesight began to waver, directing my full attention towards exiting the front door. I let the clutch out clumsily and catapulted Kasey and I into the open night air, feeling the cool breeze lick my face.

To our immediate left were several moving lights heading towards us. They were merely an obstacle at that point, and I didn't let them affect my riding as I sped off down the pathway, bathing them in thick, putrid diesel fuel excrement.

It took several precious seconds to hear and feel bullets whiz past us, though riding without headlights kept us undetected. Although this aided our escape, it offered the difficult task of navigating through rugged bushland, losing several litres of blood in the pursuit of freedom.

When I spotted the dam, I turned right, heading down the path to Roxborough Park, which acted as a corridor between Chalk Farm and my own property: the designated meeting place.

It was a long stretch to travel, so I killed the engine and opted to roll in the direction of the meeting place, with no indication as to where we were headed. My eyelids weighed heavily, and I began to slip through the crevices into a land in which no one could follow.

Tentative movements up ahead caught my line of sight, but it wasn't enough to pump blood through my body up to my brain and respond with any decisiveness.

A wall of blackness rose and consumed me. The bike leant towards the ground, skidding several metres along the dirt path on its side, ceasing to move on the edge of a weed-infested embankment.

The bike had impaled Kasey and I to the ground. Pained squeals from Kasey were only just audible as she attempted to shift the bike off both of us, her skinny arms straining under the weight. Our friends emerged from the darkness, running down to help Kasey and me.

By then, lights rained down from the sky, scanning my property, Chalk Farm and beyond, for any sign of life. It was becoming too close for comfort. Hands grazed my face and my side. Zoey began to repair my wounds. Eternal slumber intoned lamenting lyrics, and it beckoned me to her. The miraculous healing powers pulled me in another direction. Had it not been for Zoey, I would have been a rancid, festering corpse several times over.

Zoey's angelic face was a light force that beckoned me out of my painful sleep, as her starless hair swayed gracefully in the crisp moonlight, spreading her warmth over me. Kasey cried, her spluttering attempts to form words, lost in an infinite abyss in a parallel world.

Zoey's delicate hands caressed my open wound, shaking my body to its core as jagged jaws of death threatened to gnaw at my existence. I spluttered, coughed and heaved. With all those actions came the ability to breathe thick bouts of air once more. My eyes were a beacon, alive and truly open in the charcoal night.

Zoey withdrew her hands from my wound and focused her eyes to mine. Relief was all I saw in her moments before her face contorted into a hideous mask of pain and exhaustion. Her body buckled, and she collapsed onto me. I held her as tight as I could, her chest rising and falling in rapid succession, accompanied by faint breaths. The wound upon her arm glistened under the kiss of the moon, expelling the deadly disease that had pushed me to the gates of heaven.

I tore off my blood-stained, shredded shirt and wrapped her arm in a makeshift bandage. Mia touched my shoulder.

I was startled out of my transition from patient to healer and back to reality.

"Cooper, we need to leave now. They will be coming."

"Mia, how did you not see this happening?" I asked her, flustered and angry.

She took a step backward, abashed.

"Um, I think I've told you before. I can't help what I see, and I did not see this happen to you," she huffed in a frenzy.

"C'mon, Cooper, you need to come now," Gil called.

Mia turned away from me in betrayal as I hung my head in shame and exhaustion. It was my fault. I knew it, but I wanted someone else to blame for my stupidity.

Gil led the group towards a destination that he had not divulged to me. Zack and I trailed behind, cradling Zoey in our arms, whispering to one another about what was going on.

Kasey kept close to me as I struggled with Zoey's weight. She looked well and truly exhausted but was tethered to me through our mutual experience.

I stole a glance at her, and she looked deep into my eyes. I understood her. We required no words to appreciate the significant development of our friendship. Her beautiful exterior was a masquerade for intricate layers of strength and conviction.

I smiled and turned to face the path ahead.

Hadn't I been minutes – no, seconds from death not so long ago?

Hadn't sweet Zoey become my very own heroine, pushing that putrid monster of death up against a wall?

Zoey: she had saved my life, yes.

But, then again, it felt as though she saved my life everyday: the simple act of living alongside me brought me out of the shadows. It seemed as though the certain emptiness that had been present since the death of my father was slowly being filled once more in a different way.

We had always been friends, close enough to enjoy a movie on a weeknight, close enough to join our group for a drink in the city on the weekend. But it was always me who reached for something more. Had I been that stupid not to see that she had always been wanting to reach back?

Or had fate intervened and allowed our hands to come together and entwine forever?

I guess that fate had a hand in what had been occurring; the choices that we made were critical to our final destination. It could've taken just one choice to give fate a reason to abandon us. I hoped that it never came to our choices being the end for us.

The fallen angel in my arms murmured.

I held her tight and tried to keep up with Gil at the front.

After allowing us all a break, I asked him where we were headed.

"Think about it, Cooper: who's place is the closest to your own house?"

It dawned on me.

I replied as goose bumps ran across my body in excitement, "We're going to find Dani!"

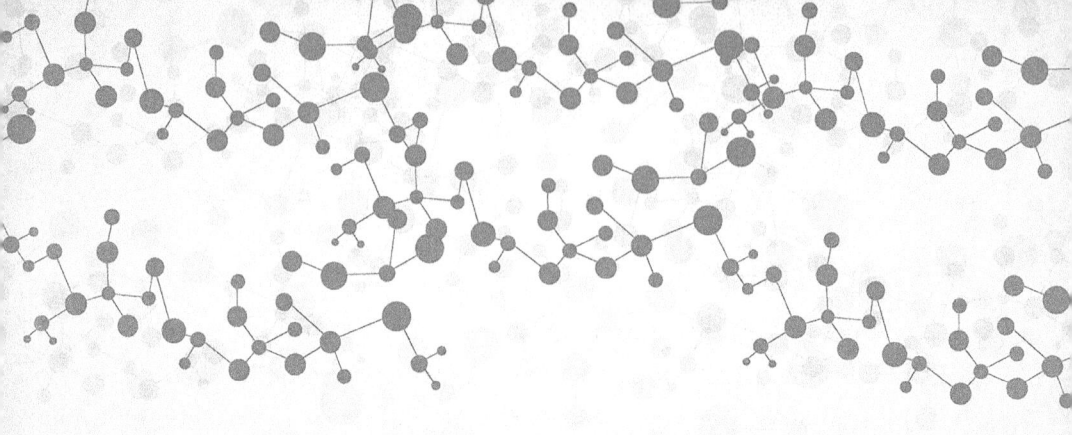

# CHAPTER 20

W e resembled a caterpillar: legs moving forward in tandem through the dead night, following Gil through twists and turns that would lead us to Dani's house. I was nowhere near the front of our small convoy, shackled by Zoey's weight.

Zack, who had indulged in a protein and weight gain binge before the crash, was forced to take over the burden.

"I'm thankful for you becoming the Hulk," I puffed.

He laughed. "You know, even though we've been hanging out in the bush, I don't think my camouflage is that green."

At this stage, no one knew that Dani, Nikki and Whitey were possibly on the run. As Gil led the group, he explained how we had both discovered their photos plastered next to ours, implicated in criminal activities.

"What do you mean by 'criminal activities?'" asked Pj.

"Well, basically, they have labelled us as terrorists in order to somehow make people or clones aware of our existence. We have been dubbed 'The Evil Eleven'," replied Gil.

"What is that bullshit?" Zack shouted, flicking his furious switch on.

"How the fuck are we terrorists? They are the ones that have terrorised us. Man, when I see 'em, they're fucked."

"Could you fucking swear anymore, motherfucker?" Pj teased.

Zack shouldered Pj, sending him off the path into a tree, still giggling despite sporting a leafy beard.

Zack's behaviour confirmed the Hulk-like similarities.

Gil ignored the antics. "We still have to sit down together and go over the documents we found. The way it is now, they don't know that we have uncovered anything, so they probably think it's safe to go ahead with the plan. First thing to do is to double check on Dani, just to see if they are okay or if they have moved on to somewhere new."

Gil slowed to a crawl and halted us in a circular formation. In the distance, the lights of the helicopters pulsed chaotically as if spurred on by an international DJ's final song at a summer rave.

"We are towards the back of Dani's property now, and I reckon the best way to go about this is to hit the abattoir first," whispered Gil.

Pj chuckled. "The abattoir you say? Mmmm delicious."

"Oh, I really don't like being near that place," Kasey complained.

Gil remained composed.

"Well, I would have thought it made a decent place to stake out her house and hatch a plan for what we could do next."

"Honestly, that does sound like the best plan – I mean, we have encountered a lot worse than an abattoir in the past few weeks."

It was hard to disagree with Desh.

At that moment, it was clear how silly it was to be afraid of a simple abattoir. We had been in dire, deadly and detrimental situations twenty times worse than sleeping in an abattoir for the night. It seemed as though, little by little, our fears were changing. Our adult lives were being shaped as we took small steps away from the innocence and liberty of university life into the turmoil of kill or be killed situations.

I searched the feeble darkness once more, as Zack rested Zoey against a tree, panting and exasperated from the walk.

"Gil, are you even sure we are here?" I pointed into the distance.

"I couldn't even see my own dick if I were naked, let alone the abattoir!" Pj joked.

"So, the same as if you were in full sunlight then, hey?" I came back at him with a twinkle in my eyes.

Most of the group laughed aloud, including Pj, as he stuck his middle finger up at me, losing his wide eyes to a goofy smile.

Gil paused, the light-hearted joke washing over him. He was thinking of a way to make me believe what he was seeing. But I already knew what he was going to say as he began to say it.

"I guess it's a little like what you, Zoey and Mia can do. I have noticed I can not only feel where we are, but I can see, like, some sort of map within my mind. Ahh I don't know . . ."

Pj piped up, "Dude, I wouldn't be feeling embarrassed about it; you're our own personal navigation system!"

Gil brushed all revelations aside for the time being and concentrated on moving us in threes towards the abattoir. "Now, Coops, come with me first, and we'll suss out the area, just to make sure no one is there first."

Kasey interrupted. "Do you think Dani and Nikki will be there?" "Kase, I don't know; that's why we'll check it out and see. We'll be back in a couple of minutes, just to give you the okay to follow."

I picked up Zoey as gently as I could to start moving. Every so often, she groaned at the inclination of the path ahead. Impeded by Zoey's weight, we still reached the abattoir in no time. Made of cedar wood, flakes of white paint hung loosely from its tired, weathered face. One window was speckled with dust and neglect; a solitary crack in the corner extended its fingers towards the centre. The corrugated iron roof was stained red with rust as it bled from the wound of time. As the ribbons of sunlight floated off into the gathering darkness, Gil's steady hand extended towards the door.

I heard a distant shifting of bodies, unnatural movement from behind the closed door. Gil drew his hand away and spun around to face me. He mouthed something indecipherable in the dusk and pointed towards the door. Something or someone must have been inside. It would only be a matter of good fortune if it turned out to be Dani's cat scampering for rotten intestines from a recently dismembered cow corpse.

I nodded at Gil, raising my eyebrows. This was my attempt at letting him know he would have to go in first, as Zoey burdened me.

He understood well enough to bite the bullet and open the door, ready to introduce the large tree branch in his hand to a life of bloodied vengeance and beat-downs. Gil lowered the stick as the door creaked open. The metallic smell of blood hung low underneath the scent of old timber and stale air.

I stole a quick peek over his shoulder.

The moonlight spilled onto the floor from the cracked cup of the sky, shedding pale light on two bodies cowering in the corner.

"Dani? Nikki?" Gil inquired.

Twigs and leaves fit like a crown upon both of their heads. Scratches shaded the creases on their knees while fear was an elegy written in their eyes.

Together, Gil and I exhaled.

He rushed into the room to tend to them. Hindered by Zoey, I lumbered inside after him, placing her across the table where countless animals had been hacked to pieces.

If she were awake, she wouldn't enjoy that thought. Opening her mouth, plump lips smacked together three times, before she resumed her fatigued but rejuvenating slumber.

I crouched to embrace the stunned and relieved young ladies. Nikki cried into my chest as Dani rubbed her back. She bent her thin, cracked lips into a thankful smile as a tear born of happiness slid down her cheek.

Gil and I helped them up from the ground, which gave us a chance to survey the damage upon them.

Nikki, who often applied several layers of makeup to rival Kasey, had, instead, countless blotches of dirt, blood and grease splattered upon her precious skin. Her light brown hair tossed into a loose ponytail, splaying out in all directions, knotted and furious. Her once lovely summer dress, skewed to the side with the loss of an all-important strap.

Dani seemed to take the harsh conditions like a grain of salt. Her face was muddy and dirty; however, her orange-red hair maintained its natural condition without the aid of product or accessories.

They had taken notice of dear Zoey, passed out upon the table. They'd seen her in states like this before; however, alcohol had been the main culprit. Their eyes moved from her to us and attempted to satisfy their curiosity.

"What happened to her?" Dani quizzed.

Remembering the scene from a couple of nights before involving healing powers, a knife and an angry Zack, I thought that inundating them both with that information may prove a little overwhelming. To be honest, our group hadn't fully understood what had happened to us either. *Would we ever?* I thought.

"Long story, but we'll get to it soon enough," I said.

"Where are the others?" asked Dani. "I mean, we heard lots of different things on the radio at night." She pointed to a dusty radio in the far corner. "But you can never believe everything you hear."

"Very true!" I exclaimed

"In answer to your questions, the others are waiting towards the back end of the property. We just needed to check here first and make sure it was all safe," said Gil.

"Oh, of course, it's more about thinking than doing these days. We've had a fair bit to learn from our experiences," replied Dani.

Just as Gil directed me to alert the others, Mia burst through the door with a wide grin.

I asked, "How did you know . . ."

The rest of the group converged as quietly as they could on the new, old company. Sharing hugs, smiles and whispered words of joy.

We sat down together on the stark, hardy floor of the abattoir to share the events of the prior weeks. Despite the smell of death lingering in the air, our senses came alive with the discovery of our friends.

Nikki and Dani sat patiently through our highs and lows, our debates about what happened and the embellishing of the heroic feats we'd accomplished. Funnily enough, we didn't discuss our gifts with them. After the other night, we didn't feel comfortable bringing it up. There was still so much in the unknown.

Finally, we reached the present time, where we gave up the stage so Nikki and Dani could enlighten us on their own travels.

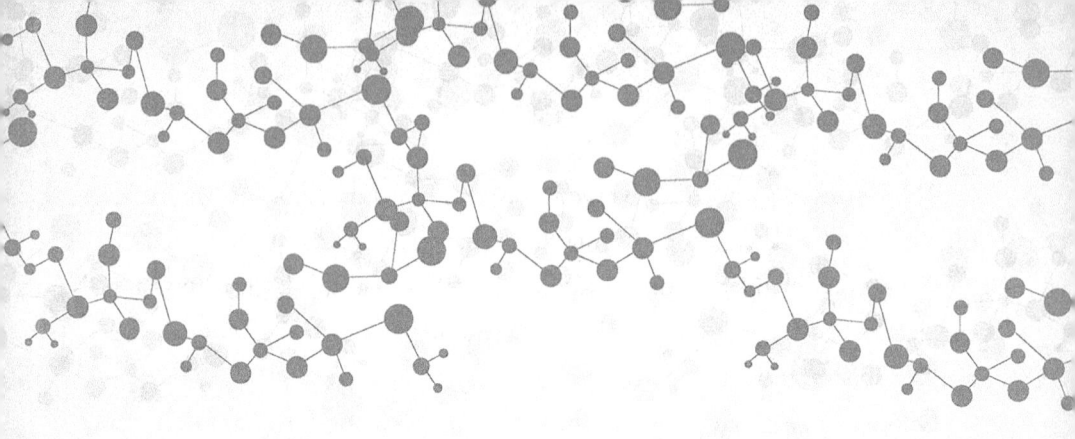

# CHAPTER 21

*ikki and Dani's Story*
Nikki woke late in the morning of uni games. She hadn't wanted to sleep in. Rather, she had dreamt of skipping through the airport with two or three bags in tow. But alas, the dream was not to be. Her parents had decided to punish her. *For what? For enjoying the company of her boyfriend, Matt, the night before? Even though they hated him, mainly for the colour of his skin, why couldn't they just understand that it was love?* she thought, hopelessly. It was the kind of love that would see them exchange vows, have babies and be together forever, she insisted to her subconscious. At least, that was Nikki's plan.

Nikki had first been introduced to Matt at a mutual friend's birthday party and hit it off with him almost instantly. But her parents were quite prominent in the local Aboriginal community and were far from pleased that she was so taken with a "white fella." The way they said that made her skin crawl. Matt tried very hard to immerse himself in the community, learning about their cultural practices, but the scars of generations tend to run deep.

Nikki hadn't always valued her heritage, which is why her parents were so hard on her, but it was a double-edged sword. The more they pushed, the more she traded in smoke ceremonies for social smoking or corroborees for night-clubs. Even though Nikki's parents' approval was not forthcoming, their relationship held strong for two years. Matt had done his very best to treat Nikki as the princess she always believed herself to be. He purchased several sparkling reminders of his love, adorned her with affection in public places, decorated her cakes in edible diamantes and he even knew what diamantes were. And with the important little things came the fact that he practically never left her side. Matt never really thought anything of this. He was content being her prince or – as several of his friends joked – her servant.

Their relationship didn't waver at all until Matt decided to leave school and join the army. At times, Cooper, Zack and even Dani didn't believe that their love would be strong enough to withstand long distance and impending war situations. However, much to their credit and the astonishment of outsiders, their relationship remained stronger than ever. Matt was stationed at a base not far from Cooper and Dani; however, Nikki was not permitted to visit during weekdays, so Matt would see her each weekend to make sure his princess was content.

Nikki suddenly remembered her phone call with Cooper the night before. *As one of my best male friends, you'd think he'd be more supportive of me, right?* she thought as she shed her satin pyjamas on the floor of her lavish en suite bathroom. She knew that, as the warm water tiptoed upon the smooth surface of her face, Cooper would be enjoying himself, halfway to their destination by now.

*Ah, you know what? I'll just go to Dani's today and have a girly weekend with her. She is a true friend,* she mused.

Nikki exited her thirty-minute shower, smelling of rose water and pink grapefruit, oblivious to any effect on the environment and set up in front of her second best friend: the mirror. She applied moisturiser to smooth out the creases and correct the slight imperfections upon her youthful face. Nikki cared about her appearance, making sure to spend time focusing on her makeup. Foundation, eye liner, eye curlers, eye shadow, lip gloss, lip liner, concealer, blush – all cluttered around the porcelain sink, stained with a soft brown sheen. Her skin glowed with the deep shade of a mature melaleuca tree. She took pride in this part of her heritage. When many of her ancestors were made to feel less, she felt empowered, richer and fuller as she pursed her lips at the mirror.

Nikki walked into the wardrobe, surrounding herself with shirts and dresses that ranged from current season fashion to those that took up space and gathered dust. She flicked through the items: coat hangers latching onto the previous one, desperate to gain affection after years of rejection. She settled on a flowing summer dress, dark blue and purple blotches entwining with one another in an obscure pattern. She gathered up a day bag, scrunching up a change of clothes into a ball and thrusting it towards the bottom, in case she decided to stay over at Dani's house.

Nikki locked the door with a dangling diamante key chain of the letter N. Her designer sunglasses sheltered her hopeful hazel eyes from the desperate sun, resting just below her full cheeks. As Nikki strutted down her bricked driveway towards Dani's house, she adjusted her top, pulling it up so that she wouldn't betray her perfectly demure image. Satisfied with the way she presented herself, Nikki resumed the journey to her best friend Dani, checking her phone a little too often for signs that her friends cared about her absence. They did not contact her, for they had greater things to worry about. As her friend's plane descended into the bush between Sydney and Cairns and Gus's eyelids closed for the last time, Nikki arrived at Dani's door. She rapped her delicate knuckles on the heavyset, wooden olive-green door and waited for her best friend. Dani answered the door in grey tracksuit pants that billowed at the ankles and a slightly unbuttoned flannel shirt, exposing her generous bust. Dani had always exuded a natural beauty that didn't require makeup. Nikki sometimes resented her for this but took guilty pleasure knowing that she had a loving partner while Dani was single.

Dani's bright orange-red hair was tied back in a messy ponytail as she pressed her body into Nikki's embrace.

"Hey, honey, how are you feeling this morning?" she asked, twisting her head to one side.

Nikki thought for a moment, stealing a glance at her phone displaying no new notifications.

"I'm a little annoyed, but I'm looking forward to hanging out with you today."

It was true. Nikki was genuinely excited to "hang out" with Dani in a desperate attempt to occupy her mind. She stepped past Dani into her house, running straight for the couch and sinking deep into its embrace.

"What movie are we going to watch first, Dani?"

Dani approached the kitchen bench before bringing popcorn and lollies to the coffee table in front of Nikki.

"Well, we've got a choice between these three."

Dani surfed through three saved romantic comedies on her streaming playlist, which always proved a hit on girl days and nights.

Nikki pointed to *The Sweetest Thing* and clapped her hands in excitement as Dani clicked play on the remote.

The movie ended, and Dani's younger brother came into the lounge room, complaining how his favourite show was meant to be airing quite soon.

"Just get out; go for a walk or something . . . or I'm going to get Mum," he whined.

"Oh, Chad, just settle down please. We'll go out the back for a bit. It's fine, just let us know when you are finished," Dani reasoned.

Chad poked his tongue out at both of the girls as they made their way out the backdoor.

"Is he always such a pest?" Nikki inquired.

"No, I think he is just annoying me to get to you." Dani laughed.

"Ewww!" Nikki felt ill at the thought of Chad ever feeling something for her.

They rounded the corner behind the abattoir and continued their conversation.

"Thank you for hanging back with me instead of going to uni games," Nikki said, eyes sparkling with appreciation.

Dani met Nikki's stare, comforting her with a warm smile, her copious freckles burning in the golden sunlight.

"Hey, I would do anything for you. You know that."

Nikki thought of talking about an incident she had with Matt just two days ago, but just as she was about to speak, a shrill scream pierced the air. Their heads spun around towards the sound. Uniformed men came from all angles and stormed the house, smashing windows and breaking down doors. Dani clamped her hand hard on top of Nikki's mouth, stopping her from screaming. She tugged her inside the abattoir and shut the door. Nikki's strap on her top was caught on a stray nail near the door and snapped off as she hit the cold concrete floor.

"Don't speak a word; don't even cry, Nikki," Dani pleaded.

Nikki was shaking but managed to nod her head enough that Dani was satisfied. Dani peered out from the murky window of the abattoir at the unfolding scene. Chad and her mother were surrounded by men in uniform, semi-automatics silhouetted in the dim light of the house. A few of the men and women looked related from where she was, but she was unsure. As she thought about what her family could possibly have done to deserve this, the clones opened fire on them. She reeled back from the window and found herself sprawled next to Nikki in complete shock.

"Oh, my god, oh, my god, oh, my god," Dani said, shaking with fear in rhythmic tune with Nikki.

"What happened, Dani? What happened?" Nikki wailed, shaking Dani.

But Dani could not respond. Nikki's questions twisted and turned in a multitude of hertz as her rational mind pushed through the panic and the adrenalin to give her clarity. Her family had been shot right in front of her. She stood up, shrugging off Nikki and moved to the window again slowly. Her breath grew stale on the glass.

A couple of clones carried the bodies out and dumped them on the lawn next to the swimming pool. They pointed into the distance, and it was then that Dani realised it wasn't just her family's life that would be over if she didn't do something to save herself. *This is the first place they'll check if they knew that I was home,* she thought. Dani had to gain control of her emotions to live. She was rational most of the time – calculating. She labelled herself one of the more intelligent of her friends, so there was time to grieve later. She had to move now.

"Get up, Nikki," Dani demanded.

"I can't. Oh, my god. I don't want to . . ." Nikki sobbed.

Dani bent down and placed her hands on Nikki's bony shoulders. "Look at me. If we don't leave here now, we're going to die. I can assure you of that," she said forcefully.

Nikki didn't say a word, though she rose up off her feet, and Dani took her to the window.

She pointed. "When we see all those bastards leave from sight, we run behind the abattoir to the bush down there," Dani commanded.

Nikki returned a weak nod. In minutes, the clones shouted and barked instructions. "You two go bring the truck around." Dani and Nikki readied themselves for the most important race of their lives. Clones rounded the side of the house, and off they went. The door burst open, blinding Nikki and Dani with a brilliant white light. They sped off towards the bush shielded by the abattoir. The clones came back from around the side of the house and they thought they saw the door of the shed out the back swinging in the breeze.

"Excuse me, Sergeant Tonks One?" the first clone asked.

"Yes, Laura Seven?" Sergeant Tonks One replied.

"What is that place down the back? Do we need to check out if anyone is in there?"

"It looks like a shed or an abattoir, and it would be safest to clear everything on this property. I'm waiting to receive the plane manifest to see if the young woman was on it. If everything went according to plan, she is on the plane, and it's going down as we speak. Nothing more to it," Sergeant Tonks One explained.

Before the clone could respond back to Sergeant Tonks One, another clone came through the house, shouting for the Sergeant.

"What is it? I'm busy," Sergeant Tonks One whined.

"Sir, there has been a problem with the plane."

As the wind rushed by, blurs of green and brown splattered onto the canvas of the moment. Fear pushed them to run further and faster than they had ever gone before. Logic returned to them, and they slowed as they searched over their shoulders at the vacant dirt path leading to dense bush. The abattoir appeared as a small speck on the horizon.

Dani and Nikki found a sheltered area filled with bushes, leaves and dead branches amidst the thick gumtree covering.

"Cover yourself with these leaves," Dani pleaded, flicking leaves in Nikki's direction.

They collapsed upon the earth; dust particles spinning and twisting around their red faces. Eucalyptus infused with the salty taste of sweat. They didn't say any words to one another, they needed to get air back into their lungs before they had anything else to contemplate. But as far as they were concerned, running for their lives was indeed the furthest thing from their minds not less than half an hour ago.

The next few days dragged on, and grief never took hold of Dani; her strong will to live and her determination to learn what was happening to her world had pushed her forward. Unfortunately for Dani, Nikki had been a nervous wreck, constantly asking to call Matt, needing reassurance. At times, Dani just wished that Nikki had stayed at home that fateful day. Throughout the many days shifting between the bush and the abattoir, Dani and Nikki learnt various things about the "people in uniforms." In an attempt to check the safety of the surrounding properties, the houses around Dani had been taken in much the same way. Sentries and people with guns patrolled the perimeter of the properties with no way to get inside the houses or get close to figuring out what was going on.

While Dani and Nikki were in the abattoir, they overheard a muffled conversation between two clones on their lunch break near the shed.

"We are leaving tomorrow, aren't we? Back to the base?" asked Laura Seven.

"Affirmative. Orders from the big man, apparently," replied Drew Four.

"So, when the families come here to their new homes, they just go about the same kind of business, right, as if they were the real family?" Laura Seven pressed.

"Yes, from what I have gathered. Look, stop asking questions, and let's just do our job. If anything, we need to worry about this plane situation," said Drew Four.

"What's the newest development with them, then?" asked Laura Seven.

"They're now on the loose. Stole one of our trucks, and even though we tracked it down and managed to crash into it, it is believed the occupants got away. They're said to be hiding out around this vicinity, actually," Drew Four said.

"Who would've thought that some teenage nobodies could potentially ruin everything?" Laura Seven contemplated.

"They are no match for our army," Drew Four said with a sense of finality and strength.

At this point, Dani had given up hope of any sort of rescue at all. It hadn't dawned on her that the conversation she had stumbled upon was actually directly related to her, as Cooper and his friends were doing their best to derail the clones' plans. That night, she closed her eyes and curled up in a ball in the corner of the abattoir. Nikki clung to her leg and convulsed with the onset of another nightmare. Helicopters buzzed in the distance as she tried to sleep. Hope was nowhere to be found until Gil and Cooper walked through the door. Dani and Nikki's luck would soon change . . . or so they thought.

# CHAPTER 22

fter Nikki and Dani revealed their story, we accepted the significance of reuniting. We were, however, without those familiar counterparts, who would find themselves at parties conversing with us all: Gus, Jasmine, Whitey, just to name a few. Tragedy was now a vex upon our energies, stifling the muted celebrations of adding to our wandering troupe. It was undeniable that there were still pressing issues at hand. The video camera weighed down Mia's pocket, and she removed it with a sigh that bore a tremendous weight.

Silence greeted the stale abattoir air as we gathered around the small LCD screen, awaiting the plot of the clones. Mia flicked the camera on. We hadn't used this old technology for a long time, but it was evident that the battery life was not as fickle as our current devices.

The 'wanted' poster flickered across the screen, showing each face for several seconds. The group watched with their mouths open in disbelief that the clones had labelled us the "The Evil Eleven" terrorists. The term "terrorism" in the 21$^{st}$ century evoked a manic sense of fear, which could turn the most stoic souls to fire. We knew from experience that the media and various social networks were likely buzzing and trending with this "news." The goal was to create a widespread mentality that capturing us would make the world a safer place. When we love so dearly and fiercely, fear can coerce brutal acts of violence. So, when love is at the centre of the violence, there is no predicting what could happen. The media knew this. The clones knew this, which is why they fed fear via the outlets and networks, spreading it into every crevice, limiting our freedom, allowing regular citizens and human beings to unknowingly fight in a cause on the same side as the clones.

The mention of terrorism meant war. Maybe we already knew that it needed to come to that in the end, but as the documents idly flashed by on the screen, they meant more than words. Hard evidence. Difficult realisations. The end of an era. The beginning of adulthood: our spiritual awakening.

The documents that featured in the next few frames took time to filter through, which is why Zoey and Desh took turns in reading aloud to us all. Document one contained step-by-step directions on the clones' movements, where they had been and where they intended to be in the near future.

The documents were laden with terminology that we did not understand. However, the message was clear in the documents:

January 27th – Initiate the cloning of residents from Region 1. After gathering various hair, skin follicles and other samples, posing as property inspectors, policemen, nurses, doctors or council workers, they would go back to the lab and create and grow adult clones in birthing pods.

March 24th – Initiate the takeover of residents in Region 1 (Outer Western Sydney, from Pitt Town to Penrith). The takeover would entail killing the human occupants of houses and replacing them with their clones. Days would follow, where the clones would adopt their everyday lives so as to not arouse suspicion in various regions that were scheduled for subsequent takeovers.

From March 24th – The plan seemed to be quite similar to what occurred in Region 1. However, the first region – which, of course, was our own – would be tested for the longest duration. Initially, the Region 1 operation would take them through to July, where they would gauge the success of the mission and make subtle changes to the routine if any problems persisted.

As the plan progressed through to the end of the year, the regions themselves would expand until all of Australia was covered. Humans who were replaced by clones that worked overseas would infiltrate other countries.

Reading through the proposed timeline set by the clones, the whole world would be overtaken in roughly five years.

Silence stood beside each of us, cupping her hand against our open mouths. So, our minds raced against rationality and incredulity. We all know who won.

How did a person without any training whatsoever stand a chance against an army?

How could a bunch of twenty-something-year-olds make even the slightest impact?

Then I remembered our gifts.

Would that even the playing field?

As far as I could tell, the gifts would be our only chance. But what about those of us who hadn't uncovered anything yet? They needed to start looking harder. Aside from that, we needed to be comfortable talking about them in front of one another. Only Mia, Zoey, Gil and I had discovered something, yet it was as though everyone was too afraid to figure out how to utilise our potential.

After the vocabulary drought came the flood of wishful thoughts and heroic streams. From "I wish we could go back to how it all was before" to "let's steal a tank and a couple of M-16's and blast our way to freedom once and for all!"

Evidently, we had reached no united direction on what to do. It was no use arguing and deliberating at such a late hour, especially when we departed the comfort of Serenity for a damp, decrepit abattoir.

I knew that both Zoey and I were feeling the effects of the escape. As her head lolled onto my shoulder, I too, succumbed to the temptress of sleep. My mind trailed off into memories of the past few weeks: how many times I had cheated death? Yet, here I remained. There was a glimmer of hope, even if it was an infant speck, glinting inside of a single grain of sand, adrift in the vast ocean.

I settled for a concrete pillow while Zoey rested her head on my chest, with only a few suitable layers of skin containing her from indulging upon my heart.

I thought that I had gotten used to sleeping in terrible conditions.

I was wrong.

My concrete pillow did not shape with the contours of my neck and shoulders.

My concrete pillow did not soften my nightmares, it barely allowed for sleep at all.

I woke up from my irregular sleep. Zoey rising and falling, caught in waves from the rapid swell of my breathing chest.

Zack and Dani carelessly whispered. I arched my head up, making eye contact with Zack.

In that split second, I could see what they had been talking over. It made me want to close my eyes once more and be back in my own bed – hell, even back in Serenity.

Placing Zoey's head carefully upon a discarded jacket, I crawled with creaking bones to Zack and Dani's side.

"What do you think you two are going to do?" I interrogated them.

"Well, Dani and I kind of have a plan to get out of here."

Desh was shadowed by shelves of tools and utensils behind Zack's shoulder.

"I think their plan might just be a way to get out of here and find somewhere relatively safe," Desh said, validating Dani and Zack.

"I know you are all a little reluctant to pick up and move again, but at the end of the day, we aren't safe here," Dani chimed. "The clones are up at the house; it's so dangerous. Besides, I honestly cannot stay here anymore. I'm going a little mad."

"All right, Dani, tell me what you think is going to work?"

Dani swallowed hard.

"Well, normally, clone Dani – damn that sounds weird," she mused. "Anyways, Clone Dani leaves the house at about eight to be at uni by eight thirty."

She paused.

But, as my gift became stronger, I could finish her thoughts, so I knew what was coming next.

"We," pointing to Zack and herself, "will crouch behind the car seat, and as she starts the engine, we'll . . . kill her."

I already had digested this; however, it still remained daft and dangerous, as vengeance burnt like a chaotic flame in her eyes.

"Look, before you even say anything, Zack and I are taking the risk here, with Desh giving us a bit of cover," Dani protested. "You don't even have to do anything but watch."

"Have you ever killed someone before? It's one thing to contemplate it but actually going through with it, well, it changes you," I warned.

Dani's expression softened, but her eyes held tight to a horrific scene she could never forget.

"Cooper, I am changed already." Her voice was as soft as turned earth in spring.

I nodded gravely. We had all seen too much, experienced too much to be the same as before.

"All right, fair enough, but you know what? Regardless of whether we're all in the thick of it or not, we, as a group, are still being put at risk."

Dani motioned to complain. I raised my hand to stop her.

"Having said that, I will help you, but we need to figure out what our next moves will be before the killing and car stealing!"

"Yeah, I get it," Desh began, dejected. "We all felt it before looking through those documents."

"That it seemed like all a bit much?" I said, finishing his sentence.

"We'll get to all the details about what happens after we've spoken to everyone."

I pointed at Zack. "You've got this guy in your brain trust for a major plan? This guy!" I stammered, teasing.

Zack shrugged his shoulders. "I do what I do."

"God help us all," I said with potent sarcasm.

Desh came forward, "Well, we've also talked about it with Zoey. Maybe she can explain to you how it's all going to go down.

"Zoey!" I whisper-shouted. "But she is always the first to fall asleep!" I challenged.

"She came to while you were asleep." Desh reasoned with me.

I turned my head and scowled at Zoey, lying on the floor in the corner, still wrapped in the blanket of a deep sleep.

She murmured something indecipherable and turned over onto her other side.

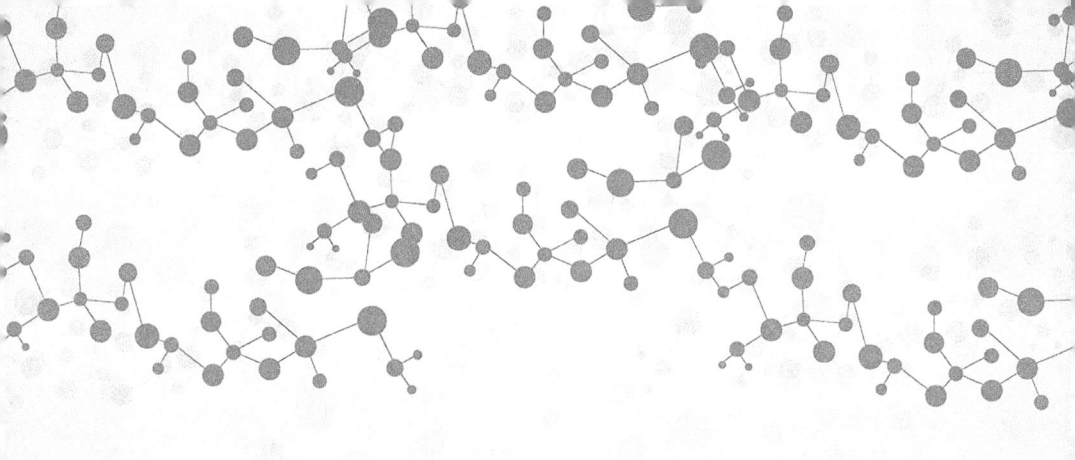

# CHAPTER 23

I crouched in the bushes with Desh, wondering why I had agreed to do any of this. The whole plan was nuts.

But, sooner or later, we had to make a stand against the clones, and this happened to be the first step in doing so. It would test the value of our newfound gifts, as well as our willingness to step outside of our comfort zone. All great stories of triumph came from humble beginnings.

So it began, with me in the thick of it all. All thanks to my smartypants love interest, Zoey. The little schemer had thought up several ways to foil the clones, not worrying or bothering me with any of the details.

As I lay my head down on the concrete pillow in the abattoir, she had woken up to find Dani ruminating in the corner. Midnight was primetime for developing a genius plan, and the two had quite the conversation.

I checked my pockets for the heavy glock. It waited patiently: three bullets growing restless inside its wavering womb. Drawing my hand away, my arms dangled at my side.

Crouching in the bushes were two unshaven men in unwashed clothes. We were accused of being terrorists, and based on stereotypes, if anyone walked past us, they wouldn't need to look twice. The only thing we were missing was a flashing neon sign that said "Terrorists Open for Business" and an arrow pointing to our exact location.

I tried my best to focus on the task rather than worrying about anyone discovering us. Tuning my eye upon the garage door, I willed it to hurry up and open.

My vision consisted of Dani and Zack now crouched in the backseat of the old four-door hatchback parked inside the garage, knives and tools from the abattoir glistening proudly in their hands.

I imagined Zoey, Mia, Gil, Nikki, Kasey and Pj were also watching from afar, waiting patiently for something to occur. The garage door barely contained the engine beginning its baritone ballad.

Uneasiness engulfed me, and I realised why. Footsteps sounded over to the right of us across the main road. We spun our heads around, standing upright, attempting our best 'we weren't doing anything wrong' impressions. Clearly, it was not an award-winning performance.

The man caught a glimpse of us and lowered his eyes to the footpath. His eyes.

Damn. I couldn't see them to gauge whether he was an enemy.

But it became all too suspicious. I turned to the garage upon the automatic door's release. The roller doors revealed Dani's car and two silhouettes visible from the back window.

My hand wandered to the pregnant pocket of my pants, placing a finger on the trigger for a sense of security. As the car pulled out of the driveway, I, too, pulled the gun out of the garage of my pocket to keep at my side. However, my sweaty, unreliable fingers lost their grip on the handle, and it crashed onto the pavement in a clutter of noise.

As I bent down to retrieve the weapon, an unexpected bullet tore through the air, implanting itself into the mailbox only centimetres above my head. Debris and dust flew into my face, but I gathered my composure quick enough to commando roll away onto the other side of the letterbox. I regained my balance and saw Desh crouching on his knees, aiming into the distance.

Pressed against the mailbox, Dani let the clutch out hard, manoeuvring the car into a semi-circle and opened the door, inviting me inside.

"Get in, Coops!"

I dove inside the car without another moment wasted.

My body thrashed across the backseat, landing on an object that felt disgusting. Realising what I was laying upon, two shots were fired outside the confines of the car. One bullet crashed through the windscreen, shattering shards of glass onto Zack and Dani. They both recoiled, shielding their faces.

I shot up, searching for Desh. He was now standing, gun pointed into the distant bush at what can only be described as a speck of a clone. He didn't need to worry about the preservation of bullets, for he only needed one. The speck disintegrated, fizzing away into the fiery depths. Dead.

Around the corner, the man we had seen previously came running towards us, eyes blazing, gun drawn. Desh turned with lightning speed and felled the clone before he could release his finger from the trigger.

The very atmosphere was distilled by a dead calm. The bodies up ahead did not quiver. The engine of Dani's car provided the only musical accompaniment to the chaos, humming a monotonous, repetitive drone.

Desh remained in the same position; gun drawn, pointing to an expired target in the distance, blinking profusely and breathing hard.

"Desh!"

We all bellowed from the car.

Our combined cacophony of voices startled him out of his trance as he motioned to swiftly leap into the car. He found himself sprawled next to the mutilated corpse of Dani's clone. The human Dani then sped off down the road, leaving Desh rubbing his eyes, as if something was obstructing his vision.

"Are you okay, man? How the fuck did you do that?" I yelled, adrenalin forming my speech.

"Yeh, yeh. I'm fine," he replied, shaken.

Desh had managed to fire two perfect shots to send the clones into oblivion.

How could that have happened?

He had no training at all. His effort was astoundingly heroic.

Rubbing his eyes and blinking viciously: was he trying to remove an eyelash, perhaps?

Dani floored the pedal, which jolted me around in the backseat, slamming into the beautiful mess of a corpse next to me. The speedometer told me that we were easily eclipsing one hundred kilometres per hour.

"Whoa, Dani, Dani, settle down on the accelerator! We're way clear by now!" I called out. The adrenalin fuelling Dani's escape to the point where she hadn't realised we were clear of danger. However, as she sped through residential areas, she would most certainly attract police on the lookout for terrorists.

She eased her foot off the accelerator.

"Oh, shit. I'm sorry . . . I'm just still a little on edge." She exhaled, voice quivering.

Zack chimed in, "Yeah, bro, my goddamn face was just pelted with glass, so excuse me if I want to hurry the fuck up and get to Desh's place."

"How much longer, anyway?" Dani inquired.

Desh and I responded in chorus.

"About two minutes."

For the purposes of our spur-of-the-moment plan, we were going to Desh's house to take his station wagon, accommodating our small terrorist cell. It would be The Evil Eleven's little engine that could.

Dani pulled up several metres up the street. Zack turned to me.

"Okay, show time."

I breathed in deeply. It was all up to me now. The scent of lemon myrtle wafted towards me as I stepped out of the car into the glamorous morning light. Rows of yellow bottlebrush lined the streets while rainbow lorikeets darted in and out of the low branches, feasting on the golden delights.

Desh rolled down the window and handed me three sturdy keys.

"This should convince her that you are legitimate."

*No problems,* I thought. All I had to do was convince a clone that I was here to borrow Desh clone's car. My feet dragged against the gravel as I inched closer to the house. Passing the neighbour's driveway, movement in the garden outside Desh's house caught my eye. My gun nestled contently inside my jacket pocket.

I knew I looked a little dishevelled, with a borrowed shirt, dust on my face and several more days of beard growth than I was used to. We didn't have any razors handy in the car, so this was the best I could do.

Would it be good enough?

I swallowed hard as Mrs Ugdashi emerged from the midst of a hedge, her clippers sparkling in the sunlight. Her eyes locked onto mine, and I forced a smile. My years of high school drama class needed to kick in right about now.

The green eyes bulged and glowed against her mellow walnut skin.

All clone eyes always had that green glow. I guessed that this was the real reason for my power: to tell a clone from a human being.

She smiled, recognising me.

"Oh, hi there, Cooper Two. You shouldn't be out of university at this time, let alone for a while," she said before lowering her voice. "The human Cooper is causing havoc around here." She brushed her hand through her hair; predominately black, with a constellation of grey stars shining with a wise aura.

I was up and close with his mother's clone, feeling her breath tickle my flustered face.

"Oh, it's okay, Mrs Ugdashi, my next tutorial isn't for at least another two hours, so I was checking if Desh One was on the same schedule as I was."

"Oh, Cooper Two, you should know he doesn't come home during long breaks; he stays in the library to study!"

"Oh, well, I'm just getting used to understanding the kind of friendship he and his friends have because I just want to be the best I can for this new world," I strained to sound convincing.

Did beads of sweat dance across my forehead?

"Yes, Cooper Two, it would be even more difficult for you after being released from the birthing pod just last night, right?" she reasoned in that haunting monotone.

This caught me off guard.

"Yes . . . but . . . I was fully briefed, of course."

I smiled, cheeks taught, lips together.

"Could I just run into the house and borrow his literature text for some extra study tonight? I hope that's okay." I swallowed hard.

"Oh, definitely. Feel free. Oh, by the way, who dropped you off here?" Her green eyes twinkled with suspicion.

I was normally quite nimble on my feet, but this was not playing out how I expected.

"Oh, the bus stop at the top of the street."

Mrs Ugdashi replied, genuinely surprised, "Oh, is there a new bus stop there?"

"Yes, just up there." I turned my back and pointed down the street.

Almost instantly, a bullet whizzed past my arm, catching Mrs Ugdashi in the middle of the chest. I spun around and saw her aggressively poised to strike me with those damned clippers. She hit the freshly mowed grass with a gentle click.

I looked at her with a gaping mouth. Breaths were short and erratic as she attempted to defy the grip of death. Her blood was a single spring rose blooming in the midst of a lush green pasture.

Her gardening was well and truly complete, as Desh skulked towards us from across the street, gun now securely tucked away inside his pants.

He grabbed my arm and led me into the house before I could utter an appreciative word. His eyes glistened as he glanced over the body, statuesque now on the front lawn of his house.

My fingers fumbled as I attempted to unlock the garage door with Desh's keys. Desh snatched them from me, revealing the inside of his garage in one swift movement.

"Signal to Dani to start moving off towards Orleans Reserve to pick up at least two of the others, and we'll be right behind her!"

I ran down the driveway once again, glancing at the clone of Mrs Ugdashi, lying peacefully on the lawn. Surrounded by what appeared to be delicate red petals.

I knew better.

Frantic, I signalled to Dani, and she flicked her high beams at me before screeching up the road and out of sight.

Desh had already reversed onto the road, leaving the garage door open and the body on the grass. I climbed in, catching a glimpse of the next-door neighbour peering from a drawn curtain at Desh and I speeding off in the direction of Orleans Reserve to meet the rest of our crew.

# CHAPTER 24

"Cooper?" Desh inquired.

I turned away from the blur of the window.

"Yes, mate?"

"It's happened to me, too." His tone was sombre.

"What's happened?"

He looked at me between surveying the road.

"I can do something like you can."

The light bulb flickered inside me, recalling his exceptional ability with a gun: the surprise on his face as he shot and killed three clones from a distance.

"It's like I have a knack for aiming a bullet wherever I want, even if they are miles away. I see a green target that helps me to aim, and I can zoom in or out with my mind."

He broke off suddenly. Words suspended in the air were almost tangible, circulating into the reality of the moment.

"Dude, don't you think I'm more than aware of these . . . phenomena sounding a little unbelievable? But if it's happening, then you can't deny it," I reasoned.

"Yeah, I guess so."

Desh muttered, eyes staring at the road.

I looked at him closely. Although he had stifled enthusiasm about his new discovery, his eyes told me what bothered him. A realisation that by sending a bullet through the clone of his mother meant his real mother was almost gone.

"Look, we're here."

He motioned towards Dani's car that was parked at the other end of the entrance to Orleans Reserve. Our dishevelled little group huddled around the car after jogging several kilometres just to meet us there. By now, clones would swarm both Dani's and Desh's houses. Their noses sniffing out our scent, their pack readying themselves, snarling at the onset of the hunt.

We pulled up next to Dani's car. Zoey, Kasey and Pj climbed into the back with us. The rest piled in with Dani and Zack.

*Hang on. Who the fuck was that?* I thought.

A young man who was not part of our entourage was left without a seat, attempting to find his way into Dani's rickety car.

I opened the door, inclining my head to get a look at this foreign stranger.

It was Whitey. He turned his head towards me. A frayed, off-white bandage draped over just one eye. Blood had dried in a crusty gathering on his grubby, freckled cheeks. He brandished an oddly disturbing smile.

"Cooper!" he exclaimed, hobbling towards me.

"What the fuck happened to you?" I managed to spit out.

Animated, Whitey yelled, "Oh, man, they nearly got me ay!" He pulled away from my shoulder, drawing in closer to my face.

His breath reeked of pickled onion, and his pale skin almost glowed from the lack of sun.

"They tried to cut out both my eyes for experiments, but I got away. . . Well, at least with one good eye!" he cackled.

"I just can't believe you're here." My joy was masked by unanswered curiosity. "But, mate, it's so good that you are, and that you're okay," I managed; knowing that time drew a narrow stare and stamped her foot impatiently.

"We've got the station wagon, so we'll put one of the other guys in the boot. You can just prop yourself up in the backseat and rest up; your head . . . and eye . . . must be killing you."

Whitey replied with sincerity, "Oh, thanks, Coops. You are a legend of a bloke."

I patted him on the back, his stark black hair scruffy atop his head, as he bent into the backseat of the station wagon.

"Pj, come here," I called out to him.

"Coops, what's the go?"

"You're going to have to lie under the blanket in the boot to accommodate Whitey, if that's fine with you."

"You know me. I'm basically the nicest guy anyone has ever known. I do things that Jesus himself would never –"

"Cut the shit and get in the boot." I pushed him towards the back, and we shared a chuckle.

Just before closing the boot hatch, Pj beckoned me towards him, and I leant in.

"How about all these new additions to the crew? We've basically got a full team again. Could start up a clones versus humans league."

Ignoring yet another joke, I asked, "How did you guys find Whitey?"

"On our way here. We were running blind through the bush and almost literally crashed into Whitey. He was stumbling around quite obviously, all messed up from the . . . ah . . . pirate situation." Pj covered one eye, and I shook my head. "But yes, massive relief that it was him and not another clone."

Zack yelled from the other car. "Look, I don't mean to be a negative Nina, but we need to get going. You can have a little secret meeting later."

I slammed the boot on Pj, donning another stupid grin, and ran towards the driver's seat to take us to the next destination: a place I knew all too well. I revved the engine, glancing at Whitey in the backseat.

*This is so bizarre,* I thought. At the same time, I felt content in an odd way. Three fresh faces in the group meant adding bodies to our army.

Spinning the wheel and turning out of the carpark onto the road, Gus filled my mind and said, *Don't forget that time is always against you, my friend.*

The seconds ticked by, and from the ashes of my youth, tentative wisdom sprouted in its place. A sturdy trunk would serve me well, decorated with flowering buds. *But it has only just sprouted, Cooper. Work with time as a friend, and it will become what you need it to be to survive.*

Gus responded to my thoughts.

*Yes, but when your tree of wisdom is strong enough to withstand winter's bitter breath, you are too old to do anything with it.*

In other words, when I truly understand life's lessons, death will be there, ready to whisk me away. I needed to stop these thoughts and let this car whisk me away to a different destination.

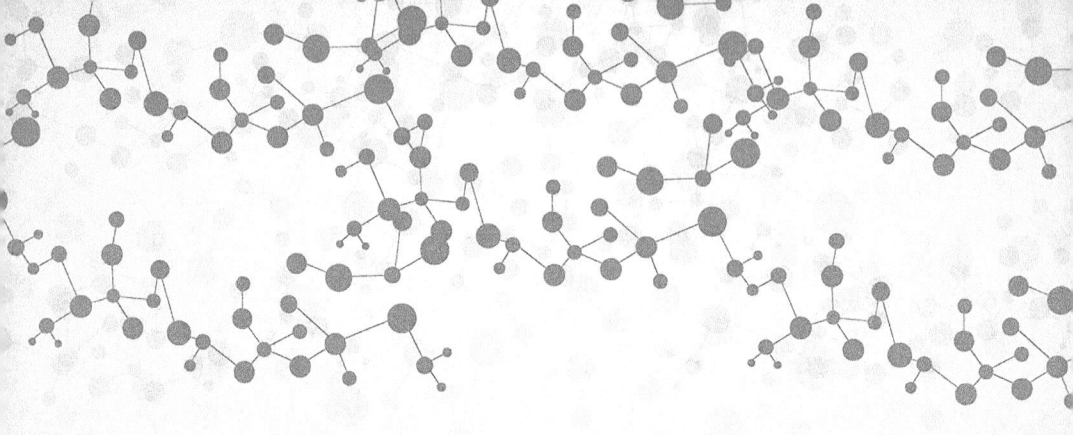

# CHAPTER 25

Uncle James was as cynical and as jaded as they came. He swept his thinning black and grey hair neatly across the top of his head, a wispy fringe falling just above his eyebrows.

"Cooper, I've just dealt with the biggest motherfuckers in the world. I should just tell 'em to get their heads out of their fucking arses." He spat bitterly on his way to the garage. A knitted green jumper fitted to his slim figure, as colourful as his language.

In the last few years of high school, it became increasingly difficult to find an enjoyable job that did not crush the soul.

Cue Uncle James. He owned a successful archery supply, manufacturing and distributing business from his home. A managing director, production manager, receptionist, secretary: the complete multipurpose employee.

On an odd family day after my father's death, where we had gathered around the stained red oak table for lunch, Uncle James asked me over for a chat.

"Cooper, I was just having a yarn to your mother over there," he said, pointing to Mum huddled in the corner as she spoke with Aunty Sakura. "And it seems that finding a job in this godforsaken hell hole is hard for someone your age, am I right?"

I nodded slowly.

"Well, how would you like to help me make some arrows for a bit of cash in your pocket?" He flicked the blue pocket on my jacket.

Making arrows didn't sound appealing to me; however, at the mention of cash, my ears pricked up.

"Yeah, I'll give it a go, Uncle James," I squeaked.

The next week, I started and never looked back. I'd learnt a lot about the archery trade in my time; fletching, vanes, fibreglass arrows, carbon arrows, adhesives, cleaning adhesives off your fingers, just to name a few. As you could imagine, it was not the most exciting job in the world. However, the part I liked the best was spending time with my Uncle James. Since I'd lost my father, he became the most prominent male figure in my life, and I looked up to him.

Uncle James showed me the importance of loyalty to family, picking up my Grandma from places none of his other brothers would. Uncle James showed me the way in which I needed to control my temper, watching in horror as he sent countless arrows crashing against the wall in utter frustration. Uncle James showed me that, although the world was a selfish place, I didn't have to conform to those standards. Uncle James showed me that it was always okay to fight for what you believed in and keep your loved ones safe. And for many years, he kept me safe after Dad had died.

Now it was only a matter of casting his protective nature over the house where he lived and worked, as it needed to keep me safe once more. I knew Uncle James would not be there. The week we left for our trip, he went to New Zealand for an archery convention and a long holiday. He was not due back for a while, which gave him time to survive whatever was going on here. Hopefully.

Aside from the vacant and spacious abode it provided us with, it also contained – well, let's face it – archaic and fantastical weaponry but weaponry all the same.

I suppose if Uncle James had not been on holiday, I wouldn't have thought of setting up shop there, but it was far enough from the danger zone, which gave us a false sense of security and comfort.

As I rounded the familiar streets, I thought of how it was a totally different situation now. Coming here was not about earning money, it was about staying alive. Stopping at the multi-lane round-a-bout on Godfrey Road, I was at ease, reclining in the driver's seat, carelessly confident that we had surpassed all the danger.

I suppose my arrogance brought a preordained moment of clarity to me. Blue and red flashing lights twinkled in the rear-view mirror. My heart leapt onto the dashboard, flapping like a dying fish on the banks of a barren stream.

I pulled over in a side street. A chorus of expletives resounded around the car. Dani's car zoomed past us, their sullen faces pressed up against the windows.

When I lost sight of them, I lost sight of our futures.

My rear-view mirror whispered to me, informing me that the officers had emerged from their vehicle. Boots clicked on the road as they made their way to my driver's side window. Zoey, Kasey and Whitey's mouths extended and descended, anxiously shouting at me. I did not hear a word.

All I could think about was how the policemen would perceive us: a full car of bloodied, soiled young adults with "guilty" written across their foreheads. If not for my licence, it would only be a matter of time before the policemen realised who we were.

My eyes focused upon the back window, blurring the disquieted trio in the backseat. Colourless, amorphous shapes bobbed buoyantly, attempting to impede my sudden fascination with the boot, idly housing a potential hero: our only hope.

Someone knocked at the window. Time returned to its regular pace as I turned, slipping my hand between the door and the seat to release the lever that unlocked the boot, rolling down the window with my other hand.

"Good afternoon. This is just a random breath test," the officer mentioned, peering menacingly into my eyes with his overwhelming green irises. I thought he instantly placed me, but a flicker of uncertainty resided within his stare.

His partner poked around Desh's side door, peering at the worse for wear passengers gathered in the back.

The officer on the driver's side caught my attention once more.

"Can I see your licence, please, while you count to ten in the direction of this apparatus."

He shook a bulky electronic device in his hand and pushed it in the direction of my face.

"Sure," I mumbled, fumbling for my wallet.

I handed my licence to him, catching a glimpse of the boot opening and closing soundlessly, in the rear-view mirror.

The officer read my name, and all at once, the recognition seeped in. He met my own eyes as if to let me know he had me, well and truly. With a hideous, haughty smirk, he reached for his gun, which was meant to be holstered at his side. Unfortunately for him, he grasped at nothing. He looked up at me, dumbfounded. I was equally in as much darkness as he. Snapping out of it, he yelled to his partner, "Dean One, it's them, it's them!"

Dean One reached to draw his gun to stop our movements.

"Dean One, I've lost my . . ."

BANG!

I screamed and jumped in my seat, smacking the top of my head on the inside roof of the car. The officer's body crashed violently onto the bonnet and slid down, half of his head ripped open, blood pouring towards an asphalt grave. Pj stood proudly above the fallen officer, gripping the gun that he had somehow swiped from the unsuspecting clone.

By this stage, Dean One had his gun fully drawn and had forgotten about the idle bunch sitting in the car. We were just as stunned as he was and had no idea what Pj was about to do next.

After all, he was standing there, tall and proud, locked in a ferocious staring battle with a clone who had a gun who would shoot him in an instant.

Dean One fired first. And I guess this was the interesting part: the bullet did not hit Pj. It slammed into the mortar and brick house several metres across the road. I didn't even see Pj move. The air whooshed into the car like a forceful gust of wind. Pj sailed at super speed around to the other side of the car.

When I opened my eyes, Pj had doubled back around and was standing behind Dean One, gun pointed at the back of his head.

"Drop your weapon, fuckhead."

Dean One, flabbergasted, stuttered.

"W-w-what the hell?"

"Yes, my friend, it seems you are fucking with the wrong kind of people."

Pj released the second bullet of the afternoon into Dean One's skull, spraying clone DNA all over the car and his face.

Kasey screamed. Pj stood there, wearing a wicked smile. Desh and I sat mouth agape, peering through the windscreen decorated with tiny bits of brains and blood. Dani and Zack raced up the street.

Dani came to a halt towards the front of the car on my driver's side, carefully surveying the chaos Pj had created. I suppose she sort of set Desh and I into motion. We regained some form of cohesiveness and consciousness by stepping out into the cool fresh air.

"What the fuck are you guys doing, just sitting there? There are cars stopped at the lights. They'll be here any second!" Dani yelled, clearly exasperated.

"Let's get rid of this mess!"

Pj had slipped the gun into his pocket and bent down with Desh and I as we collected the bodies, throwing them in the police car's boot. Zoey sat in the backseat of our car, scratching her head and staring blankly at the car seat; this was what she did when she was stressed. Zack knelt at Kasey's open door and patted her awkwardly as if she were a dog.

*Very reassuring,* I thought.

Pj couldn't stop talking, but I was obviously quite distracted loading bodies in the boot, so I only heard little things like "Hey, shit, man! Did you see that?" and "Dude, ha ha ha! I fucked them over big time!"

Zoey interrupted his barrage of incredulous phrases, yelling out from the car.

"Pj, it's about time you put a cork in it. What you have done, is create a huge mess for us, so I would shut your pathetic mouth and work on getting out of here."

Pj smirked and shrugged his shoulders, attempting to keep his pathetic mouth, as Zoey put it, intact.

Zack smiled at me and raised his eyebrows, as if to say, *Fair call.*

Pj had to add one last point. "I did save everyone, though. Just saying." He held his hands in the air, submissive.

Zoey smirked as she turned away.

We gathered around the police car, with the boot shut tight, as the traffic lights turned green and cars sped past us. Eyes peered our way from countless windows, but no one ever pulled over.

Once it was clear, we opened the boot of the police car once more, scurrying to remove the police uniforms from the clone cops. We could use them for a disguise in the future.

I got into the driver's seat of the police car, insisting that our first concern was to rid ourselves of the vehicle, as it would no doubt contain several tracking devices. The others followed me to a quiet park only a few minutes from Godfrey Road.

Dani provided us with a petrol can from the back of her car. Desh, Dani and I doused the car and all its contents, eradicating it from the present world.

As the scorching flames licked the afternoon sky, we set off to Uncle James's house, leaving the two clone policemen to surf the skies as ash, until their very essence vanished into endless space.

We turned into the quiet cul-de-sac, arriving at Uncle James's house, the sounds of sirens disrupting the suburban wasteland. I motioned for Dani to park in the driveway. Delicate memories flooded my mind as I stared at the heavy light brown wooden door, beckoning us forward at the bottom of a steep driveway.

I repressed the memories, praying that Uncle James was happy and healthy in New Zealand. Glancing around for any possible problems, I nodded at Pj and Desh as we strolled down the driveway to the spot under the second pot plant, where he hid the spare key.

I shifted the terra cotta, scraping the ground as it revealed the copper key that allowed us entry into the house.

As I picked up the key, I turned to Pj.

"Can you please tell the others to head into the house and make sure, when I open the garage door, Dani just drives right on in?"

Pj and I both turned opposite ways to our destination. The shining copper key turned smoothly, sending a thumping click that echoed in the hallway of the house.

The door swung open, inviting our weary souls into a new and impressive fortress. I focused my attention on concealing Dani's car, navigating through the kitchen and dining area to the wooden door that separated the garage or workshop space from the rest of the house.

It would only be a matter of days before the clones migrated into the surrounding homes. However, we assumed that we were in no immediate danger, as, of course, the current owner of the house was away on holiday.

As Dani rolled her car into the garage, faint smoke lingered across the treetops and surrounding houses. The sirens wailed in constant distress. We had to remain cautious in the coming days.

I closed the garage door and followed Dani into the downstairs area that linked the lounge room, dining table and kitchen. The weathered almond floorboards creaked under our feet as we shuffled around the dining table. It only seated six people, so the others leant against the cream kitchen bench, sullen and, frankly, exhausted.

"So, this is my uncle's place."

I extended my arms in an outward motion, pointing to the tired brown cupboards, fencing the mustard tiles inside of the not-so-modern kitchen. Soft murmurs and grunts of mild appreciation died around me.

"Well, have a look around. Choose a room or place to set up whenever you are all ready, and after the day we've had, just relax for a bit."

"Amen, brother," yelled Pj.

"I wouldn't get too comfortable Pj. You have a lot of explaining to do," warned Zoey.

"Did we miss anything?" Nikki squeaked.

Dani smiled. "Nikki, I think that perhaps something happened to these guys after their plane crash."

Nikki looked puzzled, pouting her lips and wrinkling her nose.

"We'll have plenty of time to talk about this once we've settled in," Mia reasoned.

Mia found me across the room and spoke with her eyes, *I didn't see any of that. I'm feeling a little useless.* Tears formed like rock pools at low tide.

I shook my head and frowned.

Her eyes spoke again, *I've been feeling uneasy, though; something big is about to happen. I'm just not sure what and when. I'm worried.*

Zack interrupted my stare, walking towards me and pressing his hand into my chest, pushing me into the kitchen.

"So, Whitey is with the group now. I don't know if I'm that happy about it, to be honest."

Zack had never seen eye to eye with Whitey. In fact, Zack had flat out often referred to him as "an annoying, little try-hard."

I accepted that Whitey did try hard, but it was all part of an innate desire to fit in.

"Man, that's a little harsh. Look, it's another number to add to this fight. I wouldn't be complaining," I said.

"Yeah, I guess. I'm interested to hear this story, though." He turned to Whitey and yelled, "Hey, Whitey, come here for a second."

Whitey stood up gingerly and hobbled over to us.

"Fellas, how are we?" he said, his faint freckles cradling his lopsided smirk.

"Hey, buddy, so, tell us this story: how did you bump into these guys?" I gestured to the group.

"Well, this is by far the luckiest part of my little story: I had given up hope of hiding and of any help coming to me, so I literally thought I would try to find the person closest to my property."

"Which happens to be Dani, right?" Zack chimed in.

"Yeah, so I left when all the 'replacement clones' – I guess you call them – went to work or uni. I just hid behind trees until I spotted all of them; Dani, Nikki, Mia and Gil wading through the bush, basically mimicking what I was doing. Honestly, I never quite believed in fate or luck or whatever until today." He breathed, relieved.

"Wow, that is pretty lucky!" Zack feigned a wholehearted chuckle.

*What were the chances?* I thought. Someone or something was obviously looking out for our group. Even if Whitey's eye was damaged, he was another asset to the team.

My chuckle was a lot more sincere. "Good to have you here, Whitey, it truly is." I gave him a firm handshake, and he winked at me with his good eye.

"You are a sight for sore eyes, boys!" He laughed at his own joke before Zack and I could recognise the dark humour.

"The dad jokes are in full swing already. Well, don't mind me. I'm off to have the first shower," I said, remembering to get in early before the hot water ran out.

"Leave some for the rest of us, princess! This is your second one in nearly three days!" yelled Zack.

As I walked towards the stairs, I playfully stuck my finger up at him.

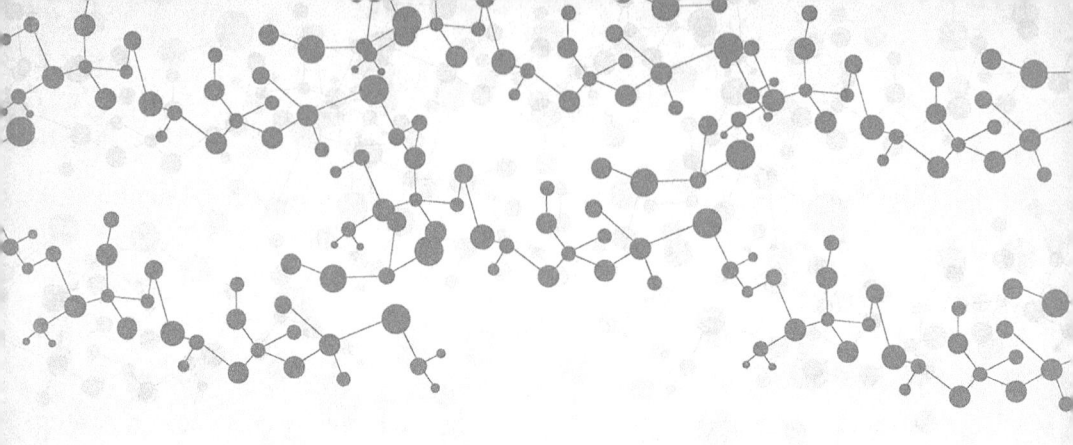

# CHAPTER 26

There was a spring in my step as I skipped buoyantly down the stairs. The hot water had soothed and revitalised not only my damaged and dirty skin but also my weary existence.

As I reached the bottom of the stairs, several voices and glasses clinked from the kitchen. Were they already cooking up a lovely family dinner? As I entered the room, their broad smiles hit me like a truck on a busy highway. They had ransacked Uncle James's alcohol collection. The caution that I had established less than two hours ago dissipated with the premise of finally acting our age. It was time to let go after such a tumultuous twenty-four-hour period.

Whitey walked over to me with a freshly opened beer in his hand, and I took it eagerly. He winked at me with the one functioning eye, his shadowed pupil appearing as a beacon, darting wildly against the backdrop of an iron oxidised wonderland. I smiled forcefully, attempting to hide my disgust.

Whitey turned to the others. "To all those no longer with us and to all of us who are here, together and alive. Let's keep it that way!"

We all bellowed our cheers, clinking glasses with anyone nearby. Hence, we began the only real party since we had left for our trip.

I squinted wearily around the room, through half a bloodshot eye. The sunlight illuminated part of the room through a crack in the curtains. The sudden desire to head to the bathroom caught me off guard. I managed to open my other eye and, with a furrowed brow, peeled the heavy blanket off my underwear clad body. As I planted my feet on the wooden floorboards, I steadied myself on the bedside table.

The room spun, but I did my best to place one foot in front of the other, progressing slowly towards the en suite bathroom. The taste of sweet candy had turned bitter on my tongue, my mouth parched. As I washed my hands, I glanced at my sorry reflection in the mirror. My eyes still had that morning look to them, thin strips of blood tainting the pure white sclera of my eye like twisted branches reaching for the clouds on a still, autumn afternoon.

My hair was unkempt and untidy, either sticking flat to the top of my head or emanating from my scalp in an unusual conical sculpture of chaos. Aside from the obvious styling issues, I clearly also needed a haircut. I shrugged. There was much more in this life to be worried about than the outward appearance.

My head, for one, still hurt, so I splashed water into my mouth and onto my face then headed back to the bed. I slumped back under the covers only to notice murmuring and movement next to me. Twisting my head around, Zoey was there, scantily clad. Her shoulders relished the freedom from a black lace bra dangling provocatively from the bedpost. I turned away from her, my mouth ajar in astonishment.

I focused on a spot right ahead of me; the apricot walls had diminished in their vibrancy, and a nail protruded halfway outside of the wall, abandoned by the painting that had once hung there. The nail appeared to be the centre of attention now that the painting was gone. The day had come for the nail to assume its position as the focal point glorified by the absence of its suitor. It helped me plunder my memory banks to figure out what happened the night before.

Zoey's arm reached over to embrace me and I succumbed to the comfort of the mattress and her endearing presence. Her fingers spread out slowly over my chest like digging into soft white sand.

The nail became submerged once more beneath the allure of something magnificent. She was dozing, as I glanced at her supple face, imbrued by patches of makeup from the previous night. All at once, memories came flooding into my head, spilling fragments of the night into my lap. There was the first drink, cheers, followed by the second drink. There was the third drink, accompanied by Zoey on my lap. There was the fourth drink as my hand rested precariously on the inside of her leg. Somewhere between the fifth and sixth drink, we migrated to the private sanctuary of the lounge room. My hand remained exploring the terrain of her legs and inner thighs, while our mouths collided in forays of passion.

Lust was an orbweaver spider, and we were tangled in her web as we stumbled towards the stairs. Our hands were vessels exploring the raging seas, circumventing shallow waters for greater depths. Zoey crawled like a ferocious tiger stalking her prey, as I lay backward on the jagged stairs sacrificing myself to her, hypnotised by eyes that didn't bother to hide desire. And in my drunken state, I grinned wildly and stupidly, as we inched our way up the stairs, sliding uncomfortably, kissing haphazardly.

My back crashed through the open door of the room, and I dragged Zoey in with me. By now, our kisses had become so forceful that our teeth occasionally clattered, our lips pressed together, creating a wet barrier from the repulsion of oxygen. One hand of mine pulled recklessly at the strands of Zoey's matted hair and the other hand carelessly unbuttoned her low cut peach shirt, discarding it on the ground, focusing on unbuttoning her jeans to reveal violet cotton underwear.

She stopped kissing me to look down, as her hands fumbled with the top button of my jeans. My lips rested against her forehead, absorbing her tiny beads of salacious sweat, our breathing and need for one another, vigorous. As I let my trousers fall to the floor, time slowed, and our intensity faded for a moment, as we realised what we were doing.

The room spun, but my heart was swimming in a glassy lake. The area was still, with stifled foreboding, with twinkling anticipation. Zoey's eyes danced provocatively, and with tentative, alluring movements, her hand reached down. I followed her lead, moving towards the cotton fabric, damp with expectation. Her mouth moved to my ear, and she exhaled tiny breaths, decorated with raspy moans of delight. And then the intensity returned. Time resumed its regular speed. I practically tore off her underwear. Removing her black lace bra, my shirt, her underwear, my underwear. Months of clawing at cages, months of scraping the walls of anticipation and desire, suddenly forgotten. I grabbed her knotted brown hair once more, pulling her head back and exposing her neck. I lunged forward, licking and sucking the curves trailing down to her breasts, flicking my tongue against her hardened nipples. She dug her nails into my back, and I grunted with a primitive need to explore every part of her. She giggled, and I pushed her onto the bed.

"I've been waiting for this for so long," Zoey exhaled, exasperated with excitement.

I drew my kiss from the outlines of her neck, moving up to the dimensions of her cheek, shading meticulously until my open mouth and tongue met hers. Our mouths locked together perfectly, and we breathed in gusts of wind that ripped the roofs off houses, that decimated branches of sagely oak trees, that became a hurricane with the potential to destroy life as we knew it. But it was not life that we destroyed. Something new was made. We moved together, breathed together and fused our beings together in the simple act of drunken sex.

As I stared at Zoey, who slept rather peacefully, I regretted the way in which our drunken state initiated our first sexual encounter together. But

I revelled in the fact that we had commenced a union, a togetherness that would hopefully continue. Zoey stirred as my unmoving stare entered her dreams. Her eyes were cradled by pastry puffs of fatigue. Her cracked lips slowly formed a satisfied smile and thrust it upon my reminiscing gaze. She pushed her arms out from underneath the blanket prison and held them out for me, and I willingly embraced her warm, comforting body.

"Morning," she whispered in my ear.

I shrunk back and searched her face.

Her eyes smiled courteously back at mine.

"Morning, you."

She dragged me back down to her, hands entwined around the back of my neck. We kissed so deep, that I felt it throughout my whole body; warming, cool and everything in between. Her lips moved to my ear. "I want you all over me again," she whispered as she moved her hands down.

"Mmmm, looks like you're also quite interested."

We made love once more. This time, as the morning sun caressed our naked bodies through the window. We were sober, aware of everything, and it was beautiful. I learnt many things that morning: more so about the power of reciprocal love. I learnt of the way in which one simple action can bind you to a person for life. Two hearts tethered to an unbreakable chain of newly discovered love. Whatever happened to us down the line, we would always have that moment. A moment of love when it was untainted: simple and all consuming.

# CHAPTER 27

The weeks passed without any assault on our existence. But in the same breath, no valuable news came our way. A routine of day-to-day life was put into place as we prepared for war. We set up the archery workshop and operated it together in shifts. During the first week, I had to train the group to manage the equipment and learn the production procedures.

Uncle James had ordered enough basic stock to work through about two solid weeks, and I oversaw the production of different arrows, including carbon, fibreglass and a number of wooden arrows with different degrees of girth and length.

Why did we do this? Because our bullets had dwindled and there was no way to acquire any new ones. It would alarm the authorities if several of us, known to the media, entered an ammunition store. Although it seemed that archer battle techniques were obsolete, we agreed that the arrows and bows were better than nothing at all.

The days after Pj killed the two clone cops, sirens lamented their loss. Helicopters circled from skies above and we were on edge because of it. TV and internet were a bad idea, but it was a novelty we had not possessed for months, so it became our coping mechanism. The bad part was seeing crime stoppers advertisements about 'The Evil Eleven'. The bad part was every trending hashtag on social media led back to us. The bad part was realising that we were not escaping anything while we were connected to that world.

I disconnected rather quickly after that. So, in my spare time, I buried my head in books. I would often curl up in bed, drag the blanket over my body and let myself be transported to another world. On other days, Zoey and I watched movies on my uncle's laptop, snuggling and exploring one another physically, as you tend to do in a new relationship.

Zack, Pj and I would play video games on an older console we found stuffed inside one of the drawers underneath the TV. Whitey and Kasey pestered the rest of us to play board games. Dani, Mia and Nikki decorated the house as best they could, making it "homely" for us all.

Sitting in the backyard one afternoon with Gil as the rainbow lorikeets chatted around us, we watched Desh shoot arrows with perfect accuracy into the bullseye of a target.

The lilly pilly hedges bordered the garden, with a verdant green. Small bulbs of red berry bliss adorned the hedges like decorations on a Christmas tree. A crepe myrtle shed its bright pink leaves into the bird bath in the corner, staining the water like a pink salt lake.

Zack joined both of us, sitting down at the faded teak table.

"This guy is a machine," he declared as another arrow thumped into the target.

"I'm glad he's on our side," joked Gil.

Changing tone quite suddenly, Zack spoke up, "I'm worried about my family. Have you both not thought about it?"

I cleared my throat.

"I have thought about it constantly, especially since I've had a run in with my clone counterpart."

"This kind of stuff is not easy to deal with; things were going fine, then BAM! Change decides to fuck with you," Zack growled.

"What do you think has happened to them?" Zack suddenly lost the bravado, his voice weakened by fear and love.

I couldn't answer this. Or rather, I believed that I shouldn't answer the question. My pessimistic nature turned to only one answer: your family, my family, Gil's family are dead. It was something that I didn't want to accept just yet; my grief became crystalline flakes in the protective winter of my heart. The fire of finality would not burn these walls until this was over.

Gil spoke while dark thoughts encircled me. "You should know, Zack, that wherever they are at this present moment, it does not matter. Love, faith and family is always within you."

Zack laughed condescendingly. "Is this you pinning religion shit onto me?"

Gil put his feet up on the table and sighed.

"That's not what I was getting at, but while we're on the topic of religion, you should get a tattoo of the Virgin Mary. Maybe she'll protect you and your family, then."

I burst out laughing at Zack's expense. Gil coming in hot with the burn!

Zack had enough tattoos covering his body, anyway, and as we chuckled our fears away, I had a suspicion I knew what Gil was trying to say to Zack.

He wasn't trying to say, "God is within. Look inside yourself, dear child." He was trying to tell Zack; sometimes we build our lives from the memories of our loved ones, carrying pieces of them to help strengthen the foundation.

"Well, apart from all the worry over these last couple of weeks, it's good to just chill here right now, I guess," Zack concluded.

"I swear, man, you are the chillest dude I know," Gil exclaimed.

Zack sat back and put his arms behind his head, in the universal "chill" position.

"Chill city is where I live," he boasted.

"You live in dick city, buddy. Get a grip. Go do something useful, like helping Desh with retrieving the arrows," I joked as I pulled my chair back from the table.

Gifts or powers? Who knew how to label them, let alone describe how any of it happened to us? Still, deep down, I wanted to find an explanation for what it all meant. So far, the only two of the group who hadn't identified any power were Zack and Kasey.

Every time I tried to bring anything to the surface with Desh, he would always brush me off and say, "It's not the right time for this discussion," and storm off into the backyard. I didn't understand the secrecy, not then, anyway.

So, I made Mia my point of call for unwrapping our gifts, so to speak.

"Don't you think we've waited long enough preparing for our little fight? We should be honing these new skills or gifts and using them against the clones."

"Yes, I guess we've waited a while, but if everyone is not comfortable making a big deal about it, we should just wait longer," Mia suggested.

"Not you, too!" I spat back.

Mia's brow bent inward. "I just think that, if we all agreed, then, yeah – let's tell Dani, Nikki and Whitey. But then again, what do we tell them? We don't know anything yet!"

I suppose she was right. We didn't even know how to use them.

"Okay, fine." I exhaled, defeated. "Why don't we just gather a small group who are willing to practice these skills until we're stronger and understand everything better?"

"I think that works." Mia smiled.

I was offended when Zoey said, "No. I'm happy just hanging around here; I already feel comfortable with what I can do." She shrugged her shoulders and continued looking at the laptop.

"Well, it's nice that you are so sure of yourself, but some of us want to learn a bit more." My voice rose with intensity.

"That's great, Cooper, then go do that." Zoey stood firm.

Shaking my head, I left her in the room. There was no point arguing with her when she was set in her ways. Pj and Mia, however, were both keen to explore their gifts.

Pj ran laps down the street, away from Dani and Whitey, who had become suspicious that we weren't explaining the extent of what we could do. We timed him, recorded his reactions and broke down his overall technique. We discovered that Pj wasn't operating at super speeds; rather, it was as though he was manipulating the space and time continuum. His vice, though, was that when he couldn't use his legs, time would not slow for him.

Mia focused on absorbing positive energy from the world. She read various yoga and meditation books, and watched videos to find a balance to her power. She began to tap into the dreams of others while they slept, exploring the cognitive connection later at night. This explained why, earlier in the bush, she was able to transmit her dream to me. She could not control the dream though, she only experienced it.

Within the real world, she only saw slight glimpses of trivial occurrences like someone hanging out the washing, or someone swimming in the pool. Whenever she experienced a vision, her eyes would become vacant clouds with a grey haze, rendering her still and statuesque. Her power grew through training and practice, but she knew there was a long way to go.

When it came to my own gift, I tried to see the positives. I searched 'learn mind-reading techniques with six easy steps' and 'read minds like a psychic in just ten minutes' on the internet. All of that was fiction, so I delved into the study of telepathy.

Telepathy, generally, was about projecting your thoughts into someone else from a large distance. I had already explored this with Mia, and it worked quite naturally between us.

My gift worked in conjunction with direct vision, so it was only about receiving thoughts and feelings, never about controlling others' actions.

Was it possible to extend my gift further and search other minds, as Mia had been able to connect to other's dreams? What if I could begin to make people do anything that I wanted?

The last question made me shudder. It seemed like too much power. How could I know if anyone who interacted with me was doing it of their own free will or not?

The movies and stories where heroes with superpowers saved the world didn't often delve into how many times they might question their actions. I was trying to better understand who I had become, yet I was on the cusp of such great power that it actually scared me.

The angel and the devil both sat on my shoulders, dangling their legs from great heights, not even bothering to utter words. Even *they* knew the limited direction that this path would take me.

Angel would say, *You can stop the war, you can end poverty, you can stop terrorism, you can eliminate crime.* The devil would say, *You can be rich, you can be doted upon, you can have anything you desire.*

Decisions you make when you have significant power must come from a divine place. I'd already crossed the bridge of faith and didn't see anything on the other side. But spirituality was not necessarily faith in the religious sense. Spirituality is more than a man-made congregation of those who had lost hope and were seeking salvation. It was more than an ideal to grasp, when humans became timorous, scowling at death; it was an overall acceptance of a deeper meaning of the end, of a cyclical nature, one often only understood by those who consistently search for something more.

The spiritual connection that I had to nature, to the earth, to animals: they called to me with a forceful voice in the deep recesses of my fractured soul. It was to that divine spirit that I was admonished by and bound to. So, I had to remain true to that, to acknowledge that, if I were to nurture a power so potent, I would not be swayed by such an encumbrance, but rather, be a master of power itself.

I knew that I wasn't strong enough yet to wield such power, so I mainly worked on the distances between what I could read from eyes as well as body language. I had only developed a small amount of distance. However, my control and invasive technique had improved significantly.

But again, it was one of those things. I didn't want it to become part of everyday life, discovering what Zoey was feeling when she wouldn't tell me she was angry with me. Part of the excitement of relationships was just that: discovery in the most human way possible. Otherwise, I may as well have been a clone.

In life, there comes a time when reality sets in. No matter how many pages of books took me elsewhere, it could never stop the inevitable. Someone knocked on the door, and I placed my book down on Zoey's side of the bed.

"Come in." My voice was hoarse.

Gil and Desh entered my room.

"Hey, Coops. We thought we'd run something by you," said Gil.

"Yeah, no problem, guys. Let's hear it." I gestured with my hand.

Gil and Desh sat on the end of the bed, and Gil began.

"Desh and I have been chatting about something, only between the two of us for a couple of days now, and we want to notify only Nikki and yourself."

I frowned, wondering why only Nikki and I were important enough to know.

"Okay, can you tell me why I'm so important?" I replied tentatively, realising instantly that I would most likely be telling Zoey anyway.

"We are using your power and also your acting skills," Gil said.

I cursed myself for always volunteering for the ensemble roles in the university musicals.

"Great, using me for my power again." I rolled my eyes. "But, seriously, why aren't we discussing this with everyone?"

"I don't think everyone has a right to know what we're working on," Desh fired back

"I just think we have to be calculating about this plan; it is the big one," reasoned Gil, calming Desh with a look of a disapproving parent.

Ignoring Desh's desire to want to be the leader, I thought it through for myself. In the corporate environment, it made sense to initiate plans and implement change through small committees and communicate to the masses later. Maybe Desh was using his business knowledge in this situation, also?

"Okay, I'm in, but let's not leave everyone out of the loop for too long," I pleaded.

Gil winked at me. "All good, brother. We'll let you know when we're ready to discuss our plans with the others."

Gil resumed talking. "We've been working on a plan for getting at the clones, and the start of it involves yourself, Desh and Nikki."

I chuckled incredulously. "And how is it that you have avoided the danger?"

He laughed back. "Every dangerous operation needs a sane and calculating mind."

To the sound of our dying laughter, Desh began to explain his plan to me.

When they both left me in my room again, I couldn't focus on my book anymore. I stuck a photo of my mother and sister into the current page as my bookmark and stared at that familiar place upon the opposing wall with the protruding nail and processed my thoughts.

I thought about the many things that brought the plan together and decided that I would put some elements of it into motion that day. Taking myself to the en suite bathroom, I stood in front of the mirror. I somehow looked a little older. Or was it my expression? A certain resolve, a weariness that had not been there before.

I eyed the clippers that were now resting in my hand and considered the state of my hair: wild upon the terrain of my head. So, Desh says that, for the plan to succeed, I needed to shave my head and grow a beard.

The chaotic buzzing resounded off the tiled walls as I steadied my hand to shave my head. A lock of hair drifted aimlessly towards the floor like the last leaf failing to resist the winter chill.

Change was upon me.

# CHAPTER 28

Kasey had curled up in the corner of the lounge, the nail of her forefinger rested on the edge of cracked, pale red lips. Her hair was tied up in a messy bun, ash blonde streamers trailed down towards hunched shoulders. I picked up a chequered blue and white tea towel hanging beside me and threw it, hitting her on the arm. She turned to me with a sour look on her face.

"What is your problem?"

Making my way over to the lounge, I shrugged, "I'm just saying hi."

"Well, could you do it in less of an annoying way – "

I extended my arms wide, inviting her in for a bear hug.

"Get off me," she spluttered in between giggles.

The bear-like embrace evolved into a cute puppy cuddle, as I kept my arm across the top of her shoulders so she could nestle into me.

"Why are you watching this depressing shit?" I scowled, grabbing the remote with my other hand and changing the channel.

"We need something like this, I said, settling for the Food Network.

"What is it with you and food shows?" she laughed.

"Food has such a deep connection to culture and who we are; it brings people together, don't you think?"

"I suppose so, but what is the point of watching people cook? Doesn't it just make you, like, hungry for something we can't have? Especially in a time when we are basically living on canned goods, frozen food and rice?"

"It kind of just reminds me how much I miss my mum's traditional Eastern European cabbage rolls she used to make. It's good to have those memories now that . . . things have . . . changed." My tone migrating into sombre territory.

"Cabbage rolls?"

"Yeah, look, I don't think they would take your fancy all that much, but it just brings me back to the good times, to family."

"Okay, well, one day, you should make it for me, and we can, like, have our own new family connection."

"We totally need to do a family meal thing, actually. That could be good for us. Oh, you just reminded me: I might need to do a late evening run to the shops to get a couple more supplies."

"Well, you definitely don't need to worry about anyone recognising you with that god-awful haircut." She rubbed my spikey head of hair, and her genuine laugh made those beautiful blue eyes sparkle. It had been so long since I'd seen them shine like that.

"Um, says fountain head over here." I returned the favour by flicking the strands of blonde hair pouring over the top of her head.

"Noooo, don't say that." She frowned and crossed her arms, shifting away from me.

"I'm only joking, Kase." I reached out to bring her back into my embrace. "You know you don't need any of that bullshit to enhance your beauty; you shine without any of that."

Tears twinkled and threatened to trickle down her cheeks, but she swallowed hard and whispered, "Thank you, Cooper. That is sweet."

Kasey looked at the TV and smiled, autumn warmth painting her cheeks. We watched a chef travelling into the jungle and using local ingredients to make dinner for his hosts. Words weren't spoken between us until I noticed her shifting uncomfortably.

"Are you alright?"

She pouted and crinkled her forehead, "Not really. Like, I've just been thinking about how . . . well . . . everyone has this new gift or power or whatever you want to call it. And I'm like, just the same old me."

"Kasey, I know it must be frustrating for you to be in a position like that. Everyone is changing around you; the world is changing around you. But take it from me, it just feels like it adds to the weight of responsibility. I kind of feel like, now that I have this thing, I'm expected to somehow help change our fortunes. Does that make sense?"

"No, like, I get it. But I just feel a little . . . worthless with what I bring to the table."

"Honestly, I don't look at any of us and think these abilities define who we are. When I look at Pj, I don't think we should enter him in the Olympics so that we can win a bunch of money. I think this is the guy who makes us laugh when we need it."

"Yes, but I used to be special. Guys used to think I was worth something. I had over ten thousand followers on social media and —"

"Kasey, that isn't real. Those guys notice you in a bikini at the beach or in a short skirt at the club. We see so much more in you: the way you make me my tea of choice every morning because you've noticed my schedule, the way you let us watch TV shows that you don't normally like but give them a go," I said, pointing to the show we were watching, "the way you have organised the girls' yoga classes as a way to keep connected to each other, the way you took Mia in and gave her a little makeover last week, just to make her feel better. I could list so many ways that you are special. I just wish you could see yourself through our eyes."

Kasey crumpled into my chest, letting tears flow as she brought her arm around me, squeezing into a healthy hug.

"Cooper, you have such a way with words."

"Well, I am nearly finished with my communications degree, so you'd hope that I would have a certain . . . affinity with them."

Zoey came into the kitchen for a drink of water and saw Kasey and I laughing together on the couch.

"Oh, let me get in on this action!" Zoey sang, as she crashed on top, pulling all three of us together. We laughed harder than we had in months.

Desh and I were in the car, turning onto the main road. We had decided to visit a shopping centre closer to the clone base.

"It's fine," Desh said. "We will just get a couple of new staples like bread, rice, cans of soup, and then we can watch the base from afar for a bit."

"Yes, but won't anyone ask us about why we were gone for two hours?"

"Honestly, just stick to the story, and it will be fine."

"You know I hate lying; I'd just prefer to be straight with everyone."

"Well, sometimes not telling someone the truth will save them a lot of pain in the end." Desh spoke with a cold finality.

I looked out the window, as the local radio station settled the awkwardness between us. The shopping centre whizzed past us, and my neck twisted around in response. Did he not realise he missed the turn off?

"I'm sorry. I know we just passed the shopping centre, but I just want to see the base first. We can get everything on the way back."

I didn't bother protesting and just fused myself into the seat.

Protruding from the earth, a huge clock tower confidently surveyed the entire base like a lighthouse beacon shining onto a calm, glassy ocean.

As we drove beside the base for the first time, the clock tower eyed us menacingly, warning us away from the danger inside. We turned left down a street and meandered up a hill, the car sweating at the steep incline. Taking another left not long after, we wound up in the street Gil had given us directions to. You couldn't fault his judgement; it was a perfect place to take in the base. But the view was daunting, and if we were skittish and concerned before, then we were experiencing a whole new level now.

The clock tower was clearly the focal point, but there were several worn buildings that appeared to be barracks, positioned in multiple rows on either side of a winding concrete path. Larger buildings congregated towards the back end of the property, the moonlight silhouetting the newest building of the lot, triple the size of the others, stark white and unscathed compared to the dreary barracks. We peered through our binoculars. This was definitely the cloning facility. It had a large security presence surrounding the building, as well as the highest tech components attached to entrances and exits. Our eyes shifted to the left, where a contrasting building stood tall. There was still a high security presence around the second largest building, but it was clearly a place that they wanted to keep in darkness and in shadow.

Desh and I took some photos and used the video camera to capture a topical view of the base. Taking a few deep breaths, I was quite nervous about how or when we would enter the base and . . . do what? I felt so small. A horrible realisation overcame me; this was too much for us.

No. I couldn't think like that. We didn't have a choice. I needed to continue training and working on my ability. There wasn't any room for panic or fear; I had to be positive.

"See, that wasn't so bad after all, right?"

"I wasn't worried about scoping out the base, Desh, I'm just not all that fond of secrets between everyone. This is our new family. I just don't want any bad blood between us."

"Look, Cooper, something is telling me it's not the right time to let them know everything. I just want to research and prepare, and when I'm confident, we can tell them together."

"Okay." I shrugged, flexing my fists in my lap.

The words "When I'm confident, we can tell them" irked me.

I hated it when people didn't consider the feelings of everyone involved. In this instance, I knew I wasn't going to get anywhere by bringing it up with him. Some people switch off parts of their personality to deal with the situation at hand. Something told me that Desh's cold demeanour may have been a protective sheen he chose to cast over his heart.

What had happened in his life that made him like this?

I tried to push my power harder than I ever had before; it encircled Desh as he stared out at the road. I saw a flash of Jasmine's face, a heart beating fast, pulsing love through clasped hands, a stabbing feeling of pain, love unrequited, death interrupting a future he wanted, the bullet through the heart of his mother.

Then I was back to myself. I shrunk down into the seat again.

When you feel so strongly, and you lose something, we tend to build a wall around us, so it keeps us contained and safe. But safety means we don't take chances; we don't open ourselves to potential. As a result, we stay levelled, never knowing the heights of happiness because, once we know them, we can easily fall into a crevice and never return. I sat there in the car, not knowing if I would choose the absence of emotion to protect me or try to build love again with broken tears and emotional cement. Who was I to admonish Desh for the way he dealt with things? We are all human, so we are all flawed.

Desh and I walked through the door at nearly 10pm, carrying reusable shopping bags full of at least a week's supply of food. Gil welcomed us and helped put items away.

"Cooper, come here for a second," Gil beckoned.

I was ready for bed, but I thought I'd indulge him by moving over to the stove where he stood. He opened the lid of a large steel pot and pointed inside.

"Kasey made this for you, and she tried to stay up until you got home, but well, she fell asleep on the couch."

Twisting around, I saw Kasey curled up in her favourite corner of the couch; a red throw blanket draped across her shoulders. I turned my attention to what was in the pot, and to my surprise, it looked like my mother's cabbage rolls. Tears welled in my heart first and then tumbled out of my eyes.

Gil nodded his head and rubbed my back. "I know, right? She spent most of the afternoon putting it together for you. I am just amazed by the care she shows us almost every day."

I could hardly speak. "Yeah, I mean, this was very sweet."

"I'll leave you to try some. I'm tired and need to get to bed. Maybe just –"

"Gil, of course. I'll show my appreciation."

Smiling, he and Desh walked up the stairs to their room.

I heated the cabbage rolls on the stove, the smell of simmering tomato, flakes of garlic and pinches of paprika ate away at memories I wasn't ready to revisit and grief I wasn't ready to let in.

I set two bowls on the table, steam rising like a cobra to the music of a solemn soul. Moving to the couch where Kasey lay, I couldn't help but smile. Maybe she did discover her power after all. Was being too considerate an ability? Generosity often withered when we were stressed and anxious, but she kept her new family at the forefront of her thoughts. She definitely didn't take our friendship for granted; a quality that I needed to improve upon. I placed my hand on her shoulder; her head shot up, eyes taking a short time to focus in the dim light.

"Oh, Cooper, you're back." Kasey's voice was raspy and quiet.

"I reheated some of the food for us to eat together."

She rubbed her eyes daintily and yawned.

"In fact, wait a second," I added, bounding to the table, grabbing the bowls and bringing them to her on the couch.

"Let's have dinner in bed." I smiled.

Kasey sat up straighter, her feet squished against my thighs. She took a bowl without saying a word; her weary eyes watched me as I took my first mouthful. As my taste buds registered the food, I closed my eyes, and I was transported back to my own couch at home: mother banging those pots and pans, the lingering taste of sweet paprika and tomato swirling inside me. This wasn't an exact replica of the dish, but it still took me back there. My heart and soul both nodded in appreciation.

"So, is it close, at least?" she inquired with a hint of concern.

"It's perfect," I said, kissing her on the cheek and holding back tears.

Kasey's shoulders relaxed, a beaming smile spreading across her face.

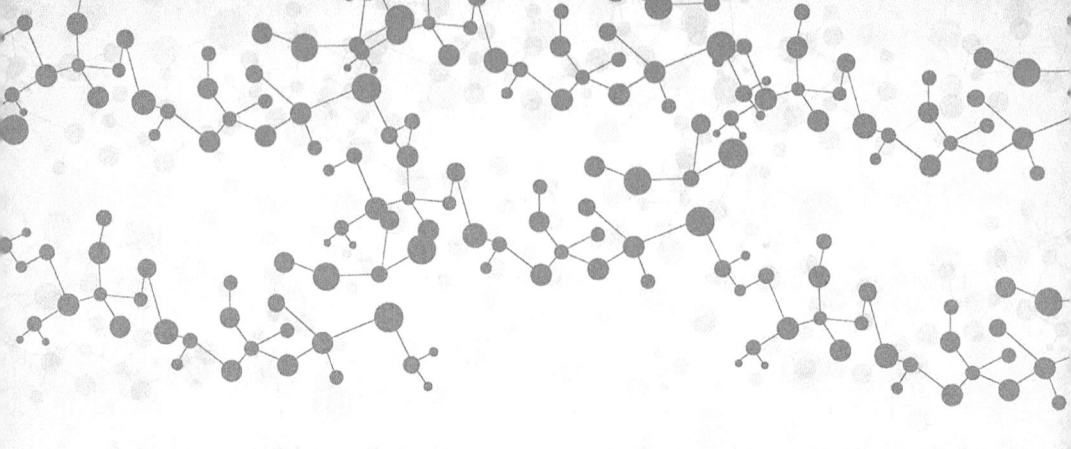

# CHAPTER 29

"So, how is it all coming along, computer wizardess?" I inquired, resting my hands upon Nikki's shoulders as I stared at the computer screen.

She flinched at my touch but then relaxed. Without turning to look at me, she replied, "Well, the digital ID cards and physical tags are nearly finished. We will just need to find and break into a printing place sometime over the next couple of days to print them."

Not so long ago, the idea of breaking into a business would have been an absolute no-no.

"Yep, okay, well, it's looking great." I pointed towards the screen that contained the ID documents for Officers McMahon and Redhi.

"It's taken long enough, though," Nikki exhaled, "and the hacking of these details into their system is difficult, too, but I will be able to navigate my way through it," she said with confidence.

Her uncharacteristic abilities impressed me.

"How did you learn all this again?" I inquired.

"I'm studying the computing course at uni, Coops, c'mon."

"I'm aware of that," I said, with a tinge of frustration in my voice, "but they don't teach you this stuff in that course."

"Well, you know that Matty is employed by the army as their web defence expert, right?"

Matty was, of course, her boyfriend, "Prince." I hadn't paid attention to details before, but I nodded.

"Well, yeah, he just, like, taught me basically all of his training 'cause I was just interested in everything he did."

She sighed and looked wistfully beyond the computer screen out the window.

"I take it you miss him, Nikki?"

She turned to face me, tears quivering.

"Of course."

She buried her head in my shirt and sobbed. Halfway through her unexpected change in emotion, she jerked back from my embrace and muttered something inaudible before running to the bathroom in a hurry.

She returned to me, flustered and wiping the corners of her mouth.

"This house or the crappy food we've been eating, must be making me sick because I've been throwing up just about every morning!" she croaked.

"You must be pregnant!" I exclaimed in my best joking voice.

We both suddenly stopped smiling, realising that it could indeed be true.

"Wait a second. When was the last time you even saw Matty?" I asked, hoping I was way off the mark.

She drew her thumb and forefinger to her chin, scratching it feverishly.

"Well, he was there two nights before everything happened." Her voice wavered.

"Jeez, Nikki." I gathered my thoughts. "Well, I suppose that was at least a month and a bit ago. I mean, wouldn't you have known if you'd missed a period or something?"

Her eyes darted to the ceiling, exploring her mind for a memory.

"You know what, Coops? I just can't remember even having it for a while, and I was close to telling Dani what happened with Matt, but the clones came, and I just didn't," she said, putting her hand to her mouth.

"What happened with Matt, Nikki?" I said, concern evident in my tone.

Nikki hesitated. "It's actually a little embarrassing . . . like . . ."

"C'mon, Nikki, it's me." I turned my hands upwards.

"The condom broke," she blurted out, brushing a wavy strand of dark brown hair behind her ear and scratching her neck nervously.

"Holy shit," I breathed.

"Holy shit, Cooper."

An intermittent silence fell between us, where we both didn't quite know what to say next.

"Well . . . just . . . get back to this work. Don't overdo it, but make sure we have everything finished so that we can go to the chemist and printing shops tonight maybe and figure everything out." I stammered without a breath.

She nodded and grimaced, slowly ambling past me towards the computer screen. I turned to leave but not before she called out to me.

"Cooper, keep this to yourself, please."

Her worried eyes sang to me, and I nodded, avoiding her penetrating stare. The power was getting easier to control, so I had already seen inside her mind. The following thoughts, flickering over and over:

*I must be pregnant. I can't believe it. I wish Matty was here to make everything ok. I wonder where he is; if he is still alive.*

I could not soothe her racing mind; I hoped that working on the officer IDs would perhaps give her the chance to concentrate on something else. The resumption of my own work continued, fletching vanes onto the remaining carbon arrows we had in stock. Whitey accompanied me into the garage workshop.

"So, why the random haircut, Coops?"

I remembered not to bring anyone else into the plan just yet.

"Oh, you know, I think a bit of a change is good, and it can't hurt just looking a little different if we go to the shops and whatnot," I explained, nonplussed.

"It all seems strange, though, considering you and Desh did the same thing, as well as having little meetings with each other," he spat bitterly.

I forced myself to chuckle condescendingly, instilling doubt into his mind.

"Mate, you're a little paranoid, aren't you?"

Whitey's one remaining eye narrowed for a fleeting moment and relaxed as he moved to slap me on the back.

"Oh, I'm just checking what the hell is going on around here. I guess I'm just tense from waiting around for something to happen. I just want to take those clones down, man!"

"All in due time, Whitey, we will find a way," I reassured him.

He rolled his shoulders twice.

"I am ready anytime," he declared, shadowboxing against a cardboard box opponent.

Smiling briefly, I focused on applying a green-coloured cock feather to the shaft.

"Hey, Cooper, what's all this about powers and things like that? How come I don't have anything?"

I looked at him.

"How did you hear about that?"

"C'mon, I saw what Pj did! It was incredible. Something is going on with him — that is obvious — but how about you and the others?"

"Well, not everyone in this group can do anything different. My . . . thing is that I can kind of interpret someone's feelings, I guess."

Whitey nodded, considering the power with a furrowed brow.

"I don't understand how knowing people's feelings can be useful. I think you drew the short straw, mate." He laughed innocently.

I stopped fletching the arrow and stared into him.

For some reason, nothing happened when I looked into his eye. I tried to see a weakness I could exploit, to get him back for digging under my skin. But there was nothing. I shook my head, realising that my hold on the power was only good when I had two eyes to look at perhaps, and lied to his face.

"Ah, whatever it is, it's been given to me for a reason. I just don't know what that is."

I'd always felt a certain jealousy over some of the others, like Mia and Zoey, who could do something cool. My power seemed so bland and boring in comparison. But it didn't have to be, did it?

I shook my head free of the devil. No, it was good enough for me. I just needed a little more training to work on seeing the feelings from just one eye and through body language.

Whitey smiled and put his bony, pale hand on my shoulder.

"That's why we are here, buddy. It's about trying to find a reason for everything we do."

I smiled at him, letting my annoyance dissipate with a simple gesture.

"I'm going to watch TV for a bit, man. Let us know what you want for lunch, and I'll make some for you, okay?"

"Cheers," I replied as he limped out of the garage.

I resumed my work, and as always, my mind continued to tick over. That was the problem with monotonous work: it didn't require any sort of mental stimulation. And so, I went from one inconsistency to the next, one fear to the next, and it trapped me in a vicious cycle. Imagination played two roles in my life. It was there when I needed to dream of something better, but it plagued me when I thought of the many negative contingencies that might be around the corner.

Imagination led us to far-reaching galaxies and provided an avenue in which to channel our negative emotions. But it also pushed against actually setting us free. It kept our emotions in stasis. It glued us to the ground. I held the art of imagining so dear to me for so long as a means to get me through tough times, but the more I did it, the more I lost the ability to deal with what was in front of me. As with everything, a balance was required, as I certainly didn't want to lose my sanity to a wandering mind.

Dinner couldn't come quick enough, and I used it as my cue to whisk Nikki away from the group.

"I think it's time we set out to the print shop and maybe take a detour to the chemist," I whispered, taking her by the arm.

She nodded. "Okay, I'll meet you in the car after I change."

On my way to the car, I ran into Gil and asked him where the nearest print store and chemists were. He closed his eyes and drew directions for me on a blank piece of paper. I shook the paper in the air as if it were a trophy, yelling thanks as I headed towards the car to wait for Nikki to join me.

We kept to ourselves during the car ride, both of us with our own things to worry about: Nikki with her impending pregnancy and my agitation over not being able to tell anyone else about our plan.

I parked the car in a side street not far from the local shopping centre, which contained a chemist on one side and a laser printing store on the other. We had become so accustomed to breaking and entering into various shopping centres over the last couple of weeks that, like so many of our new traits, had become part of everyday life.

Nikki and I double-checked the perimeter, making sure that no security guards were on patrol. Splitting up, we hugged the shadows and began to blacken out the inquisitive faces of the security cameras with a trusty bottle of black spray paint.

After we had secured all possible points of discovery, we cracked a window using a jumper to mute the sound, our elbow creating the force to penetrate the resilient glass.

The glass splayed onto the vinyl floor, twinkling a delicate lullaby that could have awoken the sleeping citizens rather than contained them to slumber. Pausing several moments to confirm our covert success, we directed our attention towards the back of the laser printing store, tucked away towards the end of the row of shops. Nikki entered the store through the exposed window to undertake her computer whiz business. Everything she did had a veil of pregnancy around it, and I was afraid for her and her unconfirmed, unborn child. I couldn't understand computers like she did, so all I could do was skulk around in darkness, watching for danger, feeling like a complete asshole.

My eyes were falling heavily upon my cheekbones until Nikki's shoes shuffled along the concrete path.

"Hey, everything is done." She held up her bag as she strutted past me.

"Even the –"

"Yes, Cooper," she called out in a muted voice, "Even the pregnancy tests."

"You got more than one?" I inquired.

She turned around, waiting for me to catch up. Her twinkling hazel eyes narrowed towards my own.

"I've seen enough rom coms to know what I need to do. I have three, if you must know." She threw back her head, dark brown ringlets of hair launching like a rocket into the air and crash landing upon her shoulders as she continued her brisk walk.

I needed to tread carefully with Nikki, as well as the path back towards the car. So, I gave her a simple answer with no hint of my bitter tone.

"Okay, no problems." I bit my tongue, hoping her little onslaught had not gathered any more steam. We drove back to Uncle James's house without a pinch of aggression between us. Upon returning, no one batted an eyelid. Most of the gang were engrossed in an action movie, squashed together on two separate couches. So, we went straight to my en suite bathroom. I, of course, waited on the bed while Nikki literally peed on a stick.

As I twiddled my thumbs, waiting for Nikki to come out, a couple of people ran up the stairs. Zoey burst into the room with Dani and Kasey at her heels. She jumped on top of me, throwing her arms over my shoulders, kissing me hard as I fell back onto the bed.

"Hey, you, where have you been?" she laughed. "You missed a decent movie night!"

Dani and Kasey leant against the doorway, beaming.

Before I could answer her, the toilet flushed, and Zoey's eyes darted to the bathroom door, narrowing as she attempted to develop x-ray vision, as well as her healing powers.

Nikki revealed herself; a forlorn figure draped in a hopeful and euphoric sheathe. I knew it before I looked into her eyes that she was pregnant.

Zoey attempted to scrutinise me for having Nikki in our bathroom, but her gaze shot towards the pregnancy test. Like a grenade, it dangled dangerously in Nikki's hands.

Nikki's eyes were swimming with unrelenting emotion, and it spilled out as Dani and Kasey rushed forward to take embrace her.

"I'm pregnant!" she wailed, sobbing uncontrollably, the test exploding as it fell to the floor.

Zoey totally forgot about kissing me, about the animosity she may have felt for Nikki being in our bathroom. She ceased our comfortable embrace to console Nikki. I picked myself up off the bed and watched the girls form an unbreakable circle around Nikki, soothing her with their "don't you worries" and "everything will be okays."

I assumed that the words meant nothing — rather, the arms around her meant a whole lot more. I shifted my weight on the bed, observing them until the circle opened up like a lotus flower, planting her in the clay pot of security and warmth, assuming the position in the garden bed next to me.

Nikki looked at me with her red, raw eyes, and I smiled, placing my hand on hers, squeezing it before retreating my hand to my lap as the girls crowded around her.

I went back to twiddling my thumbs.

"Babe, I don't quite know why you're crying, you know? You are pregnant, and you are in love!" Kasey explained.

"I'm happy. I am, but where is Matty? I can't contact him. I can't even tell him that we will be . . . parents. This is not how I pictured it," Nikki wailed, clearly distressed.

"Tonight, Nikki, we will celebrate this as normal people would. We will have some wine . . . while you watch us, of course, reminiscing about how your life will never be the same again!" Kasey bellowed a shrill but excitable laugh, and the girls joined in with her.

"I'll get the wine," said Kasey.

As she started toward the bedroom door she pushed a forefinger into her rosy cheek, "Um, where is the wine kept again?"

I rolled my eyes. "It's in the garage, Kasey."

"Be back soon." She flashed her brilliant white teeth, winking at us all just before she drifted out of the bedroom. The light would often frame her in the most complimenting of ways, dazzling us all with her beauty as she left the room.

I resumed my position at the head of the bed while the girls talked over Nikki's feelings and reassured her with the same sentiment over and over, adjusting the words and phrases.

Now bored and annoyed at the way the girls had interrupted my own comforting session with Nikki, I studied the room's features again. Cooper craved to be the heroic comforter, the seemingly sensitive shoulder to cry on, but this was one of those times when the opposite sex could not fathom the hardship.

My thoughts turned to Kasey.

"I'm just going to see if Kasey needs help with choosing a suitable wine," I muttered.

They didn't even hear or notice me as I trampled out of the room.

I clambered down the stairs. Zack and Pj were chatting in the lounge room, so I raised my eyebrows in an absentminded greeting.

Pj poked his tongue out at me as I made my way towards them.

"How do you do, sir?" Zack inquired, imitating a posh English accent.

"I'm fine, squire. How do you do?" I replied, matching his old English impression.

"We're just chillin' and talkin' shit."

Our fake posh conversation was now over, it seemed.

"Oh, that's nice, and I guess you're feeling better, then. I've noticed that, over these past few weeks, you've been a little . . . well . . . angry," I replied.

"Yeah, I guess . . . but you know I've always had a bad temper," he said matter-of-factly. I recalled times in our past when people would upset Zack so much; he would bruise and swell his knuckles, punching trees.

"Yeah, but it's been a little more," he continued. "You know, it's about time I admit that all my family is dead, all my nieces and nephews, my poor Mum. Goddamn, it's all fucked up." I watched him as he talked. A vein in his neck crawled like a gluttonous slug towards his forehead, pulsating and exhaling the embers of rage.

Pj being Pj turned to Zack and embraced him in a bear-like hug, tight and sweaty.

"I love you, man. I love you!" Pj growled and rocked him to and fro.

I couldn't help but laugh.

Zack shrugged him off and walked past me towards the toilet door.

"I'm gonna take a piss." He grabbed the door handle and yanked it off the door. He seemed confused as it hung defeated in his right hand.

Pj and I looked at each other and burst out laughing.

"The Hulk is back!" I shouted across the room.

Zack turned to me, shrugged his shoulders and pushed the door in.

"Ohhhh, that guy needs to do some yoga or something," Pj advised.

"Yeah, he's an angry little man; let's keep an eye on him, alright?" I stated.

"No worries, mate. That's why I've been doing my bit every afternoon." He winked.

At that moment, guilt seeped into my veins like a tapeworm exploring new terrain. I had been concentrating on the plan, the gifts, on my relationship with Zoey and my own issues with self-assurance and disquiet but neglecting the connections I already had.

At that moment, more than anything, I just wished for normality. So many people speak of their desire to be famous, to be a hero, to change the world. It meant more to me to resume a video game with Zack, to play a sport with Hayden, Craig or Gil, to watch Zoey from afar at a party, to get drunk with Kasey and sing karaoke – just to have things the way they used to be. It was so easy to wish and to imagine parallel universes, but the stark reality gets you in the end. It terrorises the vibrant, shimmering mirage that clouds your vision, glazing over your wondering stare.

"Alright bud, I'm gonna grab a drink of water." I broke away, that guilty feeling clouding the moment and sending me into a self-reflective state once more. If I wanted the old times, then I would have to give up what I had with Zoey. Would I ever do that now?

I filled up my glass, peering out of the window into the unknown disorder of the backyard. Before I knew what was happening, Mia had grabbed the soft skin behind my arm so hard it made me flinch and pull away. I let go of the glass of water, and it rolled inside the sink, water gurgling into the drain. She was pulling me violently towards the garage door.

Her eyes were ablaze with dread and concern. "Mia, what the fuck is this –"

The last vision of Uncle James's intact house was of Whitey, staring patiently and calmly out at the pool in the backyard. The TV was on, playing a beer advertisement.

Then a menacing shadow materialised upon the plate glass, growing larger with each millisecond that ticked by. The shadow became a body, catapulting through the window, shattering it into millions of delicate pieces.

Whitey covered his head, as glass rained down upon him and the lounge. As the clone, who wore night vision goggles and a helmet, landed on the almond floor, he turned to face Whitey and raised his gun. I screamed out as Mia dragged us into the garage and shut the door, leaving me sprawled on the cold concrete floor with an open mouth and a million questions.

# CHAPTER 30

Mia thrust a gun into my shaking hand.

"No time to explain."

I had seen enough, and I guess she had, too. She damn well knew about this.

"What was that noise?" Kasey shouted, a bottle of premium white wine in her hand.

My head reeled up towards her direction. I picked myself up and ran to her. Bullets slammed into the garage door from out the front of the house, smashing into the wall behind me as I fled to Kasey's side.

The bottle of wine crashed to the floor as a bullet entered her upper thigh. She cried out in shock and fell upon several arrow boxes in the corner of the garage.

"Mia, get over here!" I yelled desperately over ricocheting bullets darting like flies throughout the garage.

Kasey raised her leg into the air, clawing at the atmosphere and fanning her wound, yelping like a wounded animal. Mia ran past the car's bonnet and cowered behind the shelving unit. No more bullets penetrated the steel garage door; the clones were probably inside the house by now. But my attention was focused on Kasey's leg, bleeding profusely. She gritted her teeth against the wrenching pain, but it wasn't enough to contain her whimpers. I ripped my shirt off and gave it to Mia. She created a tourniquet over the wound to stop the bleeding.

Turning to the wooden garage door that led into the interior of the house, I noticed distinct movements. Pointing to the door, Mia understood my warning, clasping her hand over Kasey's mouth. Shadows under the slit of the door rocked back and forth like branches in a modest wind, confirming the presence of danger. I cocked the gun as the door handle bent inwards, carefully contaminating the darkness of the garage with suppressed light.

As soon as I laid eyes upon a target, I fired off a shot. The designated target cried out and crumpled to the floor. It didn't move. I waited for at least a minute before I dared to move.

I whispered to Mia out of the side of my mouth.

"Make Kasey comfortable, then come with me."

"What?" she squealed.

"We have to check on everyone else, Mia!" I almost shouted, scowling at her.

Mia recoiled her head and her expression faltered. I didn't release my stare.

"I need her to be safe from whatever may still be in there." I pointed towards Kasey and then the house.

"Go . . . with him," Kasey croaked.

Mia turned to Kasey before she followed at my heels. "Babe, we'll be right back."

Kasey turned on her best charming smile as we left her bleeding and pained in the corner of the garage. I stepped over the clone, dormant on the garage floor, pushing back the oak wooden door to enter the house. The windows were smashed to bits, with glass littering the floor. I turned my eyes towards the lounge, seeing a body sprawled face down on the beige pillow. It was not Whitey. However, it was the clone that smashed through the window. The last time I had seen him, he was poised to kill Whitey.

The TV had several bullet holes in the LCD screen, now dotted with RGB spots in cracks where the bullets had splinted but had not completely smashed the screen. The fiery winter wind blew the white lace curtains in the kitchen like a scarf flailing in a gentle storm. Mia was hot on my trail as we skulked around the kitchen into the hallway, tiptoeing around the broken glass and bullet casings.

A piece of glass cracked behind me, and I spun around, about to release a bullet into another clone, but it was Desh. In a moment of such terror, I nearly dropped everything and burst out laughing. There he was, coated head to toe in a black uniform, shaved head, a full beard on display, poised threateningly with his bow and arrow.

"Desh, what the hell?" I exhaled, relieved.

He ignored me but lowered his weapon.

"Where are the others?" he asked.

"We were just thinking the same thing."

He turned to Mia.

"Thanks for the heads up. I think I killed seven before anything went down but at least four made it through."

"Hey!" Desh and I both turned, ready with our weapons.

But it was only Pj. Though he held a bloodied knife.

"Zack and Whitey are in the lounge room," said Pj, pointing to the room just five metres ahead, "but both of them have been shot."

We rounded the corner and saw four bodies. Whitey was perched up against the lounge on his stomach, holding a pillow over his shoulder. Zack sat up against the lounge between two clones. One clone had a sliced throat, the other held his own head in his hands. Yes, he was actually holding his own severed head, blood still squirting, muscles and tendons protruding from his jagged, wounded neck.

Even I knew, as I stared at the open wound, that the damage inflicted, had not been caused by a knife. The fragments of flesh lay exposed like a blossoming iris in the midst of a generous spring. My eyes darted to Zack. He looked up at me, almost drunk with the loss of his own blood from a wound I couldn't see.

"I don't know what happened." He laughed hideously as his eyes slinked back towards the ivory carpet.

His hands were the only parts of his body stained with blood. Had he ripped the head off the clone? It couldn't be.

Pj interrupted my thoughts. "Listen Coops, they need Zoey. Is she upstairs?"

"Ah, yes," I replied, my voice hoarse, my thoughts still plaguing my responses.

I cleared my throat. "Yes, they should be upstairs . . . at least, I hope –"

"They are all in the bathroom. I told them to hide in there together just before I went out onto the roof."

"I'm sorry, you what?" I spun towards the Robin Hood Desh.

"Well, Mia told me what was going to happen, you know, an ambush, so I took to eliminating as many as I could before they could complete their task."

I was stunned into silence. I turned angrily towards Mia. Her eyes swam with sorrow and sadness, but she was certain she had made the right decision, with Desh possessing the power to aim. But why did she tell Desh and not just yell throughout the house?

"Whatever, I'm going to grab Zoey and get this shit sorted." Pj turned and bounded up the stairs towards the girls locked in my en suite bathroom. Zoey's embrace seemed the perfect place to reside, but I, instead, turned to Mia, continuing my penetrating search of her emotions. I didn't get far. I heard the worst possible combination of sounds I'd ever heard.

First, it was Kasey's muffled scream emanating from the garage, "Coooooooper! Helllllllllppppppppp!"

And then the unmistakable sound of a gunshot. I turned and ran blind. All I wanted was for Kasey to be okay. I had left her alone, bleeding and anxious. Rounding the corner, I spotted the clone we had mistaken for dead, perched upon his elbow; a menacing gun levelled out in Kasey's direction. My stomach lurched, and my heart sank. I came down hard upon his body and swiftly moved the gun to his temple. I caught his wry and tantalising smile just before I shattered his skull into hundreds of brittle pieces across the garage floor.

I lay halfway across the limp body after the blood had sprayed into my eyes. Bringing my knee up to my face, I wiped the blood away across the dark trousers, contorting as a necessity. My eyes found and focused first upon Desh and Mia's shocked faces in the doorway of the garage; however, they were not looking in my direction. My eyes followed theirs. Nothing was okay. Kasey was not okay.

She was still slouched over the boxes of arrows that she had fallen upon originally. The glass bottle of wine had now fused with the blood she had lost, creating a sombre orange puddle that lapped at her twitching ankles. One hand rested against her chest as she spluttered and choked on the blood that gathered in her throat. I tripped and fell as I attempted to stand up, smashing my head onto Dani's car bonnet. My own pain was the last thing I cared about. Shaking off the clumsy blow, I called out Kasey's name as I fell to my knees beside her dying body. I looked her over from head to toe and raised my arms above her delicate body, unsure of where to rest and which part to attend to first.

Kasey's blue eyes were dazed and large under the weight of her fighting spirit. She expelled timid tears, and they trickled down her cheeks. As she attempted to speak, it was evident that her breath was apprehensive, amidst the strain of staying alive. Kasey grasped my hand with desperation, begging me to stop the pain.

"Cooop —"

She couldn't help but release a sickening choking sound into the dead stillness of the garage. My own eyes stung with angry tears.

"Stop talking, honey," I breathed, saliva and nasal mucus dripping down my face. "Talk to me with your eyes." I was fighting my tears as I clutched her hand.

As her eyes darted from her wound to my face in frantic bursts, she tried to speak to me as best as she could with those eyes. *"Cooper, I'm scared. I'm so scared."*

I placed my hand on hers, stemming the flow of blood from her chest. Her nose ruptured, as a trail of blood caressed the top of her lip. A soft calm washed over her eyes for a small moment.

*"Just focus on killing them and staying alive. Promise me you won't stop until they're all gone?"* Her pupils, wide and worrying.

Spitting bits of saliva and tears onto her dying face, I whispered, "I promise."

*"Cooper, I'm so scared. Don't leave me please. Hold me. Hold me. This feels wrong."*

I knelt down on the arrows, the glass from the wine bottle digging into my knees, but I didn't care. Her blood swirled into my skin, sending the last of her life into me. The smell of wine made me light-headed as I placed my shaking arms around her body. She started to cough, and her hand loosened pressure on the wound on her chest. Blood leapt onto my face from her mouth. Her chest wound became a fountain, pushing and prodding to release her soul from the body. Sound returned, and Desh was yelling into the house, "Bring Zoey here now, bring her here!"

Kasey was dying.

Mia had slowly moved to my side, an open palm clasped around her own mouth, spilling tears onto her small black shoes. I could feel Kasey rise and fall to a quicker pace and tempo, squeezing my hand harder and digging her nails deeper into me as she did. Until suddenly, all resistance left her; all her energy faded with a final hissing breath.

I arched my head up, her blood dripping from my face as I tried to shake her back to life.

"Kasey!" I yelled. "Kasey!"

Her limp, defeated hand fell from her chest, where she had attempted to close the wound. Blood flowed down her torso in heavy spurts until it was obvious that we would never get her back. Desh pushed me aside, and I let myself fall into the shelving unit and crumple into a sobbing heap. My voice was pained, my mind hazy with the grief and utter shock that had latched itself to my broken soul, in a horribly real and ruthless moment.

All my friends were there now. Slow motion returned. Everyone was yelling, crying, pointing, shouting. Zoey's face was white; she was barely able to stand. She flopped onto the floor. They pushed her hands down onto Kasey's wound, and her eyes went into the back of her head. A jolt pierced her body and she cried out in pain. Zoey fell back into Zack's arms, but he pushed her back onto Kasey. She tried once more, with a pained effort. She slapped her bloodied hands onto Kasey's wound, screaming for it to work, but this time, she was shocked by the repulsion of death and passed out on the garage's cold floor.

After crawling to her, I embraced her, sobbing.

Zack yelled, "Why the fuck did she just pass out! Wake her up, Wake her up."

"Leave her alone, you prick! It's over!" I screamed through bursts of tears.

I held my love, Zoey, close to me, and I cried into her shoulder. There was no way I was letting her go. Desh took Zack by the arm and led him away towards the boot of the car. I heard him throw things, smash things, but that faded into the background as he moved further away from us. I poked my head out from Zoey's shoulder and glanced around at the horrible scene. Mia had her hands clasped inside Kasey's as she sobbed. Nikki and Dani were locked in an embrace, crying hysterically. Whitey was slumped against the car's bonnet, running his hands through his hair. Zack and Desh leant against the shelving unit now, speechless. Zack's fists were clenched. Gil's fringe covered his red raw eyes covered by his fringe as he stood over Kasey's body, sobbing and uttering words of prayer. Pj paced anxiously, hovering between Kasey's body and the car.

We were all broken. Our perfect family was no more. Kasey was dead.

# CHAPTER 31

Streetlights fizzed past our car like fireworks on a still night. We crammed inside Dani's car, sullen grief binding us in silence. As I imagined Kasey's body in the boot, coldness creeping over her, I thought of what had transpired in that last hour.

We had all gathered in the garage, stunned into solitary notions of sorrow due to Kasey's sudden departure. But human brains do not rest when confronted by emotional trauma; they continue to tick away like the dusty hands of a grandfather clock. Collectively, our brains decided to fire synapses targeted solely on safety. We realised that, if clones had stormed the house, it was a certainty that there were several more waiting in the distance for a confirmation that our group had been taken down.

There was no other choice but to collect Kasey's body and rest her in Dani's boot alongside the police uniforms and a deflated spare tyre. We closed it like a casket, shielding her from our hopeless stares. It took no less than five minutes to gather what we needed from the house, leaving so many creature comforts behind. Zoey rested her head on my shoulder, shivering with exhaustion, grey because death had reached inside of her. My hand held tight to her knee, procuring warmth from her presence and soothing my own aching heart. Whitey sat opposite me while Nikki took the passenger side next to Dani. In the rear-view mirror, I caught a glance of Uncle James's house shrinking away in the background, darkness coating it in dark, hateful varnish. Clone neighbours stood on their lawns, watching us drive away, unsure of what to do.

As we drove along the main road, army trucks threatened to expose us on the other side of the unbroken lines. However, I, for one, couldn't care less. My thoughts were all about death. The brevity of life was tainted by its defiance. Sure, in comparison to the inhabitants of the earth, one single life may have been fleeting, but death shrunk the timeline of lives and moments.

We required the comfort of an available sheltered area for a night, and the car took us far enough, searching riverbanks, shopping centres and car parks. Ultimately, we settled on Morgan King Reserve, which provided cover in the form of playground equipment.

As we pulled alongside the vacant bush area surrounding Chalk Farm, both cars expelled our bodies into the night. I wandered towards the gathering of the group, dragging a weakened Zoey beside me.

"What are we going to do from here?" Gil asked, as sirens blared, and helicopters dominated the air space.

"I say we ditch the cars and move ahead on foot," Dani declared.

"Where will we go, Dani?" Zack whined, exhausted.

"They know our cars, it's far too risky," Dani pleaded with a desperate inflection.

"Dani, I'm sorry," Zoey started, drained but coherent. "We're not going to leave our cars here and run off when we have no idea where to go."

"Do you have any suggestions?" Nikki stepped in front of Dani.

"Yes, I do, as a matter of fact." Zoey scowled at her.

When Zoey had told us where she thought to go, it made a lot more sense than abandoning our only form of transport. Reluctantly, Dani and Nikki put their tails between their legs and submitted to a new plan.

"What about Kasey?" Nikki whimpered.

The insects left us with the only soundtrack for contemplation. At that moment, I felt the call to bury her: to let her go and give her peace.

I started towards the boot. "Well, who is going to help me carry her?"

Zack, Gil and Whitey stepped forward and followed me.

"Wait, we're going to bury her here?" Nikki was mortified.

"Yes, Nikki, it has to happen this way." Desh put a soothing hand on her shoulder, she bit her nails and turned away. Dani gave her comfort, and she took it willingly.

No doubt everyone felt the grief reach in and squeeze their core. No doubt everyone felt guilt for leaving her here, but it was here, or it was nowhere. We just couldn't predict where we would be in the next hour, so she deserved to be laid to rest somewhere acceptable. An open reserve would have to do. Promising myself that I would return and give her a service that she deserved allowed me to continue to bury her that torrid night.

I flipped the latch to reveal Kasey's forlorn figure, drained of life in the boot. Her wavy blonde hair strewn carelessly across her right cheek, falling atop pursed lips that separated at the moment of her death. Her body was flaccid, arms flayed against the spare tyre, knees bent inward, speckled with glass stars and dried blood. I held back tears, biting my bottom lip too hard and lifting her into the cool night. We carried her towards the edge of the park and laid her on the bare earth.

We had no access to a shovel, so I called Pj over.

"Find a shed close to here, and bring me a shovel," I requested sharply.

"Why me?" he started.

"Because you can somehow run like the wind," I said matter-of-factly.

"Fair enough."

With that, he left remnants of his musk: sharp notes of sweat, leather and bergamot hanging in the air as his body departed. It took no less than two minutes for him to return with a shovel in his hands.

"Took longer than I expected, but here you go."

He thrust it into my hands and walked calmly towards the group, gathered atop the faded play equipment. I took it upon myself to dig the grave and, when anyone attempted to help me, I pushed them away. It was as if I thought this one last act of kindness would soothe my soul. It didn't. But it gave her a bed to rest her body in as her spirit soared into our bleeding hearts, keeping her with us forevermore.

I greeted the early morning, digging a grave, thinking of the last promise I had made to Kasey. A promise that would ensure I would do all that I could to survive long enough to see the clones abolished. For the final thirty minutes, I accepted Zack's help. He did it with ease — too much ease. He must have located the power of super strength within himself. Thoughts turned to guilt once more, guilt about burying her in a temporary grave, guilt about her actual death. Why hadn't I double-checked that the clone was dead? Why did I leave her all alone? I knew even then that those questions and the remnants of guilt would haunt me for the rest of my days.

As the sun rose into the sky, I buried a sweet friend into the ground and said my final goodbye to Kasey. Dirt and gravel kissed her face, tainting her beauty in death. I found a yellow flower nearby and took its life to give Kasey a final gift. My friends stood beside me as the shovel lay slack against the earth. I wiped my eyes on my shoulder sleeve as they each placed a flower of their own on the disturbed earth. Zoey nestled into my right side, her hand resting against the inside of my elbow. I wanted only to be back in the house, living our normal and comfortable lives, where Zoey and I could hold each other for hours without any repercussions.

As I strayed several thoughts to Uncle James's house, I started to question how everything had gone wrong. How did the clones know we were even there? We didn't leave any clues, did we?

Sure, there was that one clone who had witnessed the death of Mrs Ugdashi One, as he or she peered out of their house. We had killed the clone cops and set their bodies alight – was it then? Had someone identified us at one of the trips to the shops? Life as we knew it led our minds to paranoid delusions, to conjured fears that seemed far from the truth. But really, who knew?

Well, Mia could know, but her power had proven to let her down somewhat. How could she not have seen Kasey's death? Had she seen all of our deaths and attempted to save the majority of us by sacrificing Kasey? Even poor Zoey, using her fingers to draw delicate circles on my arm, looked utterly defeated. She had discovered that her power had no effect once the heart stops. We had never noticed that before.

As humans, we realised that our powers had limits, too. We definitely weren't comic book superheroes searching for a successful migration to the 3D reality form. Our powers were not strong enough to cause maximum damage to the entire cohort of the clones. Kasey's death had been a perfect example; we each had the chance to use our powers to defeat the clones, but we only managed to kill a few and save the majority. But nearly was not good enough because one of us was dead. It could have just been me, but it seemed as though we all believed that Kasey should've been saved. It was clear to me that even some resented members of our group, like Zoey, who couldn't heal her, like Mia, who didn't see what was about to occur, like Pj, who could've run to her and beaten the bullet. I didn't resent anyone. I knew that each of us would have done anything we could to have her back. I guess I only resented myself.

The sun brought light to people who didn't want to be found. It brought clone children into the park environment to frolic with liberty and careless smiles: two things that had been taken from us. As the sun became an ally to our enemy, we walked with purpose towards the car, intent on moving elsewhere.

Gil navigated us to the township development site, where several new houses were being built, in an area called Lakewood Grove. The houses in the quieter streets were nearing completion, which meant that we had exclusive access to concealment.

No clone neighbours had moved in yet. Zoey's idea was a good one for temporary cover.

Pj and Gil fiddled with the locks for several minutes, trying to get us inside. Zack calmly walked over and punched through the door handle. A hole in the dark blue wood materialised, and the conquered door bowed down, as its king passed by. We opened the automatic garage door to store the cars, so as not to raise suspicion. As we crammed inside the house, the smell of adhesive and timber was everywhere; the slick white tiles were only laid in the kitchen area, so we each chose a spot on the rough concrete to congregate. Some of us cried, some of us searched the half-painted ceiling, staring at holes where new down-lights needed to be installed, some of us just . . . were.

I rested my back against the brittle wall and cried. My arms held Zoey into the cage of my chest. Her tears crept through the cotton bars of my shirt, staining my skin and leaking into my soul. She hardly ever cried, so I knew that this was unbearable for her: a limit to her power and the failure of saving Kasey. That is how I fell asleep for the first time after Kasey's death. I didn't dream at all. I ingested the darkness and willed it to fill the empty spaces in my heart so that no other love for anyone or anything would take the killing intent away.

We endured the new dawn with puffy eyes and aching hearts. There was no way of acquiring any food or supplies to sustain us, but we had every intention of figuring out a long-term plan in the development houses.

Gil stood at the window, looking out into the abandoned street that usually bustled with tradesmen. A Sunday was the day of rest, even for clones. I sidled up next to him. He closed his eyes, incantations peppering his breath. When the whispers died, he turned to me.

"When in trying times." Gil turned his palms up towards the heavens and winked, smiling warmly.

"Any advice or still radio silence?"

"Very cheeky, Cooper, very cheeky." His hand squeezed my shoulder, a gesture he did often. "How can I help you, by the way?"

"Nothing specific. I guess I'm just doing the rounds and seeing how everyone is."

"Well, to tell you the truth, my faith has been tested more times this year than I can count. And now, sweet Kasey . . ." His voice wavered.

It prodded the tears that now sat permanently behind my stare. Memories flooded me. Cabbage rolls, blonde ringlets brushing her cheeks, beaming smiles at the airport. Swallowing the sadness with a large mouthful, I continued on.

"It must be hard, Gil. I'm not sure how you continue to stay the course, especially with everything that has happened."

A long pause settled the space between us. He often reacted in this way, gathering thoughts to elicit a more dignified response.

"I have to search for whatever the truth is. People will always say there is a bigger purpose, but right now, I don't care about that. I'm not looking to find any justification so that I can be okay and have some sort of solace. I'm hurt, and I'm trying very hard to understand and see past the grief to find meaning."

Gil tried to give me his heart and mind, pursuing truth, but I pushed for a consolation prize. "But, if God is real, why would He let them kill Kasey?"

"He didn't. A clone took it upon themselves to take her from us," he said.

"Okay, but why can't He intervene? Why can't He save someone who doesn't deserve death?"

"I wish that a miracle occurred. I sometimes get so angry that a sweet soul like Kasey doesn't survive, while other people out there, who might be the scum of the earth, get a free pass. It's the beauty and the horror of free will. Anyone can decide to use their interactions for good or evil."

"So, then, why do we praise God when something goes right and absolve him when shit goes wrong?"

"If we continue to ask why we are lucky, we will never appreciate the life we have . . . if that makes sense. So, in the same way, we can't bury ourselves in the tragedy of it all and drive ourselves crazy, thinking why or why not. At the end of the day, our capacity to understand everything as human beings is limited. We can't reach beyond what we know to rope in these answers." Gil ruffled his fringe and brushed it behind his ear.

"But that seems weak to me, like, we just have a 'get out' clause that says, 'We are not divine, so we cannot understand the divine way.' So, I guess every shitty thing that happens is a truth so beautiful we will only comprehend once we die. It basically gives God or religion a hall pass, fucking around on us whenever He or it feels like, until death comes," I argued, agitated.

"Well, I guess in that regard, we view things similarly," Gil reasoned. "But I'm not bitter about it. Faith makes me a better person; it gives me direction and comfort, and if that's so bad, then send me to hell, I guess." His laugh was tired and strained.

Every justification felt hollow to me. But it soothed Gil. So, it was important that I didn't push too hard. My own pain and anger didn't need to claim another victim.

"Sorry for the intense conversation. I just wanted to see how you saw things. I'm just finding it hard to accept all of this."

"I welcome the discussion. Anytime we do this, I am able to strengthen my beliefs because I feel like I can justify it to you, so please don't ever apologise. The main thing though, is that we find something that works for you." The shoulder squeeze returned. *Had his hand even left my shoulder?* I wondered.

"As for Kasey, one day our souls will reunite again. Maybe we will talk about what we shared here on earth, or maybe we will look forward to the form of eternity that we can explore together. Either way, the truth will reveal itself when I'm ready. Until then, I'll try my best to honour Kasey's legacy by embodying some of her strengths and hoping that in death she has seeded new gifts to us all."

A hint of a smile etched itself into my stone-like face. Kasey had a special ability, after all. She would have liked that. Although Gil had something that worked for him, as I squinted to the depths within myself, I wondered what would work for me.

Death had a tendency to crash the party of my life on several occasions now: my father during my formative years and my close friends as I leant into adulthood. Still, the formula for dealing with grief was not written on parchment, rolled into a bottle and buried in the sand, waiting to be unearthed. The complex chemical construction of each individual ensured its custom delivery was hooked into veins, spreading throughout the body like a virus. Some viruses, as we know, can wreak havoc on a host while it can make a dainty dent in others. It is just luck of the draw. With grief, it appeared to be no different. I seemed to stay a little longer steeped in the black tea of depression.

I had several moments alone during the day to think of some of the events that transpired at Uncle James's. It felt as though Mia had learnt the art of deception and manipulation with her power. Never before had she been one to lie or shy away from honesty, but I was upset that Mia had divulged her knowledge to Desh to search and kill the clones, rather than letting us all know that we were in danger. Our powers had given us certain types of authority over given situations, and evidently, we weren't perceived as equals anymore. I noticed a significant development in our group dynamic, where our powers formed various alliances.

Mia and Desh's bond anchored them. Mia believed that Desh held the key to saving our existence. I don't know why it had become that way because my belief was that we needed all our powers to work at the same time. Segregating ourselves was the furthest from my mind in our quest for dominance. The people in our group involved with divisions made it all the more dangerous, with the possibility of a mutiny and severe communication breakdowns. Any type of disruption to the group formation threatened our lives.

As I thought about divisions, I realised that even I was guilty of this. I was involved in Desh's plan with Gil and Nikki, excluding everyone else from that knowledge and input. Searching the living room in the barren house, Mia and Desh talked in whispers. Zoey, Nikki and Dani had embraced in a trio of strength, while Zack, Pj and Gil were talking over future plans. Whitey had become withdrawn from the group after the incident.

Whitey: that lucky son of a bitch. How could he have survived the clone attack? He must have been struggling with the realisation that he had to kill a living being. I could see the gears in his mind, churning and filtering the horror he had witnessed in the last twenty-four hours or so.

"Are you alright, mate?"

My question startled him out of his internal back and forth.

"Don't sneak up on me like that, man." He bit into the fresh sourdough bread roll. The sunlight pushed through the kitchen window darkening his freckles, as he scratched at the growth of coarse black hair on his cheek.

"Whoa. I'm just checking on you. You seem a little on edge."

The surrounding air settled a little, his shoulders relaxed with a couple of deep breaths. "Sorry, Cooper. I just can't believe what happened. I'm not strong enough for this."

"You took down a clone who had the drop on you. You're definitely strong enough."

"Man, luck spared me. I had an empty beer bottle on the table, and I just used whatever I could to knock him down. I'm not like you guys. You are all obviously more special than the rest of us." Whitey's forehead wrinkled, and he adjusted his black eye patch, as if he needed to wipe away a tear.

"Whitey, we're all just doing the best we can." I moved forward to embrace him; he stiffened against me, almost unsure of what to do. Some guys were not comfortable showing affection with one another, but I was not one of those.

His hand tapped me awkwardly on the back, so I let go. He mustered a pained smile and said, "Thanks, Cooper. You're right."

I soon forgot about Whitey as my eyelids became a casket, closing and sealing me in a deep slumber. That was the first night in a long while that Zoey didn't snuggle up with me, as she kept close to the girls.

As my dream materialised in shimmering segments, I searched around the room. I was in Whitey's house, and I was not alone. Gus stood behind the kitchen bench, leaning forward with his elbows on the granite table.

"Cooper, you need to see what you have been ignoring for so long," he declared.

I tilted my head to the side, wondering what he meant, as he gestured towards the kitchen floor. I followed his finger, walking around the glossy white kitchen bench. The smell of disinfectant was thick in the air. A body lay on the ground, sprawled against the bottom cupboard containing what was most likely, the pots and pans. Blood had dried in splatters across the white laminate above his head, where a bullet hole was evidently the cause of death. However, this was not the most interesting part of the body. The eye sockets were both empty, containing only traces of the retinal blood vessels and the optic nerves flailing in the wind like the tail of a kite.

I was confused as to who it was, but I suddenly pieced together the familiarity of the kitchen, the room and the sunken body. It was, of course, Ben White's body. This didn't make sense at all. I knew it was a dream, of course. Any dream with Gus was a guiding light for what to do in reality, so, naturally, my eyes sought him.

"Why have you brought me here?" I asked.

"I needed to show you what your eyes have failed to identify."

I stared once more at the decaying corpse, unable to understand.

"Your power works in conjunction with the eyes," Gus sang to me, pointing to the empty sockets on Whitey's face.

"They cloned him with his real eyes, therefore, you cannot see that the Whitey that has become part of your group is indeed a clone."

I shuddered. It couldn't possibly be true. But then again, couldn't it?

I started to recognise several signs that proved that there was something wrong. How had he survived the onslaught at Uncle James's? How had the clones found us? Why was he always asking me about our powers and our plans?

With my mouth agape, Gus was concerned with a different sense: sight.

"Open your eyes, Cooper, and wake up before it's too late," Gus pleaded.

# CHAPTER 32

**M**y open eyes squinted into the darkness of the house. Rapid breaths echoed off the half-painted walls. My dream startled me, but I was now faced with the crippling anxiety of reality. Ants were nerves crawling all over my sweating body, their pincers prickling my flesh. My hands were weak and clammy; my chest was constricted and pulled tight. My heart beat against my skin, furious and determined.

Was this anxiety making me paranoid?

Hearing faint scratches across from me, I didn't think so.

At once, adrenalin took hold of my body, abolishing the presence of the arrogant anxiety. I spun around in the enveloping shadow of the night, snatching up the gun that lay beside me and flicked the torch switch on in one swift movement. A beam of light penetrated the seething darkness, shining in the direction of where the noises had originated.

He froze in the paralysing spotlight.

"Drop it, you piece of shit, or I'll shoot you dead!" I yelled.

The torch illuminated my worst fear.

Whitey held Gil by a generous clump of his hair, pulling it back so tight that his scalp turned white. Whitey pressed a large kitchen knife against Gil's throat, trembling and toxic. It was clear that Gil was half-asleep; a vague look had spread across his pale face, eyes squinting towards the light emanating from my torch, but groans soaked in fear splashed the soundscape. I stood slowly, still pointing the torch and gun towards them. Gasps and screams erupted from the waking bodies in the house, but I only had eyes for that counterfeit piece of shit: Whitey's clone. I yelled again, as rage and malice pulsated throughout my body, emphasising each and every word.

"Put that fucking knife down, or I will end you."

Perhaps I was so consumed with rage that I never even noticed one of our guns in his other hand. I only had a moment to contemplate what to do: possibly harm Gil trying to kill Whitey or wait to see what Whitey would do.

The torchlight lit up his functioning eye, and I swear something inside him went dark; his soul flipped a shadowed cape across the hope that I had desperately held, suspended in Gil's beating heart. I had waited a moment too long. He didn't seem to think about his actions. He tore across Gil's neck in one swift movement and flung the gun at the torch in my hand. As the torch greeted the cold, hard floor and pointed into the kitchen, darkness consumed the space where Whitey and Gil had been. Scraping and scratching replaced the silent stand-off, and an almost unnatural fizzing sound tore through the air.

I fired two shots in the darkness, smashing the windows, bullets ripping through wooden frames. I ran blind with hatred towards the sounds of Whitey's feet shuffling outside the house. Oxygen seemed thicker and harder to digest as the rage took hold of my being. We were both outside, but he had stopped across the road and turned to face me as I, too, halted on the edge of the gutter. The moonlight highlighted his evil, cryptic smile and penetrated into my raging existence. I shot a bullet across the road, and it slammed into Whitey's shoulder. Crying out in pain, the force sent him reeling backwards. He ceased his gloating immediately after, but turned and ran into the night laughing.

"Pj! He's getting away!" I screamed.

After precious seconds of waiting, I fired into the distance and screamed, only to find a hand close around the gun, clicking in frustration. I turned around, and it was not Pj. It was Zack.

I didn't cry this time.

He searched me, but I had become a madman. He motioned to hug me, but I pushed him aside with a violent outburst, screaming "fuck" over and over. It was a guttural sound, a primitive rage sullied by heartbreak. I brushed past Mia, who stood in the doorway gazing out into the night. I didn't look at her. I didn't want to look at anyone.

As I walked into the main room where we had been sleeping, the group had formed a circle around a body on the floor. I squeezed into the circle and stared at Gil, rage simmering inside of me. It could have been the brilliance of the torchlight shining onto his face, but he was nothing more than a ghost drenched by the tsunami of death. His eyes were open, imploring our stunned faces. His throat had been ripped apart by Whitey's blade, a cut so deep that it exposed his trachea. The dark burgundy waterfall no longer coursed down the traverse of his chest, it had gathered into a placid lake around the mass of his head.

I collapsed onto my knees, kneeling in his blood with Zoey, who had attempted to save him, her hands stained with his blood. I passed my own hands across his eyelids, shielding the moonlight from his eyes for the last time. My head lolled onto my chest, defeated. We remained there, silent and sobbing for several minutes, until Pj walked through the door.

"I heard gunshots. Is everything –"

The sentence died in his mouth, just as Gil had died before our eyes.

I had never felt this angry before, and that was saying something. I knew my temper was tragic, but this was something else, something beyond control, even.

I didn't even turn to face him.

"Where the fuck were you?" I hissed.

"I . . . I . . . was out," he stammered.

"Is Gil . . ." he started.

"Yes, Gil is dead," said Desh with careful composure.

"How did it happen?" Pj was agitated and nervous.

Zack answered, "Whitey —"

"It was a clone of Whitey," said Mia.

"Whitey was a clone? Why didn't Cooper know?" Pj asked, turning towards me.

"Because, Pj, my power works with both eyes. The one that Whitey had was his real eye," I bellowed, frustrated at my power more than anything else.

"Fuck." He breathed and paced the lounge room's perimeter.

"Are you going to tell us where you were?" Nikki asked through free-flowing tears, Dani cradling her.

Pj hesitated. "I was doing some . . . research."

"Don't give us this cryptic bullshit, Pj. You left us alone and, well, now look what has happened!" I screamed, my voice hoarse and breaking.

Mia attempted to silence the problem. "Cooper, you don't need to —"

"Shut your fucking mouth, Mia. Don't tell me what I can say or what I can feel. Gil is dead and now, we're compromised 'cause Whitey is free," I snapped.

"You know what, Cooper? I'm not going to take this. Honestly, fuck you." Pj stormed off into the kitchen. Mia, hurt by my words, followed him while the others stayed around me, afraid of my unapologetic anger. Zoey rested her hand on my leg. My eyes saw her gesture, but I did not bury my toes in the sand of adoration. I, instead, let my hatred burn the book of hope in the extensive library of my life. Pages leapt into the air and carried me off into the corner of the room as the remaining group tidied the blood from Gil's body and the floor.

"Hate to say this, but we need to leave," Dani said as she surveyed the damage to the room and our egos. Desh walked towards me, Pj and Mia trailing behind. I kept my bulging red eyes hidden from their sight.

"She is right. Gather up the rest of the stuff and . . . Gil. We've got to get going. Who knows where Whitey is headed right now and who he is about to tell," Desh commanded.

Before I knew it, the group was placing the second body of our friends into a boot. I did nothing to help. I stared from afar as thoughts collided in my head. I was sulking, and my friends knew it but good luck to anyone who scolded me for it. I was jacked up for a fight. Even if it wasn't anyone's fault, it wouldn't stop that feeling. Zack came and pried me away from the corner of the house as tenderly as he could. He said nothing, and he didn't need to. Words were not his strength, but presence was his dictionary. As I slumped into the backseat of the car, I rested my head rested upon the cool window, and my eyes searched the dead of night. Though, it was Gil and Kasey who were dead.

My hope dangled on a branch in a decimating storm. Hope that I would survive long enough to perhaps one day start a family, finish my university degree; be somebody. But it was pointless to deny death entry into the theme park of my life. Death was ever changing, so age and height restrictions, or longer or shorter lines, wouldn't matter. Death had many ways to threaten the population of the park.

Hope hadn't stopped Whitey from embracing who he was, from ruining the life of yet another one of my friends. Wasn't it funny how humans were always in denial, always wishing for the positive over the negative? Our lives were bound by denial and death: medicine gave us denial, imagination gave us denial, a positive outlook gave us denial. We kept denying we would die until we were truly faced with death. We made up a lie about heaven to satisfy parts of that denial-labelled fear. But it all ended the same way.

My friends in the car slowly edged away from me, doing their best to ignore the wrenching rage that was so clear in my eyes and written boldly in the lines on my face. Is this what it was like to be Zack? It would be more difficult to let the anger subside because, this time, not even Zoey's touch could help me; not even love itself could stop the hate from closing its hand around my heart. On a battlefield, with your heart as a weapon, those consumed by love often survived and persevered. However, the hearts that were raped of love by a malice so deep and profound would stop at nothing to obtain vengeance.

I removed the pin from the grenade in my heart and let it rest in my hands, awaiting the obliteration of all my hatred. It was all about the heart now and it was the only real weapon I had left.

# CHAPTER 33

We remained in a quiet street, waiting in our car. My head no longer rested against the back window. Instead, I positioned it towards Zoey and Dani in the front as they ran a play-by-play of what we needed to do. A timid light bulb twitched inside my mind, burning and bursting as we drove in the darkness, searching for a place to stay for the night. I was not thinking of the option to fit the present moment. I was searching for the days and nights that would soon come. Wouldn't we all be in a better situation if we were able to regroup for a longer period?

In the cul-de-sac of the more developed suburb next to Lakewood Grove, only one house appeared deserted at that hour of the night. Desh and I navigated our way around the house as per instructions from Zoey and Dani to search through what appeared to be the bedroom window.

An older-looking man slept peacefully under floral patterned blankets.

"Is he a clone?" whispered Desh.

"I can't tell, man. My power works with the eyes only . . . and his eyes are closed," I responded, disheartened.

"So, that's why you couldn't identify Whitey, right?"

A flash of his distorted face filled my mind for a second, a memory that would haunt me forever. I narrowed my eyes into a scowl, remembering Gil, lifeless in the boot of the car. I often had the capacity to dwell on such images, creating anxiety and restlessness. Shaking my head, I let the images fall away into the murky waters of the past. Anxiety would not cloud my desire for safety that night.

"C'mon, I have an idea," I said, dragging Desh into the street once more.

I opened the car door where Pj sat.

"Get out, Pj," I calmly demanded.

"What do you want from me?" he said in a bitter tone, crawling out of the passenger's door.

Desh interjected. "We need your help."

As we crept around to the side once more, we informed Pj about what we needed him to do.

The three of us arrived at the backdoor and attempted to pick the lock. This was not the moment for Zack's strength; we needed subtlety. The door's metallic body rattled in the static night air, a hushed warning that we needed to summon our thief skills to achieve the element of surprise. But the handle came down without resistance, and the door eased open. Relief was in my eyes as I nodded at Desh to move inside. We crept past what seemed to be the combined kitchen and dining area, littered with boxes of microwave meals and discarded cans of cat food. We continued on down into a hallway connecting to the main bedroom. The walls of the hallway were a mosaic of this man's life, ranging from youthful faces in black and white photographs to colour portraits with weary faces and broken dreams.

As we stood at the entrance to the man's bedroom, we noticed the faint outline of an en suite bathroom. Desh and I headed towards the bathroom carefully and as silently as our bodies and the floorboards would allow while Pj sped off towards the kitchen to gather utensils.

Aside from the heavy breaths and the deep snoring from the old man, Desh and I made it to the bathroom unscathed. We got comfortable inside the shower, fully clothed, of course, as it gave us a perfect view of the old man snoring peacefully through a crack in the bathroom door. We left it open enough to watch Pj initiate the plan.

Pj crept into view; in his outstretched hands, he held a bottle of balsamic salad dressing, as if it were a trophy celebrating his lifetime achievements. And just maybe, as all the years of pranks and irresponsibility cultivated into a single act of heroism, why wouldn't he have seen the salad dressing bottle as a symbol of his accomplishments?

As he leant over the old man, he emptied the contents of the whole bottle onto his unsuspecting face and sped off into one of the other rooms off the hallway. The old man yelped and groaned as he came to grips with being the victim of one of Pj's infamous pranks.

He bolted up, wiping his eyes and asking the darkness, "Who's there? C'mon, you coward. Show yourself!"

As the minute passed, he grunted inaudible complaints and curses, coughing and spluttering as he discarded his bed covers and headed towards the bathroom. *He is quite nimble and fleet-footed for an older man,* I thought.

He opened the door while Desh and I stood firm behind the faded blue shower curtain, waiting patiently. Standing in front of the bathroom mirror, he wiped his face clean, his wrinkled and scarred hands obstructing our view of his eyes. I couldn't tell if he was a clone or a human being.

"What has happened here?" he mumbled to himself.

As balsamic dressing dripped down his face, he extended his bent fingers towards his nasal cavity, sniffing the substance in an attempt to uncover what it was. His brow was creased, and a confused look emerged on the reflected glass of the mirror as his hands moved to the tap.

I stared into his eyes, and sure enough, tentative wisps of green erupted from within his pupils, until they became brilliant, glowing empty sockets. I nodded at Desh, but as he raised his gun equipped with a homemade silencer, my anger forced its way through my spiritual wall.

"Give me the gun, Desh," I said from my mind to his.

His head turned, and he looked at me, confused.

"Give me the gun," I repeated, this time firm and definite.

He cradled the gun in his hands, but he was reluctant to let me take his sleeping child away. His eyes were cloudy, yet his shaking hand raised the gun towards my outstretched palm. I snatched it before my power wore off, then I let my control go. Desh was himself again. The pistol murmured as it released the prized last bullet into the back of the old man's head. Blood splashed upon the mirror like a war between a gumboot and a puddle, glass shattering chaotically into the sink. The washbasin, garnished with delicate pieces of brain.

What was left of his body crashed against the edge of the bath, slumping towards the bathroom mat, oozing thick bursts of blood onto the yellow and brown tiles. Desh snatched the gun from me, my eyes twitching at the inclination of the killing. At the release of my anger onto a clone, I stood there, consumed by vengeance.

Pj burst through the door.

"Geez, man. Could that have been any louder?"

I brushed past him without saying a word, with the intent on bringing the rest of our mates into the haven and running away from a confrontation with Desh. Opening the front door, I was careful not to appear conspicuous to fellow neighbours or others who may have been patrolling the streets. I motioned for Dani to park the car in the remaining spot in the garage and for Zack to park the station wagon across the street. The cool night air did its best to soothe me, and my anger was slowly subsiding, replaced by a gnawing guilt.

Was it because I had killed a clone to replace the life of Gil? I didn't think so. But it sure had done something positive for my grieving process. But not the guilt. I had used my power for the wrong reasons. I had not only abandoned my spiritual soul, but I had let down the memories of Gil, Kasey, Gus and my whole family. As we gathered the rest of our supplies and filed into the house, Desh and Pj cleaned the bathroom. The overwhelming guilt drenched me more than ever, as they were cleaning up the mess I made. Often, a sense of lethargy and apprehension overrode my guilt. I had often forsaken the effort to help Mum or Brooke clean dishes and tidy up the house, but I needed to make an effort here, I needed to work on changing for the better.

"Can I offer a hand?" A weak smile humbled my face.

"No, it's fine." Desh avoided my eyes.

I walked away, following Dani and Mia to give Desh some space. They carried the load of our personal items into the house, while Nikki, Zoey and Zack searched the house for anything conspicuous. We also searched one another; conflicting emotions seemed to pulse throughout us all. We couldn't bring ourselves to speak, for words could not purify the tainted situation. The division of rooms encouraged us to communicate once more. However, it was a matter of saying, "Here, you have this one, and you have that one."

Nikki and Dani took the master bedroom; the second bedroom was left to Zoey and me. Desh took the study while the lounge room housed Mia, Zack and Pj.

As Zoey moved off towards the bed, she whispered to me.

"Babe, are you okay? Come to bed with me, please." Her eyes pleaded innocently and pitifully.

I wasn't okay. She was the only one that could open me up. But could I tell her the things that I didn't even want to admit to myself? The way I craved vengeance, the way I wanted to kill these living beings for the things they had done to the people I loved. I'd watched enough documentaries to know that, in various habitats, animals will kill animals to survive and to live on. It was nothing sinister; it was nature. But somehow, it felt different as humans fighting the clones.

Could I explain to her the way that grief had rooted itself into my core, twisting my tear ducts into deformed sculptures of hatred and horror?

I couldn't let weakness take hold of me; I would repress and attempt to deal with something without the help of someone else.

"No, I won't go to sleep yet," I muttered.

As I turned away, I saw Zoey's shoulders sink towards the floor of her expectations, and her eyes glistened mournfully. A nuclear bomb of despair obliterated any twinkle of hope they once possessed. I was attempting to leave my emotions behind to deal with the clones, and if I wavered for a second, would I be able to continue to do what I did? Did love weaken me?

I walked towards the study to talk with Desh. I needed to clear my mind of guilt, at least.

"Desh, how are you feeling?" I inquired tentatively.

"Cooper, I don't know what happened in there," he muttered, pointing to the bathroom, "but I don't want to ever feel that again. I had no control and . . ." he shook his head. "Just don't do that again, no matter how shit you feel." He peered into my soul.

"I'm sorry, man." I was genuine. I felt like I had sold my soul. "It won't happen again."

He nodded. "Now, to business."

"Well, yes. Whitey knew we were planning something, and he knows what we look like now." My voice, strained.

"I've already had time to think this over, and I think our decision not to tell everyone has proven to be the best idea of all." Desh brushed aside the beige curtain and stared into the street.

"So, we need to continue with the same plan?" I asked.

"Of course, there is no way that Whitey could've known what we were going to do," he replied, turning to face me, resolve burning in his stare.

"Okay, so do you think we should communicate it to the rest of the guys now?"

"After we bury Gil, I think it's time they had something to work towards, rather than living in fear and living for nothing but running."

It was clear that we were now on the home stretch. After apologising once more, I wished him a goodnight.

I squeezed in next to Zoey, accidentally rousing her from sleep.

"You okay?" she asked in a husky voice.

"Yeah, I'm fine," I lied.

In fact, I knew that I rarely communicated my feelings willingly, but wasn't a partner meant to be different?

"You can tell me if and when you ever need me, you know," Zoey whispered.

Maybe this was the moment that would make our relationship seem real. After all, your partner is the person you are meant to confide in, the person who is meant to know your hopes, dreams and fears. Up until that moment, our relationship was the only normally progressing aspect of my life. Day after day we got stronger, knew one another better and became comfortable in each other's presence.

"Zoey?" My weak and broken voice appeared so unrecognisable in the small, dense room.

"Yeah?" she replied, turning to me, resting her hand on my leg underneath the blankets.

"Can we just lie here and not talk, please?"

Zoey didn't need to answer. She rested her head on the top of my shoulder as my arm carved a path underneath her neck. Her slender arm reached across my body, choosing one of my ribs to rest upon. She squeezed me, sending her love throughout my body. I closed my eyes tight, fighting back tears.

My heart soared with love into the night air, as it twinkled with the death of my friends and as it glistened with the malevolent face of anger that had unwillingly become my own face. I flew with my heart that night, spreading wings that were burnt by the heat of hatred. Right then, I knew that love held the true power: the power to save, to heal, to see, to feel, to know, to give strength and to provide hope for something more. The love I had for Zoey gave me enough strength to show her my weakness. She became my tissue, absorbing grief and providing me with a resolve to continue.

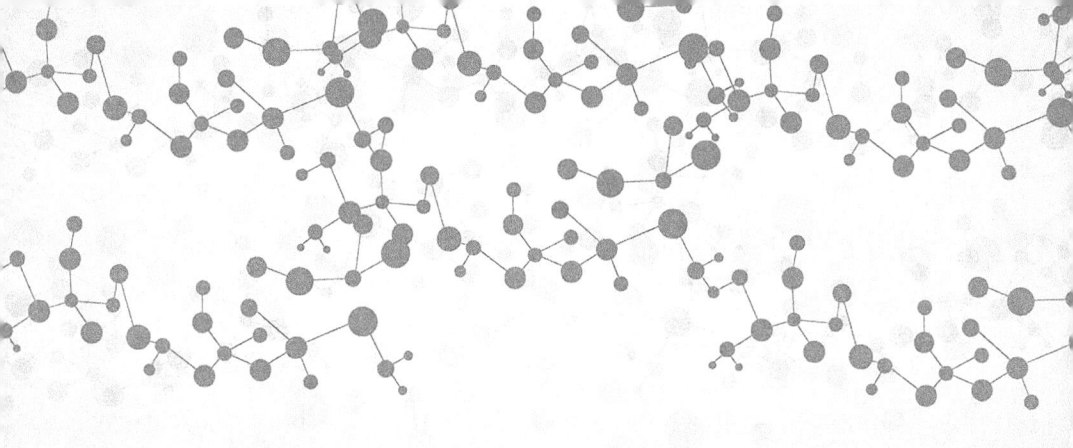

# CHAPTER 34

I walked into the backyard in the morning, employing several of my friends to combine their physical strength to dig a grave for Gil. It was shallow, but it was enough to shield him from the horrors of the world and prepare him for the beauty of what he believed in: the promise of a heaven.

As some of us finished our breakfast, consisting of fresh bacon, eggs and toast in tense and sombre silence, one of the most disturbing events of the last month occurred. Pj, Zack and Mia walked into the kitchen carrying their backpacks.

Pj spoke first.

"We're leaving," he said.

"What do you mean you're leaving?" inquired Zoey.

"I mean, we're going, and I don't know what else to say."

"I think there is a lot more to say," remarked Desh, perplexed.

"I'll speak on behalf of the boys. We're sorry guys, but at the end of the day, I know that Zack and I need to leave with Pj for anything to move forward. Things are not working with us anymore, and I think some of us need space from one another," reasoned Mia.

"Yeah, but I thought that sticking together was what we needed, especially after all this," cried Nikki, pointing to Gil's fresh grave in the backyard.

"I was leaving no matter what, 'cause some people don't see eye to eye with me." Pj dangled a fishing line right in front of my face.

I knew this was directed at me, and I took the bait.

"Well, if we knew what you were up to, maybe we could help one another, but you are so cryptic about it all. So, how could we possibly believe you are doing the right thing?" I yelled.

"You are just blaming me for Whitey's getaway. So, maybe, it's better if I'm gone for good, then you can't blame anyone but yourself," he spat back.

"What does that mean?" I hissed.

"Well, we've all done something wrong, haven't we? I wasn't there in time. Zoey couldn't heal Kasey or Gil. You couldn't see that Whitey was a clone all along!"

"Fuck off, Pj. At least I was here, not doing whatever you were doing."

"If you must know, Cooper, I was figuring out how to get into the base, since you and Desh were discussing little secrets amongst yourselves! Why is it okay for you but not okay for me?"

"It's okay for me 'cause I never abandoned my friends in search of anything. I was always here, working for a greater cause."

"Yeah, well fuck your secrets. I'm out."

Pj started to make his way out the front door as I stood.

"Where the hell are you going, Zack?" I yelled, my eyes burning into Zack.

"Dude, just calm down. I'm going 'cause I don't want to leave them alone. It's all sweet; we'll keep in contact," he reasoned, squeezing my shoulder.

"How, Zack? We don't have any phones." My tone was condescending.

"Mia will see, and she will know when we need to meet up again." He smiled a weak, apologetic smile.

Zack was my best friend. He was leaving me to make sure other people were okay. He was meant to worry most about me. These selfish thoughts clouded my mind. Zack hugged me, as I stood there, rigid and fuming.

*I'll meet you in your dreams,* Mia whispered with her eyes then kissed my cheek and followed Pj out the door.

The remainder of the group gathered on the welcome mat, farewelling them as their car drove off down the road.

"Fucking pricks," Zoey muttered as she turned back inside.

I slammed the door and escaped to the privacy of my room.

If only Gil was alive, he would provide me with the faith to get through any situation. If Kasey was here, she would make me realise the important, simple things in life, like living day-to-day, smiling and laughing. But they were both dead, and we were in this situation because they were gone.

I punched the wardrobe door, letting out a groan of frustration as my right fist met the wooden obstacle. A small, splintered dent revealed itself as I drew my fist back towards my body. The skin had broken away, leaving bone-white flesh and slowly but surely, tiny specks of red pierced the surface. Blood formed a pool, overflowing down the back of my hand and fingers. I didn't care for my own blood. Instead, I wanted to spill the blood of every single clone.

They had done this to us. They had torn our friendship apart.

I turned towards the bed, burying my body in a blanket grave in an attempt to shed the feeling of anger that festered in the pit of my stomach. This was my life now: how fucking depressing.

Time could administer control in any given situation, and it had sought an adversary in change. They were joined at the hip, barging through life, through people, through friendship groups and redirected futures with just one moment.

Before this situation took place, Pj and I had never fought, yet there we were: locked in a disagreement over something seemingly insignificant but horribly existent in that specific chapter of our lives.

Change had taken the best of life from us. As we grew older, we lost our high school friends to engagements, to unplanned pregnancies, to weddings, to different lifestyles, but Zack, Pj and Gus had remained resilient with a strong bond. Change had never threatened our friendships until now. The death of many, the introduction of clones into our lives, the constant threat of injury or death and the emancipation from our parents through incomprehensible means.

Pj's betrayal, in my eyes, could've led to frustration that my own power could not stop Whitey from infiltrating our group. No matter what Pj said he had accomplished for the group, I never would have left us alone. I never would have left us without letting someone know what was going on. When selfishness arises in a person, you know that issues with doubt and trust soon follow. It's selfishness that drives us to do things that only glorify our actions, neglecting the group but satisfying the individual.

This is why I believed it to be a betrayal. His actions had jeopardised the group, and the group was all I cared for. They were my family.

Turning to the bedside table, I scanned the old man's belongings: a couple of bottles of medicine, an adventure novel, a watch.

I stopped dead at the watch and reached out to pick it up. A green flash spread across the surface, and I immediately recognised the watch from a dream I had.

*"As a reminder, you will soon find a timepiece. Take it and wear it to remember that time is always against you."*

*Gus stopped and looked straight into my eyes. I could not see into him. An invisible force stifled my power.*

*I had so many questions for him, but the words suffocated at the back of my throat.*

*"Do it for all that has been lost, if you won't do it for yourself."*

282

*He turned to his left and blew out the candle.*
*Pitch black.*

In a weird way, what Gus said seemed more relevant now than ever.
*Do it for all that has been lost.*
Pj, Zack, Mia, Kasey and Gil.
They were all gone in some way or another.

Strapping the watch to my arm, it beeped to confirm that it registered my core temperature. This seemed like a fancy watch for an old bastard. I wondered what else it could do. My search was cut short as a faint knock on the door rung out. I called them inside, expecting it to be Zoey. I knew she would be on my side.

Instead, Desh walked inside with Zoey.

Zoey came forward, kissing me and put her arms around me as I sat on the bed.

"They are in the wrong, Coops. Don't worry, I'm always going to have your back." Her voice was strong and decisive.

Petite in stature, Zoey roared with the ferocious strength of a lioness. Love gravitated towards her fierce, beautiful intensity. As I so easily crumpled into a mess, there she stood, resolute and supportive all in the same breath. In her strength and in her faith, I drew out those very qualities within myself.

She smiled her sweet, comforting smile. "I'll leave you to it." She turned gracefully, leaving Desh and me alone in the room.

"Cooper, I think we've got to do this as soon as possible," he declared, thrusting a newly washed police uniform onto the end of my bed.

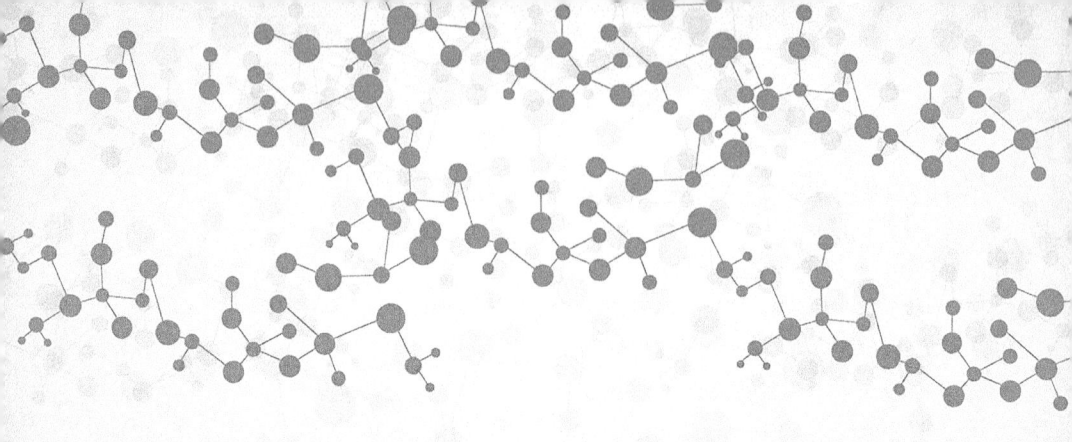

# CHAPTER 35

W e drove through the police station gates, the uniforms rigid with starch, sticking to our sweating bodies. We looked different to how we appeared just one week ago, when Whitey murdered Gil in front of our eyes. Our beards had grown significantly, our eyes had narrowed into a complex, reaffirming stare, filled with resolve and determination. My short hair was bleached blonde and horn-rimmed glasses adorned my eyes. Desh had shaved his head with a razor to the skin. A bristling, dark moustache quivered underneath his nose, and he shielded deep, brown eyes with sturdy black sunglasses.

My restless heart pounded against my chest like a caged animal, defying the rules of containment. I watched Desh as he drove, seeing into him and identifying the trepidation in his eyes. This was as crazy as we could get. We were driving into the heart of the enemy, doing as Whitey had done to us: infiltrating the clones to gain an advantage.

How many times had we already cheated death? How many times had we let our simple desire for normality override the need to remain safe?

As our group diminished with the death of several friends and irrespective arguments, life and even the potential threat of death itself, appeared as a genuine possibility. But we had to ride into this one, fearless and valiant in our pursuit of normality.

"Hey, guys, you must be . . ." A sturdy, tall young man ruffled several papers.

"Officer McMahon and Officer Redhi?"

Desh spoke clearly and confidently, offering his hand to the young officer, who had a fresh buzz cut and a clean-shaven face, highlighting a strong jaw and a will to match.

"Yeah, mate. How are you doing?"

I nodded my head towards him, not in the mood to be excessively polite.

"Nice to have you on board, fellas. I am Lieutenant Harwood. Come follow me, and I'll show you to your office."

We followed him as he walked and chuckled. "You have some higher ups looking out for you, that's for sure. You have an office on this site for a month or so, and you don't even have to report to anyone here. That's very rare for a couple of officers on secondment."

"Yes, well, your department is held in high regard, especially in the search for terrorists. We have heard that being inside this fine institution will benefit our own investigations."

Desh attempted to appeal to the young officer's ego.

"Well, she's a good gal, the chief – runs a tight ship."

"Oh, I'm sure she will make us feel like one of the crew, right?" Desh humoured the young officer.

Lieutenant Harwood chuckled with the sweetness of a warm cherry pie.

"Well, it's a pleasure to have you guys here. Those little assholes need to be caught." His welcoming tone was obscured by his intent to, ironically, capture us.

Before he left, something caught his eye. "Oh, you got one of those watches, too?" He gestured to my wrist.

I recoiled, surprised. "Um, yes, I'm not too good with this technology stuff, though."

"I know the feeling. Do you receive those special updates?" He appeared like a bubbly child on Christmas morning.

"No, I can't say I do," I stammered, still confused.

"Oh, here." He took my arm. "Just swipe across the screen and tap twice, and it should activate the notifications . . . Okay, there you go. All set," he declared.

"What will I receive now, exactly?" I asked, searching him for information.

"All the latest developments from head office, latest terrorist rumours, tips on how to pretend to be human. I'm surprised you didn't get trained on the equipment," he quipped.

"No offence, but I usually tune out when we learn about these gadgets. I've got plenty more important things to worry about," I replied condescendingly. Desh shot me a grave look.

"No worries, McMahon. Look, I'll let you get back to it." Harwood motioned to leave.

"Thanks, Harwood, for helping me out. You're a good man," I added, with a hint of appreciation in my stare. Desh and I walked into the office, and Harwood closed the door upon our little operation. The door became the mouth of the beast, and we were firmly fixed within the belly.

Desh smiled uneasily. "Too easy, Coops — apart from the 'I'm better than you' routine."

Just as he uttered those words, the chief came in pacing to and fro, never once acknowledging the courtesy of eye contact.

The blue uniform was tight across her belly, buttons groaning to keep everything contained. Large sweat patches appeared as she moved her arm upwards to adjust the hat sitting lopsided across the top of her head.

Beady eyes glowed with the hint of self-importance. Puffy lips held the gloss of a recently sipped can of lemonade, swishing in her swollen hands.

"Right-o fellas. We all know why we are here. The people up top are keen for some further inroads into the 'Evil Eleven' – or is it the 'Evil Eight' now? I can't keep up. I guess it still has a ring to it." Her voice was in a race with her words.

We both nodded.

Her speed did not decrease.

"Anyway, here are your badges and service weapons, and on this induction sheet, you will find personal access codes to our facility here, complete with wifi, VR access and networking."

"Now I understand you won't be taking orders from me here. However, I would still ask you to inform me of what you are doing, so I feel like we're working together here."

"That sounds more than reasonable," quipped Desh.

As she turned to leave us in the cramped office space, she spoke once more.

"Oh, and just before I leave," she looked up at us, cheeks flushed with stress. "I checked in with Lieutenant White yesterday."

My spine tingled at the mention of his name. I tried to stifle my surprise.

"Lieutenant White?"

"Oh, surely you've heard the stories; he was the one who knocked off a couple of their numbers. I've received some of the reports that he has written; the revelations are crazy, something about them possessing some supernatural strength."

I looked towards Desh with a worried expression on my face that the captain mistook for being incredulous.

She thrust a folder of documents onto our separate desks.

"Here is all the information, plus all the other documents you request-ed with the plans of the base and all that other stuff. Just make sure you let me know if you need anything, but as far as I'm concerned, you have your mission. The rest of us have ours. We should do our best to concentrate on that, don't you think?"

She searched us.

The green haze enveloped her plump figure.

"Sure," I said. I had to contain the hatred in my own eyes from seeping down my chest and onto the floor and roping her being into oblivion.

"If you ever wanted to visit Lieutenant White to improve your investigation, he is up at the base where you'll be conducting your interrogations anyway. Although, he may be busy with the introduction of phase two quite shortly." The excitement in her voice could not be contained.

We had at least two weeks before the killing of innocent humans began for phase two. We had to finalise our attack before then.

Desh replied this time. "Yes, we'll be having a significant hand in the phase two developments, Chief. We'll do our best to shake the hand of Lieutenant White for all his efforts."

"Well, good luck with that," she chuckled, "He is the closest thing we have to a celebrity around here! I'll leave you both to it."

She slammed the door. Desh and I looked at each other, resembling the same person: a steely gaze, intent on completing our job there.

When I walked through the door, Desh excused himself and went straight to bed. The sting of raw onion and sizzling olive oil was strong, even in the hallway. Dani was in the kitchen prepping meals for everyone.

"Playing mother, are you?" I quipped, standing at the kitchen bench in front of the chopping board.

"Make yourself useful and pass me the chopped onion while you're there, son," she said without cracking a smile.

I moved around to the stove and put them into the pan myself.

"Sous chef extraordinaire?" My voice was playful.

"No, no, just a delinquent child trying to impress his mother."

The onions sizzled, disguising my timid laugh.

"What's on the menu, by the way?"

"It's not going to be as immaculate as anything Kasey used to put together, but it's just a quick vegetable stir fry."

"Hey, don't downplay it. If it wasn't for you putting in the time to do this, we wouldn't have much of anything."

Dani's smile was as warm as the flame on the stove.

"Listen, I'm glad you're here. I was wanting to talk to you about Nikki."

"Yeah, of course, go ahead." A flicker of concern flashed across my face.

"I know you've been busy with all the plans and the whole saving-the-world thing." Her tone was light, but we both knew the grave nature of our task. "But just keep another set of eyes on her, and if anything seems a little off, just step in to help. You know how needy she can be, and Matt used to pick up a lot of the slack there. Now that he is . . ." She double-checked the area, making sure Nikki was not close by. "Now that he isn't around anymore, you and I might have to step up."

Dani had already stepped up in a huge way. Any pregnancy concern that Nikki had resulted in Dani searching for books online and reading tips and tricks to help. Dani would find an acceptable alternative to any meal that Nikki didn't want. I realised I hadn't been doing enough, wrapped up in my own issues.

Sure, there was the "saving-the-world" thing, as Dani put it. But there was also exploring the exciting world of love and lust with Zoey. There was also the late-night anxious thoughts that would inhibit my sleep. There was also the resentment of our other friends who left us in the midst of a war. Everything I had to deal with was, of course, valid, but not leaving any room to help others was of great concern to me. It was, in fact, a huge disappointment, and it didn't feel like 'me.'

I nodded. "You're right. You're absolutely right. You've been a rock, and I've been nothing more than an overhanging branch. I've got to do more. I'm sorry."

"Cooper, stop." Dani reached her hand around to the middle of my back, and her eyes found mine. "I didn't say you weren't doing anything. I just know she values you and, well, you are very good at making others feel at ease; kind of soothing their troubles."

If you were a good friend, you needed to be there even when you weren't at your best. I had lost parts of myself to the siren songs of hate. My eyes were red with revenge, and it had stained my heart. I needed to remember that we didn't do this for glory, nor to stoke the fires of resentment. We did this for love. Love lost, love gained, love that was to surely come.

"Now, give me those carrots, please." Dani pointed at the bench.

I delivered them to her empty hand.

"I'm going to do more." I nodded my head with a determined stare.

"Look, just the carrots are fine. Relax, buddy."

We both started laughing, playfully pushing each other and seizing a positive moment amidst the darkened times.

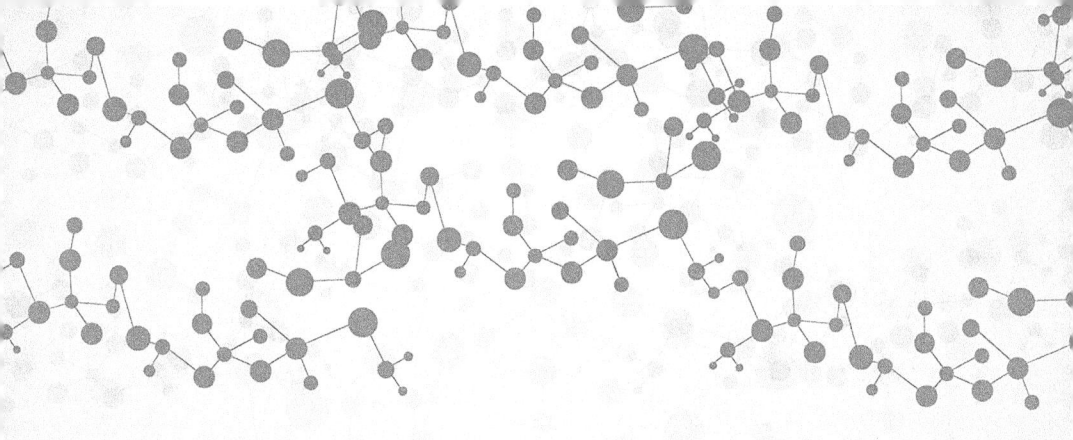

# CHAPTER 36

Each workday of the tiring week, Desh and I, sporting unfamiliar new looks, ventured into the bruised and beating heart of the enemy. The clock tower at the base was as imposing as ever, glaring down at us as we walked down the path to the holding cells. Whitey had become second in charge at the facility, but he was locked inside an ivory tower, a hero to the clones. We didn't need to concern ourselves with him yet. Our focus was on visiting the person who had started this all.

Wasting away as a prisoner in the holding cells, it was difficult not to harbour some resentment towards the man. He was one of the most intelligent and well-regarded scientists on the planet. But he had lost his way.

The Australian government, who attempted to establish themselves as leaders in clone and genetic technology at the time, approached him with promises and an offer he couldn't refuse. But the government's true intention was to develop a cloning programme that would be used to harvest organs for affluent humans and build an army of expendable fighters. The government was oblivious to just how bad it had gotten.

Since the press conference several months ago, his speckled silver hair had turned a ghostly white and lay frazzled and slovenly upon his head. The genius in him didn't handle the months of isolation well.

The first day we visited him, his drooping eyes arched up. A large crack ran through the centre of his bent oval spectacles. "What do you want now?" he croaked.

"Gordon Grey, I presume?" I asked, mustering all the confidence I could.

"Is that who I am? I forget these days." His reply was lethargic.

"Look, we don't have that much time, Grey. We need to discuss an urgent matter with you," I pressed.

"Oh, by all means, don't worry about poor old me, please 'discuss' away."

He threw his hands in the air.

"Have you heard of 'The Evil Eleven?'" I stopped suddenly and corrected myself. "'The Evil Eight' – I mean." A hint of darkness clouded my confidence.

"Of course, I have. You people come in here each and every day to ask if they're working with me."

"Stand up and approach us here please," Desh directed from behind my shoulder.

Grey obliged, frailty clinging to him as he limped towards us. He stood there, a man draped in shame and guilt.

I lowered my voice. "If you want to redeem yourself, then you will start by telling us everything that you know."

He scoffed and started to retreat.

"You'll do this because we are part of The Evil Eight."

Lowering his eyes towards us, silence fell upon the cellblock. He stared at the camera behind our shoulders and back at us. He whispered, poking his nose through the cold iron bars.

"You know they can see you. How did you even get through?"

"You'll be surprised at how much facial hair, some hair dye and a simple haircut can alter the appearance."

"This is a trap. I know it." The fear in his voice reverberated off the prison walls.

I had to think of a way to calm him down.

"I promise you, Gordon, that this is not a trap." I thrust my hand through one of the bars and offered it to him to shake.

He stared at it blankly. It was an overt "human" gesture, a gesture that he probably hadn't seen in a very long time. He clasped my hand, searching me for strength but found nothing that would transfer into him. Defeated and broken, he had no other choice but to accept that we were, in fact, his only chance out of prison.

"Okay, fine. I will do my best to assist. But how do you intend on breaking me out of here?"

"It's not that easy, Grey. We came here today to give you the opportunity to fix your mistakes by helping us first."

"How do I know I can trust you?"

I sniggered. "This goes both ways, Grey. We need to be able to trust you as well, and that means you need to tell us everything."

He seemed unsure.

"Look, we can give you an opportunity to think about it, and we'll be back tomorrow to see if you'll join us in the fight or if you're just too weak and settled on giving up." I did my best to manipulate an already broken man.

"I'm not weak. I just don't know if you can actually defeat them; there are way too many now," he protested.

"Just think about it, Grey."

And, with a sense of finality and assertion, Desh and I turned, leaving him grasping the cylindrical bars. Admittedly, I was worried about my tone with Grey. Was I too harsh on him? Would my attitude have pushed him into the arms of the enemy? I hoped that he would see reason and redemption.

Just as we emerged out of the prison building and onto the path towards the exit, an alarm pulsed loudly from where the cloning facility shone brightly in the afternoon sun. Fear choked me for a moment. Did we set it off? Had Grey turned us in already? We both put our heads down, focusing on getting out of the clock tower's gaze. Several clones ran past us towards the facility. One in a white biohazard uniform was coming in the opposite direction and bumped into my shoulder, nearly knocking me over. He didn't even stop to say sorry. Clones were absolute assholes.

"Don't worry," Desh said, "at least we have a clear path out of the base now."

I looked at my watch beeping with notifications. *Disturbances in the cloning facility. Alarm. Alarm.*

Thankfully Grey hadn't outed us already. It was something else.

We got into our car, the sound of the alarm fading as we drove away.

Thankfully, Grey relented, but even though we visited frequently, it didn't subdue his agitation. The more information he divulged, the more anxious he became, worried about a negative outcome. Empathy swam in careful circles within me, staying at a shallow depth. The man believed he was doing extraordinary things in the name of science. Clearly an intelligent man, coated in naivety.

"All is not lost, though," he whispered to Desh and me, his eyes constantly darting from the cameras, to our faces.

He created beings with the best intentions, but he knew that, often, the best intentions led to the greatest failures. Grey had taken insurance against his own best intentions. The humble beginnings originated in Kota Kinabalu, Malaysia - where he worked on cloning the famed orangutans. Once he was successful, it wasn't long before he discovered the formula to replicating the human form.

The first attempt proved unacceptable as a severe mutation occurred, of which he was required to terminate immediately. Then, contrary to his own belief, the perfect clone emerged upon the third attempt. A true specimen: mirroring a human in extraordinary detail. There was, however, a noticeable difference between the clone and the human. The clone did not possess the memories from their original source, and this was because Grey had taken advantage of a loophole. Through long hours studying DNA coding and modifications, Grey merged magnetic components in the DNA double helix, in the place where their memories would form and grow. It was "our" failsafe against clones if they were to develop control over the human form.

A failsafe that would have grave consequences for the clones on a mass scale if it were activated. Poor, ignorant Grey initially enjoyed having an inferior version of himself around to teach science to, to absorb countless amounts of information and basically mould into the perfect version of himself.

When Grey's clone had studied human interactions and popular culture, he would often "help" Gordon Grey himself with female companionship. Grey's clone would present a smooth demeanour at an initial meeting, something that Grey did not possess. Once Grey's clone had taken the female to his bedroom, he would excuse himself to the bathroom where the real Gordon Grey would be hiding. Grey would then enter the bedroom as himself, to "close the deal." His clone would watch from the bathroom, resentment towards his mentor festering within. As well as learning the importance of their scientific research, Grey's clone was also trained by the army for hostile situations. Things went pear-shaped when Grey's clone had become curious of his origins and whether his existence was a means to an end. When Grey's clone's brain capacity development increased, thoughts of his existence and notions of existentialism were bound to creep into his mind. Upon realising that humans were to harvest clone organs and conduct further research, hatred of the human form began to boil over, until he himself conducted experiments by killing fellow human soldiers, replacing them with the same DNA code that had been written for his race. He brainwashed new clones into targeting humans as an enemy.

Before long, he had command of a large battalion and had locked poor Gordon Grey into a cell for life, condemning him by revealing the inner workings of his mind. Grey pleaded that the harvesting of organs had never been the true reason for his birth, but Number One or "The One," as he was affectionately known, would accept none of it. He wanted dominance; a trait that was so very human.

Our week with Grey had revealed much and brought some insecurities about the human race to the surface. We contemplated our own reservations about what we'd already done and what we were going to do. At the end of the day, one must acknowledge that the clones were indeed life forms in their own right. However, they did stand to threaten the existence of the human race. Even if they were made in our image and even if we didn't always show enough care and empathy for one another, we still couldn't allow our own destruction. Unfortunately, clones possessed the interesting side effect of wickedness, rendering them all malevolent in their actions and reactions. It may have been the high magnetic coverage throughout their brain that changed the way they dealt with issues. I assume it was like their evil side, as poor Dr Jekyll discovered.

There we were, apparently the deliberators of life, deciding who lived and who died according to our own moral code. Wasn't that how God was supposed to run things anyway? By ticking the boxes of those who had lived a "pure" life as opposed to the ones who were lustful, jealous and "bad to the bone." Things weren't as black and white as that. Zoey always told me that I was too obsessed with the extremes in life, and I seldom find the "in-betweens."

But life and its definition could never be black and white. Life is calculated through a collective process of understanding each and every being. The fact is, we are all different versions of the same species, and we are all alive, therefore "living." The defining characteristic of life is biology. However, the most important aspect of judging a life is calculating the reasons behind what we do. Most humans could accept harmony between other species and variations, until something threatened their own existence. By default, our intentions are merely to protect what we hold dear, and our innate desire or instinct is to survive.

But the clones were, with the capability to perhaps live among us as equals, repelling harmonious sentiments and prescribing violence and authority to obtain dominance. Effectively, the debate on judging life is done, for if you do not respect life in all its forms, then do you have reason to participate in life?

Each night, Desh and I returned home with a "burn" mobile phone recording of our conversations. The group would gather around, listening intently. When they all dispersed, I would spend some time with Nikki, helping research baby names, finding the best swaddles and discussing the best eco-friendly toys on the market. What seemed like only an hour each night made a huge difference to Nikki's outlook. Dani would walk past us and wink at me, or throw an exaggerated smile my way, but it was clear that it also meant something to her. Little did she know, it impacted me, too. The fight to preserve who I was, was just as important as fighting for our right to live. What was the point of fighting so hard for a life that you ended up tainting with hatred? The softer, loving part of who I was would not be claimed by the other fierce and unrelenting side.

The final night, we returned home to discuss what our plans should be from then on. Dani was at the head of the table, silent and waiting for us to sit down together. Something was going on, as I noticed several sheets of paper spread out before them, accompanied by pens, plans and stern expressions.

Desh and I kept our own council and took our seats. As Dani laid out the plans in front of us and spoke, our faces wore the same expression: relieved, determined and anxious, all in one. We had been waiting for this moment for countless months, losing members along the way, and the end beckoned. It would be one more weekend of restless training and planning before we would launch our final attack upon the clones' existence.

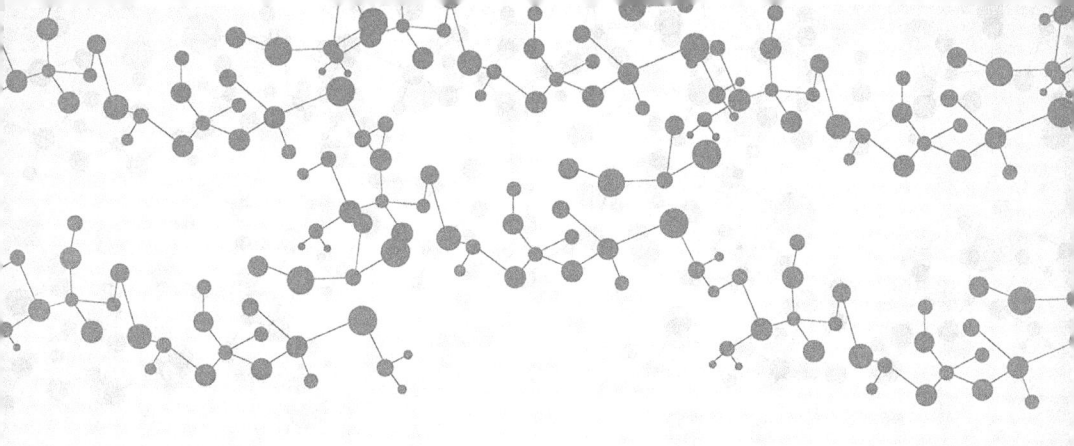

# CHAPTER 37

I looked through the lens of life as if I were Mia. The rest of the group shrunk as the car lurched forward, leaving them behind on the doorstep.

Guilt latched onto her heart, and the threat of tears called loudly. Instead of crying, she closed her eyes and searched for the future. Green and purple swirls spun around in the darkness, combining together to bring an image to light.

Straining, she cast a question into the fold: where do we go? Street signs flashed, roads and buildings flickered; a house in a field of trees shimmered gold. Her hand opened the door. Pj sped past her checking the house, her own sombre smile in the mirror to her right. This was their temporary home.

I woke with a start. It seemed that Mia was trying to communicate with me via dreams. I smiled, pleased knowing they were safe.

Little did we know it then, but often, the most careful preparation and meticulous planning could not account for fateful interference. Let's face it, the mystery of life itself: the inability to predict what would happen. Admittedly, we didn't have Mia to alert us of any danger in real time.

I lay in bed, struggling to sleep after making love to Zoey. Sleep was always much easier for her. She usually fell into a comatose state, rousing merely to scratch various parts of her body and grunt with unconscious annoyance. Turning to the wall speckled with decaying ivory paint, I fixed my eyes upon its shedding scales floating like autumn leaves towards the soil of the house. These were the moments where anxiety would eat away at me. My thoughts circumnavigating my pitiful mind, racing around the murky outskirts of worry and fear.

I imagined my parallel being; an intrepid, heedless specimen of perfection and grace, yet grounded by a determined and focused resolve. I imagined him, and I envied him. I envied his beauty within the confines of the shell. I envied him for the fact that I could never be that good, that perfect.

I was there, lying beside the love of my life, approaching what could be the defining moment of my existence to date, and I didn't even want to savour it. I didn't want to know heroism or explore the intricacies that grandeur could provide. I didn't want to know anything but simplicity. Searching Zoey, her mouth was open, and she hissed the melody of a mournful moccasin snake. I reached for her hand, making sure that I wouldn't have to fall asleep without touching her in some way. And just as I had realised those many nights before, love was not what made us weak. The ability to love gave us the ability to fight for something more and have faith in something intangible.

Love, hope and faith grew from the same seed planted inside of yearning hearts at our inception. The soil of my own life seemed nutritious enough to encourage cultivation, but here appeared the crossroads of the seasons. A time when nutrients were often spent or saved. I fell asleep, watching a seedling grow into a towering tree, stretching into the heavens further than my peripheral sight would allow. Mia was there with me, but it wasn't as clear as it was before.

She planted the seedling in rich, moist soil, and time passed, allowing it to tower over both of us. But as we looked at the treetops, Mia smiled and pushed her feelings into me. It appeared that she missed her friends over the last few weeks, this one being the most difficult that she could remember. Countless moments were spent trying to rationalise with Pj, calming his impulsive desires to seek revenge. Mia still felt as though the plan to destroy the clone birthing units at the base was nowhere near ready. She wished Pj had learnt from the previous week.

I moved my lips.

"Mia, can you show me what happened last week?"

She shook her head with sadness in her eyes. "My strength is wavering. Tomorrow, I will show you everything."

Zoey woke me early, which became the routine of most mornings. She was too restless to accompany herself, so I needed to be roused to entertain her.

"Babe." She taunted me with kisses on my neck.

"Zoey, c'mon?" I croaked.

She reached inside my pants.

I guess sleep wasn't that important after all.

As I put on my uniform after our morning entanglement, Zoey cocooned herself in a pure white sheet, staring at me.

"This is the worst part of the day for me. The part where you leave," she whined.

I turned to my right and caught the reflection of her frown in the mirror, then a grimace on my own face. I wasn't used to seeing myself in the mirror these days, let alone registering myself with bleach blonde hair and a police uniform. It was still quite bizarre.

"I think it's safe to say that the best parts of my day are being around you. I'm starting to resent almost everything else," I complained.

"What do you mean?" Zoey cocked her head to the side.

"Well, I can't sleep knowing what has happened, what we've done, what we're going to do. Not to mention Pj, Zack and Mia. I just want everything to be back to normal again."

She looked up into my eyes again, with careful consideration.

"Cooper, ever since I've known you, you have taken things so deep. Probably too deep sometimes that you threaten to erase any positive stuff from your world."

I came to sit on the end of the bed. "You have become my positivity, sometimes the only reason that prompts me to wake up."

"Let me finish, Cooper," Zoey snapped, annoyed at my impatience.

"There are times when we cannot do anything but accept our disposition, and even though it's okay to be upset, it's time you learnt that, instead of fighting against what shit situation we're in, you need to move forward. That is what defines us; the ability to adapt and overcome."

She was right. But I couldn't just repress the anxiety or calm the nerves and become the perfect optimist. I was predisposed to feeling sorry for myself. How could I click my fingers and suddenly frolic through rainbows and dive into pots of gold?

I grunted. "Alright then." I kissed Zoey on the lips and made a swift exit out the door without looking back.

In the car with Desh, I recalled the hard truth that Zoey had decided to lay upon me. Often, I wasn't quite ready for hard truths, especially when they tore at my inconsistencies. But Zoey attempted to teach me life lessons, not only with wise words and sentiments but with actions: the way she loved, the way she gave me strength, the way she was concerned for my feelings at a time like this, the way she became selfless, making me her priority. It was all the things I thought I would never be able to learn from life; things that I thought I would never learn from experience. Yet, there I was, with evidently a long way to go, but someone pushing me to get there every step of the way.

My innate being was primed and pumped full of pessimism, though a conduit had developed, conveying love at its richest and finest, down into the darkest depths. Change was all around us, and adaptation was the key to survival, so not only did we need to adapt to our physical playground, but we also needed to be open and willing to accept any challenges to overcome, learn and to be truly whole.

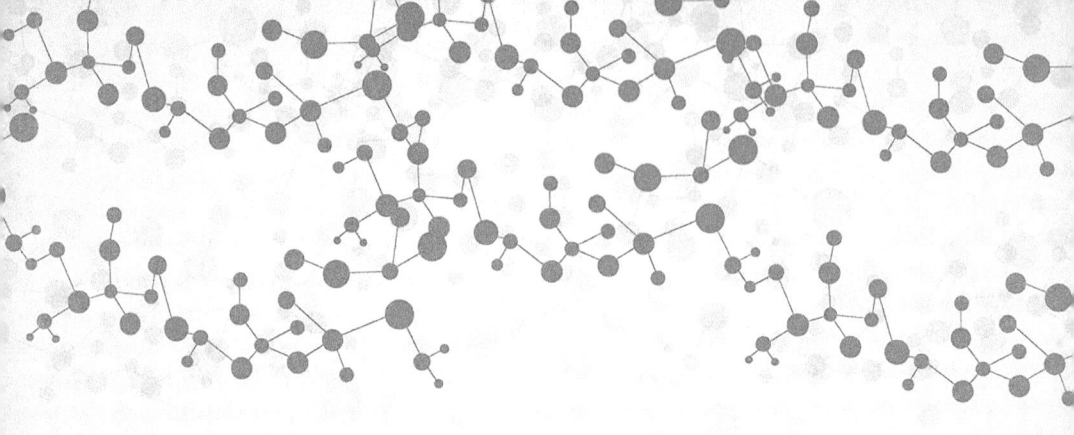

# CHAPTER 38

There she was, surrounded by complete blackness. Almost suspended in the air.

"I've been working on what I can do, so that you can see it, too. I'm going to show you moments of the past, built from our memories. It's not exactly how it was, but I've recreated it as best as I can for you," Mia said.

"How come I'm the only one you're sharing this with?" I asked her.

"For some reason, our powers speak to one another."

"I suppose we've known this from the start."

"Try not to hate Pj too much." She smiled and vanished, my vision replaced with the scene before me.

Mia was now standing with Pj and Zack. A hole cut into the fence of the clone base. The dense bush along the fence line, shielded them from prying eyes.

"I've searched for this moment in the future, and I can't see what happens past getting through the doors. I know that I can't follow you into the facility, though, so I'm sorry." Mia frowned, dejected.

Zack was clearly frustrated at Mia's lack of foresight, but he strained hard not to show it to her. They stood here because Pj had pushed. "We need to act now and not just wait around for them to start moving onto another phase." He had said.

Even though Pj wanted confirmation that they would be safe, it didn't seem like it was going to change what he was going to do. Inaction and failure crossed the desert of his mind often enough that he built his own oasis. But was it only a mirage? Pj didn't care. Paradise beckoned beyond those white walls, and he would find it, making up for all the things that had gone wrong over recent weeks.

Mia suddenly spoke up excitedly. "In ten seconds, the door will open, Pj. That's your chance."

"Got it. I'll run in and out with a uniform for Zack." He turned to Zack, "You get changed into the uniform, go in through the front door, and I'll follow after you. Simple," Pj whispered hastily.

The door opened, and Pj was gone.

The scene shimmered into darkness and reappeared as Zack changed into the uniform. The biohazard helmet covered his face so that he was unrecognisable, which was the main objective. Sliding the ID badge into the clear plastic pocket, he was ready to go. His approach was steady, but underneath the suit, sweat dotted his forehead, fogging up the Perspex cover of the helmet, obscuring his eyes.

The guards nodded absent-mindedly as he flashed them the ID badge. The doors opened with a high-pitched beep, sending what appeared to be a small gust of wind inside of the facility. Zack was comfortable that Pj was now inside, so he placed one large boot in front of the other, clicking loudly on the metallic pathway surrounding the facility. His first urge was to take the helmet off, look around and to take in the view, but he resisted. Instead, he peered through his fogged peripherals at the scene before him. The interior seemed to glow with a pure white light. Watching from above it reminded me of a private hospital in a wing for the elite: sterile and soulless.

Hundreds upon hundreds of domes filled with liquid were lined in perfectly spaced rows. It was clear that these were the birthing pods, containing clones at earlier stages of their life cycles. Clone bodies were suspended in the pods, their eyes shut tight, a breathing or feeding apparatus fixed to their mouth, akin to an umbilical cord, pumping them full of the nutrients they needed to reach full term.

Pj had positioned himself in the blind spot of the cameras, peering out at what was before him. The birthing units seemed to go on forever, but with his speed, he anticipated that he could get to at least half of them before having to escape. Zack was still gazing out at the scene before him while Pj watched and waited.

Zack composed himself, breathing in several times before setting his sights on the control panel at the end of the metal pathway. His shoes sounded a death knell with each step. Entering the control room, he stepped up to the main switch, took a deep breath in and plunged his fist into the sturdy steel box. It crumpled and twisted. Power surged and fizzled out. His part was complete. He turned and walked briskly out of the control room, as tiny droplets of red from his bleeding knuckles, coated the metal rungs of the pathway.

Pj heard the power die down and took his cue. The doors to the hall with the pods opened, and he sped through them, floating down the stairs in a flash and finding the first birthing unit's mechanical umbilical cord. With his knife, he severed the connection to the pod. Nutrients and life-sustaining liquid splashed onto the ground beneath him. He was way too fast to get any on his shoes, and he raced off to the next one to do the same. As he got to the second row, the alarm sounded throughout the facility. Anger flared inside him. He hadn't gotten to half of what he wanted to.

Zack cleared the facility just as the place was thrown into chaos with the alarm. He bumped into a police officer's shoulder on the same path, his helmet still foggy with fear. Keeping his head down, he walked off as fast as possible to meet Mia.

Mia heard the alarm go off, and she shook with worry. Her nails went instinctively to her mouth and her teeth knew the routine. Zack arrived not long after the first nail met an untimely demise.

"What happened?" Mia blurted.

"I don't know, I just got the fuck out of there." Zack spat back, breathless.

A jolt of wind disturbed the air between them. Mia's hair rose and fell, obscuring her eyes from registering Pj, who was now right next to her.

Although frustrated by the final outcome, he had managed to push through the fire escape and find his way to the back end of the base.

"Piece of cake." Pj smiled, hiding his frustration with confidence.

"Can we go now, please?" Mia pleaded.

"Yeah, I think we need to regroup back at the house, don't you?" said Zack.

Pj, Mia and Zack turned and walked through the vacant bush to their car on the other side of the metal gates.

The vision died, and Mia stood in the darkness once more.

"I'll be seeing you very soon, Cooper." She smiled with a twinkle in her eye.

I tried to hold on to ask her what that meant. But I woke up, looked at the watch strapped to my wrist. 3am. I knew that I wouldn't sleep after that.

As Desh and I waved to Gary — yes, we were on first name basis with the security guard — we didn't exactly appreciate that this was the second last time that we would ever enter the army base. The day itself did not seem any different. The sun didn't shine with an exaggerated finality; fallen leaves did not follow the wind like mindless minions into an impossible battle with gravity. The clouds perhaps concealed the faded blue sky from our view, but nothing gave us an indication that this day would be our final battle with the clones. The penultimate day, where we would eradicate the enemy who had surfaced from complete obscurity and ruined and changed our lives forever.

We opened the large khaki-green door and entered cellblock five, passing through all necessary checkpoints on our way to see Gordon Grey. Our intentions were to notify him of our final plans and prepare him for the escape, as we had promised.

That very promise drew a grave amount of tension from our group. Not since Pj, Zack and Mia had left did we feel so much indecision. Half of us believed we should leave Grey behind and rescue him afterward, but it was not guaranteed he would survive that way. I felt somewhat indebted to him for telling us how to kill all the clones with one specific action. Although he had created them, he was basically a passenger in a driverless vehicle, destined for collisions of a terrible magnitude. It all came down to Desh and me to decide his fate. Since it was essentially humans against a different species, we felt compelled to take Grey under our wing.

We approached his cell, and he was facing the wall on a cold steel chair.

"Grey," I announced confidently.

He didn't move.

"Grey, it's us. Why the hostility?"

He turned to face us in the terrible dim light. His disconsolate and dejected eyes spoke before the words fluttered into the damp cell. I turned sharply, narrowing my eyes into the darkness. I was frantic. Where was he? A gun emerged from the shadows before I saw his body as Grey's words met my ears.

"He found out about it all. I'm sorry. I'm so sorry."

He appeared taller now. Maybe it was because he was revered by so many of his own. Maybe it was because he held a gun and Desh and I were in such a compromising position, grasping for remnants of shattered dreams and foresight. He raised an eyebrow, and a callous smirk like a scar that trailed across his cheek. Whitey's clone spoke.

"Don't reach for your gun, you will be dead before you even try."

I knew he was right, and I gritted my teeth. "Desh, don't do anything, hold tight."

"Yes, indeed, hold tight, you brain dead simpletons. Who do you think you are, riding in here like goddamn heroes?" he chuckled heartily.

"You pathetic humans can't fool me, and now, you . . . will . . . die," he stated with aggressive finality.

What the fuck could I do? I was done. This was something we hadn't anticipated. What a way to die. Shamed in our first phase by the prick that had already decimated our group.

When you begin to face your own demise, the world slows down almost to a halt, and you breathe in deeply, with nothing but a seething acceptance left to accompany your final few seconds. Just when this acceptance was all I could taste, in all its putrid bitterness at the back of my throat, a decisive gust of wind blew through the open door of the cellblock section.

I imagine that Pj saw it quite differently, but it was my eyes that witnessed Whitey: confident and bold in one moment, toppled over in the next, his gun strewn across the floor, thumping into the iron bars of a cell down the hallway. It took him quite a while to adjust from such an impact with immense velocity. Ten metres further into hallway, Pj stood over him menacingly, revelling in his dominant status. Zack yelled something indecipherable as he speedily marched past Desh and me, mouths agape.

Zack launched himself to the sound of Whitey's desperate, elongated "Noooooo!" gliding as a hot-air balloon across a vast landscape. His clenched fist raised and primed for maximum contact.

Once his feet landed upon Whitey's spindly kneecaps, he brought his fist down upon our enemy's face. A sickening, moist crack resounded throughout the cell block as Zack's fist buried itself into the floor;

Whitey's leg's twitching chaotically; rearing after his synapses had been severed forever. Zack arched his head up calmly, dug his fist out from within the grey floor and stood on steady legs. Flicking skull fragments from within the gaps in his blood-soaked fingers, he looked to the carcass and sent an almighty kick into its side. It sent what was left of Whitey's clone, sliding across the floor, thudding into the iron bars of the cell adjacent to where they kept Grey.

We each wandered over carefully, stunned to see Whitey's clone wrapped tight in the pale cocoon of death. As our eyes met after surveying the corpse, we nodded to one another in extreme appreciation. Our longing for the friendship we had forgotten drew us closer than any disagreement we ever had.

Togetherness meant more at a time like this than holding grudges, and let's face it: Pj and Zack had saved our lives. God knows how, but they had. *Hang on a minute,* I thought. Without mentioning an apology or gratitude, I croaked, "Mia?"

Pj answered me, "Isn't she damn useful to have around, hey? I guess, if it wasn't for her, you could consider yourselves . . . dead."

"Not just her, mate. If it weren't for all of you, we'd be dead." I swallowed my pride. It severely scarred my throat on the way down. Without acknowledging my somewhat disguised apology, Pj and Zack both extended their pointer finger towards their ear, listening to something. They wore earpieces. Pj and Zack switched into stealth mode, looking lively and alert.

Zack communicated first, "Come on, boys. Time to roll. Follow us."

"Wait, what about Grey?" Desh pleaded.

Grey sat on his chair still, stunned into complete silence.

Zack walked over to the bars. Gripping them with both hands, he pulled them apart to create an opening for Grey to fit through.

Grey rose up cautiously from his chair and headed towards freedom.

"What *are* you two?"

"No time to explain, old man," yelled Pj.

Zack came to Grey's aid and helped to carry him upwards and onward through the maze of the army base. We stopped at several sections for minutes at a time until the person on the other end of the earpiece gave us the go ahead. Before we knew it, we had made our way towards the truck and were piling Grey, Zack and Pj into the back.

"What do we do now?" I yelled frantically to the immediate group as I got the car moving towards the exit gates.

"Go and collect everyone. It's time for the action now. This is it, Cooper. It ends today," Pj yelled from the back.

Desh and I looked at one another and nodded in acceptance.

This was the day, then. No looking back now.

# CHAPTER 39

As we pulled into the driveway, Pj and Zack ran out from the back first into the house. Everyone met them with open arms at the front door. Mia cut through the rest of our friends and stared at me from across the lawn. Her lips formed a careful smile, and her eyes formed sentences to my rather special sense.

*Dare to dream, right?* Her thoughts traversed the distance between us.

I nodded, a pitiful smile bleeding onto my face. Severing the distance between us, I hugged her warmly. Zoey interrupted by taking me in her arms and burying her face into my chest, looking up at me with those swirling amber eyes.

"I'm over this. I want this to be done."

"You and me both." I rubbed her back as she, once again, pressed her face into my chest, thankful Whitey had not taken me from her.

"Maybe we should head inside so I can tell everyone the final parts of what needs to be done?" Gordon Grey croaked as he stood awkwardly with his hands in his pockets, agitated.

I let Zoey go and walked towards Grey, hospitably showing him into the red-bricked house to the sounds of whispered concern. We gathered around Grey at the head of the table, Nikki and Mia to his left and right. Mia spoke before anyone, with her communications device still wrapped around her head like a blackened halo.

"We have exactly nine minutes before we need to leave, so we have to brief everyone and get the show on the road."

"Wait, can you see what's going to happen? We're really going to win this?" inquired Dani.

"No, I don't know exactly what will happen. I'll get flashes closer to the moments, I'm assuming. But at this point, I know that if we don't leave in about eight minutes, we won't have enough time to surprise them," she revealed.

"Okay, well, then, I must begin now in order to end this disaster today, once and for all," Grey declared.

"Who is this guy?" Nikki inquired innocently.

I rolled my eyes as Zack had to explain who "this guy" was before Grey was able to tell us anything.

Eight minutes later, we bundled ourselves into the police wagon. Desh rode in the front with me while the rest of the group, including Zoey, Grey, Nikki, Zack, Pj, Mia and Dani, were locked into the back.

Desh and I were still in our uniforms and would need the disguise to get back into the base. Nerves buzzed through the vehicle as we approached the familiar security gates for the second time that day. We searched the skyline for the clock tower that had become the centrepiece of the base. It was the clock tower that would soon become our immediate focus, standing tall and mighty, surveying the grounds beneath, reminding us that time was always watching us, but now holding everyone's fate in its hands.

Desh and I arrived to speak with Gary once more.

"You boys left in a hurry before, everything all right?"

"Yeah, the chief was on our backs with reports and all the paperwork stuff. You know how it is," I quipped casually.

"Yes, I do – all too familiar with me."

Clones were sticklers for paperwork. Who knew?

Desh rolled forward, past the remaining guards, each one waving us on. The clone army barracks lay up ahead, and we parked just to the left of them. We had researched that, at 1400 hours, they would be deserted, as the squadron were training in the fields. We opened up the back of the wagon, and the others stepped out into the afternoon sun wearing matching janitor uniforms. A booming, agitated voice floated across the base. "Would Lieutenant White report for duty at the Delta Building immediately?"

The watch on my wrist beeped and alerted me with the same message.

Our hearts aligned as one, beating ferociously, as we began to take heed of just what we were up against. At least the clones had not located the body of Whitey's clone, so we still had time to manufacture the plan.

Each of us had been assigned to a specific role, separating ourselves into smaller groups due to lack of weapons and protection. Zack and Pj acted together as the integral part of the plan while Zoey, Nikki and Dani took cover on the left side. Dani and her rationed gun led us to the right-hand side, accompanied by Grey and Mia, with the final gun resting in my pocket. We checked our communication devices given to us by Mia, as we bid farewell to Desh, who had a sniper rifle salvaged from the police station and a quill of arrows slung across his back. He would take up a sniper position at least one hundred metres from the barracks in the northwest building called the Alpha Building. The Alpha Building contained cleaning and maintenance products, utensils and other stock inventory, so it was most likely deserted at the time. As we waited within the bushes, pretending to mix paint, Mia suddenly went rigid like an ice sculpture.

"Mia, are you okay?" I inquired.

She blinked twice, her vacant stare fusing with the point of convergence between the future and the present.

"I have to go," she said.

"What? Where do you have to go?" I stammered.

At that point, Desh came through to us on our devices.

"I'm in position. It's go time."

Before I could respond, Mia slinked away, her bob of mahogany hair swaying in the sun.

"Just remember this," she commanded, "Zoey must go with Zack, and Pj needs to stay here."

Just like that, she turned and ran off past the car.

I called out to her. "Mia, what do you see?"

My voice trailed off into nothingness as I lost sight of her, behind the barracks and the buildings beyond.

Mia was gone, and I couldn't believe it. What had she seen?

I had no time to dwell on why she had just left us as the comms exploded with life once more.

"Pj here, do we move in or what, Cooper?"

"Cooper here. No, change of plans: can you come back here and swap with Zoey? Mia thinks it will work better that way . . . Just . . . pretend like you have forgotten something and swap."

He was hesitant, and rightfully so. I sure as hell didn't want Zoey to be thrust into Pj's job. I wanted her out of the action; I wanted her preserved not only because I loved her but because, if any of us were injured, she held the key to our survival.

However, I had faith in Mia's ability enough to blindly trust her counsel.

"Alright, then. I'll be down in a minute. Get Zoey ready to swap."

I searched across to the left, where Zoey's group had gathered. She had narrowed her eyes at me, as if asking, "What the fuck is going on?"

I shrugged my shoulders and tried to mouth, "It was Mia. I'm sorry."

She rolled her eyes, but her features softened, accepting that I was not at fault. As Pj came into contact with Zoey, he passed her his mop and bucket and wished her well. She carelessly tied her hair in a bun at the top of her head. Zoey's eyes spoke to me just before she left my view. *I love you.* She smiled, so I attempted sign language to redirect the sentiment.

Gordon Grey cleared his throat as if to embarrass me.

"C'mon, Grey, what do you want from me?" I snapped.

"Oh, me? Nothing at all." His tone was of surprise and expected innocence.

I wrinkled my brow and grunted, staring at Zoey and Zack making their way towards the clock tower. Our final plan was underway.

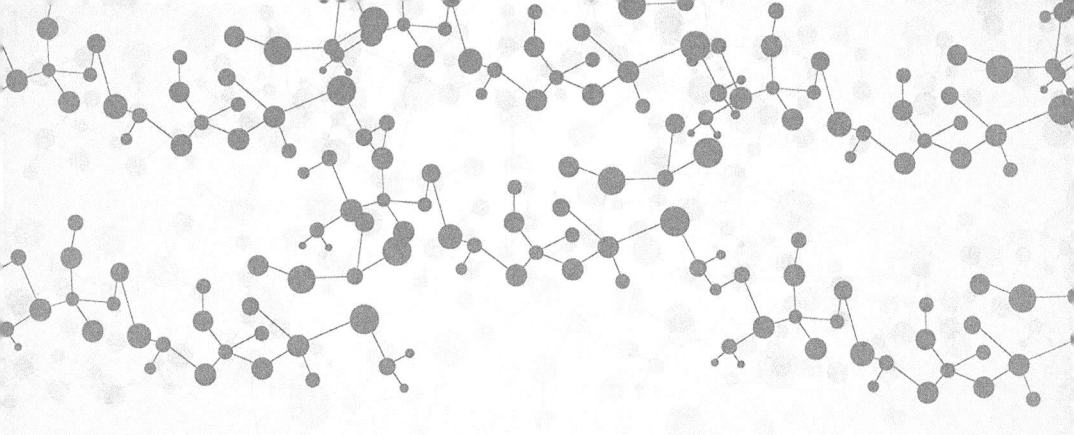

# CHAPTER 40

Various cleaning utensils weighed down the janitors: buckets, mops, spray bottles, rags and the like. However, they walked with a definite purpose towards the imposing guards. From where Grey and I crouched, the guards were not only physically superior but were sold with extra parts: menacing machine guns, utility belts containing grenades, hilted knives and other threatening objects I couldn't quite make out. Zoey and Zack would have to be seriously convincing while Desh would need to exercise perfect timing.

The guards motioned forward first, holding their outstretched hands to halt the janitors. Zack held up his bucket and spoke to the clone.

"Hello. Reporting for cleaning duty."

"Cleaning duty?" The guard replied, unsure.

Zoey pointed towards the door. "We have been sent here to clean and scrub the base and stairs of this tower." She motioned to the clock perched atop the tower.

Normally, Zoey was a terrible liar, but maybe the monotone in her voice would actually aid her in this attempt. Several seconds went by, where I imagine we each held our breath as one, as if ceasing our flow of oxygen would prompt luck itself to materialise in between their conversation. As fate would have it, the guards held a conversation between themselves, which we could not hear on the communication devices.

"Did Lieutenant White not tell you that, this morning, the schedule had been moved to an earlier time due to the cockroach and rat problem at the base?" Zoey interrupted their conversation with an impromptu improvisation.

Maybe she was getting better at this.

"Lieutenant White has been missing for several hours now," the other guard replied.

Zack chimed in. "We saw him just an hour ago; he was leaving to complete some important work off base today."

Zoey took over from Zack. "Look, we could always just show you the mess on the floor, and if there is none, you can send us back. At the end of the day, we are just following orders."

The guards seemed to linger with their decision until one of them turned to the electronic alarming system and fumbled with an access code. The door to the tower opened. Zoey stepped inside, pointing to something on the floor. That was enough for Desh to send two silenced bullets streaming across the length of a football field into the heads of the clones who had turned away from us.

Their blood splattered the outside grey wall of the tower and their legs buckled as they came crashing to the earth. As soon as they hit the ground, Zack moved to drag and throw their bodies into the base of the tower. Zoey searched around to check if they were in danger, while cleaning and scrubbing the blood splatter off the walls. Her janitorial work was second to none. No alarm bells rang out across the grounds, so it seemed that the first part of the plan was a sweet success.

Just as a wave of satisfaction carried me on its crest to a perfect shoreline, a squadron of clones emerged towards the left-hand side of where we were camped out. That wave of satisfaction swelled into a bubbling mass, dumping me onto jagged coral reefs. My eyes darted to where the others were crouched just opposite us, and it was an absolute nightmare in action. To everyone's horror, Nikki decided to stand up from where she was hiding, now in full view of the squadron. I couldn't believe my eyes. My ears followed suit as she screamed out.

"Matty, Matt!" she called, bristling with excitement.

She ran out towards the man she believed to be her partner. Strong chin, his hair the colour of wet sand, but the eyes weren't Matt's. The emotionless green eyes had firmly fixed themselves upon Nikki, sizing her up as a target. Dani ran after her, as the clone she believed to be Matt stepped outside of the formation and raised his gun towards Nikki without a flicker of recognition. The rest of the clones took their direction from him, identifying Nikki as a target and an enemy. Nikki stopped dead in her tracks, dark hair rested on her shoulders, comforting her as death was sure to follow. She cocked her head to the side, and a bemused look covered her innocent, supple face, as clone Matt's gun fired.

In desperation, Dani launched herself in front of Nikki, orange hair flailing in the wind like a burning flag. The bullet greeted her in the centre of the chest with a sickening thud. The force threw her up against Nikki, sending them both towards the ground. The splatter of Dani's blood dotted across Nikki's cheeks. Nikki had her arms tangled like twisted tree roots, bent and crippled in shock, as she looked up from the ground.

Nikki did not have time to register the condition that Dani was in. As I stood up, gun in hand, extending it towards the clones, Pj sped through the air, lifting Nikki off the ground and carried her away towards the entrance to the clock tower. Dani hadn't moved from the ground. She had become a still river of peace and piety, weightlessly sacrificing herself to the skies. I stared for too long. The clones dropped one by one as the menacing Desh cloud rained and hailed bullets upon them. Grey pulled my shirt and pointed to the clock tower. "Run!" He bellowed.

He started off before I could tear my eyes away from Dani's body, crumpled and fragmented in defeat. I willed poor Dani to stand up, to shake, to do anything, but it was no use. She would never do any of those things again.

The clones then saw me standing there, advertising my willingness to be gunned down, so they did what any ruthless enemy would do. They opened fire on me, too. That was enough to convince me that running towards the clock tower was perhaps more productive than raising the dead with a stare. I just had to hope that Desh was able to cover me well enough.

An alarm imitated my footsteps as they thumped into the earth, making my way towards the clock tower. Bullets buzzed past me like bees in a field of sunflowers in spring. I saw the finish line not that far ahead. The field marshal's beckoned me into the door. Zoey called out the loudest, fear and dread circling within those amber eyes. I almost believed that I'd survived: I'd made it through unscathed.

But then, the right side of my body screamed in agony; my breath fizzled like a firework and skirted off into the distance as my right lung sank to the bottom of the ocean, collapsed and unhinged to my body. My knee jerked, and I fell forward, smashing my head into the metal door and ricocheting into the darkness of the tower base. By the time my body had come to a complete stop, I was flickering in and out of consciousness, more so than the last time I had been shot. The combination of pain so intense, blood loss and a totally deflated lung, left me with a short supply of available oxygen.

I panicked as adrenalin turned every light on in my body, energising my remaining functioning organs to stand up and fight. My eyes were wide, my fingers became talons clawing at anybody and anything as I searched for oxygen.

My angel came to kneel by my side. The face of her, my blood-stained healer, grimacing in anticipation and in toil as she placed her hands on me. That regular healing sensation flowed through me and second-by-second, regular breaths returned. The shimmering haze of impending death no longer obscured my perception. My breath was still a ravenous rapid river, devouring oxygen, but Zoey let go of me and rested her head back against the stairway's entry. Her wound expelled the threat of my death as the dark red liquid dripped down her arm and onto my skin, marking me with fortune.

I looked up at all their eyes shining brightly in my direction, like speckled stars on a limpid summer night. "I'm . . . okay," I murmured, my hoarse voice resonating in a low frequency around the domed base of the tower. The outside door was sealed shut; Nikki and Zack had helped disconnect the number pad system installation so that no other clones would easily follow us through. The ping of bullets died, replaced by the shouting and commanding voices that came through to us as an indecipherable murmur.

"Let's finish this," Pj said.

Silence met his statement. Zoey's head bent down towards her chest as she extended her hand out and squeezed mine. I slowly arched my back up until I was sitting up, sliding in closer to Zoey.

Nikki started with a shaky voice, "Dani . . . what about Dani?"

I'd been shot. I had nearly died, but Dani. Poor Dani was outside on the grass, penetrated by bullets and encased in a heroic death. I swallowed my grief, knowing it would come again later. We had a small window to finish the clones, and every one of us needed to bury our emotions.

"Nikki — she's gone. I'm sorry, but we have to finish this. She did that so that we could win. It's what she would've wanted," Zoey said, cold and breathless.

Nikki sobbed, and the hard truth was not what she needed to hear to stifle her grief, but maybe it was enough to encourage her to move forward.

Zack and Pj moved over to where she stood trembling and wailing, and they put their arms around her while Grey fiddled awkwardly with his hands in the corner of the room. It was a brief moment of warm solidarity, but Zoey was right: we had to finish this. As Pj let go of her, he looked around at Zoey and me and then to Grey in the corner. "Alright, ladies and gentleman, shall we?" He said, motioning to the steep spiral staircase that ascended up towards the crux of the tower itself. We each nodded, determined to finish the job.

Both Zoey and I struggled to walk as our legs were terribly weak, beginning our ascension to the end. We followed Pj, who, even with his speedy abilities, traversed up the stairs with elegant intensity. We were near to the inside of the clock itself, as the brass dome ceiling took shape ahead of us. The panels were thick and sturdy, with large bolts fastened to each section of the ceiling, trailing down to the walls surrounding. Engrossed by the a new environment, my sense of peril had been dealt a serious blow, with images of a perfect ending feeding me a banquet of delicious dishes.

As Pj reached the top before the rest of us, he turned and extended his arms. "I have reached the –"

A machine gun fired, and his legs buckled underneath him, sending him sprawling forward down the stairs. I raced up to catch him before he fell upon his neck and spiralled all the way to the bottom.

"My fucking legs!" he screamed.

I placed him down at the top of the stairs. He winced and breathed in short bursts, trying to deal with the pain. I reached for the gun at my side as I searched for the culprit.

It was our first encounter with Number One himself: the first clone and the orchestrator of all things clone-like.

Grey spoke first. "Number One, what are you doing?" His tone reeked of disappointment, like a disgruntled parent.

"Well, the last person I expected to see here was you, until I saw your empty cell and Lieutenant White decapitated." His deep and chilling voice resonated within the dome.

The lines and wrinkles on his face were not as deep. The once grey hair was now dyed a deep black, like a void in space.

"And this little human travesty, who thinks he can defy physics itself, by travelling at supersonic speeds, what can he possibly do without the use of his legs though?" he cackled.

Pj moaned and shivered. Even with his khaki pants on, you could see that several bullet holes had decimated his quite extraordinary legs, now shredded to the bone, bloody and useless.

"It's nice to come face to face with the enemies I have heard so much about, yet I'm disappointed in the way that your end will be so easily administered." A thin, evil smile cursed his face.

"This is not the end; there will be plenty more of us . . . you have underestimated the desire that humans have to maintain their dominance over any species. We are too proud to let you take us without fighting for it!" I yelled, Zoey and Nikki by my side.

"Quite the contrary, Cooper, I believe that is your name. Your human pride is what got you into this mess in the first place. The fact that there is no regard for anyone but yourselves, the way that you will use every and any living thing just to satisfy your own selfish needs. It only took someone like me to stand up and say that it was wrong. Someone who had a voice!"

"You don't speak of pride; you speak of selfishness, and not every human who is proud is selfish . . . They will do what they can to benefit the lives of others. Not every single human is the same, and that is what makes the world what it is. Not any one person is meant to be perfect, and if we were, we would never be fulfilled."

"Would you be fulfilled harvesting our organs to prolong your existence?" he responded.

"No, I personally wouldn't, but this isn't about *my* beliefs. I'm going to do everything I can to stop you and save the people I love. If that means killing another being, then that is what I'll do."

Nikki finished my point for me. "Everything we do is to preserve love."

"What is this 'love' you speak of? I have no recollection of ever feeling sentiments like this. Where is proof that love exists? What is the formula for this 'love?'"

"You don't have to have a formula and reason for everything, Number One," said Grey. "Sometimes in life, intangible elements need to be accepted and implemented into our lives. Without those intangible occurrences within us, we can't call ourselves human; we become almost robotic. If only I could've taught you how to comprehend and accept that which cannot properly be explained," Grey mused mournfully.

"For that, I'm sorry." Grey hung his head as I watched Number One carefully.

I stared into his eyes, and I pitied this being, so evidently close to our physical stature and nature, but so far behind, mentally and spiritually. Ideas of grandeur and prevalence rendered the clones deluded because they couldn't feel emotion, because they couldn't accept anything but equations and formulas for life.

How could we have expected them to know? We are young for a reason. We develop not only physically, but we develop qualities; we learn how to reason and deal with the complexities of life. It was almost as if the clones were as dense as toddlers. His eyes told me that he couldn't understand the concept of being sorry, and he would or could not accept it. As far as Number One was concerned, we were obstacles standing in the way of achieving perfection.

"Mr Gordon Grey and his little entourage, you will now explain to me why this place is so important to you, or I will kill you all and forget that there may ever have been a problem."

Grey hesitated. "I don't think it's something you will want to hear."

"If you don't tell me, I will kill you all, starting with this one here, who apparently can't die. We will see how far she gets when her head is separated from her body." He pointed to Zoey, who didn't flinch but reached for my hand and grasped it tightly behind my back.

I thought about Desh. But not about where he was or if the clones had found his hiding spot. I thought about the night that I swore I would never try to take control of someone's mind again. That was a lie. This was the moment to break that promise. It was over unless I did something. I found his eyes, and I tried to find a way in. But something called to me.

"Cooper, search the room," she said.

My eyes wandered the room for the voice, for anything that could perhaps give us an advantage. I'd given up hope until I thought I saw something concealed behind the computer lab. It was Mia, crouched beneath the desk, holding a shining metal blade. How did she get up here before us? She must have located a back entrance, and that was why she had left earlier!

Mia crept forward a few inches and held her arm out taut, ready to strike. I decided to speak to Number One to keep his focus on what was ahead of him. "I pity you, because you will never know just how beautiful life could have been, if only you were able to feel." I squeezed Zoey's hand.

"So, I and the rest of the group will tell you nothing," I declared forcefully.

"So be it, you have chosen your fate." He raised his gun in the air.

I bellowed, "Do not shoot your gun!"

His eyes grew wide, and his hands began to shake. Was it taking effect?

It didn't matter. Mia launched herself through the air, almost gliding with the grace of an eagle. Her hand clenched tight around a large and beautiful blade. Mia sliced his Achilles tendon with a brutally swift movement and crashed onto the hard floor. I raised my gun in the air, stepping forward. I let Zoey's hand slip, wanting to fill him with bullets as he fell. Due to the shock of Mia's attack, Number One's finger pressed down upon the trigger of his gun as he catapulted to the ground. Bullets flashed past me.

He lost his grip on the gun as he hit the floor and fell on top of Mia, sending it bouncing and sliding across the brass floor. I made it to him just in time to see him smack the back of his head and wince out in horror as he realised he would never walk again. But I would make sure that he would never breathe again. There was no thought of hesitating this time around; I sent several bullets thudding into his head, each shot tearing another part of his brain from his being until his face was merely a mess of blood and bone. Death had been delivered to our biggest threat.

I exhaled, satisfied and relieved that all was over until Mia rose from the floor, next to the dead Number One, pushing past me in such haste. I turned to see what she was concerned about. Zoey was nowhere to be seen, but the group had started descending the stairs, crying out in panic for her. I thought to myself that it couldn't be true. That Zoey had to be okay.

Love was the only thing that mattered. Wasn't that the lesson that resonated most throughout this horrible ordeal? But there she lay, slumped across two stairs, bleeding and battered from her left thigh stretching out across to her right breast, punctured by several bullet holes from the automatic weapon; Number One's final accidental trigger squeeze.

"No!" I yelled, running down the staircase.

Zoey coughed and spluttered. Her face twinkled with a delicate blood Morse code, scribing a message of regret for a future ruined.

"Cooper, I've been shot . . . Oh, I'm so sorry," she moaned.

Tears flooded my eyes. It couldn't be; she wasn't meant to die. She was meant to live happily ever after with me. I broke apart knowing that in a few moments; I would never hold her again. I would never feel her warmth against me. I could never kiss her, make love to her, connect or talk with her. It was all taken away from me in that very instant, when several bullets had marched up her thigh, stomach, ribs and chest and lodged into her delicate organs.

"Cooper, I love you so much," Zoey croaked. "You made me realise that nothing was ever as good before there was you." Her breath slowed like a river's current, diminishing to a trickle across smooth, weathered stones.

I was about to respond as best as I could, with tears flowing down my face, but a metallic *ping* struck the stairs next to my outstretched right arm. I shot a glance down. A single bullet rolled in circles, blood-stained and battered, but now, outside of Zoey's body. I wrinkled my brow, tears continuing to disturb my face, until I heard the same sound again. Another bullet rolled off her stomach and bounded towards the bottom of the staircase.

Immediately I understood: she was healing herself.

"Grey, go to the computer. It's time to initiate the final process," I demanded.

"But, Zoey, is she —"

"She is healing herself. Just go now, so we can end this already," I said, wiping my tears.

"Seriously, what *are* you people?" he breathed before being whisked away by Zack.

Nikki, Mia, Zack and Grey went over to the computer while I stayed with Zoey, as one by one, the bullets left her body and the wounds closed over.

"I was so scared I was going to lose you." My voice was still quivering.

Zoey laughed a little. "Well, now, I guess you're stuck with me forever. I actually can't go anywhere!" She was relieved.

I placed my arms underneath her, and we embraced at the top of the stairs. I whispered in her ear, "I will love you forever then."

Her cheeks expanded with a powerful smile.

Grey was busy typing away on his computer and muttering indecipherable words and phrases to himself.

"Can you explain what you are doing?" inquired Nikki.

He pushed his broken spectacles further up the bridge of his nose. "Yes, yes, I'm just logging into the network, syncing every tower that we erected in the country with the magnetising application. As you know, my failsafe against the clones is implemented within their cellular connections. Their blood vessel endothelial cells, to be exact, have been engineered to be different to our own. Instead of the cells being stuck together molecularly, they're stuck together magnetically. So, in essence, these giant pulsed magnetic waves will throw them all out of whack, resulting in a simultaneous explosion of their blood vessels. Which, of course, results in major haemorrhagic death." Grey marvelled at his own genius.

Nikki was often confused with difficult concepts, but her brain basically haemorrhaged, trying to comprehend what Grey had devised.

"Ummm, okay, then," she chirped, "As long as they die; whatever."

A time bar materialised on the computer screen as the whole area of the dome began to tremor. "As you can feel, the large magnet is being switched on as we speak, gathering momentum." Grey began to yell over the noise. "It will now link with every tower in Australia." The time bar filled at a rapid rate, but even over the baritone hum of the magnet, we heard a commotion at the bottom of the staircase. A massive explosion rocked the tower, and several angered shouts and bellows travelled across the magnetic waves to our ears.

"Your magnet better hurry up. I think the clones just broke down the door," Zack exclaimed.

He was right, although the constant humming of the magnet intensified, shaking the dome and causing even us, difficulty to stand, we still had no clue as to how the clones were reacting. But then, we saw their heads as Zack and I leant over the railing, looking down the staircase. A clone caught our eye, and bullets whirled past us towards the top of the dome. As we threw our heads back, we noticed that all the metallic objects in the room were beginning to quiver and retreat to the domed walls in total submission. The rings on my fingers slipped off, Zoey's Necklace was ripped from her neck, Zack's buckle snapped off his white leather belt and thudded into the wall.

The clones' guns were out, pointing towards us, but as they ran up the last set of stairs with us in sight, their weapons were escorted violently to the walls. The clones stood in front of us for a second, not knowing what to do. Then, the effects of the magnet began to work its magic on them. They each twitched and screamed, others clawed at their own flesh. It was terrible to witness and many of us simply turned away. But I could not.

First, their extremities turned purple as their small blood vessels pulsed with extreme agitation. Their fingers swelled dramatically, accompanied by screams of horror. As clones fell to their knees, waves within their skin fragments pulsed like a water mattress, as the purple made its way from the fingers all the way up their arms. Tears began flowing down their cheeks in red rapids of agony; the fluid in their ears burst like the first rain of the monsoon. The blood of impending death trailed from their nostrils.

If they hadn't died from a brain haemorrhage by then, they choked on the vomit and liquefied organs spurting out from the bowels of their ruined existence. Minutes passed, and when their screams died away, the others turned to see the damage. The bodies were still intact, twitching upon the ground, their orifices still seeping and their dead eyes stained with blood.

We all ran down the staircase with Zack carrying Pj, the magnetic wave still emanating from the tower as a precaution. The distance was covered up over to the next tower, and it was like a chain reaction from there, all the way around Australia.

As we surfaced onto the grounds of the base, bodies littered the earth, some had bullets burnt into their skin, or arrows embedded in their flesh, others were magnetically killed.

We had done it. We had found a way for our simple group to kill all the clones. We noticed Desh up ahead, briskly walking towards us, sniper gun hung low in a relaxed grip, arrow and bow slung over his shoulder. He was stunned, searching the distance for an enemy but finding only his better friends. We all ran towards him, embracing together as a group. Even Gordon Grey celebrated with us. We stopped short of cracking open the imaginary champagne bottle that lay in Uncle James's cellar on the blood-soaked floor and walked over to where Dani's body lay.

"I think she deserves a proper burial in a place away from everything here," Nikki said, kneeling down and placing her hand across Dani's open eyes. Nikki sobbed heartily, and we each came to stand beside her, shedding tears of our own for all the fallen members of our family, both in our new life and in our old one.

We carried Dani's body into the back of the police van, resting her on towels and pillows from the barracks. As Desh and I made our way into the front of the car, Grey held up a mobile phone.

"I take it it's fine to use this now?" he asked. "There is no one that can track this anymore."

"Yeah, I assume so. Why, who are you calling?" I inquired wearily.

He held a pointed finger in front of my face, dialled a number and waited with the phone at his ear.

"Hello, Prime Minister? I need to have a long conversation with you."

# EPILOGUE

For three years, I thought that I could put it all behind me. I left my diary entries in Serenity, but memories were tattooed onto my skinless soul. True solace was found moving on into a life that would be considered relatively close to normal. But how could I think that normality would reign supreme?

There is always something that tests our true nature. And in this particular case, I only hope that I passed the test and chose correctly.

Once touted as an ability or a power, I would deem it now and forever as the unfortunate curse. The curse of knowing what I knew, seeing what I could, which put me in the position where only I could make the choice. During the clone years, that choice was often reactionary. But it was different this time.

I suppose that the events of the previous three years must be explained in order for me to get to the present moment.

After that fateful day, having defeated the clones, we all attempted to get on with our lives. Grey explained everything to the Prime Minister and the Australian government. They were sceptical until they saw all the evidence.

Obviously, we, the group of "terrorists," were exonerated of all charges. As a result, a massive conspiracy swept over the country and the world. It didn't help that media outlets swarmed our houses searching for answers; it didn't help that every blogger, vlogger and virogger (a virtual reality blogger) attempted to contact us at our email addresses, social media accounts and even at our workplaces. No prizes for guessing who assaulted someone first!

Eventually, the government had to come clean about what went on, due to extended family members found dead or reported as missing. It became public knowledge that the clones, originally manufactured by the government, posed a serious threat to national security and their future well-being. Subsequently, the existing government stepped down, many front and backbenchers resigning from their posts effective immediately. I guess, to a degree they had no real choice in the matter, as a large part of the population had to blame someone.

It sparked a mini revolt against those in power; statues came down; government buildings were damaged and ransacked; politicians were attacked in the streets. For a while, it looked like we escaped one hell for another. The media backed off from our doorstep after realising that we were the "heroes" of the whole operation and were now anti-lambasting, begging us for exclusive interviews by throwing excessive amounts of money at us. We all agreed to decline until the time was right.

As a new party of government took over, they brought in our little group to assist with the growing concern over the anti-establishment revolution. Our group was seen as a way to instil peace in the wider community: show that even we were happy to work with the government.

In truth, we may have been pawns in a larger game; however, our concerns over the safety of our country were more important than our pride. So, we took a stand with the new government to ensure that better transparency and communication found the community, that secrets like this would never plague us again. They also brought us in as specialists in the field of clone tactics and extermination. At first, we didn't believe that any survived. But the more we thought about it, the more we realised that several clones could have been hiding in a "dead spot" and concluded that it was better to be vigilant. A counterattack with knowledge of their own DNA flaw would not have been good at all.

They employed us formally as consultants only a handful of times a month while we worked our full time jobs. The consultancy fee was quite handsome; however, money was not an issue – as you will find out soon enough. Desh and Mia had been the only part of the group employed full time for the government, each in different roles. Mia headed the clairvoyant division within the Australian Intelligence while Desh became the head marksman on covert operations for locating clones, as well as regular wanted criminals or terrorists. Our appointments came from the Prime Minister himself, as we didn't want to divulge the extent of our abilities to anyone else.

I was brought in to assist in confirming that a proposed clone target was actually a clone. They would show me a video recording of the man or woman in question, and I would see whether they were or weren't. There were only a handful of cases over the three years that required immediate action where a clone had evaded their magnetic termination.

We are often able to see both Mia and Desh; however, video, holograph or VR conversations were more regular, as their jobs often ensured they worked tiresome and irregular hours. Desh's missions were confidential, even to our group. Mia provided us with cash bonuses now and then. She was often able to predict the lottery numbers and made sure to win large sums to provide the group with "rewards."

We have each invested our money in companies and real estate, which ensured that we were set up for life in a diversified portfolio. The way we saw it: it was a reward for our perseverance and dedication during our dire situation. In that regard, we had a right to try to enjoy what life we had left. Fame was something that the majority of us didn't want to exploit. Our powers were still very much a part of who we were, but we were determined to keep that hidden from everyone outside of the smaller group. Once the media dropped off our radar and our five minutes of fame had expired, we were basically left to our own devices. The occasional person at the shops or on the street might look at me twice, but it was merely a fleeting thought of, *that guy looks familiar.*

We never missed an anniversary of Gus, Dani, Kasey and Gil's death, always gathering together to visit the reserve and the house where Gil was buried, which we bought and converted into a lovely little chapel for the community.

Zoey had changed her career and was now working as an intern at a veterinary hospital twenty minutes from home. Using her healing powers discreetly and for a positive purpose, she gave many animals a second chance at life. I once asked her if she would consider working at a hospital.

"This whole ordeal started because humans wanted to prolong their own existence by using something unnatural. Death is a natural thing. I guess, if we don't have death, we can't appreciate life," she sighed, the weight of decisions clearly affecting her.

"That's not to say I won't take a trip to the children's hospital on the odd occasion and volunteer for the kids." She winked at me.

After the clones' saga, we took some time working on a normal relationship. I lived in my family home by myself, while Zoey did the same. However, after six months had passed, we booked a holiday overseas. It was the first time we had travelled on a plane since it all started. We were both quite shaky but made sure to entwine our fingers, taking strength and comfort from one another. We spent a few days trekking the rainforests in South America, and while atop a mountain, I dropped to my knee and revealed a sizeable diamond ring and a certain question.

As life does, it has a tendency to flow forward without warning. October last year, we tightly tied the knot, and that day had been as perfect as a day could ever be. There was no one else that I wanted to be with and our bond, formed in unfortunate circumstances, was unbreakable.

I have become a communications specialist, working for a mental health charity organisation. It helps fuel my passion for writing and keeps me focused on charitable purpose and helping those who are struggling.

Zack stood next to me at my wedding as my best man. He found himself a nice lady about a year after the clones: Catarina, a sandy-haired IT consultant, sweet-natured and balanced. She was a good foil for Zack. They are quite comfortable now, and he is starting to work through his anger issues. When mixed with super strength, it's definitely not an ideal combination. He started working in a sauce factory, packing boxes, putting his strength to use. I often ask why he doesn't do something more beneficial to the world. He always replies that he is sick of caring so much and would rather just partake in a job where he doesn't have to think at all. I guess I understood the toll of what we went through. It made the best of us lose hope in the joys of life, compared to constituting a vibrant appreciation for it.

Speaking of which, Pj started to lose the plot as soon as normality returned to our lives. Unfortunately, for the first two years, he battled addiction to alcohol, cocaine, ketamine, whatever would dull the memories. It strained his relationship with the group.

Luckily, he got clean. Zack and Catarina had lined him up with a finance job at a prominent bank, and he is now on his way up, a massive part of that transition. He hasn't lost his sense of humour, often playing pranks at those in his office, utilising his speed. He made many lifestyle changes, and is now focused on healthy habits, eating well, exercising and meditating. It was great to see. Now, he was a healthier lad with his hair neatly combed from left to right. More often than not, a slim-fit charcoal suit with a bright and obnoxious bow tie saw him through the city days and nights.

Nikki had her babies. Yes – plural – she had twins: Jessica and Danielle, of course, paying homage to Dani who died for the three of their lives. Nikki lived down the road from Zoey and I, and I would constantly play father figure to the kids, loving them at times, as if they were my own in the absence of Matt. Nikki was the only person in the group to ride the fame wave. She was an "influencer mum" with social media accounts on all the new platforms, driving forward the idea that widows can do it on their own and live a successful life. Her company, Singled Out, provided well-being courses directed at those who had lost loved ones and were dealing with single parenthood. If she didn't put her time and effort into that and take a step back, her world would have crumbled.

Zoey and I were always there when "freak outs" would occur or when she wouldn't come home on time from an event because she had drank too much, her publicist putting her into a rideshare car and sending her back home. Being some of the only parents who survived the clone invasion, Nikki's mother and father stepped up to her side and showered the two twins with love, giving Nikki much needed support. In fact, the remaining members of the Indigenous community rallied around them and highlighted why being a part of the mob was so important. It was a deep love and care that no other community I knew was able to show or prove with action. Nikki started to recognise the importance of the community a lot more, and it filled the hole in her heart left by Matt's death.

Once the government was up and running, Gordon Grey did his best to fade into the shadows, but his curiosity got the best of him.

"Last time we spoke, I told you to drop it," I said, my voice rising.

He was nervous, even over hologram chat. "Look, I honestly don't care about notoriety anymore. I think I've proved that, by staying away from you all: the government, the media – basically living a recluse life, I'm more than capable of keeping secrets, and I have not said one thing about you to anyone. I'm just one of those people that likes to solve mysteries. Besides, I need something to do!" he reasoned. "So, let's just do some bloods and a bit of after-hours research, and we can find out about how you have those abilities."

I suppose our group had just accepted the difference within us, but never thought to question why it had happened. Admittedly, a certain curiosity got the best of me because I allowed Grey back into our lives to investigate the "mystery."

He discovered that the clones had laced our food on the plane with a new chemical compound that Number One had sequenced. Something that was new to the periodic table. Usually, the chemical compound would attack part of the human molecular structure, but instead of it breaking down, it activated something within us.

Zoey and I invited the group over for dinner one evening to hear about the results.

As Grey explained it, "It's like if somebody walked into a house that had never been lived in, but all the electrical wiring was there and ready to go; they switched on a light, and all of a sudden, it was functional.

"Why do some of us have different abilities then?" Zoey pressed.

"Well, it's the same as blue eyes, brown eyes or even predisposition to genetic diseases," he said.

"What does it all mean for us, then?" Zack's prominent brow wrinkled.

"Look, I'm not going to play this down. This is essentially the next step in human evolution. Ironically, created by a clone." We all shared an uneasy laugh.

"Even though all of us here know, I won't be publishing any of this information; somewhere in the government files is the blueprint for this. And I'm not saying it might come within our lifetime, but I would predict that, at some stage, this will find its way into someone's hands."

I turned to Desh. "Could you take care of it?"

He shook his head. "I have the same type of access as you and Mia. Unless all servers and the cloud are destroyed, I don't think we can do it." Mia nodded in agreement.

"Look, if I know one thing, it's most likely buried deep. As I said, it's not something we have to concern ourselves with for a long time. Not unless anyone is thinking of having kids anytime soon." Grey raised his eyebrows, and everyone turned to Zoey and I.

We both yelled at the same time. "No way!"

"Well, we won't know what this means for the next generation until they're here, so, as I said, I'll keep everything under wraps. But if any of you start to notice any other changes outside of the last few years, I'll investigate some more."

Now comes the horrible truth. The way that life cannot operate without catastrophic peaks and troughs.

It took three signs over three years to understand. I ignored the first two, and when I think about it now, I may have not wanted to believe; I may have convinced myself that if it was out of sight, then it was out of mind.

The first sign occurred at our own wedding reception. On the dance floor, towards the end of the night, Zoey was across the room dancing with her work friends, and I was sitting at a table with Desh and Zack.

I noticed little Jessica or "Jesse," as we liked to call her, slip and fall on the dance floor, landing heavily on her arm. Rushing to her side, I made it there first while Nikki and Zoey looked over my shoulder at her. Little Jesse was crying uncontrollably, holding up her arm towards us, a heartbreaking frown so potent on her tiny face. At an external glance, we could tell that it was broken. Zoey knelt down and pressed her hands across Jesse's arm and immediately felt a jolt surge through her hands until she had to let go.

She turned towards me, shaken and perplexed.

She tried again and failed. Our first assumption was that, maybe after we eradicated the clones, her powers would fade, and this was the first indication of this occurring.

This was not the case, and the first sign was ignored.

As Dani and Jesse's birthday came around, I started to realise how often Nikki would have to reprimand Jesse for constantly doing the wrong thing to Dani. At one particular moment, Nikki yelled at Jesse and sent her to the naughty corner. As Jesse turned to walk past me to the corner, her eyes flickered a hateful glance at her mother. I put it down to the terrible twos.

I should have known better; I ignored the second sign.

So, there we were, moving towards the last sign, which happened not so long ago. The kids are three years old, and I often played the part of dutiful babysitter or pseudo daddy. Zoey and Nikki were out getting their nails done. The first hour ran smoothly, as they cuddled up to me, watching the new animation movie streaming on the TV. As they got restless, I told them I would grab them some sweets from the cupboard. On returning to the lounge room, Jesse smacked poor Dani in the face with a toy, quite brutally for a young child. I yelled from the entrance to the lounge room, "Jesse, No! Put that down!"

Holding the toy high up in the air, she froze. Twisting slowly, her small, but feature-filled face came into view, and I dropped the mixed bag of lollies to the ground in total disbelief. A green haze enveloped her eyes as she stared at me, wondering why I had called her name. As I stared deeper, my mouth arched wider, butterflies slowly scraping my unassuming bowels. I saw a profound hatred that could not have existed within a three-year-old unless they happened to be a clone. Suddenly, everything was clear: Jesse was Dani's clone. I didn't know how it had happened. Immediately, only one thought circled my mind: how could this possibly be true? I gathered myself in whatever pathetic way I could, and I stumbled over to Jesse, who still held the toy above her head, ready and willing to strike. Taking the toy from her grasp, I knelt down level with her, and I stared right into her eyes.

"Jesse, you are not allowed to hit Dani like that."

She tilted her head towards me, green eyes tantalising and disturbing.

"Why, Uncle Cooper? Dani is being bad."

Her answer astounded me.

"Because we don't punish people if they do something bad, Jesse. It's more bad to hurt people the way you're doing. Now, I'm sorry, but you need to sit in the naughty chair and think about what made you do that and how to do better next time."

She made her way to the naughty chair, perplexed. As she sat down, she rested her chin on her hands and said matter-of-factly, "I just listen to my insides, Uncle."

I gathered the whimpering Dani off the ground and held her close to me, the little fountain of light brown hair shaking as she cried into my shoulder. I paused and stared at Jesse, the green haze fading from her stare.

*Did I see things? Or was this the truth?* I wondered.

When Nikki and Zoey came back home, I was frazzled, so I dragged Zoey back home with me immediately. As she went to have a shower, I searched for old files on my computer.

Because Desh and Mia, even I, had been granted top-secret access to the "clone files," I spent several hours combing through everything and anything to prove that my assumption was correct. I was intent on finding something, but I was also hopeful of being wrong. All hope escaped me when I came across a document from no other than Ben White's clone, detailing the mission he was given. It was buried beneath several pages of seemingly convoluted information. Ben White's clone conducted intro-fertilisation upon Nikki Hopkins within the first week of becoming acquainted with the group. In a lab they fertilised one of her eggs with Matt's sperm, split the embryo and cloned it. Discarded the true twin, then implanted the split embryo into her womb, creating identical twins: one regular human baby and the other, a clone.

I was still staring at the computer screen for at least half an hour after I had found it. What was the possible conclusion to the situation? I would have to try to teach her to be good. Was that even possible? Another thought popped into my head. I might actually have to kill Jesse. As I considered that the horrible thought might become an actual possibility, my mobile phone buzzed persistently in my pocket.

Mia didn't even say hi.

"Cooper, you just can't do it. You can't!" she wailed.

I sighed but said nothing. My stomach churned. Mia had seen something happen in the future as a result of this discovery.

"Cooper, we can teach Jesse to be good. Nikki will be in ruins if you do this to her."

"Mia, don't you think I've not considered other options? At the end of the day, I'm going to try to do everything I can to avoid this."

My voice quivered with frustration, but more than anything, deep despair and heartbreak.

"Cooper, what can I say to convince you otherwise?"

"Nothing, Mia, look, I have just found out, I just want to go to bed and sleep it off." I was defeated.

I hung up before she had a chance to respond, and I walked to my bed. Zoey was already sleeping, but I roused her when I got underneath the covers.

"Coops, is something wrong?" she asked.

She knew. That is why I loved her. I never lied to her, so I told her what I had found and what I was thinking.

"You can't kill a toddler, can you? Let alone little Jesse!" The thought pained her.

"I don't know Zoey," I sighed, "As you know, Jesse has been like a daughter to me, to us even, this is just beyond imaginable."

In the dreary darkness of our room, her forehead creased with concern as she attempted to find the most logical solution; she was always good at problem-solving. But this was different.

"There's no easy answer," she began, "I'm trying to be impartial, but the thought of anyone hurting her is making me want to cry. I don't even know what to say or what advice to give you."

"If I have to kill her, it will ruin me, Zoey. You need to know that I won't be okay. . . maybe ever again," I confessed, tears spilling down my cheeks.

"For better or worse, wasn't it?" She pulled me close, referring to our wedding vowels.

"Forever and always," I replied, burying my face in her chest, shuffling deeper under the covers to hide from the world and a choice I didn't want to make. I knew that I couldn't ask Zoey to help me do this; I didn't want to burden her with the death of a child. Besides, she gave life, she didn't take it away. It was my burden alone because only I could see Jesse in her true state.

I called Grey the next morning. "Hey, would it be possible to develop a cure to fix the clones' evil disposition rather than just killing them?"

"Cooper, in the background, I've run sequencing data to see if this was possible. At this point in time, nothing works. I'm sorry to say." He sounded tired.

I hung up the phone, feeling like I had weights attached to my ankles, and I was sinking in the ocean.

One week later, Nikki called me up on a whim in the afternoon, asking me to babysit. She had a pre-booked hair appointment she had forgotten about. I accepted, knowing that fate had arrived. A moment that would give me a choice to make. Which path would I take?

How do you kill a child and make it look like an accident? It wasn't something that a sane mind considered every day, that was for sure. Nikki kissed both of her precious children on the head as she left to visit the hairdresser, muttering something about leftover food being in the fridge. It kind of washed over me in a sprinkled haze. I noticed seven missed calls from Mia, so I switched my phone off as Nikki's car sped off into the street. I stole a glance at both children playing quietly in the corner with their respective toys. Walking over to the backdoor, I peered outside the window into their backyard, thinking about whether I could do it. The faded wooden deck looked like it needed a coat of oil to spruce it up, the grass browning with the heat of the summer sun. A terrible knot twisted within my stomach, when I noticed the dark blue pool water shimmering with the gentle breeze. It was an inviting pool of death: no safety barrier while the garden was being landscaped. Was this the moment I had been waiting for but also dreading? The question that kept playing over in my mind was one I'd heard in conversations about time travel, about saving lives by destroying just one.

"Would you go back in time and kill Hitler as a baby?"

The answer was always a resounding yes.

I turned back to the kids. Dani played peacefully with some animals in a plastic meadow while Jesse dismembered a doll with that familiar green tinge wrapped around her like a snug blanket. I left Dani playing alone, taking Jesse in my arms. Tears were painting my face a pale red as I walked out into the bitter air in the backyard.

"Why are we going to the water, Uncle Cooper?" Jesse inquired, youthful naivety tainting her.

I started to hyperventilate as we reached the edge of the pool. My hands were shaking; I felt faint. Holding her out in front of me, I looked at her for one last time.

"I'm sorry, child. I love you, but I have to do this."

By now, she had realised that she was not safe. Her green eyes pulsed with incomprehension, with fear and betrayal. But it was not the last thing I saw in her. I saw the innocence only a three-year-old could possess; I saw her beauty, and I saw the memories we shared flood the foreground of my mind.

She surely knew what I was doing now, as her fear penetrated through my guilty grip into my heart, like a carving knife into tender meat. My tears blurred the windscreen of my life, and I hurled her into that pool of death. A short, shocking, piercing scream filled the air until, with a diminutive splash, Jesse entered the dark depths of the backyard swimming pool as her liquid tomb.

I shook, fighting off the realisation that my friend's child was dying before my eyes, by my hand. I was crying uncontrollably. Screaming into the sky. Breath was scarce. Panic set in. Ripples in the pool became less and less, and she appeared as an indistinguishable blob at the bottom of the pool.

Terrorists and tyrants were often born evil, weren't they? Something happened in their lives that sent them on a path to destruction. Jesse had evil written in her DNA, but would nurture prevail if she were given the chance? Didn't she deserve better? Deserving of my optimism to push through and inform this choice.

She wasn't Hitler, and it wasn't written in the stars that she would become evil. More than two choices flooded me. You could force Grey to find a cure, even if it took his whole life. You can teach Jesse about everything, train her to be nice, watch closely and you can let her live.

The icy water slapped my face as I dove in. Scooping Jesse up in my arms, I pushed and pushed to the surface. Spilling out onto the edge of the pool, I rolled Jesse onto her side. Her small face white, unresponsive, betrayed by the closest thing to a Dad that she had. I pushed myself up over the edge and tilted her head back while parting her lips. My open mouth covered Jesse's, and I breathed into her, encouraging a response, wanting us both to have a second chance. I pushed down a little too hard on her chest. I eased off, screaming out in desperation. My hands trembled from the icy water or from the tight grip of anxiety, of guilt, as precious seconds went by without a response. Death threatened to close in on Jesse, and it dawned on me that there was no way I could carry on after this. Rancid petals floated on the wind, fate's demonic voice calm and clear. If death took her, it would also have me. I brought my lips down upon hers again and puffed three times into her nose and mouth.

She coughed and spluttered; water and bile flowed from her. I quickly flipped Jesse on her side, thumping her on the back, pushing my fingers into her mouth and removing any blockages. Once she had finished coughing, the screaming began. I pulled her close to me, both of us crying, both of us relieved.

I held Jesse in my arms, as I walked to the house muttering sorry over and over. Her face distorted as she wailed for her mother, shivering and devoid of breath. Dani stared at us from behind the glass door, absolutely petrified and on the verge of tears herself. Her brown teddy bear, dejected as she let it slip through her fingers bouncing on the grey tiles.

Pushing the sliding door across, I yelled over Jesse's screams, "Dani, please get me a blanket! Hurry, hurry!"

She leapt into action and brought me the red and white knitted blanket from the lounge, and I stripped Jesse of her wet clothes and wrapped her tight in the blanket. I held her close to me, rubbing her back and trying to soothe her. Dani was nearly as white as Jesse. Her hands were clasped together, shifting uncomfortably as she fought against the shock of seeing her sister so distressed. "Get Uncle Cooper his phone please, I need to call the ambulance."

As the ambulance got ready to drive off, Nikki turned to me with red raw cheeks from crying, "I don't know what you were doing, or why you weren't paying close enough attention, but you nearly fucking killed my daughter, you prick!" She slapped my face once, and I didn't move or protect myself. I let it sting me.

"Nikki . . ." I stammered, but that was all I could get out, as she yelled obscenities at me and struck me again. Mia had arrived just after I called the ambulance, and she was trying to calm her down, but I just turned and walked to my car, without saying another word, as Mia coaxed Nikki into the back of the ambulance.

Dani's big brown eyes watched me as the hulking vehicle took off and sped down the street. The police had already interrogated me, and I lied easily. The tears I cried, though, were painfully real. Mia walked to the car and gestured for me to put my window down.

"I just called your wife, and she will meet you at home in ten minutes. I won't tell Nikki what you did but go home and check your phone messages when you turn it on." She turned away and left me staring at the dashboard.

"Mia," I called desperately.

She returned, but her look burnt holes into me.

"Just don't." She glared at me, swishing her burgundy hair and leaving me alone in my car.

After ten minutes of replaying the event over and over in my head, I pushed the ignition switch and sped off towards my home, glaring at the pool in the rear-view mirror. No words could justify anything I had done. Nikki loved Jesse, even if, deep down, she knew that something was wrong. Who was I to take that love, that connection away? Come to think of it, who did any of us think we were to meddle so severely in the lives of others? What makes us believe we have the right to inflict pain and suffering into anyone's life? Even if my cause was for the benefit of all humans, others might not see it that way.

When I got home, Zoey let me crumple into her arms, let me stay in bed for days, let me feel what I was feeling and didn't judge me. It made me think that Nikki loved Jesse for *who* she was and not *what* she was. I was a monster, yet someone still loved me. I was just glad that I came to my senses and saved her.

It all happened a week ago, and as I sit and write this, I remember quite clearly the haunting image of Jesse's eyes, her beautiful green eyes begging me to save her and not to give up on her. I don't know what the repercussions will be for the world, but I have to believe she can be saved.

I know it's mandatory to end a manuscript where the world is perfect and beautiful and joyous, so this is evidently a slight letdown. I'm livid, and I'm depressed and I don't think I will ever be the same. But life is like that: a perpetual spiral of challenges, obstacles and experiences, each from which we must learn and develop. It is the integrity of our character that shows us who we are, who we could be and what we can achieve.

So, I guess time will heal my wounds, my guilt, my relationships, as it has a tendency to do, but it's those moments in between: the waiting room limbo that tethers itself to the greatest sadness. I suppose I deserve a certain chance at happiness to end this chronicle, this section of my life.

Mia's messages on my phone were ravaging; hateful, despiteful, accepting, but it was one line that I particularly remember, especially now.

*Now that you have chosen this path, the only way you will find forgiveness and happiness, lies within Zoey. I'm sure that when you look into her eyes you will see.*

I took that to mean her heart. The way her love soothes me and comforts me and makes me truly happy. But I was wrong. An hour ago, I came home from work. Zoey was sitting on the edge of our bed, the cream coloured blanket ruffled, the faded violet throw pillow in her lap. On the bedside table a candle burned with a quivering flame, sending the calming scent of lavender and nerolina throughout the room.

She smiled at me as I walked through the door. A smile that diffused sadness, a smile that was a winter night in front of a fire. The smile was a flame spreading up into those amber eyes and I saw the secret. True elation had found me, after what felt like years of self-hatred. It was time to let go and let her smile become my own.

Inside Zoey was my baby girl. She was the size of a walnut, but the breadth of change that she evoked within me could not be measured. I showered her with kisses, cuddles and yelps of joy.

Mia had said to me that she couldn't see what lay ahead for Jesse. But she has seen glimpses of how close we become. Maybe that was a good sign? It showed that, at least at some stage, Nikki forgives me, and I can start to nurture Jesse and develop her "goodness."

At the same time, I decided that I needed to give up my job and work with Grey to develop a cure. I knew nothing about chemistry, but I needed to be there to push him; all my working actions would be used to save Jesse.

With the knowledge that we are all somewhat safe from peril, I just want to focus on living a simple life with Zoey and our new family. I want those who I love to be safe and not have to endure what we did in that horrible year. I want my choice to end up being the right one. I want nothing but the best for my little girl.

They say time will tell. But I won't let it dictate my life any longer.

Time will say what I want it to say.

I'm seizing the moment, and I'm only looking forward.

# ACKNOWLEDGEMENTS

I would like to start by acknowledging the Traditional Owners, Custodians and Elders of the Darug Nation, both past and present. Most of my writing occurred on Darug land and I wanted to pay respect to all Darug community members living on and off country and show my support for the Darug Nation and its people.

Firstly, I would like to thank you for buying this book or for choosing to read it. By doing so, you are not just reading a story. You are supporting me, you are validating my dreams, you are allowing me to express myself without reproach. Whether you connected with it or not, I really appreciate your interest in what I've created and I hope that you might support my future projects in years to come.

Secondly, I would like to thank the many people who helped bring this story to life. As a writer, you are constantly seeking growth and development within your craft as well as absorbing advice to better the story. I was blessed with some wonderful writing advice from my beta reading team Elise, Emily, Kate, Nick and Bianca who provided critical points that pushed me and gave me the tools to help take the story to another level. Special mention to Kate who essentially coached me on various ways to enhance my writing skills, helping me realise a potential I was unsure if I had the ability to reach. Thank you for believing that I could. Emmie, for being a writing Oracle, who not only took the time to tediously rework lines with me, but also assisted with every aspect of the self-publishing journey. Giving me advice that bettered my writing craft, consoled me during moments of weakness and doubt, and was there to raise me higher when I was at risk of sinking. Words don't really reflect the amount of gratitude I have for your guidance, support and friendship during this stressful time.

To all the team on bookstagram, who have been like my own online entourage. They are a constant support, ensuring that I wasn't alone and that I felt seen and heard. Renee, Liz, Tanya, Jayse, Vie, Jess, and Kimberley to name a few. In general, it must be said that the bookstagram community is really such a positive place for writers to engage with others who feel passionately about the written word.

To all the friends who have read the manuscript over the years and who have provided feedback, encouragement and support, I thank you deeply. Manesh, Issy, Jack, Alex, Trisha, and Jessica among countless others. To the people who have helped with various technical elements of this book; Dr Evan, Dr Jaime, Issy and Elise; thank you for your expertise.

To my editor, Samantha, I thank you for answering all the millions of queries I had, guiding me through the difficult task of putting a magnifying glass over my work, and being the final piece to the puzzle that would give this story the breath of life it needed to survive in the wild.

To my proof-reader Nick, you have followed every creative endeavour I've touched with the vigour of no other. I know that even before I release anything, you will be one of the first people in line to shout your support from the treetops. I don't know why you're in a tree, but either way, thank you for that and thank you for the skill you bring as a writer and journalist, to operate as the last level of defence for this story, before it needed to fend for itself.

To my artist Beyza, I'm utterly grateful that I was able to find someone so creative and talented to come up with the artistic renditions of these characters. You delivered everything I asked for and more, and I have no doubt that your positive attitude will serve you well in the future.

To my friends who are at the heart of this story: Jarod, Gus, Jesse, Sharon, Manesh, Pete, Whitey, Juan, Frankie, Hayden. It is a testament to the time we spent and the memories we shared, that our interactions are now documented for all to see. You are all dear to my heart and I thank you.

To my family, Mum, Dad, Sabrina, Cici: Over the years you have each played a big role in ensuring the story continued. From Mum instilling in me that my dreams should never die, To Dad reading, providing feedback, and helping to open doors for me; Sabrina for entertaining my character art ideas leading up to publication; Cici for researching, seeking advice, and finding inspiration that would help me succeed. Thank you all.

Thank you to Lou, my wife, who has supported all of my creative endeavours over the years. From the very early days of the manuscript you were able to contribute some really valuable ideas, interesting plot points and brought a logical element to the story that I often couldn't see. Being a partner to a dreamer is also no easy feat, so I thank you for being an ever-present force ensuring that our family is secure and content as we search for the dream in the wilderness, safe and sound. For giving me the gift of our daughter, I will always love and revere you.

I thank you, Amelie, my incredible daughter. You made zero contributions to the manuscript, mainly because at the time of publication you were two years old. However, I thank you for increasing the vibrancy on the canvas of my life. I thank you for being the reason I wake everyday and I thank you for giving my existence true meaning. The publishing process has been a selfish thing, but wrapped up in it, are hopeful aspirations that I have for you. I just want you to chase your dreams and know that I'll always support you, hell, I'll carry you nearly all the way to ensure you find what you're looking for. A quote from one of my favourite TV shows, scrubs is, "Nothing in life that is worth having, comes easy," but when you have supportive people around you, willing you to get there it will be a little bit easier at least. I could write another 300 pages on you alone, but I'll finish with - I can't wait until you're old enough to read this and maybe take inspiration from it to achieve something of your own. I love you.

Lastly, I just want to thank my writing heroes. Although they may never know of me, or this story, without them it might not exist. John Marsden & John Wyndham for the beginning phase; Gregory David Roberts for showing me that writing can be meaningful and beautiful; Kathryn Barker for getting me over the finishing line and allowing my confidence to grow.

# CONNECT WITH JP McDONALD

Website: www.jpmcdonald.com.au

Instagram @jpmcdonaldwrites

Tiktok @jpmcdonaldwrites

Facebook @jpmcdonaldwrites